THE CASE OF THE DEVIOUS DAUGHTER

by

Cathy Ace

FOUR TAILS PUBLISHING LTD.

PRAISE FOR THE WISE ENQUIRIES AGENCY MYSTERIES

'…a gratifying contemporary series in the traditional British manner with hilarious repercussions (dead bodies notwithstanding). Cozy fans will anticipate learning more about these WISE ladies.'
Library Journal, starred review

'If you haven't read any of Cathy Ace's WISE cozies, I suggest you begin at the beginning and giggle your way through in sequence.'
Ottawa Review of Books

'…a modern-day British whodunit that's as charming as it is entertaining…Good fun, with memorable characters, an imaginative plot, and a satisfying ending.'
Booklist

'Ace spiffs up the standard village cozy with a set of sleuths worth a second look.'
Kirkus Reviews

'…a perfect cozy with a setting and wit reminiscent of Wodehouse's Blandings Castle. But its strongest feature is the heart and sensitivity with which Ace imbues her characters.'
The Jury Box, Ellery Queen Mystery Magazine

'Sharp writing highlights the humor of the characters even while tackling serious topics, making this yet another very enjoyable, fun, and not-always-proper British Mystery.'
Cynthia Chow, Librarian, Hawaii State Public Library in Kings River Life Magazine

'A brilliant addition to Classic Crime Fiction. The ladies (if they'll forgive me calling them that) of the WISE Enquiries Agency will have you pacing the floor awaiting their next entanglement…
A fresh and wonderful concept well executed.'
Alan Bradley, New York Times Bestselling Author of the Flavia de Luce books

Other works by the same author

(Information for all works here: **www.cathyace.com**)

The WISE Enquiries Agency Mysteries
The Case of the Dotty Dowager
The Case of the Missing Morris Dancer
The Case of the Curious Cook
The Case of the Unsuitable Suitor
The Case of the Disgraced Duke
The Case of the Absent Heirs
The Case of the Cursed Cottage
The Case of the Uninvited Undertaker
The Case of the Bereaved Butler
The Case of the Secretive Secretary
The Case of the Unfortunate Fortune Teller

The Cait Morgan Mysteries
The Corpse with the Silver Tongue
The Corpse with the Golden Nose
The Corpse with the Emerald Thumb
The Corpse with the Platinum Hair
The Corpse with the Sapphire Eyes
The Corpse with the Diamond Hand
The Corpse with the Garnet Face
The Corpse with the Ruby Lips
The Corpse with the Crystal Skull
The Corpse with the Iron Will
The Corpse with the Granite Heart
The Corpse with the Turquoise Toes
The Corpse with the Opal Fingers
The Corpse with the Pearly Smile
The Corpse with the Amber Neck

Standalone novels
The Wrong Boy

Short Stories/Novellas
Murder Keeps No Calendar: a collection of 12 short
stories/novellas
Murder Knows No Season: a collection of four novellas
Steve's Story in "The Whole She-Bang 3"
The Trouble with the Turkey in "Cooked to Death Vol. 3:
Hell for the Holidays"
Wax in "CrimeFest: Leaving The Scene"

PRAISE FOR THE CAIT MORGAN MYSTERIES

'…Ace is, well, an ace when it comes to plot and description.'
The Globe and Mail

'Her writing is stellar. Details, references, allusions, expertly crafted phrasing, and serious subjects punctuated by wit and humour.'
Ottawa Review of Books

'If all of this suggests the school of Agatha Christie, it's no doubt what Cathy Ace intended. She is, as it fortunately happens, more than adept at the Christie thing.'
Toronto Star

'…a mystery involving pirates' treasure, lust, and greed. Cait unravels the locked-tower mystery using her eidetic memory and her powers of deduction, which are worthy of Hercule Poirot.'
The Jury Box, Ellery Queen Mystery Magazine

'…a testament to an author who knows how to tell a story and deliver it with great aplomb.'
Dru's Musings

'Cathy Ace makes plotting a complex mystery look easy. As the threads here intertwine in unexpected ways, readers will be amazed that she manages to pull off a clever solution rather than a true Gordian Knot of confusion.
Cathy Ace's books always owe a debt of homage to Grand Dame Agatha Christie…the blend of "cozy" mystery, tragic family dynamics…
pure catnip for crime fiction aficionados.'
Kristopher Zgorski, BOLO Books

Dedicated to my sister, Sue

18th JANUARY

CHAPTER ONE

Henry Devereaux Twyst, eighteenth Duke of Chellingworth, was terribly worried about his unborn child. Attempting to rid himself of his concerns, he reminded himself that his firstborn constantly proved he was a strong, healthy boy. Indeed, during the tea for family and godparents held just a week earlier to celebrate his first birthday, Hugo had managed to scoot himself across the sitting room to an area beyond the large Aubusson rug – his usual 'domain' – where he'd firmly wedged himself beneath an intricately carved, and heavy, Jacobean settle. Extricating him had proved a rather stressful process, with poor Stephanie coming close to tears.

As if summoned by his concerns, his darling wife appeared at the door of the library, pushing Hugo in his pram. For once his son was blessedly quiet, and Henry peered down at him as he slept, amazed – as always – by the perfection of his cheeks, his lips, and his chubby, curling fingers.

Stephanie whispered, 'He's adorable, isn't he?'

Henry rolled on his toes with pride. 'Indeed he is. And how are you feeling now, my dear? Still a little under the weather?'

The duchess sniffled. 'I think the worst of my cold has passed. Now all I have to do is endure this stuffy head for a while, then I dare say I'll be back on top form.'

Henry replied quietly. 'I hope so. You need all your strength for...' He nodded toward his wife's midsection and added, 'You know.'

Stephanie chuckled. 'Everyone knows now, dear – there's no reason to not mention my pregnancy any longer. Though I must say that I'm glad my parents have gone back to their place in Spain. The constant chatter about my "condition" – as you insisted upon referring to it – was beginning to grate on me. And with your mother and Mavis off to

Scotland, to join Clementine and Julian there for a couple of weeks, we won't have to endure any more dinners with "guests"…though I do appreciate the fact that your mother's hardly a guest in what was her own home for decades.'

Henry nodded. 'Indeed. I've already told Edward we'll dine in our apartment this evening, and that we only require three courses.' He noticed that his wife looked slightly taken aback by his words. 'You did say that five courses were making you feel a little bloated, dear. So I thought I'd take the initiative.' He could feel panic rising in his gullet; he feared he'd done the wrong thing.

As Stephanie's hand gently touched his arm, he felt immediately reassured. Her words bolstered his spirits further. 'Thank you, Henry, you're quite correct – entertaining with five courses has taken its toll. But now, with Christmas and the New Year celebrations behind us, and all our guests having departed, we can get back to more healthy habits. I'm extremely relieved that you didn't catch my cold, but we have to be careful – I believe I need to build up my immune system as best I can, in natural ways. Val Jenkins is popping over tomorrow, before elevenses, and it's something she and I plan to discuss.'

Henry was puzzled. 'Didn't Val mention at Hugo's tea that she was off to the wilds of…somewhere? Isn't she making soup out of bizarre ingredients for another one of those *Curious Cook* TV things?'

Stephanie sighed in the way that made Henry nervous. 'She's been in Anglesey for a week, not in the wilds of anywhere – though Anglesey has a wonderfully wild coastline. She's been filming segments for a series of short videos about ancient cooking ingredients, but she's coming tomorrow because she's my friend, and because she's also a qualified nutritionist. I want to call upon that part of her expertise. She, Cook Davies, and I, will come up with a plan of action to ensure that all the food we eat from now on helps my body to do what it needs to do in order to give this new life the best possible start.'

Henry felt queasy. 'We? I, too, shall be eating…nutritiously?' He wasn't sure if he liked the sound of that.

Stephanie chuckled quietly. 'Oh Henry, don't panic. I know how fond you are of certain dishes, and how you're quite traditional in your preferences, so that's why Cook Davies will be there – so we can come up with compromises, where necessary. Though, let's be honest, it might not do you too much harm to lose a few pounds, eh?'

Henry felt himself suck in his tummy, though he hadn't meant to do any such thing. 'I dare say you're right,' he replied. Grudgingly.

Stephanie gazed at her son, nestled in his pram. 'He'll be too big for this soon, Henry. I know he's already standing a little, and able to scoot and crawl at quite an alarming pace, but we'll have to come up with a new system for transporting him around this big place, until he can walk properly.'

Henry agreed. 'Yes, he's already grabbing the furnishings to help him balance, but…do you mean we should get him a…pushchair for getting him from A to B within the Hall? That sort of thing?'

'Indeed. I understand they're available with three wheels nowadays, and that they're able to accommodate quite rough terrain, which would be useful when we begin to take some extended walks around the Estate. Val and I have already spoken about increasing the amount of exercise I get, and walking around the Chellingworth Estate seems the ideal way to achieve that.'

Henry was astonished. 'But it's the middle of winter…is that…is that even healthy? You'd be horribly cold, and you'd probably get wet every other day at least – if not every day. I cannot imagine that would be good for Hugo.'

Stephanie tutted. 'For heaven's sake, Henry, children do go out in all weathers, you know. As long as Hugo's well wrapped up, there's no reason to believe that getting a bit of a pink nose now and again would put him in some sort of mortal jeopardy. None of us would be parading about in the nude – we'd all be appropriately attired.'

Henry dared, 'And by "all" you mean…the three of us?'

'Of course.'

'Yes, of course. Excellent idea. I'll talk to Edward about airing out some of my, um, waterproofs. I dare say I have some…somewhere.'

'It's already in hand, Henry.'

'Of course.'

CHAPTER TWO

Carol Hill watched the kettle in the little kitchenette in the office, knowing she was being foolish, because her attention wasn't going to make it come to the boil any faster. Forcing herself to walk away from it, she gazed at the view through the tall windows of the converted barn where the women of the WISE Enquiries Agency worked. It was unusual for Carol to be in the place alone, and it felt cavernous in a way she'd not experienced before.

Christine Wilson-Smythe, who'd been living in the apartment that had been built into the eaves of one half of the barn, had decamped to London, where she was staying with her parents – the Viscount and Viscountess Ballinclare – until the imminent arrival of the child she shared with Alexander Bright. As she thought of it, Carol could hardly believe that Christine was about to become a mother. She shook her head as she considered all the risky behaviors Christine displayed that showed she clearly imagined herself to be immortal. That would all have to stop, once she became a mum. As Carol knew only too well, the arrival of a child meant that life changed immeasurably…forever. Her smile grew as she realized how wonderful it felt to know that she'd be Albert's mum, and David would be Albert's dad, for the rest of their lives. What a delight. And what a responsibility.

'That tea's not going to make itself, Car…'

Carol's head snapped around at the sound of the arrival of her friend of many years, and colleague for several of them, Annie Parker. Both women looked toward the steam billowing from the kettle. Carol tutted. 'Took my eyes off it for two minutes, and there it goes. I'll make tea while you…look, stop hopping about, Annie, and just go, will you? You're clearly desperate.'

'Ta, doll,' called Annie as she headed toward the loo.

Carol made a full pot, completely forgetting that there'd be just the two of them at the office that morning, then decided to allow the plate to remain piled with biscuits on the basis that she and Annie deserved a treat; they were about to hold the fort because Mavis MacDonald had agreed to accompany the dowager Althea Twyst to Scotland, where Mavis would then split her time between Twyst House itself and the homes of her two sons, both of whom lived not too far away from the Twyst residence, in Dumfries.

Annie bounced into the office and kicked off her shoes. They rolled in the general direction of her desk.

'Quiet here, in't it? With Chrissy gone, and no Mave, it'll be just you and me for the next couple of weeks, doll, so…do you reckon we can cope? Oh, lovely – let me loose on them Jammie Dodgers.' Annie collapsed onto the sofa beside the coffee table and grabbed a biscuit.

'They're supposed to be for our potential client, too, Annie,' chastised Carol, knowing full well that she'd end up having to top up the supply of sweet treats before their meeting convened in half an hour's time. 'And get your feet off the sofa – you know Mavis doesn't like that.'

Annie giggled through the crumbs. 'Mave's not here, she won't know.' She pulled her ringing phone from her pocket, and almost choked. 'Gordon Bennett! Talk of the devil. Do you think Mave's got cameras hidden in here, Car?'

Carol spluttered tea as she watched Annie sit up straight and brush crumbs from her chest when she answered the phone. 'Hello Mave? Haven't you and Althea gone yet?'

Carol watched Annie's face make wicked shapes as she listened, then said, 'I'll put you on speakerphone, Mave. Car's here.'

With Annie's phone on the table between them, Mavis's familiar Scots' accent wafted toward the beams high in the roof above them. 'Ian's driving us as I speak, and Althea's promised to be quiet while I have a quick word with the two of you,' she began.

Carol and Annie exchanged a knowing smirk when Althea's voice cut in with: 'But I have to say hello, Mavis. It would be impolite to not do so. How are you, Annie? Missing your parents, now that they've gone back to Plaistow?'

Carol thought she noticed…something…cross Annie's face just before she replied, 'Nah, not so much. They're always at the end of the phone, and Eustelle's got the hang of using the FaceTime thing, now, so I can see them whenever I want, as well as hear them. It was nice to have them staying at the pub with me and Tude for as long as they did, but they've got lives, too, and I dare say we're all glad to get back to normal.'

Althea added, 'And are you and all your family well, Carol? Poor Stephanie's had a dreadful head cold. I do so hope she'll rally soon, and I hope she's not passed it to anyone else.'

Carol replied, 'Mam and Dad are fine thanks, though David says he reckons he's got a cold coming on. But he's been saying that for a week now, and nothing's materialized, so I dare say he'll survive. And I'm in the pink, as is Albert, thanks. Have a lovely time with Clementine and Julian, Althea. We look forward to hearing all about it when you get back.' She knew that time was short, and also how Althea could witter on.

Mavis cut in, 'Aye, we'll do that. Now, let me say what I wanted, then you two can get on. Carol – I've sent you an email…'

Carol dared to jump in with: 'I saw it Mavis, and I have no questions. It was very…comprehensive.' She visualized the ten pages of notes Mavis had sent, and rolled her eyes toward Annie, who silently shook with mirth on the sofa.

Taking a deep breath, Annie added, 'And I got mine, too, Mave, and I also have no questions. We'll be fine. It's quiet here, we'll catch up with everything you listed, and we won't let you, or our company's reputation, down while you're away. Oh – and Chrissy sent a photo this morning of her and Alexander, which I'll text to you. It's a bit…well, you know, it's one of those studio portrait things, so they're both all dressed up and that, but they both look fantastic in it, of course. I'll do it when we disconnect, okay?'

A moment of silence at the other end of the call was followed by a sharp, 'Ach no, Althea, now look what you've done – there's jam all over the table. Could you no' have waited? We've been on the road no more than half an hour.'

Carol shrugged at Annie and said, 'You've got a table…in the car?' It made no sense to her.

Althea chirped, 'We each have one. They fold down. Lovely bit of walnut they are. I was putting jam on a scone, and the knife came off the side of the plate, that's all. There, see, Mavis – it's all gone now.'

Mavis could be heard saying, 'Put the jam in the door pocket, beside the flask of hot water. Yes, dear, there. See? It fits nicely. Or you could have put it back into the picnic basket on the seat between us. No, don't…well, yes, it is better there, I suppose.'

'So…bye for now then,' ventured Carol. 'Safe travels.'

Mavis sounded unusually dithery when she replied, 'What? Aye. Now, Althea, what are you doing with that clotted cream…'

The call disconnected.

Annie observed, 'I remember, back when I was a kid, I never even used to get to the end of the road on a bus trip with the school without opening my sandwiches. Althea sounds about the same.'

Carol couldn't help but chuckle. 'Sounds a bit more grand than any bus we ever had for our school trips. Tables in the back seats? Places for flasks and picnic baskets? How the other half lives, eh? Well, one percent of the other half, in any case. I dare say they're in one of those massive, gleaming black cars from the Estate.'

Carol was surprised that Annie sounded so blasé when she replied, 'Yeah, Mave told me they were taking one of the Bentleys. Didn't think her car would make it.'

Carol nodded, and blew across her tea – quite unnecessarily, because it was almost cold. 'So – what do I need to know before Barbara Newsom turns up?'

Annie topped up her own tea, and grabbed another biscuit. 'She's brilliant, Car. I mean, I honestly don't know what I'd have done without her. Best counsellor ever. Well, the only one I've ever had, but, you know what I mean.'

Carol smiled warmly. 'Well, she certainly helped you get through what I know was a difficult time, Annie.' As Annie opened her mouth to speak, Carol added, 'Yes, I know we're good friends and that we can, and do, talk to each other about anything – but there comes a time when a friend can mean well, but just can't help like a professional can. The way seeing that man in Swansea dead at the foot of his stairs hit you, it was clear it was time for some structured input, and I'm so glad this Barbara was able to give you that. And, now that she's signed you off, so to speak, she wants us to…well, do what, exactly? Has she said?'

Annie shook her head, licked sugar off her lips and said, 'Nah, not really, Car. I haven't seen her in, what, five or six months? We both agreed I wasn't really going to benefit any more by continuing with her – and the way she set me up to be able to cope on my own's been brilliant. But I sort of miss seeing her…the person, not the counsellor, you know? Lovely woman. She's so clever, Car – a truly bright, sharp woman. And she never took no nonsense from me…wasn't ever stroppy with me at all, but strong, you know? A big woman…not wobbly-big, but…well, I reckon she knew what the inside of a gym looked like, and in great shape for her age. In her early sixties already, I'd guess, but her hair always done nicely, and always well-dressed, you know? Strong-spirited, too. Well, I'd need a strong woman to relate to, wouldn't I?'

Carol had to smile. 'You could say that, Annie, yes. So…we'll see what she wants when she gets here, I dare say. Which should be any minute now. Let me freshen up this pot for us, and get the water ready in case she prefers coffee, and we'll be all set. But…maybe the shoes should go back on, Annie – you know, for the sake of professionalism.'

'Turning into a right little Mini-Mave, you are, Car,' called Annie as Carol headed toward the kettle.

Carol's back was toward the door when she heard it open. Then she heard Annie exclaim, 'Gordon Bennet! Barb – what the 'ells 'appened to you?'

She turned and was surprised by what she saw: a thin woman, wearing clothes that drowned her, stood in the entrance, and she appeared to be grasping the door handle to keep her balance. A sallow complexion was topped by a slightly greasy steel-gray helmet of hair, and the woman seemed to be out of breath. Both Carol and Annie rushed to her aid, and steered her to a safe seat on the sofa. If Carol had been in any doubt that the woman's appearance had shocked Annie even more than herself, she only had to take one look at her friend's concerned expression.

Annie was all aflutter, and poured tea – with three sugars – for her one-time counsellor, holding it toward her solicitously. She said quietly, 'Come on, Barb, you look like you could do with a cuppa. Get that down you, then tell me and Car what's up.'

Carol noted the slack skin, the bags beneath the eyes, and the general air of unkemptness about the potential client, and wondered how the woman Annie had just described had changed so much in such a short time. She and Annie shared wordless worry as the sweet tea worked its magic.

Eventually, Barbara placed the cup and saucer on the table, and nodded. 'There, that's better. I've been having these…turns, since Richard died. Well, no, since about three months after he died, to be precise. And that's why I'm here.'

Carol noted that even the woman's voice seemed weak, and forced.

Annie jumped in. 'Richard? Your husband Richard? He's dead? I'm so sorry to hear that, Barb. When did that happen?'

Barbara Newsom managed a shadow of a smile. 'Oh, about two months before you and I parted company, Annie. But I've always done my best to not allow my personal life to color the counselling process, so didn't mention it at the time. But, since I've retired, I find I'm…well, no…let me say what I need to say, then we can begin. I need your help, because I… There you are, even as I think it before I say it, it seems…very silly.'

Annie pressed her. 'Barb, you can say anything to me, you know that. And you can trust Car, too. You know…sometimes people come to us and tell us things they never thought they'd say out loud to anyone. They have problems they've been struggling with, on their own, for ages. A bit like the people who came to you, Barb. But in a different way. So – however silly it might seem – if something's not right, or you fear it might not be right, you can tell us about it. Go on…we're listening.'

Barbara Newsom looked at the floor, and said, 'I think someone's trying to kill me.'

Carol noted the way Annie's mouth widened into an 'O' and felt hers do the same…then they both leaped from their seats as Barbara's face lost any color it had and she collapsed with a loud thump, face first onto the coffee table, her body slumping forward and rolling onto the floor.

Carol shouted, 'I'll phone for an ambulance, you make sure her airways are open, Annie. Get her into the recovery position, as quick as you can.'

'I know, I know, we both took the same training courses, Car. Oh no…that's not good…blood's pouring from her forehead. Looks like she cut it on the edge of that table. Tell them to be quick – she looks bad. Pulse is…oh Gawd, Car…it's all over the place. Tell them she's got issues with her heart, that'll get them here faster. Can you grab the defibrillator from the wall in the bathroom while you're on the phone? Better safe than sorry.'

CHAPTER THREE

Christine Wilson-Smythe sat at the large, highly polished dining table in her family's home in London, and stared at the remnants of her — very late — breakfast. She couldn't face another bite. In fact, she couldn't imagine ever wanting to eat again. To say that she felt full would be an understatement; her entire body was swollen and bloated, from the tips of her toes — which she hadn't seen for weeks — to her once-graceful hands…where, now, her engagement ring didn't even fit on her sausage-like little finger. And yet she knew that if she didn't eat, she'd face more of the endless questioning to which her mother had subjected her since she'd moved from Wales. She looked a bit pale — was she warm enough? She looked a little flushed — was she too hot? Did she fancy a cup of herbal tea? Nice and hot to shift the wind she was feeling. Did she want a biscuit? Just so her tummy didn't feel too acidic.

On and on and on it went, and Christine was using every shred of her rapidly diminishing patience to stop herself from snapping at her mother, who she knew only had her best interests at heart. As she nibbled at the crust of her toast, she reminded herself that at least today she'd get a bit of a break from all the over-solicitousness, because her parents were going to a charity luncheon that she'd been able to get out of attending herself; it was a fundraiser for a facility that provided counselling for women who'd suffered miscarriages, so it had been agreed that having Christine there, who looked as though she might be eleven months pregnant, wouldn't be the best of ideas.

Christine's mother — known in society as Lady Ballinclare, by her friends and acquaintances as Lady Fiona, her middle name, and by only her closest confidants and family members as Dierdre, her first given name — arrived in the kitchen barefoot. She was wearing a claret cashmere twinset above a chocolate-brown tweed skirt, while holding a charcoal skirt in one hand and a duck-egg blue cardigan in the other. 'Christine, I can't decide — which would be best? This blue's a bit wishy-washy, but my face looks too pink with the one I've got on. I'm thinking I might be starting the Change, and my skin's not its usual self. Which is best?'

Christine looked into the pale blue-green eyes that had always seemed to be filled with certainty when she'd been a child and noticed, as though for the first time, the way her mother's forehead was starting to concertina when she frowned, and how the smile lines at her eyes were now more deeply etched. She reminded herself that her mother and her colleague Annie Parker were both about the same age – in their mid-fifties – and she knew only too well that Annie had been suffering with hot flashes for some time now. She chuckled wryly to herself as she rested her free hand on her massive pregnancy lump and wondered why on earth women had to cope with so many physical challenges at, seemingly, every stage of their lives, while men seemed to get away with everything so relatively easily.

She gave her mother's question the attention it deserved. 'You haven't done your makeup yet, Mammy, so I think the claret will be fine, but you could cool the overall look by wearing the gray skirt, and then the crocodile shoes and bag set that match the twinset would work. And your pearls, of course. You'll look lovely, as always.'

Dierdre Wilson-Smythe shrugged. 'I'm not sure about that, Christine. I'm not finding myself feeling at all lovely to look at these days.' She sighed. 'Ah well, being a grandmother will suit me, I suppose. Though I'll not be winning any "Glamorous Grannie" prizes, to be sure.'

Christine smiled. 'Ah, go on with you, Mammy – you look grand, so you do. You're putting me to shame, and that's the truth.'

Christine enjoyed the comforting aroma of Penhaligon's 'Bluebell' cologne as her mother approached to tenderly stroke her hair; her mother had smelled the same for Christine's entire life, and it suddenly dawned on her that soon she, too, would have to consider how her personal choices would imprint themselves upon her own child.

Her mother whispered, 'Ah, you're soft in the head, my dear – you've youth and that magical glow on your side. And, before you know it, you'll be smiling in the way only a mother can when she looks at her child. Those poor women we're trying to help today might never know how that feels, which is why your daddy and I think it's worth giving them all the support we can. I've told you what I went through before I managed to have your brother and you, though I understand you can't really appreciate how that feels. No one can, unless they've experienced it themselves – and your daddy and I have, which is another reason for us doing what we do. But you're right – once I've got a bit of makeup on, I'll probably look, and feel, more myself. I'm just thinking they overdid it a bit with the light bits in the balayage when I got my hair done last time…it seems a bit too harsh, to my eyes.'

Christine was replying: 'Maybe talk to them about a bit more caramel next time?' just as her father bounded into the room.

He boomed, 'No time for talk about snacks, girls, we need to get going, Dierdre. Jerry reckons the traffic's going to be murder because of the roadworks at the back of Buckingham Palace, so we'd better allow an extra quarter of an hour…which means we need to be away in half an hour. So come on, let's get moving.' He paused, appeared to take in the scene of the mother and daughter sharing an intimate moment, then added, 'Sorry to interrupt. You look lovely, Dierdre, though I'd say the gray with the red is better. You look good enough to eat at the moment – a bit like one of those Raspberry Ruffles you know I can't resist – and we don't want the other women to get too jealous, do we?'

Christine beamed as her parents shared a hug. 'I said the same, Daddy. And you look lovely in that jacket. Is it new? I've not seen it before, I don't think.'

Her parents both smiled.

'It's as old as the hills is that one,' said her mother indulgently. 'You're not usually here, Christine, don't forget that – and certainly not when your father's taking a whole day off work to be able to do something…useful. We agreed that a City suit wouldn't be the right thing for today because we'll be in a slightly dingy community hall in Marylebone, not schmoozing on the terrace at the House of Lords, for a change. He's had that jacket since just after we got married, haven't you, Aiden? Remember when we went to collect it? Your tailor was one of the first people to use my title, and I had no idea who he was talking about when he asked if "Lady Ballinclare" had an opinion…then I realized he meant me. It gave me such a thrill…and a bit of a turn, so it did.'

Kissing his wife on the forehead, Christine's father whispered, 'Me too. I thought my mother had come back from the dead. Now – let's get going, shall we?'

As her mother left the room, Christine finally gave up on her cold toast.

'Not long now,' said her father, for the umpteenth time, as he nodded toward her belly. 'You feeling…ready?'

Christine smiled. 'As I'll ever be, Daddy. Which is to say, no. Not at all.'

'Well, there's no turning back now,' noted her father with a wink. 'Will Alexander be here before we get back, do you think?'

Christine shrugged. 'He said he hoped to be here by teatime, but it all depends on the traffic on the M4, coming in from Wales, of course. Though that shouldn't be too bad…I hope.'

Her father's hand landed gently on her shoulder. 'He's doing a lot of driving about, these days, trying to keep everything straight with all his business interests here in London, and in Wales. He'll be glad of a rest, when the baby comes.'

Christine considered her reply carefully. 'I'm not sure that a newborn's going to give him much of a rest, Daddy – though he'll not see the motorways for a while, because he'll be here, with us, for at least a couple of weeks. He promised.'

Her father sighed. 'Your mother's looking forward to having a baby in the house. You're a good girl, saying you'll do all this here, not at your new place in Wales. I dare say that's nearly ready for you two…no, three…to move into when you leave.'

'Alexander's updating me when he arrives. To be honest, it all seems to be taking much longer than I'd thought it would.'

'Well, from what Alexander's been telling me, he's aiming for perfection, which always takes time, even if it's ultimately unattainable.

But we all know it's best to get things done properly to start with, and that cottage might be your home for decades to come, so it's not worth rushing now, only to have to redo things, down the road.'

Christine smiled. 'That's not what you say when they tell you about the work that needs doing at Ballinclare Manor, over in Ireland, Daddy. Then you haggle over every penny, and tell them to patch things up as best they can.'

It was her father's turn to chuckle. 'That place has stood where it is for hundreds of years – it's not going to fall down any time soon, and I don't see any reason to do more than keep it upright. One day your big brother can decide if he wants to invest more heavily into it, to bring it into this century as far as things like the heating and lighting are concerned. But, until then – and given that we hardly use the place at all – I'll just keep it watertight, and in generally good order. It's never been anything but a rambling old place…bit of a shambles, really…but, you know – home. This house is the one we need to be sound enough for living in, and to look good enough for visitors with high expectations, so this is where the money has to go for now.'

Something prickled at the back of Christine's brain. 'You're doing alright, Daddy? I mean your business. In the City. Nothing amiss that I should know about?'

Aiden smiled broadly. 'I'm not your grandfather, nor your great-grandfather – who, between them, managed to hollow out the entire financial resources of the Seat – so you'll be comforted to know we're living well within our considerable means. Neither you, nor this child of yours, will have anything to worry about. But you can only spend money once, you know, so I need to keep an eye on it all, even if it's still coming in quite nicely, thank heavens.'

'Indeed.'

'And, speaking of keeping company with folk who've high expectations, I'd better get myself sorted out. Today's charity is an important one, to both me and your mother, but we've got to endure several hours in the company of the Fentons, and you know how we both feel about them. George mentioned there's something he wants a quiet word with me about…in fact, he was quite mysterious about it all, when we spoke on the phone. So…loins must be girded, and smiles firmly affixed to faces.'

Christine groaned. 'You poor things – the Fentons are such bores. You can tell by her beady little eyes always darting about the place that she's constantly working out how much things cost, while she's no real concept of their true value. And he's…well, does he still talk about his yacht the way he used to, years ago? As though he's more in love with it, than his wife?'

'No. The yacht's gone.' Her father adopted an expression which suggested there was a nasty smell in the kitchen, and an exaggerated, whiningly-clipped English accent when he added, "'The crowd's changed so, over the years, don't you know, Aiden. Not at all the same types as one used to mix with. Lottie and I think it's too, too bad. But we've both dedicated ourselves to learning all we can about wines, and we're rather enjoying that now…" and so on, and so on.'

Christine giggled. 'Excellent impersonation, Daddy – you should have been on the stage, so you should. Good grief, so he's one of the mad glass-swirlers and -sniffers, nowadays, is he? Does he talk about terroirs and climate pockets all the time? Alexander knows a few people of that type – you two should compare notes.'

'God help us, no. I'll leave all that to George and Lottie. And before you even ask, yes, Lottie knows the price of every blessed wine and vintage they mention, and she's constantly banging on about their cellar now, too – how it's going to be such a wonderful investment for them, their children, and even their children's children.'

Christine reached out for her father's hand. 'Oh no – they're never even going to drink and enjoy the stuff they buy? I tell you what – there's no point leaving behind a load of old wines for me and Alexander, Daddy. We'd just drink it all ourselves and be sozzled every evening, or serve it at wild parties to folks who wouldn't know the difference between a true Burgundy and a Pinot Noir grown in California. Now while I admit that – thanks to your personal tutelage – I'm not one of those people, I don't have a terribly sophisticated palate, so buy what you want to drink now, and drink it. The way we do. Not that I'll be indulging for a while myself, of course.'

Even as she spoke, Christine felt the familiar pang of guilt as she recalled how she'd been knocking back the booze pretty heavily before she'd known she was pregnant, and how terribly worried she was about how that might have affected her child's early development…not that she'd shared that knowledge or concern with her parents, of course.

'It won't be too long, in the scheme of things, my dear,' said her father warmly. 'Right, I'd better go to check on your mother's progress.' He glanced at his watch. 'We hope to be back by teatime, so we'll see you and Alexander then. You'll be alright on your own for a while? Sorry, but I need Jerry to drive us, because there's nowhere to park near the place where we're going, so he'll have to take the car off somewhere, then collect us when we're finished. But you'll phone one of us if you need anything, won't you? And you've got all the contact numbers you need in case…anything starts, right?'

'I'm not due for weeks, Daddy – just go and have fun. Oh – and give my regards to the Fentons, won't you? Ask if they can recommend something we can lay down for our child's twenty-first birthday. Something that will age well…maybe even be worth a few bob by then, so we could give a case as a gift…you know, to offset their college fees, or something.'

Her father called from the hallway, 'You're a wicked one, Christine, so you are.'

'Thank you. I don't like to disappoint.'

CHAPTER FOUR

Mavis MacDonald hadn't imagined that the drive from the Dower House on the Chellingworth Estate to Twyst House, in the beautiful Rhins of Galloway, would have been capable of becoming such a challenge so soon after it had begun. But, of course, Althea had put paid to any idea of a calm and enjoyable trip when she'd decided she was peckish not half an hour after they'd started off. And there were at least five, if not six, more hours to endure.

'I should phone Clementine to make sure she hasn't forgotten we'll be there for tea,' said Althea as she brushed crumbs from her lap and gazed out at the landscape that was passing them in a blur.

Mavis tutted. 'She knows full well we'll be there then, dear. I personally heard you tell her so three times on the telephone last evening.' She wondered if Althea was becoming a little forgetful; Mavis admitted to herself that the woman was usually a little dithery, but that there was an undeniable sharpness beneath that vagueness, so she told herself she might be being a little over-zealous in her informal care-taking oversight duties.

Althea snapped, 'I'm fully aware of exactly what I said to my daughter last evening, Mavis – but she's hardly known for her ability to connect with the realities of everyday life, is she, dear? As long as she passed the news to the staff, we should be expected when we're expected – but it's just as likely that she's not thought to mention the fact that we'll be there for two weeks, not just tea, to anyone who might need to know, or could prove helpful.'

Grudgingly, Mavis agreed. 'Aye well, we'll be there soon enough, and I dare say the people who work at Twyst House will be sufficiently professional to be able to accommodate us.'

Mavis noticed that Althea's expression grew wistful as she replied, 'Chelly and I spent much more time up there than I do, now. He liked the place. Said it was on a more human scale than Chellingworth Hall – which it is, of course. It only has ten bedrooms, after all.'

Mavis couldn't help herself. 'How will we all manage – four full-grown adults squeezed into such a tiny place? Sorry, five – don't think for one moment I've forgotten that Ian needs to be accommodated too.' She nodded toward the glass privacy panel that separated the driver's compartment from the passengers.

Althea's eyes narrowed, then she smiled. 'Ian? Oh, he'd be quite happy with a cardboard box in the middle of the road.'

Mavis thought she'd misheard, then realized that Althea was tittering. She sighed. 'Is that another of your Monty Python references, dear?'

Althea beamed. 'Oh, you're getting too sharp for me, Mavis. But, on this occasion, no, you're wrong. It was a pre-Monty Python sketch, from something called *At Last The 1948 Show*, which was a television series I dare say you've never heard of. John Cleese and Graham Chapman were in it, along with Tim Brooke-Taylor and Marty Feldman. The Python team did their own version, later on, but it's one of those pieces that's always…stuck with me, in ways other than it making me laugh.'

Mavis bit. 'And why's that?'

Althea shook her head and looked…sad, Mavis judged. 'Four Yorkshire men, obviously well-off, are discussing the concept that money doesn't make one happy by using increasingly ridiculous examples of how poverty-stricken they were as children – when they were "truly" happy. And, yes, one of the comedic examples given is that an entire family lived in a cardboard box in the middle of the road…but that's neither here nor there. I'm not going to claim that my own, relatively humble, start in life was anything like any of the bizarre situations they referred to, but I do often dwell on whether money can really make one happy…or whether happiness can only come from how one chooses to use it. And I don't mean on personal frivolities – but so it benefits others, too.'

Mavis tutted. 'Well, we're sitting in one of your Bentleys, being driven from your Welsh estate to your Scottish estate, so it seems to me you're particularly well-placed to have an opinion on how wealth can deliver happiness, or not.'

Althea shuffled about in her seat. 'You're making fun of me, Mavis, and I deserved that. You know very well I wasn't born to any of…this, but it's been my life for more than half a century, so I do – I must admit – speak of it all as though it were normal. Which it is, now, for me. However, please don't make the mistake of believing that I take any of it for granted. I do my best to give back to…well, all sorts of people, as you know.'

Mavis felt a little guilty, because she could tell she'd hurt her chum. 'Sorry, dear, I didn't mean to imply that you're someone who looks down on those with nothing. To be honest, Althea, I don't even think you understand how very much you've done, for so many, over those decades. I've only been in your life for a few years, and even I can see how many people you've helped during that time. Speaking of which – and, forgive me, I forgot to mention this yesterday – I was so busy with last-minute things…'

'Like all those notes you felt you had to leave for Carol and Annie, you mean? They're both very capable women. They'll manage perfectly well in your absence, Mavis.'

'Aye, I dare say they will, but – as I was saying – I got an email from the Lincolnshire office of the MacDonald Trust yesterday. They've managed to recruit two part-time nurses, instead of one full-time one, for their region. Both have the experience in working with those suffering from substance dependency and abuse we were looking for, and both have agreed how to split the working hours, to their – and our manager's – satisfaction. So we can get everything going in that area, now – well, next month, at least, when they both come on board.'

Mavis enjoyed the warmth of Althea's smile. 'I'm so pleased. Well done, everyone – especially you, Mavis. I knew when I established the charity that you'd be the right woman to head it up, and you are. You're exceptionally good at finding the right people for the right job, and you've selected excellent regional managers, in every case. This will be our eleventh regional office now, correct?'

Mavis nodded. 'And number twelve is on the horizon, covering my old home territory, as you know. This trip to Dumfries and Galloway won't just let you spend some time with your daughter and new son-in-law, and me with my own two sons and their families – it'll also let me get to know the man who's going to head our regional office in Dumfries.'

Althea sounded surprised when she said, 'You haven't met him yet?'

'Only by video link, which isnae bad, but not perfect. It was just a bit too far for either of us to travel at the time – with Christmas, and all that, on the horizon. But I'm confident he's the man for the job, though I'll take the chance to get to know him a wee bit, given I'll have two weeks in the area, and at least a week of that in Dumfries itself.'

Althea spoke as she turned her attention to the view outside the car. 'I hope he's suitable, Mavis. He's going to be overseeing a considerable budget, and will have to ensure we help as many people as possible, with what are – even so – bound to be stretched resources. Though maybe there won't be too many people in such a beautiful part of Scotland who find themselves addicted to prescription medications as there are in other parts of the UK.'

Mavis couldn't help but smile wryly. 'I only hope that's the case, Althea dear, though I have to say that's no' what we're finding wherever we open up. There's no way of knowing how many people suffer in silence…until we offer them a ray of hope, and they grab it. Anyway, we'll find out soon enough. He's told me he's working his way through a long list of applicants for the positions we have, so that at least shows there's enthusiasm for the idea of what we're doing – that people want to be involved with offering a helping hand. And I've every confidence in him.'

'You just want to feel him up a bit, is that it?'

Mavis spluttered, 'Do what?'

'Get to know him personally – do the "feely, touchy bits" of recruitment. Isn't that what they call it?'

Mavis pondered, 'Mebbe they do – whoever "they" are – but I think you might have used the wrong phrase, dear. I just want to have a bite to eat with the man, and enjoy a chat with him about something other than our mission, just to get the measure of him.'

Althea turned toward her chum. 'Ah – measure him up, not feel him up. I see. Of course. Can I come, too?'

Mavis snapped, 'No. Absolutely not. When you set up the charity and made me its head, you said you'd stand back and let me run the thing…as long as we talked about plans, and both agreed on direction, and such. Let's no' change that now, eh? Besides, I don't want to rob you of any of the time you want to spend with Clementine and Julian. That's why you're making this trip, after all.'

Mavis couldn't help but notice that Althea turned away again before she replied, 'Of course it is. That's what I said, wasn't it? Why on earth else would I be doing it?'

Something in the pit of Mavis's tummy suggested to her that Althea had something up her sleeve, but experience had taught her there'd be no point in confronting the woman about it – she'd just lie, crinkle up those dimples of hers, and carry on regardless. No, Mavis knew she'd have to approach this with a little bit of patience and a great deal of wiliness; Althea was up to something, she was sure of it – but what on earth could it be?

CHAPTER FIVE

The double doors at the end of the busy hospital corridor swung open, and a woman who looked young enough to be Annie's daughter approached. She was wearing green hospital scrubs and an expression that suggested she was battling exhaustion, while grasping the listening end of the stethoscope that dangled around her neck as though her life depended upon it. 'Miss Parker?'

Annie stuck up her hand, and shot out of her uncomfortable plastic bucket seat. 'That's me.'

The woman nodded. 'I'm Dr. Doraswamy. You brought Mrs. Newsom into A and E?'

Both Annie and Carol nodded. Annie said, 'My friend here, Carol Hill, called the ambulance, and followed in her car. They said I could stay with Barbara. How is she? Is she going to be alright?' Annie could feel the panic in her stomach; the paramedics had appeared calm while they'd attended to her one-time counsellor as they'd driven with sirens blaring to the hospital, but she'd sensed their concerns about Barbara's condition.

Relief washed over Annie when the doctor nodded. 'Your initial actions made a great deal of difference. Thank you. Both. Are either of you related to Mrs. Newsom?'

Both Carol and Annie shook their heads. Annie said, 'I know her…quite well. Carol just met her. I believe she has a daughter, and a stepson, but I don't know their names, or where they live. Sorry. Maybe their contact details are on her phone?'

The doctor's eyes narrowed. 'We have the details of her next of kin, thank you. But with you not being relatives, I can't tell you more. Mrs. Newsom's daughter has been contacted and is on her way. Feel free to wait, if you wish. I'll speak to her daughter – maybe she'll choose to speak to you.'

The doctor turned and hurried away, and Annie knew there was no point in calling after her to beg for more insights.

She felt Carol's hand on her arm. 'Come on, Annie, let's get ourselves a cup of something, then we can hang around until the daughter gets here. If we stay close to the registration desk, we'll be able to overhear her enquiring after her mother when she arrives…because I dare say you don't know what she looks like.'

'Mini version of her mother, so Barbara always said – but I suspect she meant a mini version of the way she used to look, not how she looks now. I can't believe how much she's changed in just six months. And I still can't get over the fact that she never mentioned that her husband had died.'

'Well, we know now, and we also know that she thought someone was trying to kill her, and she very nearly died in our office. So…there's that. Though what we should make of it all, I don't know. It's frustrating that we can't ask her any questions…and we don't know how she is, other than that she should…recover. But…from what? I mean, it was obvious there was something seriously wrong with her, but what?'

Annie nibbled her lip. 'She's lost a load of weight – her face never had that hollow look – and…well, her teeth looked too big for her mouth, didn't they? Never a good sign. Do you think something like cancer? That really takes it out of a person, doesn't it? Even if they're having it treated. Mind you, she still had all her hair, even if it looked like it needed a good wash. And that was never like her, Car – always paid a lot of attention to her appearance she did…not over the top, you know, but smart. Well turned out. I wish the doctor could have told us more, but you know what they're like. Yeah, let's grab a cup of something hot and sweet and try to nab the daughter when she gets here. She'll have to come this way, I suppose – go to that desk?'

Carol nodded. 'I've been watching while we've been waiting, and that seems to be the system. Though goodness knows how much longer we'll be here. We don't even know when they got in touch with the daughter. We've been here for four hours already – you'd think she'd have got here by now, wouldn't you?'

Annie nodded. 'Maybe they had to check Barb's records, then get hold of the daughter herself…which maybe took some time. But, yeah, you'd think. I wonder if we missed her…but, no, the doctor would have said. Oh, Car, I can't think. Look – how about I lurk here and you find us…something. There must be machines or something somewhere along that corridor. I've seen people come back with sandwiches, not just coffee.'

Carol agreed and Annie settled herself on a seat as close as possible to the reception desk, knowing she might be in for a long wait. Just as she'd realized that as soon as Carol got back, she'd need to pop to the loo, a woman swept through the automatic sliding doors who she reckoned had to be Barbara Newsom's daughter; she really was a younger, smaller, version of her.

Ignoring her nagging bladder, Annie leaped to her feet to intercept the woman, whose attention she managed to attract just as she arrived at the desk. With a gaze that took in Annie from top to toe, she raised a dismissive eyebrow, then gave her attention to the man behind the desk.

Annie noticed the tone in the woman's voice – commanding, slightly snotty – and that her accent was almost English, when compared with her mother's Welsh lilt.

'My name is Nia Williams. My mother, Barbara Newsom, has been admitted. They phoned me to tell me earlier, but I couldn't get away from my work until now. Where can I find her, please? And can you tell me anything about her condition?'

Annie wondered how anyone's job could be more important than their mother's health, and listened as the man behind the plexiglass shouted through the little grille thing. 'She's still in A and E. They're looking for a bed for her. She's being admitted for observation, overnight. If they can't find a bed, they'll keep her where she is. If you take this to the door marked "Secure – Patients Only", they'll let you in to see her.'

Annie watched as Nia Williams received a slip of paper from the little pass-through, glanced at it, thanked the man – rather imperiously – then turned toward Annie, heading for the double doors in question.

Annie thrust out her hand. 'Hello, my name's Annie Parker. I brought your mum in. In the ambulance. You're Barbara's daughter, right?' She watched as Nia's eyes, once again, swept up and down her entire body, which made her feel a bit queasy.

'And you know my mother…how?'

Annie's mind raced; if Barbara thought someone was trying to kill her, should she reveal the fact she was a private investigator? 'I used to be one of her clients. We'd met for a coffee – just as…people.'

Nia's expression cleared. 'An ex-client? I see. Yes, Mum sometimes met up with old clients, just to check in – though I thought she'd stopped all that, since she retired.'

'Obviously not,' replied Annie, then she told herself off for sounding too snappish. She forced herself to use a warmer tone when she added, 'They won't tell us how she is, because we're not you. We're going to wait until you know. We'd love to hear how she's doing.'

Nia looked confused. 'Who's "we"?'

Annie looked around; there was still no sign of Carol. 'My friend's just gone to try to rustle up a bite to eat and something to drink for us both. We've been here a while, already. I came in the ambulance with Barbara, and my mate, Carol, followed in her car, so she can drive us back to our homes when we know we can't be of any more help here.'

Nia shrugged. 'I don't see how you can help at all. Mum's with doctors and nurses now, so why don't you leave, and maybe I'll phone you. Though, to be honest, I'd say it's up to Mum if she wants you to know the ins and outs of her health, so it might be better if we wait until she's up to phoning you for herself.'

Annie had to admit that Barbara's daughter had made a good point – after all, Annie hardly knew the woman, other than in her professional capacity. But…Barbara had come to Annie and Carol looking for help – looking for people who could investigate a serious concern she had about her personal safety…though Annie knew she couldn't play that card now. She felt torn.

'Are you the other one?' Nia peered around Annie as she spoke. Annie turned to see Carol approaching, with two big cardboard coffee containers supporting precariously balanced wrapped sandwiches.

Carol looked at Nia Williams. 'Sorry – can't shake hands. I'm Carol Hill. A friend of Annie's. You must be Barbara's daughter.'

'Yes. Nia Williams. I'll leave you both now. I've explained my position to this woman. Goodbye.'

Annie saw Carol's face get a bit pink as Nia headed to the double doors, where she pressed the buzzer beside them until someone opened them for her, whereupon she disappeared.

Carol said, 'She's rude. Not even a thank you – or did she do all that before I got here?'

'Not a word of thanks. Not many others, either. She might look like Barbara, but that's where the similarity ends. Struck me as a right stuck-up old—'

Carol cut her off. 'Come on, Annie – she's probably distraught. She's no idea how her mother's doing…she's probably all at sixes and sevens.'

'Hmm…well, I was prepared to give her the benefit of the doubt, earlier on, but now? Said she couldn't get away from work. What's all that about? That's not normal. If it was Eustelle lying in A and E, I'd be at her bedside before the ink was dry on the admission papers.'

Carol smiled. 'Can you take the sandwiches, please? Ta. And as for you getting to your mother fast? Well, you'd have to get two trains to London, then the tube, but you'd have to start by waiting until someone could drive you to the station at this end, or else get a taxi. I know you're learning to drive, but you still have to have a qualified person in the passenger seat to be in charge of a vehicle, Annie…so maybe we should both be a bit more sympathetic toward Nia Williams, eh? I mean, we don't even know where she lives, or works – it could be hours away.'

Annie conceded, 'Yeah, I s'pose. Though Barbara gave me the impression that her daughter was still local. Anyway, the upshot was, we shouldn't expect to hear anything from her…Nia. She reckons we should wait to hear from Barbara herself. Says her mother's health is none of our business.'

Carol nodded, then popped one of the coffees onto a chair, beside which she sat herself down. Peeling the lid off the steaming cardboard container, she blew across the surface and said, 'Let's drink these, use the facilities, then get back to Anwen-by-Wye. My lot know I'm doing this, and I know you told Tudor, too – but getting home sooner, rather than later, would be good. And I suppose that Nia makes a fair point. I dare say you didn't mention what Barbara said about…her suspicions.'

Annie took the lid off her own coffee. 'This smells…interesting. Nah, course I didn't, Car…not professional, right? I know this isn't the place to talk about it in detail but – if Barb wasn't just imagining things, and talking a load of old nonsense – having now met her, I bet that Nia is capable of all sorts of things. Struck me as…hard. Cold. Nothing warm or fuzzy about her.'

Carol smiled. 'It's all going to remain shrouded in mystery until we can talk to Barbara, isn't it? So, come on, let's drink these, get home, and get on with what we can actually get on with, which isn't this…whatever this might turn out to be.'

Annie knew her chum was right. 'Yeah, but, for now, keep an eye on that for me, will you, Car? I need the loo, then I'll be back, and we can get going. I can't keep his mum away from Bertie for too long, can I?'

'Don't worry about Albert, Annie – he's being cooed over by a doting grandmother and grandfather, as well as his dad, and he's got all three of them wrapped around his little finger. But, yes, let's get going as soon as we can. The sandwiches are a waste, but the coffee'll be good.'

Annie felt her tummy rumble. 'Not wasted, Car – I could probably manage both of them on the way back…unless you'll let me drive home.'

She felt Carol's reply – 'I'm happy to drive, so you can munch away' – was just a little too quick, and maybe even a little too sharp, but she let it pass. One day she'd get to drive Carol's vehicle again; they'd only had that one short outing in it so far, and she suspected she might not be given another chance until after she was able to demonstrate her abilities by passing her test.

CHAPTER SIX

Alexander Bright couldn't help but smile at the expression on the man's face in the car passing him; he loved the way that his Aston Martin drew admiring glances from so many people, and how their respect for the car seemed to automatically transfer itself to him. He was glowing, inside and out, and he knew it. Life had never been better for him, and it was about to improve even further, with the imminent arrival of his child…their child…the child that he and Christine would share for the rest of their lives.

A few vehicles back, someone pressed on their horn for a couple of long minutes, as though that would make the knot of traffic dissolve. Ah well, people took out their frustrations with the world in myriad ways and, after all, it wasn't doing anyone any harm. Unlike the situation he was facing in Hackney; a development had ground to a halt due to the lack of any sense of urgency on the part of a supplier of sliding balcony doors. Until the units were watertight, none of the other trades could get on with their jobs, so every day lost because of the doors, was a day where rescheduling had a domino effect, sending ripples across other sites, where he also needed people doing certain things at certain times.

He checked his watch. Geordie – his right-hand man, in so very many ways – had said he'd be at the supplier's place in Dagenham after lunch. It was almost four o'clock; why hadn't he heard anything yet? He told his phone to call Geordie, but there was no answer. He couldn't decide if that was a good sign, or not. Should he drive out there himself? No, he'd promised Christine he'd be at her parents' place by teatime, and he didn't want to let her down. This was it – this time he was staying put until the baby was born; he'd promised that twice before, only to find himself having to drive back to Anwen-by-Wye to sort out problems with Honeysuckle Cottage, which should have been move-in ready before Christmas, then by the New Year, and now – if there were no more problems – by the end of the month.

He'd noted, with interest, that his reputation hadn't spread as far as Wales, so the building tradespeople there had no fear of him, and acted accordingly – taking their time with jobs he knew would have been completed much quicker in London, where few people were in any doubt about what might happen to their businesses, or themselves, if they didn't meet his company's demanding schedules. Which was why he was so puzzled by the situation with the doors, and why Geordie had decided that a personal visit was in order. Three days late was three days too many, and this supplier – a new one, for Alexander – needed to understand what it meant. Not that he'd be connected to whatever action Geordie deemed fit, of course…he couldn't afford that. Not now, not ever again – not with a child on the way, and then marriage to the daughter of a viscount.

The past couple of years had changed him, he knew it, and admitted to himself it was for the better. All his businesses were now one hundred percent legitimate, and – other than the odd bit of leaning on folks to make sure they understood the necessity of keeping to the timetables he set – he wasn't worried that anything could dent his reputation as a solid pillar of the community. And Geordie understood where the line had to be drawn, too. That was why Alexander trusted him. That, and the fact they'd been almost joined at the hip for so many years, with a good many reasons for each to trust the other that most people would never, ever know about.

Just as the traffic unsnarled itself, his phone rang. He punched at it as he inched forward. 'How did it go, Geordie? Result?'

Geordie sounded as though he had his head in a bucket…a thousand miles away. 'They got the message. Lorry's loaded, and on its way to the site now. I stayed until I saw it leave. And we're getting a fifty percent discount. For our troubles. You can use him again, down the road, and know he'll deliver, on time.'

Alexander dared to ask, 'No problems, I hope?'

'Not for us. A few unavoidable breakages for him. Just stock. Not limbs.'

'Good. Thanks. As always.'

'You in town yet?'

Alexander sighed. 'Sitting in traffic trying to get across to Green Park. Everything's solid. Should be there by half four, at the latest. You going home, now?'

'Just want to make sure everything gets sorted in Hackney, first – locked away safely for the night. They can start the installation first thing. Might be worth putting a few extra pairs of hands onto the job so we can try to claw back a day. Cost a few bob, but worth it, I reckon.'

'I agree. Do it. Talk to Sundeep about that. He's got a few blokes at his site who could manage it.'

'I'll sort it.'

Alexander knew he would. 'Thanks. I owe you.'

Geordie laughed. 'Not even close, mate. You know I'll never be able to pay you back for everything you've done for me over the years. So you go and enjoy some family time. You deserve it. And, don't forget, I can always organize getting some of our blokes in to sort out that cottage of yours in Wales…get rid of the shower you seem to have working on it at the moment.'

Alexander smiled. 'They'll get it done, Geordie. To them I'm just some English bloke who's doing up a Welsh cottage in a style to which they are unaccustomed, shall we say? The traffic's almost disappeared now, which is good, so – if you don't need me – I'll focus on this, and let you focus on that. Talk soon. And thanks again.'

'Bye, boss.'

Hoping that the worst of the traffic was behind him, Alexander used all his knowledge of the side streets to get to Christine's family's London house as quickly as possible. As he put his key into the lock, he still couldn't believe this was his life now – being able to walk into the home of a viscount. Him…the mixed-race Brixton boy who'd grown up parenting himself, and smuggling who knew what around south London for all sorts of criminals. Now? Now he was the personification of respectability.

'Christine – it's me!' His voice rang around the marble hall. Silence answered it.

He checked the kitchen – nothing. The sitting rooms were empty. He bounded upstairs and opened the bedroom door – no one there, but he could hear the shower running. The anxiety that had been building since he'd entered the house melted; the past few weeks had seen Christine taking long showers – warm ones, not too hot – which she reckoned relaxed her and the baby. She'd bemoaned the fact she couldn't take long baths, but feared she'd never be able to get out, having got in. He shouted, 'It's me, Christine.'

He dithered at the bathroom door. Of course they shared everything, but didn't Christine deserve some privacy? He knocked. No answer. He knocked again, more loudly, then opened the door a little. Steam billowed, and he waved it away with his hand to reveal…Christine in a heap, on the floor of the shower, the water beating on her back, which was turning pink.

It took longer than he felt it should have done for what he was seeing to register, then he sprung into action. He yanked open the shower door, reached in and turned off the water, then bent to grab Christine, but she was hard to get hold of, and her entire body was limp, her long locks covering her face…was she even breathing? Alexander felt his hands shake as he battled with her uncooperative hair, then, finally he could see her face.

Her eyes flickered open, and she managed a mumbled, 'Oh, Alexander…thank God. I slipped…I think I bumped my head. Help me up?'

'You're staying exactly where you are until an ambulance gets here.' He turned away, dialing on his phone with one hand, grabbing every towel he could see with his other. 'Let's get these all around you, so you don't get a chill…hello, yes, ambulance please…'

As Alexander waited to speak to someone he hoped could help, he felt the floor begin to solidify beneath his feet, and was relieved to see that Christine's eyes were really focusing on the towels she was using to dry her wet body. He grabbed her hand, and they gazed into each other's eyes for a moment, sharing a look of anguish, and love, and…hope.

19th JANUARY

CHAPTER SEVEN

Henry couldn't help but wonder how the meeting between his wife, their cook, and his wife's nutritionist friend was going, but he'd said he'd oversee Hugo while it happened, so that was what he was doing, though he'd decided to do so in close proximity to the private sitting room where he knew the three women had gathered.

As thoughts of his schoolboy reading of 'The Scottish Play' wafted back to him, conjuring images of three witches on a blasted heath, he reminded himself that his wife had mentioned the word 'compromise' when she'd spoken about how any decisions about the menus for their meals at the Hall would impact him, personally, and he took comfort in that. Stephanie was a wonderful woman, and he knew she always liked to do whatever made him happy, when she could.

When the sitting room door opened, Henry lifted Hugo off the floor where he'd been conversing – in his unique way – with a wheeled wooden horse that Henry himself had enjoyed playing with when he'd been an infant, and deposited him into his pram, only turning when the duchess called, 'Henry – is Hugo alright?'

He replied cheerily, 'Perfectly so. Have you ladies finished?'

'Cook Davies has to attend to luncheon, but Val's staying on for a while. She'd like a little time to play with her godson.'

As Cook Davies passed Henry he panicked; he thought he could see steam coming from her ears – her face was certainly red enough to suggest it might be a possibility, but she acknowledged him with a nod, and Hugo with a smile, then disappeared toward the kitchen, so he did his best to set his worries aside.

Henry pushed his charge toward his wife. 'Here we come. He's been no trouble at all.' Henry thought it best not to mention the fact he'd had to stop Hugo trying to eat the horse's ancient, and bedraggled, tail.

As he watched Val fussing over his happily gurgling son, he wondered why the woman had chosen to present herself at the Hall wearing an outfit that seemed better suited to a day at an athletics field; everything was stretchy and brightly colored, including her luminous pink shoes, which made her feet look enormous…like something that should be attached to a cartoon character.

His wife attracted his attention as she said, 'Val was just saying that she's been enjoying her time on Anglesey. We should think about visiting, Henry – she says there are lots of opportunities for bracing walks.'

'I'd have thought any outdoor activity would prove bracing at this time of year,' replied Henry, somewhat puzzled. 'Just opening a window is enough, let alone being outside in this wind, and with these temperatures. It's only just stopped raining.'

The lowering clouds pressing down upon the Hall – which required, apparently, every light fitting within it to be illuminated – had already made Henry feel more despondent than usual that morning.

His wife's cheery tone, therefore, felt all the more jarring, when she enthused, 'But that's the thing, Henry – by being out and about in the weather, we might feel better in ourselves. Val was just saying that there's a great deal of research being done these days that suggests one's spirits rise as a result of outdoor exercise, whatever the weather.'

Henry grumbled, 'Probably all paid for by the companies that make the expensive clothing one needs to purchase to be able to wander about in our climate without catching one's death of cold, I dare say.'

His wife's tutting made his neck feel warm. 'It's no such thing, Henry. Universities are doing the research. Val said.'

Henry wondered why his usually level-headed wife was suddenly giving everything that Val Jenkins said such weight. It wasn't like her; she usually took several opinions on board about every matter before making a decision. He gave his attention to Val herself. He couldn't help but notice her figure, given the way her gaudy outfit hugged it. There was no question she had a fine one; pleasantly slim, and going in and out in all the appropriate places. And, now that he was paying attention, he thought her hair looked somewhat different than it had when he'd last seen her, and there was no question that the woman's skin was radiant. Indeed, she seemed to be bubbling with *joie de vivre*, not something he'd noted in Val before…though he'd never thought of her as especially morose, either, just…normal. Now? Now she seemed…she seemed to fill the room with energy. How odd.

He ventured, 'Things going well at the bookshop, Val? Allowing you to take a little break for this TV thing of yours?'

Val didn't turn her attention away from making faces at her godson. 'I've got two part-timers who help out. They jiggled their hours around a bit so I could get away for the week. And we're not sure that TV's the way to go, these days. There's a chance to find an audience with short films that are available online now, so Barry said we'd give that a go – you know, instead of waiting for the TV people to make up their minds, which they seem incapable of doing.'

Stephanie added, 'You remember Barry Walton, Henry? The TV producer who worked here for a while when they were filming.'

Henry snorted, then snapped, 'I'm unlikely to forget the man who wanted to drag my family name through the mud, am I?'

'Well, Val's working with him again. They're getting along together very nicely, aren't you, Val?'

Even Henry could see that something odd was happening to Val; she turned pink, giggled like a teenager, then said quietly, 'Oh yes, we are.'

Stephanie rubbed her chum's back. 'I'm so pleased for you, Val. It's not been an easy few years for you – with your mother dying, and your father proving to be…well, not the man you'd hoped. But you've done ever so well with the bookshop since you bought him out. And now this new venture. And…Barry, of course. Look, Henry, Val's got a new lease on life, hasn't she? And she's in such good health, too.'

Val finally relinquished her spot beside Hugo's pram, and turned to face the duke and duchess. 'You've both been fantastic to me. And I know you both understood my reluctance to take on the responsibility of being Hugo's godmother, but I'm so glad I did, because now we'll always be connected. And I'm making a concerted effort to form connections these days – connections that are meaningful, and will endure. Barry's helping me to put myself at the center of my own life.

I've never done that before. When I had the restaurant, it was all about the food, then there was that part of my life when I was on *The Curious Cook*, which I enjoyed, but I always felt as though that woman was…a character, not fully me. Packing all that in and going through things with Mum was a challenge – she had to be my focus then, of course – and, after that, when Dad and I had our falling out? I had to put every ounce of energy into the bookshop. But now it's my time. I'm getting close to forty, and that's a turning point in everyone's life. The sort of thing that makes you pause, and take stock. Well, I've done a bit of that, with Barry's help, and don't like what I've seen. He's helping me to understand how I can make small changes in my lifestyle that can make big differences to my feeling of self-worth, and quality of life.'

Henry was at a loss, as he always was when people started spouting off about vague concepts like self-worth, and quality of life.

Stephanie caught his eye, and said, 'We're delighted for you, of course, Val, but don't forget that you have friends who've always known your worth, even if you've been blind to it yourself. It's why we love you, and wanted you to be an important part of Hugo's life.'

Val and Stephanie hugged, which took Henry by surprise.

Val drew back and announced, 'Well, I'll aim to improve, not change from the person you trusted, then. But, since I am a sort of part of this family, I'll also dedicate myself to doing all I can to improve your quality of life, too. Those meal plans? I'll get them all typed up this evening, and I'll email them to you, Stephanie. Cook Davies shouldn't have any problems with the suggestions I made. In fact, I thought she took everything rather well.'

'I should hope so,' said Henry with feeling. 'We very nearly lost her, recently, and that would have been a tragedy.'

Val looked shocked. 'I had no idea she'd been poorly.'

Stephanie explained, 'Henry means that she almost chose to leave our employment.'

Henry added, 'Healthy as a horse, that woman. Always has been. It's the food, you know.'

Val said quietly, 'I'm not sure about that, Henry. But, yes, she seemed to be on board, though she might put up a fight about the butter.'

Henry's ears pricked up. 'Cook Daves has always been quite rightly fussy about her butter. We only use local butter, you know, and even proper Welsh sea salt is used in it.' He noticed that Stephanie seemed to have acquired a bit of a tickle in her throat, so added, 'I used to help make butter, down in the kitchens, once upon a time. I hope to, one day, share that pleasure with Hugo. It's a magical feeling to see butter emerge where once there was none. Most satisfying – if rather a lot of work. And making the little pats? Why that was better than almost any game involving clay, or plasticine, because one could eat it.'

Val chuckled. 'You ate butter? On its own, not on anything else?'

Henry smiled. 'Well, rather a lot of it was on my fingers, but, no, nothing else. It really does melt in the mouth, you know. Even better than chocolate, I'd say.'

Val shook her head. 'Well, that might explain a lot of things, Henry, but I dare say you'll get used to the few, small, changes we'll be making. In fact, if no one tells you what they are, you probably won't even notice them. Right, Stephanie?'

Henry didn't like the way that Val winked at his wife, nor the way his wife's nostrils flared when she smiled back at her chum.

Stephanie said, 'I agree, Val. There's nothing at all for you to concern yourself about, Henry. Now – it's almost time for lunch, and I need to attend to Hugo before we eat…and I know you said you had a lunch appointment with Barry, Val.'

Henry noticed that Val perked up – if she could get any perkier, that is. 'Not lunch exactly. We're meeting at the gym for a quick session. He's helping me with my hamstrings – they tighten up after I've run uphill, so he's helping me stretch them out.'

Henry wasn't entirely sure what hamstrings were, though he at least knew they were in a person's legs. 'You could try not running up hills instead,' he suggested.

Stephanie and Val laughed for a long time about that – all the way through Val taking her leave, in fact, which puzzled Henry, because he'd thought his suggestion was sound.

CHAPTER EIGHT

Mavis had slept relatively well, given that the bedroom she'd been allocated at Twyst House had a window that let in just enough of a draft to make a high-pitched whistling noise – and the wind had blown all night long. Having heard tales of the challenges of maintaining Twyst House from the entire family over the past couple of years, she'd rapidly become acquainted with what that meant, in practical terms, since her arrival; rooms being chilly was one element by which she hadn't been surprised – and she'd packed appropriately to allow for such. However, she'd been astonished by the poor standards of the general décor of the house, and she'd noted that Althea had seemed a little taken aback by it, too.

The building itself was an odd mixture, architecturally speaking, of a rambling hunting lodge that had been expanded over the centuries by previous Twysts with varying tastes – meaning it had a classical façade, a turret at one end that looked as though it had been stuck on as an afterthought – which Althea had told her it had been – and the overall ambience was slightly spooky, largely due to the fact that its poorly fitting windows were indeed plentiful, but seemed to not let in as much light as air. However, what had completely taken Mavis aback was the spartan nature of the bathroom arrangements.

Realizing she'd become accustomed to the luxury of enjoying amenities attached to her bedroom at the Dower House, she found scampering along a chilly corridor in the dead of night to use one of two WCs equipped with toilets of Victorian vintage to be…quite unpleasant. Both were the same as each other, with a pull-chain attached to a high tank that required the strength of a seasoned weightlifter to get it to work, then – she'd been horrified to discover – when it was finally coaxed to perform its function, it made a noise that she really did fear could wake the dead. The arrangement had lost any charm it might have initially possessed by the third time she'd had to avail herself of its utility during the night. Mavis had later discovered that the room Althea was using – in the turret, no less – did, indeed, have its own, attached facilities, so she felt even more put out.

Following her hasty ablutions, carried out in a frigid bathroom located even farther from her room, Mavis had been expecting a proper Scottish breakfast that would set her up for what she hoped would be a good day. She'd wrapped herself up in layers of serviceable navy, and had arrived as cheerily as possible in the yawning hall that was referred to as the dining room. Its cavernous dimensions meant it could have hosted a banquet for about sixty people, and most of them could have fitted around the overwhelming table at which she found herself struggling to make conversation with Althea, Clementine, and Julian while they all picked at kippers and scrambled eggs.

'I've no' had a kipper in a while, and you cannae beat a good one,' said Mavis, hoping to jolly things up.

Althea asked, 'Would you pass the butter, please, Clementine, dear?'

'Here,' replied her daughter – shoving the butter dish as close to the center of the wide table as possible.

Mavis stood to reach it for Althea, and passed it to her, smiling. 'I know we shouldn't, but it's the butter that makes a kipper, isn't it?'

Althea dimpled. 'Absolutely. Don't you agree, Clementine?'

Mavis had noticed the tension between the mother and daughter since the previous evening, when a cold supper had been served by Clementine herself, with her husband's help, since the cook always left the estate at seven o'clock sharp. Unfortunately, Althea's insistence that Ian should park the car to allow her to avail herself of facilities she claimed were 'quite superior' somewhere just past the Lake District, had meant they'd missed their planned tea at Twyst House altogether, and then had all but bumped into the cook as she was leaving – making for an awkward arrival, to say the least.

Seeming to have got off on the wrong foot, Althea and Clementine had then proceeded to bang heads when it came to all the changes Clementine and Julian had made to the place since they'd moved in – that Althea could spot – and things had gone downhill from there…leading to the situation at the breakfast table, where Mavis felt it her duty to try to lift at least Althea's spirits.

Julian Treforest, Clementine's husband, ate silently, and Mavis began to wonder if he ever spoke. She'd met him before, of course, on several occasions, and he'd never been garrulous, but now he was almost mute. With a plate twice the size of anyone else's, Mavis noted that the kitchen must have become accustomed to his appetite – which needed to be large to have created such a large man. Feeling the draft around her ankles, Mavis could well understand why he'd elected to regrow, and keep, his full beard, and she could tell that the chill in the air was something with which Clementine was equally familiar; she appeared to be draped in several blankets, each of a different hue, and all as shapeless as each other. Mavis suspected it was unplanned, but Althea had almost outdone her daughter's get-up by presenting herself at the table wearing a one-piece outfit – not unlike the sort of thing an infant might wear – made of heavy forest-green velvet, with a purple mohair shawl draped around her shoulders, which Mavis knew would have made her sneeze in an instant. Althea was also wearing a hat at the table, which she, Julian, and Clementine had all, obviously, noticed, but upon which no one had commented. It was a green tweed flat cap, of the sort usually worn by men, but Althea had pulled it down to cover the tops of her ears, so it looked a little…odd, even for Althea.

Mavis was always able to sense when Althea was bursting with something, and she spotted the usual warning signs at least ten minutes before the dam gave way. It began innocently enough, with Althea noting, 'I think the color you've chosen for my room is rather lovely, Clementine. Would you call it green, or blue?'

However, Mavis feared the conversation might take a turn when Clementine replied huffily, 'It's teal, Mother. So both. Or neither. As you wish.'

Mavis jumped in. 'Coincidentally, that's the shade Annie used when she spruced up a special room at the Coach and Horses pub, back in Anwen, ahead of her parents' arrival before Christmas. It was thoughtful of you to decorate before Althea got here.'

Althea preened. 'Indeed it was. Thank you.'

Julian said, 'It had to be done…the plaster had started to fall off the ceiling, and we couldn't have that. Clemmie knew that was the room you and the late duke used when you visited, Althea, so she wanted to make the effort. We knew it was in hand before we arrived at Chellingworth Hall for Christmas, but we didn't want to spoil the surprise, did we, Clemmie?'

'No. We didn't. Though we rather expected it to be finished by the time we got back. I hope the smell of paint isn't too strong in there, Mother. They didn't finish until last Friday, and the curtains didn't go up until yesterday morning.'

'It's hardly bothering me at all, dear. And the choice of *aubergine* for all the fabrics in the room was…bold. How very like an artist to come up with such an original idea. It makes the room feel very…cozy. Like it's hugging you. In the dark.'

Clementine slapped her cutlery onto her plate. 'So it's dark, dingy, and smelly? Thank you very much, Mother. Heaven forbid I'd be able to do something for you that you actually appreciated.' She stood. 'I'll see you all later. I need to put in a full day at my studio, though why I'm bothering I have no idea.'

Mavis noted that Althea's mouth was open, and didn't close until her daughter had disappeared, when she said quietly, 'Oh dear.'

After that, breakfast continued silently, until Julian also took his leave of the two women, wished them a good day, and invited them both – should they choose – to visit him at his smithy.

Althea became suddenly magnanimous. 'Why thank you, Julian. I might take you up on your kind invitation – though I have a few local errands to undertake, so I might get them out of the way before giving myself over to more enjoyable pastimes. Maybe later on, or, if not, tomorrow?'

Julian smiled – his teeth barely showing within the nest of his beard. 'You know you're welcome whenever you want.'

Once they were alone, Mavis dared, 'You and Clementine don't seem to be hitting it off, Althea.'

Althea sighed. 'Oh Mavis, she's ruined what was a lovely room. It used to be *eau de nil* and cream, with a beautiful light in it, and an air of whimsy. Now the room where Chelly and I would make plans for our future, and talk about our young children's lives, is like…well, it's like being in a muddy hole in the ground. It's so dark, and oppressive. It's…horrid.'

Mavis's heart went out to Althea, who – even though she was brightly attired – looked pinched, and most definitely all of her more than eighty years. 'Do you really have errands to run, or was that an excuse to not go to the smithy to watch Julian work?'

Althea brightened a little. 'I really do need Ian to drive me to a few places. Would you like to come too? Just for the fun of seeing the countryside. Though I might put that off until after lunch. I really fancy a little stroll around the old place, at some point.'

Mavis declined, and the pair took their leave of each other with Althea promising to wrap up warmly before she left the house…deciding she'd walk first, then pop out later on.

Alone at last, Mavis spent a frustrating half an hour trying to get her laptop to connect to what was apparently the best possible satellite internet connection in the entire area, according to Clementine and Julian. Eventually, she set out to seek help from Billy Stewart, whose formal title of 'Rural Asset Manager' for the Twysts' Scottish estate, was – she'd been informed – ignored by all, in favor of the catch-all title of 'Steward'. She finally located him: tall, well-built for a man in, possibly, his late fifties, and dressed in a full-length waxed coat, he turned out to be extremely grumpy, rumbled instructions at Mavis through an even wilder beard than Julian's – that all but covered his face – then he stomped off, declaring he had better things to do with his time, and left her to it.

Crossing the entranceway from the side hall where she'd managed to locate the man just before he'd gone out…somewhere, Mavis – almost literally – bumped into Althea, who looked like a walking plaid sausage, wrapped, as she was, in a coat that swept to the floor, and had been fashioned from an eye-watering mustard, orange, and lime green plaid of…well, definitely no Scottish origin.

'It's just his way, Mavis,' said Althea, when Mavis pointed out Billy's less than helpful manner. 'You have to remember he's not used to any of us being here. We're trampling all around his home, and he probably doesn't like it very much.'

Mavis was taken aback by Althea's attitude. 'But this is your house, your estate – not his.'

Althea looked sad when she replied, 'I know that, dear, but we're all getting under his feet. Years and years have passed since Chelly and I were here on a regular basis. Billy's kept the whole place running – the house, the farms, the tree harvesting, the care of the loch, the rivers, and the bit of fishing that goes on there. Now Clementine and Julian have taken up residence, and they've already made a great number of changes here – not that you'd know that, of course – and now here we are, too. It must all be a bit much for him, poor thing. But he's a good man. He's worked on this estate for decades, and he'll be here until he can work no more, then we'll look after him in his cottage for the rest of his life. It's what the Twysts do, dear. He'll…acclimatize to the new situation.'

Mavis waved Althea on her way, suspecting the wee woman wouldn't be able to take more than half an hour out in the biting wind, then settled herself in the sitting room, where she was still unable to connect with the outside world, either by internet or mobile phone. She composed some lengthy emails and texts for Carol and Annie, and hoped a signal would magically appear to allow her messages to be sent at some point that day.

When lunchtime finally arrived, she found herself in the dining room again, where long-dead furred and antlered beasts with beady glass eyes watched her as she sat herself on one of the plain wooden chairs which surrounded the plain wooden table. She gazed across at Althea, who stared back at her, dimpling.

Knowing that something was up, Mavis asked, 'And what have you done now, Althea?'

The dowager adopted her most innocent and coquettish smile. 'Absolutely nothing. Well, maybe the merest hint of…something.'

'Clementine and Julian will join us in a moment, so out with it.'

Althea replied, 'We're having fish for lunch.'

'Aye, and what of it?'

'It's locally caught. Sea fish. The fishmonger's also the fisherman.'

'And?'

'I met him earlier today. He was outside the kitchen door. I got chatting to him, as one does…'

'As you do, Althea.'

'Indeed. Anyway, I learned he was from Port William, which I know is not far from where you grew up, so I mentioned your name. He's coming for lunch, too.'

Mavis was puzzled. 'You've invited a fishmonger to lunch? Have you told Clementine and Julian – our hosts? This isnae your home, Althea.'

Althea pouted. 'It used to be, and – if you want to be picky about it – the place actually belongs to the Seat, so it's Henry's. I have just as much right to invite people for lunch as Clementine and Julian do. I told the cook – that's what really matters.'

Mavis sighed, and was just about to let Althea have a piece of her mind when Julian Treforest entered the dining room, so she bit her tongue.

With greetings exchanged, Julian asked, 'Anyone seen Clemmie? I know she's invariably late for meals, which drives the kitchen nuts, but she said she'd make a real effort today – for you, Althea. I haven't seen her since she left for her studio this morning.'

Althea rolled her shoulders and said, 'I hope I'm allowed to actually see this studio she's been talking about, Julian. She seems to be rather protective of it. Does she let you in there?'

Julian placed his large body on the chair that Mavis suspected might be uncomfortably small for him, then admitted, 'Bit of a sore subject, Althea. She does not.'

Althea's eyes gleamed. 'We'll have to see about that before we leave, then, won't we, Mavis?'

Before Mavis could reply, there was a knock at the door, and upon Julian's booming – if puzzled – 'Come in' a head appeared, followed by a body.

The man was short, wiry, with grizzled steel-gray hair, and a ruddy complexion. He was wearing what Mavis could only imagine was a get-up that he'd pulled together in an attempt to rival Althea's outfit, because he was wearing a bright yellow sweater above an equally eye-watering pair of lime green waterproof trousers, and was barefoot.

Mavis watched with interest as he looked at Althea and said, 'Here I am then.'

Julian rose with a welcoming smile, saying, 'Hello there. And you would be…?' He walked toward the man, his massive hand outstretched at the end of his massive arm.

The man seemed to shrink as Julian got closer to him, then he finally stuck out his own hand and croaked, 'Francis Aloysious O'Malley. Frank, to my friends.'

Julian was almost lifting the man from his feet as he shook his hand, but Mavis hardly noticed, because she and the stranger had locked eyes, and she could see the seventeen-year-old boy she'd once known, and loved with all her heart, behind them.

She stood, and croaked, 'Frank?'

Frank looked at her and nodded. 'My wee Mavis.'

Althea pulled at Mavis's sleeve. 'Surprise!'

CHAPTER NINE

When she arrived in the snug bar of the Coach and Horses, Annie tiptoed up behind Tudor Evans and gave him a hug.

She felt him chuckle as she squeezed him. 'You know these glasses on the shelf here are reflective, don't you, Annie? You'd be no good as a ninja, you know.'

Annie kissed him when he turned. 'Maybe not, but I'd look good in the black outfits, wouldn't I?'

'You'd look good in anything – and, now that you've managed to winkle a compliment out of me, how about you do what you promised, and take over here, so I can give Aled a hand in the other bar? As you can see, it's as quiet as the grave in here, but we need to cover it. And thanks for volunteering for this. As I said, I daren't speculate as to what's gone on between Aled and Joan Pike, but she hasn't been in for three days to give him a helping hand, and that's not like her.'

Annie said, 'You know you're living under the same roof as a private investigator, don't you, Tude? If you'd asked me, I could have told you.'

Annie loved wrong-footing Tudor when she could…which wasn't often. He looked surprised, then sighed. 'Go on then, what's happened?'

'It's nothing to do with Aled and Joan Pike, or even with Aled and Sharon Jones at the shop…and that's still bubbling away, by the way. Nah, it's Joan's mother – she's having a bit of a bad time of it with her multiple sclerosis. It flares up, apparently, with no warning, and she took a turn for the worse a few days back. Joan's been giving her all her attention, which is understandable, of course.'

Tudor nodded. 'Of course it's understandable – if a person knows about it. Why doesn't anyone tell me anything these days?'

'Did you ask?'

Tudor shrugged. 'Never mind. Right, you're here, I'm in there. Love you. Thanks…oh, did you get any news about your counsellor?'

Annie felt her shoulders slump. 'Not a dickie bird.'

'I'm sure she'll phone, when she can. They might not allow phones in the hospital – you know, not mobiles.'

As he headed toward the kitchen, Annie called, 'I think those days are long gone, Tude,' then she turned to the almost empty snug and continued, 'how would anyone manage without them?'

A head bobbed up in a dark corner, and Annie shouted, 'Don't disturb yourself, Gwyn, I was talking to myself.'

Gwyn rumbled something unintelligible, and Annie picked up a cloth to start polishing glasses, rather than look as unoccupied as she really was.

When her phone vibrated in her pocket, she actually said aloud, 'Phew, saved by the bell,' which drew no reaction whatsoever from Gwyn, so she answered the call.

'Hello?'

'Annie?'

'Oh, Barb – thanks for phoning. How are you?' Annie felt the relief right down to her toes.

Barbara Newsom sounded as though she were phoning from Timbuktu. 'I've been better, but they're letting me go home. I'm just waiting for Nia to pick me up. I thought you'd like to know. And I wanted to thank you, and Carol, for getting me here. The doctor said that what you two did made a huge difference. You might…oh, Annie, you might even have saved my life.'

Annie waited while Barbara cried. It took some time, and her heart went out to the poor woman.

Eventually, Barbara was able to say, 'I wondered if you and Carol might be able to visit me. I really do want to talk to you about…you know. It's…important. Might even be urgent.'

Annie was about to reply, when Barbara cut in again – this time sounding almost hearty – with: 'This afternoon at four? That would be lovely. And yes, I'm sure a bit of cake won't hurt me. I know you and Carol have my address, Annie – but remember, like I said, it's number six Sycamore Close, not number nine…there isn't a number nine, silly you. See you then.'

Annie looked at her phone, which now lay dead in her hand, and hit the speed-dial button for Carol. Without even letting her colleague say anything, she jumped in, 'Car, I just heard from Barb. They're letting her go home – which is good, of course – but she did something weird. I think someone came into her room, or wherever she was – maybe she was still in a cubicle in A and E for all I know – anyway, her voice and manner changed, and she gave me an address. She said number six, Sycamore Close and she wants us to go to see her. She sounded as though it's something she needs done now – well, at four this afternoon. But I don't know where Sycamore Close is.'

Carol replied calmly, 'My phone tells me there are Sycamore Closes all over the UK – I had no idea it would be such a popular street name – but I expect it's the one in Brecon that she means. So she gave you her address, and invited us for four, right?'

'Right.'

'I'll pick you up at the pub at three, be ready to go. See you then.'

Annie looked at the phone which lay, dead again, in her hand. 'Gordon Bennett! What's wrong with everyone today?'

She looked up to see Gwyn standing in front of her. 'Half of dark mild, is it, Gwyn?'

'Aye, go on then. They give you brain cancer, they do.' He nodded sagely at her phone. 'And you should never keep them in your pocket. Give you cancer there, too, they will.' He took his glass, dropped the correct amount of money for it – all small change – on the bar, and ambled back to his seat.

'And a very good day to you too, Gwyn,' said Annie, then she texted Carol to check that everything in her world was alright, but got no reply, so knew she'd have to wait until three to find out why she'd been cut off so unceremoniously. Her general feeling of grumpiness wasn't helped when a blast of cold air rushed in through the door that she, and Tudor, kept meaning to fix; the inner door to the snug wasn't supposed to blow open like that when the outer one was used. Unfortunately, the cold wind was followed in by Marjorie Pritchard, who was brandishing a piece of paper, and wearing an expression that put Annie in mind of Boudica on the rampage.

Annie slapped a smile on her face. 'Hello, Marge – and what can I do for you today?'

Marjorie waggled the paper in front of Annie and snapped, 'You can tell me what this is all about. Is this something to do with you?'

Annie took the paper, which was missing all four of its corners – something she deduced meant that Marjorie had ripped it off…somewhere…probably the noticeboard outside the village hall. At its center was an illustration of something that looked a bit like the van that the Scooby Doo lot had used, except that this one had 'SGLOD SQUAD' on it, in bold, 1960s-type lettering. Above an equally lurid 'Kapow! and in among various renderings of 'Splat!' she noted random words like 'fish', 'curry sauce', 'chicken', 'gravy', 'sausages in batter', and 'kebab-burgers', and further gathered that this vehicle was going to be in the car park next to the old school in Anwen between three and five o'clock on Wednesdays. There was also a phone number with the promise of more information about 'UNPARALLELLED CATERING OPTIONS'.

She thought she understood what it all meant, but was still a bit baffled. Looking over the sheet she asked, 'Does "sglod squad" mean something to you, Marge?'

Marjorie looked at Annie as though she were very dim indeed. 'Of course, you wouldn't know – you're English. "Sglod" is Welsh for a chip. That you eat. "Sglodiau" or "sglods" means chips. It's obviously a chip shop van, but that's not why I'm asking you about it. I'm here because I want to know if you've got anything to do with this? This is absolutely not the sort of thing we want here in Anwen. Just think of the type of person it might attract. The littering alone would be a disaster.'

Despite the fact that Annie wasn't aware that people who ate chips were of any particularly worrying 'type', that wasn't what concerned her. She checked the back of the poster, which was blank, then rang the number on the front. She could tell that Marjorie was about to say something, but she put the poster on the bar, held her finger to her lips and glared at the woman – daring her to speak. Marjorie looked taken aback, but said nothing.

A chirpy female voice with a clipped accent answered her call. 'Hello, this is the Sglod Squad. How may I be of assistance?'

Annie decided to sound equally perky. 'I've just seen your poster about you being in Anwen-by-Wye – could you tell me more about what you do?'

A strong Welsh accent, and a bit of a vacant tone, replaced the upbeat welcome. 'We sell chips, and loads of things to go with them. If we don't do it, tell us, and we'll see if we can arrange it. The chips are brilliant. Big fat ones – not like those horrible skinny things you get with your burgers. Lush, they are.'

Annie pressed on. 'And when will you be in Anwen? Is that this Wednesday?'

'Yeah. Every Wednesday, from three to five, from this week on, then we go to…somewhere else, just let me check…'

'No, that's fine. And this is a new thing, is it?'

The girl was starting to sound a bit tetchy, Annie thought. 'Well, we're always up for trying a new patch, and Anwen's not somewhere we've been before. Thought we'd give it a go. Well, Liam did, though Dylan said it might be a bit too posh. But there, they're brothers, so they disagree about a lot of things.'

'And would that be Liam and Dylan…Thomas?'

The girl replied, 'No. Liam and Dylan Tanner. Why, is there another Liam and Dylan? That would be funny, wouldn't it? I wonder what their wives are called.'

Annie pressed on. 'The Liam and Dylan I know are married to Tracy and Sharon.' Annie kicked herself as she finished, suspecting she should have chosen more Welsh-sounding names.

'Ah well, I'm Celine – after Celine Dion, 'cos Mam was mad about her when she was having me – and Liam's wife is Shaz, well, Shaznay really, which we always think is hilarious. You know, because of Nicole…though I bet she'd turn in her grave at the thought. Not that Nicole's dead, of course.'

Annie had no idea what the girl meant. 'Yeah, of course not. That's hysterical.' She began to feel her lifeforce ebbing away. 'So will you all be here on Wednesday?'

'No, just the blokes. We run the office, get supplies in, sort out catering orders, that type of thing. Oh, and we all agreed to start renting out the van for events, too. Is that of any interest to you?'

'No, thanks.' Annie ended the call, and stared at her phone.

Marjorie Pritchard was almost bursting at the seams. She squealed, 'So…what have you learned?'

Annie said, 'Can you keep an eye on Gwyn over there for me for a minute, please, Marge? If he's true to form, he won't need another drink for about three quarters of an hour, but you never know – he might throw his routine out of the window any day now, and surprise us all. I've got to have a quick word with Tude about something important. Ta.'

Annie didn't wait for an answer, but turned, leaving Marjorie standing beside the bar doing a very good impression of an irate goldfish.

CHAPTER TEN

Alexander Bright looked down into the eyes of the woman he loved and hissed, 'If I have to tie you to that bed myself, you'll stay there. And I'm saying that within earshot of your parents, so you know I don't mean it in a fun way.'

Christine looked up at him, then across the hospital room to where her parents were sitting, mute, haggard, and still in the clothes they'd worn to lunch the previous day. It had been a long night, and morning, for everyone.

She sighed, and knew she'd have to give in, but decided on one last salvo. 'But I'll be bored rigid. It could be a whole month before the baby's born – unless they induce me. I will literally lose my mind if I have to stay in this bed until then. It's…it's torture, so it is.'

Dierdre Wilson-Smythe gave out a little whimper. 'Oh my darling, the doctor says you have to. You can't risk hurting yourself or the baby, can you? You were lucky yesterday. I don't know what would have happened if Alexander hadn't found you so quickly. You might have…drowned. Or worse.'

Christine's father grabbed his wife's hand. 'What your mother means is that it's clear you need to be here, under observation, until that baby's born. And that's that. Pre-eclampsia's not to be trifled with. It's dangerous for you, too, Christine, not just the baby. Time to be a proper, grown-up woman, and act in everyone's best interests.'

Christine sighed. 'I know you're right. But…oh, I feel as though some sort of parasite has taken control of me and I'm just the host. This…this baby's ruling my life already, and it's not even out yet.'

Christine was shocked when her mother got up out of her chair with such force that it rattled against the wall. She was even more taken aback when she noted the fire in her mother's eyes as she approached her bed.

In a low voice, Christine's mother said, 'Now you listen to me for a minute, madam. That's a terrible way to speak about your child, so it is. You think about this – we spent our day yesterday trying to help women who might never have the chance of having their own child. And think about how your father and I had to live through five miscarriages before we had your brother, then you. I know it's our fault, because we raised you, but sometimes you act like a selfish little brat. It's time to grow up, Christine. You're about to become a mother, so start acting like one. Now. Be thankful you've got the opportunity.'

No one spoke as Dierdre Wilson-Smythe stormed out of the room.

When her father stood, Christine could see tears in his eyes. He said, 'Your mother's tired. But she's right. We'll be outside, Alexander. We'll give you a lift back to the house, so you can freshen up, then you can come back in your own car, if you want…though I'd suggest getting a cab – there's almost nowhere to park around here. Bye bye, Christine. You're in safe hands here, we all know that. Take advantage of it.'

Finally alone with Alexander, Christine dared a quiet apology. 'I'm sorry. I didn't mean it…about our baby. I…I do love it, and want it. And I love you, and want you. It's just that…'

Alexander sounded exhausted. 'You don't have to say it, Christine, you articulate it in everything you do, and how you do it. You're fighting against losing your identity as an individual beyond being "a mother". I get it. It's not even uncommon. But…come on, my darling, you know I love you. You, for yourself. That I'll always and forever love Christine the person, whether she's being Christine the mother, Christine the lover, or Christine the alarmingly bright professional investigator who can ferret out a wrong 'un at the drop of a hat. How can I make you believe that? How can I get you to hear me?'

Christine felt the wetness on her cheeks before she was even aware she was crying. Alexander magically produced a couple of paper hankies, and she dried her face as she sniffled, 'I know…I really do. But what if you stop seeing me? What if I just become a "mother" – invisible as anything else? What if, one day, I look back and realize I lost a whole chunk of my life to…this.' She stared at her bump, then around the room that – despite the use of gray-green upholstery and a few dreamy landscape paintings on the walls – was still, essentially, a sterile box.

Alexander slumped, his head down. 'How can I make you see that motherhood isn't a loss, but something you gain? How can I convince you that we can enjoy parenting, together, for the rest of our lives? Come on, Christine, you love a good adventure – and this will be the greatest one ever.'

Christine whispered, 'But what…what if I'm no good at it, Alexander? What if I turn out to be a terrible mother?'

Alexander sat up. 'Is that what's worrying you? Deep down – is that what's frightening you?'

Christine nodded, the tears flowing again.

Alexander gathered her in his arms. 'Why haven't you talked about how you're feeling? We all think you're…well, none of us know what's wrong with you. You'll be a brilliant mum, Christine. And you and me – together – will be fantastic parents. We'll have the brightest, bubbliest, cleverest kid in…whatever school they manage to get into.'

Christine pushed him away a little. 'But we might not. You know…my drinking. Before I knew. The baby might not develop well.'

Alexander squeezed her again. 'We've talked about that, and agreed we'll deal with whatever we have to, whenever we have to. Right? So, come on…cry, or don't cry, be smiley or sad, but at least know we're in this together, Christine. But, if I don't go and change my clothes soon, you won't want to be this close to me. I'd say I look, and smell, as though I've slept in them, but being in them all yesterday, then all night here, wandering about while they tested you to within an inch of your life, means I could do with a quick shower, and something a bit less wrinkly and stinky. You going to be okay if I nip back to your parents' place for an hour?'

Christine nodded. 'Of course. But, before you go – you know when Daddy was telling you about George Fenton and his wife in the early hours of this morning? Can you just straighten that all out for me?'

Alexander settled back in his chair. 'You heard that? We all thought you were asleep.'

'Just resting my eyes.'

'Well, even so, it's nothing at all. Certainly not something you can do anything about here.'

Christine felt her jaw clench. 'George Fenton's been investing in wines for the past couple of years, and his wife, Lottie, has told him about someone she knows who opened some of the wines they're laying down – for a wedding, was it? – and they were all undrinkable. There's been a kerfuffle between the supplier and the buyer, with the supplier claiming the poor state of the wine was due to less-than-ideal storage conditions, and the buyer claiming they were tricked into spending more than they needed to for inferior products. Is that about right?'

Christine's heart soared when Alexander laughed loudly – a genuinely joyous sound that echoed in the room. 'So not asleep at all. Yes, that's a fair summary. Odd thing is I know the people the Fentons were talking about, though I don't know the Fentons myself. And I hadn't heard anything about the wine debacle. Sunny Dalton was the man who opened the wines for his cousin's wedding, apparently. He's a roofer in north London I've used in the past…though he's retired now, and his sons have taken over the business. If the sons are as reliable as the father was, they'll do well. Though, knowing Sunny a little, I'd say that the wine merchant in question had better keep their eyes peeled – I wouldn't want to get on the wrong side of Sunny Dalton, nor anyone he's associated with.'

Christine dared, 'Doesn't anybody in the entire construction industry just deal with business disputes in a gentlemanly manner? Is it really all fisticuffs and smashed-up stock?'

She noticed a flicker of…something…as Alexander replied quietly, 'Not a lot of gentlemen to be found in the business. Sadly.'

'Except you…now.'

He smiled. 'Except me, now. Yes.'

'So can you find out all about it, from the horse's mouth, so to speak?'

Alexander bristled. 'You're in here trying to finish making a healthy baby. Can't that be enough for you?'

Christine scooted her bottom up the bed a bit and decided to play nice. 'Look, I'll sit here like a good mother-to-be, but I haven't even got a book to read at the moment, so at least help me to keep my brain functioning, will you? You know how I like to get to the bottom of things, and – from what I heard Daddy saying when you all thought I was dozing – George Fenton approached him about the matter because he knew I was a private investigator. So, if there's a little something I can do while I'm lying here, why not let me do it? It won't be hurting the baby, and it'll probably help my blood pressure because I'll feel…useful. Other than in terms of helping this little one to reach the point where it's safe for it to be coaxed out. Come on, Alexander…if you could bring me my phone, my charger, and a few numbers I could do a lot from this bed.'

Alexander rose. 'You're quite something, Christine Wilson-Smythe. I love you, and I'll do at least this for you, us, and our child – I'll bring you a puzzle you can work through…if you promise to do everything the doctors, and nurses, tell you to. Deal?'

'Deal. Love you.'

'Love you, too.'

CHAPTER ELEVEN

Mavis MacDonald pulled her scarf closer around her face, and squinted against the low winter sunlight. She could hardly believe what was happening to her – it was as though someone had taken pictures of her life and twisted them in some sort of weird kaleidoscope. She was about to meet up with a slightly ragged-looking fisherman in his late sixties who'd captured her heart when she'd been no more than a bairn, in the grounds of a house that was hundreds of years old which she'd known of since her childhood, where she was now a *bona fide* guest of her close friend, the dowager duchess of the family that owned it. It was like something out of *Alice in Wonderland*…though she had to admit Althea was nothing like that duchess, nor was Stephanie, the current holder of the title.

And what about Frank? Mavis was grappling with her feelings about seeing Frank again. He was…well, exactly the same, and yet completely different. She couldn't help but notice his age – nor he, hers, she reckoned – and yet she could see the younger version of Frank beneath all the wrinkles and sagging flesh and gray hair. He still had the twinkle in his eye, the crooked smile…that chipped tooth, even. Oh, the day that had happened – she'd never forget that day. How could she?

And now here she was, off to meet him at the summer house, which was where Althea had insisted the two of them should get together to watch the sun setting. Mavis shook her head as she followed the path she'd been told would deliver her to her destination. Althea was more than a scamp, sometimes, but Mavis hadn't had the heart to admonish her, because it was clear that the dowager hadn't had an inkling about how deep Mavis's feelings for Frank had once been. Indeed, Althea had invited Frank to lunch because – as she'd put it – she'd hoped to pick up some juicy tidbits about Mavis's past, once she'd discovered that Mavis and Frank had been at school together.

What an odd lunch that had been: no sign at all of Clementine, Julian doing his best to understand why his mother-in-law had seen fit to invite a seemingly random fishmonger to join them, and Althea baiting Mavis and Frank into telling all about their teenage years. Ah…but it had taken no more than one look passing between them for both Frank and Mavis to bring that little performance to a stop. Yes, Frank had always been a sharp one, which was probably why Mavis had…liked him so much.

Pausing to make sure she knew where she was going, Mavis announced to the wind, 'Ach, who're you trying to kid? You loved him with every fiber of your smitten wee body, and you'd have moved heaven and earth to have become Mrs. Francis Aloysious O'Malley…if only your parents hadnae come between you.'

A voice called from behind her, 'If only both our sets of parents hadnae come between us, you mean, Mavis.'

Mavis turned to see Frank about twenty yards behind her. He cantered to join her – as nimble as ever, it seemed.

When he reached her, he threw open his arms. 'All I got earlier on was a nod and a smile, Mavis. Now, let me hold you as I used to, once again. Just a hug though…for now.'

Mavis couldn't think of a good reason to say no, so – for the first time in almost fifty years – she found herself in the arms of the man she'd once adored, and was surprised to discover that it felt…rather wonderful.

Pulling away, and readjusting her scarf, Mavis turned to head toward their goal. Frank fell into step beside her.

'You look a bit different than you did earlier on,' noted Mavis.

'Aye, well, I was at Twyst House with my fish van when that Althea cornered me, and I dress for the job, which is cold, wet, and fishy. Thought I'd better spruce meself up a wee bit for this. I even broke out the aftershave my son gave me for Christmas. Want a sniff?'

He thrust his chin toward Mavis, who giggled, then sniffed. 'Very nice. Though you didnae have to use the whole bottle.'

Frank laughed. Mavis laughed.

He said, 'He's got a good job, my boy. He can afford to buy me another. What did your two give you for Christmas? Duncan and James, right? Both in Dumfries, I hear.'

Mavis was surprised. 'You're very well informed.'

'Dumpee's prerogative, Mavis. I followed news of you through everyone who knew us both. You've had quite the life, my girl. Very different than we one we had planned for ourselves, anyway. Matron of the big place in London? Very swish. And now living with a dowager duchess. Who'd have thought it of my wee Mavis?'

Mavis wasn't sure how to feel about the fact that Frank knew so much about her life, though she was certain he wasn't going to have the upper hand for long. 'If you've a son, who'd you have him with? No, don't tell me, let me guess…Allie MacTavish. You always had your eye on her.'

'Allie married Alasdair. Remember him? Smelly feet. They emigrated to Australia and he's something big in sheep, now.'

Mavis laughed. 'Poor Allie, she hated animals of all sorts, didn't she? I wonder how she copes with sheep.'

'She doesnae. Cancer. Ten years back.'

Mavis shook her head. 'Too bad.'

'Aye.'

'Was it Donna, then? Donna Moore?'

Frank chuckled. 'Aye. My Donna, God rest her soul. Also cancer. Five years ago. We had just the one boy. Irvin. After her father. Good man. Also gone.'

Mavis asked, 'And where's your Irvin nowadays? Still local, like my two?'

'I wish. Canada now. Toronto. Working in finance, though what he does exactly, I don't know. He's explained it to me, but it all sounds like gibberish. How can money not be real? Just digital? I don't get it, Mavis.'

'We're too old, Frank.'

Frank paused. 'Now that's enough of that sort of talk, Mavis. I'm not yet seventy, still fishing, and selling, and there's a lot of life left in me. Haven't you heard that seventy's the new fifty, or has that passed you by in the wilds of Wales?'

Mavis play-thumped Frank's arm. 'I'm no' saying we're old, really, but I have to admit there are some things I find I've no time for, these days. I'm still working, too, though not at anything as strenuous as either of your jobs.'

'Aye, you're a private investigator. I heard.'

Mavis laughed. 'I need to know your sources, Frank – sounds like they could put me out of a job.'

'I get around. And I mean that literally – in my van. People like to chat, you know? They like to show off their knowledge a bit, even if we're only discussing a fillet of this, or a recipe for a good broth. Mind you, it'll all be behind me, soon. I've sold the boat, and the van, to a bloke from down south who's coming up here to try to make a go of it. I've got a good customer list, see, and that's what he said was worth him buying…though I did warn him it's mainly older folk who like to use me, and they're – literally – dying off, these days. But he seemed confident, so we've done it. I've sold it all to him. It'll be his – using my name on the van – in a month. I'll be off to see Irvin for a while. Get to meet my granddaughter, too. She's three, and I've nae felt those wee fingers of hers in these rough old hands of mine yet.'

Mavis felt the overwhelming need to say, 'There's something wrong, isn't there, Frank? What's got you…worried? You're not…right. Out with it.'

They'd just reached the structure that – for some unknown reason – had been dubbed 'the summer house'; it was a shed with one side open to the view across the loch…and what a view it was. The pair had been climbing steadily, and now the vista opened up in front of them, wide, mounded, and softened by the shafts of golden light which gleamed on the water.

Frank said, 'Look, there's a bench inside. Let's get out of this wind, and enjoy the view, before we talk about anything…else.'

'So there is something?'

'Mavis…wee Mavis…do you know you've always had a way with you? People must have told you, over the years. You've a nose for a problem, a secret…a way of somehow knowing when someone's hiding something from you. I dare say you put it to good use as a nurse all those years, and I bet you use it a lot as a detective. Well now…yes, mebbe you can help me out. For old times' sake.'

'I won't look at you as you tell me about it, Frank. I'll watch nature's show as you talk. But tell me everything, mind you. Don't leave one thing out.'

'It's a long story, Mavis, but I'll do my best. That being said, the headline is this: I'm frightened, Mavis. Fearful I've done the wrong thing taking that young man's money. I think he's got designs on my business that aren't entirely…honorable.'

'I'm listening, Frank…'

CHAPTER TWELVE

Carol felt the whole vehicle shake when Annie wrenched opened the passenger door and said, 'Can I drive to Barb's, Car? We've got loads of time, and the traffic won't be too bad at this time of day.'

Carol groaned inwardly, then said, 'Maybe next time. I haven't got any L-plate stickers or anything.'

Annie patted her giant handbag. 'I've got them – I've got a magnetic set I take to Josie's with me that I can stick on, then pull off.'

Carol panicked. 'I'm settled in, now, Annie – come on, we haven't got time to muck about getting you installed, we need to get going.'

Carol hated letting Annie down, but she just couldn't bring herself to be Annie's passenger again – once had been enough. It wasn't the fact that she'd been thrown around in her seat as Annie had searched for the right balance between the accelerator and the brake, it had been the wildly over-confident steering, and her friend's general inability to keep her eyes and concentration fully on the road ahead, and other road users. Carol had almost had kittens when they'd skidded to a halt at a zebra crossing where a woman with a pushchair must have seen her life flash before her eyes. No, she couldn't cope with that again. Indeed, knowing that Josie – their friend with the retired racing greyhounds – was giving Annie lessons made her suspect that the woman was a saint, or at least soon to be canonized…possibly after her own untimely death on one of the local roads.

Carol thought she could actually hear Annie sulking as they began their journey toward Brecon, and their teatime meeting with Barbara Newsom. She tried to engage her in conversation. 'So you still don't know any more about why Barbara thinks someone's trying to kill her – other than we both saw her collapse, and she's lost a lot of weight since you last saw her, correct?'

'Yeah. Nothing more.'

Carol tried again. 'Tudor alright? How are you coping with his new-found fame after the panto in the village hall?'

Annie mumbled, 'He's fine, ta. Though he wasn't very pleased about the Sglod Squad.'

Carol thought she'd misheard. 'The what? Sglod squad? What's that?'

'Chips. Chip van.'

Carol sighed. 'I know that sglods are chips – but what chip van? What are you talking about?'

Carol listened as Annie explained how Marjorie had brought the imminent arrival of a chip van to the village to her attention, and couldn't help but chuckle. 'I bet Marjorie's onto the entire social committee for the village about it now. And I dare say she's got a point about the possibility of littering. But why's Tudor so upset?'

Annie turned so she was half facing Carol. 'It's hard enough as it is to make money in the pub, without some little upstarts coming into the village with a chip van and sucking the money out of the pockets of people who might otherwise choose to spend it on a meal at the Coach and Horses. Liam and Dylan, and Celine and Shaznay. All of them.'

Carol asked, 'Who are they?'

Annie explained.

Carol mused, 'Shaznay and Liam? That's hilarious.'

Annie snapped, 'That's what Celine Tanner said, too. So…why is it so funny? I don't get it.'

Carol dared a glance at her chum, who didn't seem to be being sarcastic. 'The girl group, All Saints? Remember them?'

Annie shrugged. 'What did they do?'

Carol gave a rendering of the chorus of 'Never Ever' until Annie said, 'Oh yeah, I know that one. That goes back a bit though, don't it?'

Carol said, 'I suppose so, yes, but you did ask. Anyway, that was by All Saints and they had a Shaznay in that group, but it was Nicole Appleton – also in the same group – who ended up marrying Liam. Liam Gallagher. From Oasis.'

'Is he the one with the long head, or the round one?'

Carol sighed. 'I've no idea what you mean, Annie. He's the singer…the one who always seems to need to wear a jacket, even indoors, and looks really angry and miserable.'

'Well…that's no help.'

'Bucket hat?'

'Ditto.'

'He plays the tambourine.'

'Got it. Long head. Oh – yeah, see, that makes more sense now. One of them's called Shaznay, in the same group as Nicole, but she married Liam. Funny.'

Carol smiled sweetly. 'Now we've got that sorted out, what's Tudor going to do about it? Shouldn't a food van get some sort of license, or permission to come into the village? Is he going to check that out? Is that a local authority thing? Well, no, the Twysts own the village, so it would be up to them, wouldn't it?'

Annie mumbled something Carol couldn't catch. 'Sorry, what did you say, Annie?'

Annie sighed. 'I said I'll do some research. Which I will. And I'm going to go undercover tomorrow evening and check them out.'

Carol smiled. 'What – you mean you'll go to the chip van to find out what they sell, what it costs, and if it tastes good? That's hardly undercover, is it?'

'Well, everyone knows me around here, so there won't be any point in disguising myself, will there? What am I going to do? Wear a wig? Change me clothes? Hope everyone in the village thinks I'm some entirely different six-foot tall Black woman who wants a bag of chips on a random Wednesday night? Not going to work, is it? So I'll be going there as me, but won't be telling Liam or Dylan that my partner runs the local pub, where he sells some delicious chips himself, by the way.'

Carol nodded. 'No question that Tudor makes good chips. In fact, where does he get them, Annie? They're a decent size.'

'What do you mean "where does he get them"? He "gets them" from potatoes, which yours truly often peels for him. Then he fries them. Twice.'

Carol was surprised. 'I thought he'd buy them frozen, then cook them. Maybe he should be telling customers more prominently that they're properly handmade.'

Annie harrumphed. 'Full of advice, when it's not asked for, in't ya?'

Carol bit her tongue; obviously the Sglod Squad thing was annoying Annie…so she shouldn't push it – though that was a great name for a chip van in Wales.

'Do you want me to go to the van, too, and pick something you don't so we can compare? Or are you going to buy a load of things, then try them all?'

Annie slumped. 'Oh, Car – I don't know. I suppose I'll buy a few things. Tude said he definitely wants to try the chips, since that's the main thing they're offering. Oh – and he said I have to get whatever a "kebab-burger" is, because he's got no idea.'

'I've never heard of that, either. A burger that tastes like a kebab, maybe? Though why they wouldn't just sell a kebab is beyond me. It's just slices of meat off a big stick thing, isn't it? Easy enough to do in a van, I'd have thought. So do you want me to do it too? Tell you what…I could get something different for all four of us – me, David, Mam and Dad. We could do notes for you and Tudor. How about that? One less meal for us to think about…or argue over.'

Annie said, 'Your mother still trying to tell you what you should be serving your husband for dinner?'

Carol tutted. 'Can't get it into her head that David and I are happy to take turns, and that we like a bit of variety. Dad seems to have come round, but not her. Dare say she won't change now. Too old…too stuck in her ways.'

'You know your mother's not even ten years older than me, don't you, Car?'

'She might not be, but a woman who's spent her entire life in Carmarthenshire, most of it farming sheep, is not at all the same sort of person as you, Annie. You're someone I've drained bottles of wine with on some fuzzily memorable nights in the City…she's someone who insists upon reminding me, in detail, of how easily she potty-trained me, especially when Albert's being a bit…challenging. I love you both – but I have to love her, she's my mam.'

'You thought it would be fantastic having them to stay for a while, didn't you?'

Carol conceded, 'I did, and it is. But they don't seem to be making any headway with their search for a new home, and…well, time's dragging on a bit now. Are you missing Eustelle and Rodney after their stay through Christmas and the New Year?'

Annie turned again. 'I know you won't take this the wrong way, Car…but I was glad to see the back of them. I moved out of home when I was sixteen, and two weeks after they arrived here in Anwen, and got themselves settled in the room I decorated for them in the pub, I remembered why I'd done it…my mother can't half talk.'

Carol felt the joyousness fill her entire body as she and Annie laughed like drains as they pulled up in front of number six, Sycamore Close, in Brecon.

Annie said, 'Come on now, Car. Let's pull ourselves together…poor old Barb needs us, and this could be serious.'

Carol's eyes were still smiling when she replied, 'I know, Annie. And I've got an inkling of how important this woman became to you. So let's do what we do best – help someone who needs it…even if we hope she really doesn't.'

Annie sighed, and grabbed Carol's hand. 'You're not wrong there, doll. I hope it's all in her head…though I have to say I very much doubt it. Barb's not one for fantasizing. Look, her car's there – so that service you got to drive it back here for her after she had to leave it at our office worked out alright. Let's go in and see what's what. Oh no…I forgot to bring a cake. She mentioned cake – as cover, I think.'

'There's a madeira cake I picked up from Sharon's on the back seat, Annie. Don't panic.'

'What would I do without you, Car?'

'Honestly, I've no idea, Annie. We're five minutes early – but let's go in anyway.'

'Good idea. I'll fight you for the loo.'

CHAPTER THIRTEEN

Stephanie Twyst was bouncing her surprisingly hefty son, Hugo, on her hip, as she pondered the notes that Cook Davies had sent up for her approval. It was quite clear that the woman had put a great deal of time and effort into preparing them, however, the duchess couldn't help but wonder if the explanations were just a little too detailed, if the changes weren't being focused on just a little too much? Was this Cook Davies's way of communicating to Stephanie that what she was asking for was a big shift, rather than just a few minor adjustments, in kitchen practices?

Setting aside the sheet for a moment, so she could rebalance her son, Stephanie noticed how often an item had a little star beside it, signifying that Henry wasn't to be told about the recipe amendments being made. It amounted to about half the dishes listed. She felt a pang of guilt as she realized she was asking her staff to lie to her husband…by omission, at least. How did she feel about that? She and Val had agreed it would be best if Henry was unaware that vegetables were being sneaked into most of the baked goods he'd be served, and that both butter and sugar were being replaced with healthier options. And it appeared that those changes were – at least for now – being readily accommodated by Cook Davies, which was quite a big step forward in itself.

As she placed Hugo into his pram, Stephanie told herself that she had to stand firm – that she was the only one who could help Henry to help himself…if only because he had no idea that he needed help. He was almost sixty, overweight, took no noticeable exercise, and had developed a habit of swigging port and brandy as though they were water. At least he'd given up on his stinky cigars since the arrival of Hugo, and she knew that was an end to that, because Henry really would do almost anything for his son – other than accept the fact that he might not be around for much longer if he didn't take at least some care of himself. She didn't want a long, bleak future as Henry's widow

– she wanted to be his wife. Wanted him to live for long enough that Hugo didn't inherit the title until he was advanced in years, at least married, with his own children. And Henry didn't look as though he had thirty years in him. Sometimes, when he'd had to, unavoidably, do something that exerted him, she worried that he didn't even look as though he had five good years left.

If only she could get him to move more, but even his passion for art meant he basically stood – or even worse, sat – all but motionless in his studio while he thought about painting, painted, then reworked his paintings.

'Ah, there you are my dear…I thought you said you were going to be meeting me in the library, for tea.' Henry was at Stephanie's elbow so swiftly that she had to stuff Cook Davies's list into Hugo's trousers as she pretended to straighten his blanket.

She accepted Henry's kiss with a smile, and motioned for him to push the pram, so they could take tea together.

As they walked, Henry mused, 'I hope it's seed cake today, though I doubt it. We never seem to have that unless Mother requests it, and she'll be gone for weeks. I dare say I should have asked for it myself. What do you think? Would Cook Davies make one for me?'

Stephanie weighed her response. 'I dare say she would, Henry.' She knew that seed cake hadn't been on the list the cook had provided; how would the woman feel about changing a recipe that went back to the 1700s, she wondered? She suspected it wouldn't please her at all.

Henry sighed contentedly, 'Ah well, whatever it is, I shall enjoy it. I thought the portions at lunch were a little on the meager side, didn't you, dear?'

'I found lunch to be more than ample, Henry.'

Henry paused and turned. 'Of course…there's a little one taking up a bit of room in there now, isn't there? Though doesn't our second child deserve to be well-fed dear?'

Stephanie replied, 'Our second child will be most nutritiously fed, Henry, as we've discussed, together and with Val.'

She noted that Henry spoke too nonchalantly when he paused and asked, 'Val seems very taken with that Barry chap. Something in it?'

Stephanie couldn't help but smile; her husband was so transparent. 'She's madly in love with him, Henry. Even though they've known each other – professionally, and as friends – for years, it's only recently that she's begun to find him irresistible, she says. She can't put her finger on what's changed, but something obviously did.'

'Maybe they…grew into each other? They say people do. We did, didn't we?'

It was Stephanie's turn to pause. 'Henry, we've both acknowledged that we each found the other attractive from the outset, but also each believed the other to be unattainable.'

'True. True. But this Barry chap – I mean, even though they've known each other for some time, what does she really *know* know about him? Is he reliable? Trustworthy?'

'She's not starting a business with him, Henry, they're in a relationship. Well, she is starting a business with him, but that's beside the point.'

'What sort of business? Oh, I say, Stephanie, look – it's a Victoria sponge today, how splendid.'

Stephanie parked the pram beside the tea table and gazed in wonder at the large, perfectly pillowy confection; it could have fed a dozen people. Henry would take that to mean he could have at least two large slices. Knowing that Cook Davies wouldn't have had time to make any changes to the recipe for this particular indulgence, Stephanie told herself to be sure to take just one, slim slice for herself.

As she cut the sponge, and handed Henry his plate – would he notice she'd given him a much smaller piece than usual? – she chattered happily, to distract him.

'Val's very excited about this new video shorts thing she and Barry are working on. She told me that, with today's technology, it really only takes her and Barry, alone, to be able to produce content of excellent quality – the sort of thing that would have required sound people and all sorts just a few years ago. And with this series they've done about ancient foods, and the role they could play in today's low-nutrition diets, she and he are also launching a range of even shorter pieces about the building blocks of nutrition, which she's then going to publish as a book – to launch and sell at her bookshop, of course. The whole thing works symbiotically, and it should lead to lots of online subscribers, book sales, and then they're going to launch a whole range of clothes and accessories that will help a person to exercise as part of an overall good nutrition and well-being plan. They're calling that company Barval. An…elegant name, isn't it? She's put up a bit of cash for that part of it, because they need samples and so forth, and they have to commission the design work – but she reckons it'll be worth it, in the long run. Isn't that exciting for her, Henry?'

Henry had already polished off his first slice of sponge, and wiped a remnant of strawberry jam from his mouth with his napkin. 'Absolutely splendid, dear. Maybe another piece?'

'Why not let that one settle first, Henry? You might not need another.'

Henry laughed. 'No one *needs* a second slice of Victoria sponge, my dear, but the entire thing is designed to make one *want* one. Look – it's twice as appealing now that we've sliced into it…all that jam oozing down the insides. Yes, another slice, please, but – since you're asking me to think about my waistline – I'll leave it at that.'

Stephanie smiled as she cut another, slightly thicker, piece of sponge for her husband. She did love seeing him happy, and food really did seem to be one of the few things that had the capacity to make him feel that way.

Eyeing up the incoming treat, Henry asked, 'So would one be correct in thinking that Barry's closeness with Val has developed alongside these business plans? The ones that required her to put her hand in her pocket, that is. While he, by the sounds of it, simply gives his time, and expertise…and promises of future success.'

Stephanie paused, her cup close to her mouth. 'I hadn't thought of it that way, Henry, but I dare say you're correct.' She didn't like how that surprising insight made her feel. 'But Val's an intelligent woman – she'll have developed business plans, looked into costs and so forth. I dare say she'd share them with me, and I'd enjoy reading them.'

Henry gazed longingly at his plate, then said, 'I'm sure you're right. After all, I know you have complete faith in Val's judgement…she is the one coming up with all our new menu plans, after all. And that means you're trusting her to feed every person here at Chellingworth Hall healthily and nutritiously – a responsibility I know you'd never take lightly. Ah…thank heavens for Cook Davies's light touch with a sponge, and heavy hand with the jam.'

'Indeed,' was all Stephanie could manage as she found she was cutting another slice of sponge for herself, which wasn't at all what she'd meant to do.

CHAPTER FOURTEEN

While Annie sat beside Barbara Newsom and took in the sorry sight before her, Carol was in the kitchen, making a heck of a racket.

Ignoring Carol's clattering, Annie coaxed, 'So, come on then, Barb – what did the doctor say? What happened to you yesterday? It didn't seem like a simple fainting spell – we thought you were a goner for a while there. Just as well both Car and me are fully trained in first aid and CPR. Mind you, that cut on your head isn't as bad as it looked at the time. That's a very small plaster on there, which is good.'

Barbara was dwarfed within a capacious armchair in the middle of her yawning sitting room, and was bundled in a crotched blanket, despite the fact Annie reckoned the central heating must have been set to 'tropical'. She'd been a bit taken aback by the size of her ex-counsellor's house; it was the newest on the Close – possibly only about thirty years old – and the largest by far, looking as though it might have as many as half a dozen bedrooms over its three floors.

Barbara smiled weakly as Carol placed a tray filled with mugs, a pot of tea, milk, sugar, and a sliced Maderia cake on the table that filled the space between the massive television in the corner, and the overstuffed chairs surrounding it.

Carol said, 'I'll serve, but we'd both like to hear what they said was wrong with you…if you don't mind telling a complete stranger like me about it.'

Barbara nodded. 'You helped me yesterday, so you're no longer a stranger, Carol. You and Annie are my saviors, and I shall always be most grateful for what you did for me. There's no way I can repay you, but I can confide in you…and ask for even more, professional, help. I want to hire you. To be perfectly honest, you see, one thing I'm not short of is money, especially since Richard died, and what I need you to do is find out who's trying to kill me. That's that part said. But…as for what was, or is, wrong with me? No one knows. Not even after yesterday's little…episode. I have a host of symptoms, none of which seem to be related to each other, or else they point to so many possible diseases and conditions that I'd be lucky to be alive if I had them all. But whenever they test my blood, or the functionality of my various organs, everything comes back as "normal" or inconclusive. Well…the load of tests they a month or so ago were a little off, but they reckoned that was because I'd been on antibiotics for a week.'

Carol asked, 'Why did you need those?"

Barbara looked a little sheepish. 'I took a bit of a fall, out in the garden, and cut my leg – on the rough wall out there. More of a great big graze than a cut, really. Nasty. And I feared it would get infected. Better safe than sorry, my GP said, hence the antibiotics. Actually, thinking about it, that week was the best I'd felt in a long time…but I was soon back to what's become the norm for me. Fair dos, everyone comes up with a theory, and they do their best to treat what they think I might have. At the moment, they're focusing on the vomiting, weight loss, and my headaches. They need to address the weight loss because that can have all sorts of other side-effects, and they're addressing the headaches because I've told them that if they don't I might run amok through the middle of Brecon and do a great deal of damage to a large number of people…not that I would, but you've got to get their attention somehow.'

Annie looked at her friend and said, 'If only Mave weren't up in Scotland.' Carol nodded. Annie added, 'One of our other colleagues is a retired nurse – she's good at this sort of stuff. I know she'd give us the benefit of her expertise if I could send her some details. How would you feel about that, Barb? Fancy talking us through it all?'

Barbara said, 'No need to tell you – I've written it all down. You know how I like my notes, Annie?' Annie nodded. 'I've been documenting it all since I became aware that there was something wrong with me…so many things wrong with me. There's a little notebook in my handbag – it should be hanging up outside, in the hall. The brown one – the one I had with me when I came to see you. If you bring it in, I'll dig it out for you.'

Annie watched as Carol rose and left the room. 'How are you feeling, now, Barb? Any better than yesterday?'

A wry smile crossed Barbara's face. 'I felt quite chipper, considering, when I was driving to your office, and didn't feel bad until I got out of my car then…well, you know. Nia's taken my car keys away with her now. Says the doctor didn't think it was a good idea for me to be behind the wheel, given that I passed out with no warning yesterday, and they don't know why.'

Carol passed Barbara's handbag to her and the woman rooted around in it for a couple of minutes, then looked at Annie with great frustration and just dumped the whole thing out on the floor. 'There – can you see it? It's red. Spiral-bound. Small thing.'

Annie couldn't see anything like it, and Carol agreed.

Barbara's immediate reaction was to doubt herself. 'I thought it was in there. I thought I'd put it in there to show to you yesterday – I know I intended to. Maybe it's in my bedside table – could one of you check, please? Top of the first flight of stairs, at the back of the house – the door will be facing you. Right-hand table – that's the side I sleep. Always did throughout both my marriages, and I'm not going to change now.'

Carol and Annie exchanged a glance, and Carol said, 'I'll go. If it's not there, is there anywhere else you can think that it might be? If you don't mind me poking about, that is.'

Barbara's reply of, 'Poke about wherever you want. But it's a big house, so it could take you a while,' sounded, to Annie's ears at least, to be more than tinged with hopelessness.

'Carol's a very methodical person, Barb. If it's here, she'll find it, I bet.' Carol left, and Annie added, 'So, while we're waiting, tell me when all this started – and tell me why you think someone's doing this to you…and anything you can about who you think might be doing it.'

Tears filled Barbara's eyes. 'I was fine for a couple of months after Richard died. Well, not fine, you know, but physically not unwell. Mentally and emotionally drained, of course, but that's to be expected. In fact, it was quite a "pleasant" period of time, in a way, because I saw more than usual of Nia, who's my daughter from my previous marriage, and even Tim, who was Richard's son with his first wife. We were a widow and widower when we met about ten years ago, and we just clicked. Neither of us believed it, to be honest, but when you know, you know. Tim and Nia were both adults by then, so they didn't have a problem with us getting married – they were our best man and maid of honor, in fact, so that was all lovely too. But, you know, people's lives are busy, and they both have big jobs. Tim's a science teacher not far away, and Nia's a dentist – well, a periodontist, to be more accurate, and she is a girl who appreciates accuracy, is our Nia – here in Brecon. One of only two in a very large geographic area, in fact, so she's always very busy.'

Annie could tell that talking was taking its toll on Barbara, but was keen for the woman to keep going; she needed to get to know her as more than 'just' a counsellor.

She asked, 'So the children were around a bit more because Richard was…ill, and then after he died?'

'Oh no. Not…beforehand. Richard didn't want either of them to worry, so we kept things between us, until very close to the end, you know? Then, afterwards, they were both wonderfully supportive of me. Tim's married, with a boy and a girl, so hasn't got as much time as Nia, who's divorced. No children. She kept her own name when she married, which was her father's name, my married name first time around. Williams. Sensible, really. You never know, do you? Anyway, like I said, she was here quite a lot. Helped me with all the…clearing out. That sort of thing. And, to be fair, Tim did come over too – he wanted to pick out some of his father's things to keep, you know? But he only popped in a few times. Then he…stopped coming. But Nia? She started to drop by with a takeaway on the odd night, and we'd natter over a glass of wine…well, she doesn't drink alcohol, but I find those boxes of wine are very handy if you've no one to share a bottle with. We'd watch some old rubbish on TV, that sort of thing. It was as though we were becoming more like friends, rather than a mother and daughter, you know? And as she and I were talking things through, I decided to retire. I didn't feel I had enough emotional energy to give my best once the headaches started. I've only myself to look after, and this place is all paid for – so why bother to work? And so…that was that.'

'How exactly did your symptoms begin?'

'With the headaches. I'd get up in the morning and feel awful…thumping head, unsteady on my feet, even throwing up, sometimes. And I realized I was becoming a little forgetful…things weren't where I was sure I'd left them – like this blessed notebook, for example. I can see myself putting it into that handbag yesterday morning, and there's nowhere it could have gone.'

Annie suggested, 'It could have fallen out when we were getting you into the ambulance. I know I made a point of bringing your bag with me, so that you'd have access to your phone and so on, but your little notepad might be on the floor inside, or even outside, the office for all we know. We wouldn't have been looking for it, what with you being out cold.'

Barbara brightened. 'Of course, my phone. Oh, sorry, Annie, I've made a right mess throwing everything on the floor. Where's my phone – can you see it anywhere?'

'It's on the arm of your chair.'

'Of course it is – Nia got me this little tray thing for all my bits and bobs. Here, let me show you – I took photos of all the pages in the notebook so that I could email them to you. I could send them to you now, if you like, then you can see what I mean.'

Annie watched as Barbara scrolled madly on her phone. 'Where are they? I'm absolutely certain I did that. Maybe they're after the ones I took when Nia and I went to Builth for tea the other week. No, they're not there either. Now when was it I did that? Hang on a moment, Annie, they must be here somewhere. Oh dear…Nia's always telling me off about this, saying I have too many photos on here…she was trying to find one I took of a robin in the back garden last week just after she'd dropped me off here today…and she said she couldn't find that one anywhere either, and I'm a hundred percent sure I took that one. In fact I took a lot of him. Robins are just perfect little creatures, aren't they?'

Annie's own phone buzzed in her pocket, and she ignored it. Then it buzzed again, and she surreptitiously pulled it out. A text from Carol read: **UPSTAIRS NOW!**

Annie's mind whirred. 'I know I went when I got here, Barb, but I've got to go to the loo again. Me and tea, eh? I'll let you have a good look through that phone of yours and I'll be back in a tick.'

Barbara all but ignored her, so she left the sitting room with its overwhelmingly stifling heat, though she noted that the entire house had a refreshing, minty smell – coming from those essential oil dispenser things – which helped alleviate the overall oppressive effect. She headed up the stairs as fast as she could.

Carol hissed to her from the door Barbara had described as leading to her bedroom – and what a room it was.

'This is huge, Car – it's like our entire flat at the Coach and Horses. She's even got a three-piece suite in front of that lovely big bay window and it matches the curtains. And look at the size of that back garden out there. Mind you, even though it's a nice view, I can't see why anyone needs an entire suite in their bedroom – not when they've got goodness knows how much space downstairs, too.'

Carol snapped, 'Never mind about the three-piece suite, or the blessed view, look at this.'

She opened the drawer in the bedside table. Annie's eyes opened wide. 'Oh heck…it's like a little chemist shop in there.'

'And that's not all. The table the other side is the same, as are two drawers in her chest, over there, and come and have a look in the bathroom cabinet with me.'

Annie followed Carol into the massive bathroom that had acres of marble, and a few too many gold fittings. 'There's nothing "builders' grade" about this place is there?'

Carol sighed. 'Forget about how fancy the house is, Annie – though you're right, it's quite something – and look at this.' She opened a large, mirrored cabinet that Annie imagined would hold towels and other bathroom supplies, but it was stuffed with boxes and boxes of medications. Bottles, too.

Annie was puzzled. 'What on earth is it all?'

Carol chuckled. 'Where's Mavis when we need her, eh? The boxes all have names on them and blister packs inside them, too. Some have been started, some not touched at all. Some expired years ago, others look as though they've only recently been prescribed. They're for Richard, in most cases, but some of them in the bedroom have Barbara's name on them.'

'It sounds as though her late husband was ill for some time. We don't know what was wrong with him, but we know it eventually killed him, so I dare say he might well have been on a lot of medications. But the ones for her? Do you think they keep prescribing her different things all the time and – what – they just don't all mix well? Could that be what's wrong with her?'

Carol smiled. 'You know that Mavis runs a charity for people who become addicted to prescription meds, don't you? How about we phone her and run this past her now?'

Annie agreed. 'Look, I told Barb I needed the loo, so could you do that? Photos and so on – which we could do with anyway – and get Mave to chip in everything she knows. Or maybe she could refer us to one of the people who work for the charity, who'd know all about it? I'd better get back downstairs. Barb's saying now that she took photos of the contents of the notebook that's disappeared, but she can't find them either – though she did mention that Nia had been using her phone. Maybe Nia deleted them by mistake, or…for another reason? In any case, we should check for the notebook at the office, in case it fell out of her bag there. I don't know, Car…maybe this is all something and nothing – a mixture of all these drugs has made her as ill as she is, and paranoid with it. But I'll keep talking to her, getting whatever information I can, while you follow the Mavis angle, okay?'

'Teamwork,' replied Carol. 'Now…flush, and go.'

Annie did, and returned to the heat of the sitting room to find Barbara trying to change the channel on her TV, which wasn't even turned on.

Taking the remote control from Barbara's hand, she said, 'Let me get that for you, Barb. Fancy another cuppa? I can see you finished that one, and how about another bit of cake? So, come on then, tell me who you think is trying to kill you, and why.'

Barbara said calmly, 'Well, I've been giving that a great deal of thought over the months, of course, and – although I don't like to think it's true – I believe it can only be one of two people. It's either Nia or Tim, and I think it's most likely to be Nia.'

Annie took a deep breath. 'And why do you think your daughter's trying to kill you, Barb? You've just been telling me you and her have built a closer relationship of late.'

'Oh, we have…which would mean she'd be close enough to try it, you see? Unless I'm just being paranoid about everything. But as for why she'd want me dead – well, that would be for the house, of course, and for the money. Richard was terribly well off, you see. Started doing all that "day trading" stuff some years back, and took to it like a duck to water. Until his prostate blew up, of course. When Richard died, Tim was horribly disappointed that his father left everything to me – he'd expected to inherit. And there was a sort of falling out about that. Which made me feel rather bad about things. That was about the same time that the headaches began. At that time, I was still thinking that it was all just grief…but then I thought it might be stress, because I did get very upset with Tim, you see, and I told him that he and Nia would each get a half of everything I left when I went, but he got nasty about that. Said that wasn't fair – that most of what would be mine at my death would have come from his father, so he deserved it all. Well, poor Nia got very upset then, and she is my blood, after all, so I told Tim that if he wasn't careful he'd end up with nothing at all…or at least less than half, and I meant it. He hasn't really kept in touch, since then. That's…that's why he stopped coming to visit.'

'And have you done that – cut him out of your will altogether? Or have you written one giving him only a third, or a quarter, or whatever?'

Barabara shook her head, then seemed to regret it, looking pained. 'No – Nia was quite right about that. I was angry with Tim, and…as…as time passes and I think about it all, I am getting less angry with him. So she was right – it was best for me to wait before writing a will. If I'd done it then, it would have been a waste of money, because I'd be rewriting it some time soon. Now I think it's only fair that he gets half, which I've told Nia, and she understands that. Besides, she's got a good career, so she's not short of a bob or two. And, as I said,

Tim's got children, and she hasn't. Which makes a difference. So, when I get around to it, it'll be fifty-fifty, for each of them.'

Annie ventured, 'So, okay, you think Tim is angry with you – so might actually have a reason to want you gone…but you think that Nia's the one trying to kill you, despite the fact that the two of you are getting closer to each other. That doesn't make sense to me.'

'Tim and I never meet, let alone mix, Annie. How would he be poisoning me?'

Annie felt everything in her clench. 'Oh, so we're definitely going with poison, are we?'

'Of course. I'm taking it for granted that I'm being poisoned, so that's why I suspect Nia – she really is the only person who sees me frequently enough that they could keep doing…something that's making me this way.'

Annie put down her tea, and gave Barbara's comments the attention they deserved…which was a great deal.

'You know when I first started coming to see you, Barb, and you told me that total honesty was the only thing that could help me, in the long term? That if I wasn't open with you, then you couldn't help me. Remember that?'

Barbara smiled. 'I said I'm getting a bit forgetful, not that I've lost my memory, Annie. What – you're going to be honest with me now, and I won't like it?'

Annie chuckled. 'There she is – the Barb who's as sharp as they come. Yeah – I've got to say some things, so here we go. First off – what's with all them drugs you've got tucked away upstairs?'

Barbara waved a hand, weakly. 'Oh, poor Richard was a hypochondriac…always self-diagnosing, bothering a whole host of doctors with this pain and that symptom. Which was why, ironically, the diagnosis of what finally killed him took so long. The man was the tragic embodiment of the boy who cried wolf. Poor Richard. Poor…me. I didn't take his aches and pains seriously, either. And then…it was too late. So, yes, a lot of what's up there is what he used to call his "Just In Case" store. There's so much there that I've no idea what to do with it all. You can't just take it to the dump, like a box of old papers or something. It's so embarrassing that I wouldn't let Tim or Nia into the bathroom – I said I'd clear it out. But I haven't. Most of what's in the bedroom, on the other hand, is mine. I've been diagnosed with so many, various problems that I've been given all sorts of things to take. But I've taken almost none of them, so toxic side-effects of multiple medications isn't what's going on here, Annie – though I must say I'm impressed that you and Carol, who I dare say has discovered my little "secret", have reached that point so quickly. But no, that's not the problem.'

Annie nibbled her lip. 'Right then – so does Nia give you any supplements, or anything like that…while you're being all pally? You know – something that could be…doing you harm.'

For a moment, Annie glimpsed the fire she knew was within the woman sitting swaddled like a person much older than her years. 'I'm not a stupid woman, Annie. And I've being going back and forth on this for months. My suspicions are truly…dreadful. I know that. For a mother to think that her daughter might be trying to poison her? I keep telling myself it's all rubbish…so, to protect myself – or, more like it, to prove that it's all in my imagination – I never, ever, eat or drink anything that Nia doesn't share with me. We'll share a meal from the same takeaway containers, or we'll maybe pick at a charcuterie board. When we're out, we'll usually select different meals, of course, but they come from commercial kitchens, and I certainly give her no opportunity to sprinkle something on my Welsh Rarebit when we're in the local pub, or whatever. But…I'm still so ill. And she still…oh Annie, sometimes she looks at me…strangely. See? It's all so…nebulous, and…unlikely.'

Annie sat back in her seat. 'Look – you're obviously worried enough about this that you're taking what I'd call far more than normal precautions, so have you got any bright ideas about how your daughter's managing to poison you? If she is.'

When Carol entered the room she paused in the doorway, and both Annie and Barbara turned to face her. 'Awkward moment?'

'Nah, come on in, Car – I've told Barb about what you found, but she isn't taking a whole load of stuff that could do this to her – and she's being careful about what she eats and drinks. But did Mave have anything useful to say?'

Carol shrugged. 'Sorry, no answer. I sent her a load of photos, and a text. We don't know what her internet access or phone reception is like up there in Scotland, so maybe we won't hear for some time. But…well, it's good to know you're being careful, Barbara.'

With two cups of tea and two pieces of cake inside her, Annie got the impression that Barbara was rallying a little when she said, 'I've also asked various doctors at various times to carry out tests for mercury, lead, zinc, and other types of chronic poisoning – all of which could produce some of my symptoms, and it's none of those. All my tests suggest I'm within normal ranges for everything they can think of…but I just cannot keep food inside me for long enough for it to do me any good. And those bottled meal-replacement things are so boring, though I do drink them, because I know I should.'

Annie began, 'And you're checking that they've…'

'Not been tampered with, yes, Annie. And this is why I'm at a loss. I've grappled with it, and…I finally felt I needed the help of a firm of private investigators. Which was why I came to you. Can you help me prove it's not her…doing something to me?'

Annie and Carol shared a significant look.

Carol replied, 'I think we need to address your expectations, Barbara. It's almost impossible to prove a negative…but we might discover something concrete that's not…to your liking. Are you really prepared for the truth, whatever that might be?'

Barbara stuck out her chin. 'It has to be better than not knowing, but hoping…and worrying.'

'Right,' said Annie, 'in that case, how do you feel about not leaving this wonderful house of yours for a week or so? If you allow us to set up hidden cameras all over it, and you stay inside it – so that any interactions with you can be observed – we could watch over you from our laptops. How does that sound?'

Barbara Newsom sank back into her chair. 'Like heaven – with guardian angels. Thank you.'

CHAPTER FIFTEEN

When Alexander arrived, Christine used the buttons on the control pad to raise her hospital bed. 'That was quick. Did you even dry yourself off after your shower?'

Alexander beamed. 'Ran around spraying droplets everywhere, then threw on some clothes, and here I am, my darling. I even did as you asked, and have information for that poor little brain of yours, so it doesn't atrophy.' He swooped down and kissed Christine on her forehead, which she graciously allowed him to do.

She felt the giggle before it came out. 'You're too good to me. Sorry I was grumpy, but…well, what can you tell me about this – what shall we call it? The Case of the Whining Wine Snobs?'

She loved the way Alexander's eyes crinkled when he smiled. 'If you say so, though this isn't a case at all, and – if it were – it would be Annie who'd name it, as you well know. No, this is just you choosing to help some friends of your parents, and maybe using some friends of your significant other to grease the wheels.'

Christine mugged a salute. 'Yessir. So, what have you got for me?'

Alexander settled into the seat beside her bed and produced his phone, and hers. 'Here's your phone, and your charger, and I'll let you take notes as you choose. Ready?'

Christine smiled. 'Well, I'm not doing anything else, am I?'

'Okay. Here's the number for Sunny Dalton. It's his personal mobile number, and I've texted him to say that you might phone him. He said he might ask you to talk to his wife, because she's the one who had the dealings with the wine merchant. Anyway, you can start with him.'

'Got it. And do you know his wife's name?'

'Charlene.'

'Right. On you go.'

Alexander snorted. 'You're so much more Irish when you spend time with your parents, you know. It's delightful.'

'Begorrah! Get on with it, Alexander.'

'I thought you might want to talk to these two blokes, too. Cliff Richards – I kid you not…that's what his parents named him – big fans, I dare say, when he was born. Mind you, he has an "S" at the end of his name, unlike the singer, who hasn't – which I was never really aware of, until I met this Cliff. He mentions it. Often. Anyway…Cliff Richards is someone I've met a few times, but I can't recall where or when I first encountered him. I think he was a mate of someone I attended a few rugby games at Twickenham with, once upon a time. Anyway – nice enough bloke. In his forties I'd say – about my age, anyway. Something in the City – so you two'll speak the same language as each other. But…a bit of a plonker. Hence the wine thing. Though – apparently – he knows his stuff. Gets a bit boring on the topic, when allowed to do so. But…you did ask. He'd be your best bet, I think. However, if you can't get hold of him, then try this bloke: James Onatade. To be honest, if I had to spend time with either one of them, James is the one I'd pick – knows a great deal about a lot of things, wine being one of them. Absolutely not boring, because he can chat about almost any topic. Bright, too. But maybe Cliff's your man for this. If anyone were to have encountered a shady operator in the wine field, it would be more likely to be Cliff because James – the much more sensible one – buys wines to drink, not as investments, which I know is Cliff's thing.'

Christine was impressed. 'You've really given it all some thought. Thanks. I appreciate you not just trying to pacify me with this. I'd kiss you, if I could reach.'

Alexander leaped to his feet. 'I can make myself available for being kissed.'

Settling back into his seat, Alexander added, 'I did ask for the name of the wine merchant Sunny claims sold him the bad stuff, and I've even got a link for you to their website. There – I've sent it. What do you think?'

Christine opened the site and gave herself a moment or two to skim through it. 'Looks professional, though I'd say all the photographs are stock images – your typical glossy stuff. The lack of photographs of key players is a bit of a red flag, though their CVs look…decent. I'll need more time to be able to scroll through it all, though, so I'll do that when you've gone.'

'You're chucking me out? After I shaved, and all but polished myself to look my best for you?'

'Your meeting with Bill Coggins? You said it was important. That was why you were coming back to London yesterday – to be here for that, this afternoon.'

Alexander's face fell. 'What with…everything…I'd completely forgotten. How could I forget? What time is it? Oh, you're right, if I phone him to say I'll be a bit late, I could still make it. Are…are you okay with that?'

Christine waved at him. 'Phone Bill – give him and Nat my love – tell him I'm fine, and if Nat wants to visit she can. Her I could cope with…though I realize she's probably up to her neck with her design business and their little one. Come on, kiss me, then go. Love you loads, so I do.'

'And I do you…too. Oh, you know what I mean. Talk later. Good luck with the whining wine thing.'

Alone again, Christine settled herself, as best she could, to read through the website for HVR Wines which, as she'd suspected, offered many ways to invest in rare wines, using language that suggested – rather than promised – significant returns, as well as the ability to boast about the labels and vintages one owned. It felt…slick – maybe a little too slick?

Realizing she'd almost dropped off, she felt herself come to properly when there was a knock at her door. 'Come in.'

A head popped in. 'I've brought you something for dinner. Is now good?'

Christine checked the time on her phone – she'd obviously done more than doze for a few moments. 'Please do, though isn't it a bit early for dinner?' It was only half past five.

The door opened, and a short, wide woman in her late twenties – like Christine herself – entered. She was wearing a daffodil yellow tabard and a smile just as bright, which showcased an appealing gap between her two front teeth. 'We weren't able to invite you to make your menu selection this morning, because the doctors were with you. But the staff nurse says this would be appropriate for you and your…condition. It's butternut squash soup, with truffle oil drizzle, then a quinoa salad with beetroot, balsamic roasted chicken, edamame beans, and a bitter orange coulis. Do you think you could manage that? Dessert is crème caramel with a blueberry compote.'

Christine's mouth watered as she realized she hadn't eaten since the previous lunchtime – unless you counted endless dry biscuits and cups of tea as food, which she didn't. 'Sounds delish. Thanks. I'm Christine, by the way.' She squinted at the name badge the woman wore. 'Thanks, Priti. Will you be bringing all my meals? I think I'm going to be here for quite a while.'

The woman altered the position of Christine's bed, then pulled a hefty-looking tray-table on wheels into position next to Christine's bump. 'I think that's about as close as I can get it, without shoving it into you. Will you be alright with that?'

Christine chuckled. 'I've become used to having to work around this thing. That's fine, thanks.'

'Right, I'll fetch your tray.'

Three plates were each covered with a stainless-steel dome, and Christine couldn't help but peep under them as soon as Priti placed the tray on the table. 'It looks lovely. Excellent presentation. Thanks to…whomever was responsible.'

Priti beamed. 'I'll tell them. They're a good lot in the kitchen. As they should be…here.'

Christine knew how extremely fortunate she was to be able to have access to a private room, in a private hospital, with top-notch medical care – as well as, obviously, other services.

As Priti moved around the bed, making sure she hadn't disarranged Christine's sheets, she said, 'There'll be someone along with a hot cup of something in about half an hour. You can choose what you want when they get here. I'll be gone by then, but I'll be back tomorrow, then I have a day off. We try to keep our service rotas set up so that we get to know patients, and patients get to know us, so I'll see you often. You can use the hospital's app to choose what you want to eat from the menu there. Just go to the website and you can download it. Then we can prepare what you fancy for breakfast tomorrow. All you need to do is input the patient number from your wristband, and a few other things, and the menu you're offered is one that's been tailored to your needs. It's straightforward, but I could bring in a paper version for you before I leave for the day, if you'd prefer.'

Christine shrugged, keen to get to the soup, the aroma of which was wafting out of the tiny hole on top of its dome. 'I'll be fine with the app, thanks.'

Priti appeared satisfied that she was leaving the room in good order. 'If there's something you fancy that's not listed, you can type it in, and the nutritionist will say if it's appropriate for you, or not – then they let you and the kitchen know, and add it to your personalized list.' She leaned toward Christine and whispered, 'I happen to know that all sorts of things get sneaked into the place. There's a woman up on the fifth floor who gets pizza smuggled in – there's no hiding the smell of that is there? But try not to. They really do know what they're doing here when it comes to food and suchlike.'

Christine had to ask, 'Are you from the East End? My good friend Annie is a proper Cockney – born within the sound of Bow Bells – and you sound a bit like her.'

Priti grinned. 'Essex girl, me, but now I live out west, in Brentford. Husband's from there, so I went over to live near his lot. It's not too bad for this place – just the train, then the bus. You alright now? Someone will come to take the tray in about half an hour, when they bring the drinks – unless you buzz sooner. And don't be afraid to do that, by the way.'

Christine didn't think she'd need to bother, but thanked Priti.

'Bye for now, then, and I'll see you in the morning,' said the woman as she took her leave.

Setting aside her phone, and any thoughts of doing any research, Christine opened her pack of sterile cutlery and dunked her spoon into the velvety soup…she was going to enjoy this meal.

CHAPTER SIXTEEN

Mavis sat beside Althea in a draughty corridor at Twyst House that served as a sort of library; books lined both walls which led to a large window, which, in turn, overlooked the winter-barren garden at the rear of house, which was – at that moment – no more than a black expanse. It was a bleak area in a bleak house with a bleak outlook.

Althea twinkled at her chum. 'You're looking flushed, Mavis. Is that a result of the cold night air on your face, or because you watched the sunset while wrapped in the arms of an old flame, I wonder.'

Mavis wasn't going to let Althea get away with taunting her like that – she had to nip this thing in the bud, or she'd never hear the end of it. 'You can stop that right now. I know what you're like for meddling, so you need to understand I'll be having none of it. That you invited Frank for lunch was…enough. A nice gesture. Thank you. And it's been a pleasure to see him again – though not at all in the way you're implying.'

'I'm not implying anything. You've inferred a meaning I didn't intend.'

'Ach, get away with you, you scamp. Don't you go giving people ideas that Frank and me were canoodling out there. I tell you what, the wind was so bitter we'd each have benefitted from the body heat of the other, but we didnae do any such thing. Had a nice chat about the old days, we did. You know – who's doing what, and where, these days, and who's no longer the right side of the grass. Too many of those, of course.'

'I know what you mean,' said Althea quietly, and Mavis realized she'd struck a painful chord; Althea had received word just a week earlier of the death of one of her children's nannies, which Mavis had seen take its toll on the octogenarian.

She told herself off, then said, 'Aye, well, we're none of us getting any younger.'

'Some of us aren't getting any older, either. Which is worse.'

'Come along now, Althea, buck up, dear. This visit was supposed to give you a chance to develop some meaningful bonds with your daughter and new son-in-law. So tell me – how's that going?'

'I've read an entire book, that's how that's going, Mavis. And I'm missing McFli terribly. I know we all agreed it wouldn't be fair to him to have him in the car for so long for the drive, given those digestive issues he's been having, but now I'm regretting that decision. Paul Baker might be a true dog lover, and more than capable of tending to the needs of one small Jack Russell while I'm away from the Dower House, but if McFli were here, at least I'd have some company. Clementine's been almost invisible, and Julian's doing his best, but he's not much of a talker, is he? More a man of action, I think. I'm not sure he knows how to hold a conversation unless he has a massive hammer in one hand and a lump of half-molten iron in the other. Following his invitation, which I felt I'd better accept, I spent an hour or so watching him fashion something that began as a simple bar of metal into a wonderfully sinewy strand of ivy, this afternoon. The heat from the smithy fire kept me warm enough out in his work area, but it's not set up for comfort, so I admit I'm rather stiff now. And even when he did chatter away it seemed as though he were talking to the metal as much as to me. However, on the plus side, one thing I did glean from him is that Clementine has finally, thank goodness, seen sense about having a baby. Or not – which is, in fact, the case. It seems the penny's dropped that she's a bit too long in the tooth for all that nonsense, so she's found herself an alternative outlet for her creative spirit, it seems, hence the new studio – which is in the smaller barn behind the stables, by the way…in case you'd been wondering where she's been hiding.'

'I hadnae given it much thought,' said Mavis, truthfully. Indeed, bearing in mind what Frank had told her earlier on, Clementine Treforest-Twyst was the last person on her mind.

Althea reached over and poked Mavis – something which was unusual even for the dowager. 'Tell me all about Frank, dear. Did any of the old juices flow?'

Mavis tutted. 'None of it is any of your business, but the idea of "juices" is…quite disgusting, thank you. We talked, as I said. About folk you'd not know, so what's the point of me listing a lot of names of people you'll never meet, and telling you if they've dropped off their perch, or managed to be the reason there are twenty-odd more human beings on the face of the planet?' She knew she sounded cross, and hadn't meant to, so added – in a more temperate tone, 'It was indeed, a pleasure to see him. But…well, we can never go back, can we, dear?'

Althea chuckled wryly. 'You think you have to tell me that after my recent experiences with Ossie? I know exactly what you mean, Mavis, but we're friends, and I'm…well, I'm so bored I could pop a gasket. So, please…tell me more.'

Mavis sighed. 'The rest of us weren't put here to provide you with amusement, Althea. But I will tell you that I've agreed he can collect me tomorrow to take me to show me his boat and his business premises. Not that either of them will be his for much longer – he's already sold up, and is retiring.'

Althea rolled her small shoulders, and the tartan shawl she had bundled around her fell off one of them, which required a great deal of reorganization. As she fiddled with the massive piece of what seemed, to Mavis, to be unusually heavy cloth, Althea noted, 'There you are, you see, that wasn't so very difficult, was it? That's very interesting. When I was chatting with him in the kitchen this morning – Cook introduced us, of course – he explained how he catches his own fish, then prepares and sells them, making sales and deliveries in his van. It sounded to me as though the process filled his entire life, and that he much preferred the fishing part to the driving about part. He didn't strike me as the sort of man who'd be happy doing nothing, so what does he intend to do with his retirement?'

'He has a son, in Toronto. His first plan is to spend a little time there, getting to know his granddaughter.'

Althea seemed to have finally re-swaddled herself to her satisfaction. 'Ah. Spending time with one's family is so terribly important.'

Mavis couldn't decide if Althea was being sarcastic – given how little she'd managed to see of Clementine since their arrival – so decided to go with: 'I agree – which is why I'm looking forward to seeing my two boys next week.'

'And would you take Frank with you when you go to stay with them?'

Mavis stared at Althea, open-mouthed. 'Why on earth would I do that?'

Althea dimpled. 'You know…meet the family.'

'Ach, for goodness' sake, woman. I swear you're never happy unless your making up scandals in that wee head of yours. Speaking of which, where on earth did you find that motheaten old Tam O'Shanter you're wearing? In the bin?'

'It was Chelly's. I found it, along with several other of his hats and caps. And my head was cold.'

Once again, Mavis felt she should have bitten her tongue; she knew how being at the Scottish house made Althea feel even more raw about the loss of her husband. She wondered what the two of them had got up to at the place to make it such an emotional rollercoaster for the woman…then put such thoughts out of her head, because they'd no place being there.

'Who's he sold it to?'

Mavis was pulled out of her reverie. 'Pardon?'

'Who's Frank sold his business to? It must take a very particular sort to want to buy a fishing boat and a fish van. Someone who at least sees their future revolving around fish, I dare say, and there can't be too many of them, these days.'

'No' something we talked about,' snapped Mavis.

Althea was quiet for a moment, then said, 'Why are you lying to me, Mavis? I always know when you're lying to me…you have a tell.'

Mavis bristled. 'I do not. What do you mean by that? What do I do when I lie?'

Althea giggled, and dimpled. 'Oh my dear, you're such an honest woman that you have to make an effort to lie, and it's written all over your face and…well, no, if I let you in on it, you might stop doing it — and we can't have that. But, in any case, you've just gone and all but admitted that you were lying. So why would you lie about that? What's so important about the person Frank's selling his business to that you wouldn't want me to know who they are? Oh no…dear heavens, Clementine hasn't decided to make a living out of fish, has she?'

Mavis had to laugh. 'No, not Clementine, dear. I think that would be a step too far even for her. Your son-in-law would be more suited to that sort of lifestyle, though he'd need a pretty sturdy boat to carry him about. He seems to be bigger every time I see him.'

'Impossible, dear, he's well past the age for getting any taller. In fact, he's only got a decade or so ahead of him before he begins to shrink, like us. Well, like me, in any case. But stop trying to side-track me, Mavis – who's Frank sold up to?'

'Just some chap from down south who wants to give a simpler, Scottish life, a go, that's all.'

'So why didn't you just say that, instead of lying about it?'

Mavis sighed. 'Frank's having second thoughts. Wondering if what sounded too good to be true is, in fact, too good to be true.'

Althea sat bolt upright, her shawl falling to her lap. 'You mean a swindle? The man's not paid up? He tried to fob Frank off with…counterfeit currency? Something like that? We should do something about that, Mavis. We're detectives – we could ferret out the crook and make him pay.'

Mavis felt her eyeballs roll behind her eyelids. '*We're* no' detectives, Althea; *I* am a detective. And there's no crooks involved, nor a swindle, and definitely no counterfeit cash. Frank's got the money already. He's just a bit worried about the buyer's…motivations, that's all.'

Althea batted the shawl off her lap and onto the floor. 'Does Frank employ other people, and he thinks the new owner will sack them?'

Mavis smiled. 'Good of you to think of people's livelihoods, Althea, but it's no' that.'

Mavis watched as Althea closed her eyes and screwed them up. Her lips moved, though she uttered no words. As she studied the woman who'd invited her into her home, a few years back, Mavis couldn't help but love her – she really was quite extraordinary. In a world where 'unique' was an over- and ill-used word, Althea Twyst was a truly unique person.

Eventually, the dowager opened her eyes, with a triumphant expression. 'This part of the world's not been a stranger to smuggling over the centuries – its close proximity to both England and Ireland saw to that. And a man with a boat and a van could do a good deal by way of smuggling. He'd own methods of collection and distribution, and Frank's good name on the side of the van would be excellent cover. That's it, isn't it?'

Mavis conceded defeat. 'Aye, it is. Frank's afraid that the business he's built, his reputation, and his name, will be used for nefarious purposes.'

Althea punched the air. 'That's for being able to slip the word "nefarious" into a sentence where it was really needed – something that happens too rarely in modern life, Mavis. Well done. I suppose the only question is – what are we going to do about it?'

'No, Althea, that's no' the question at all. I've decided that I'll take a look at the boat, the van, and the business – tomorrow – and Frank's also going to show me all the paperwork he signed with the buyer. The young man's name is Danny Carmady, and he's from somewhere near London – that was all Frank could remember this evening. The money for the business is already in Frank's account, so there's no problem on that front. But he's afraid that he didn't think things through properly – that this Danny might be buying the business to use it for something other than being a fishmonger. As you said, Port William is close to England and Ireland, though – these days – it's not as though there's a defended border between England and Scotland to have to smuggle things between the two countries. Eire, on the other hand, is a country in its own right, and there's parts of it that are actually farther north than bits of Northern Ireland, and just around the corner, so to speak. Though Frank said those are dangerous waters, and he was no' sure his boat would be the best vessel to use to be getting there. But – what do I know about such things? I suggested it would be a good idea if he showed me, which is why he'll collect me here at ten o'clock, tomorrow morning.'

Althea whimpered, 'Can I come too? Please?'

'Absolutely not.'

20th JANUARY

CHAPTER SEVENTEEN

Annie peered out of her bedroom window, above the snug at the Coach and Horses. 'It's pretty out there, with everything white, but it looks like it's flippin' freezing, Tude. I'm putting on an extra pair of socks before we take the girls around the village green. That's more than frost, it's proper icy. I'll put my special boots on, too – I don't want to go for a cropper on any slippery bits, do I?'

Tudor Evans shouted from the bathroom, 'No, you don't, Annie. Not again, please. And can you call Rosie? She won't let me be in here on my own.'

'You should shut the door then.'

'I couldn't – there was one dog in the doorway, and another stacked up behind her. Just give them a call and get them into the kitchen, will you? Ta.'

'Come on Gert, Rosie…fancy a pre-walk treat?'

Wagging tails and excited tongue-dangling followed, until Annie allowed each Labrador to take a tooth-cleaning stick, gently, from her hand. Rosie retired to her bed beside the sofa with hers – guarding it jealousy in her blonde paws – while Gertie had almost completely consumed hers by the time Annie had put the packet back into the cupboard. 'Aw, Gert…you need to learn to take your time, girl.' She rubbed her hand over glossy black fur. 'I can't get over how big you two are, now – look at you.'

Both dogs gave Annie a moment of their attention, then returned to demolishing their treats, Gertie with one final swoosh of her pink tongue, Rosie with several delicate nibbles, followed by a thorough paw-cleaning, as though she were a cat.

Annie beamed at him when Tudor announced, 'Right, here I am – properly shaved, and ready for the off. I thought you were dressed already. Didn't you say something about socks, and boots? Come on…we need to get these two out there, abluted, and then I've got to be back here for a delivery at half eight. Chop chop.'

'Aww, Tude, give us a break. I'm so tired, it's a miracle I'm out of bed at all. You know what a bad couple of days I've had – I hardly slept a wink the night before last because I was so worried about Barb, and I didn't get back here from the office until gone seven last night. We had to search the place to see if we could find a notepad that Barb might have dropped there – with no luck at all – and Car and me had to sort out our kit to be ready to install all those cameras at Barb's house today. So, the upshot was, I didn't even have time for a relaxing G and T last evening, and I was all achy, and tired, and then I couldn't get off to sleep. Again.'

Tudor stopped petting Rosie, and asked, 'You're not going up any ladders installing cameras, are you?'

'Nah, Dave's coming, too. And Car's pretty good on ladders, anyway, as long as I'm at the bottom. But we need an extra pair of hands 'cos we don't know how long we'll have to do it all. Not long, maybe. So, you know – many hands make light work…and make camera installation faster, too.'

Tudor chuckled. 'Look at me here, LOL-ing. Good to know you two will have some male supervision for this part of the job, at least.'

It was Annie's turn to laugh aloud. 'You'll pay for that comment, you will, Tudor Evans. But, for now, I too have an early start, so keep these two busy while I take my turn in the shower, then let's get going. Tell you what, if you set up the coffee machine now, it'll be all ready for us when we get back. Byeee.'

She scampered off to the bathroom, knowing that Tudor would grumble a bit, but that he was much better at using the coffee maker than she was, anyway.

Finally fully equipped – she hoped – to deal with the frigid conditions, Annie clumped downstairs in her boots which, unfortunately, made her feet far too big to fit easily on the treads. Having successfully made it to the bottom she shouted, 'Okay, you can let them come down now. Thanks for holding them back, Tude.'

Rosie and Gertie writhed joyously down the staircase, and gazed at the back door of the pub willing it to open for them. Annie grabbed their leads, then hauled the door open, and was all but dragged out onto the ice-covered courtyard beyond. Managing to keep her balance, she was grateful when Tudor took Rosie's lead, and all she had to do was concentrate on controlling Gertie.

'Come on, Gert – this way. We always go this way. Good girl.' It appeared that the icy conditions had conjured fascinating smells everywhere that had to be investigated, and their progress around the green was slower than usual – with many more stops being made along the way than Annie really had time for. Her breath came in billowing clouds, her fingers began to feel numb, and she realized she'd need a better hat if she were going to have to endure more mornings like this one.

Catching up with Tudor and Rosie she managed to pant, 'I knew it was cold, but this is starting to freeze my bones, Tude. Even the girls look like they're shivering…let's get back – cut across the green to make a shorter trip of it.'

Tudor's lips looked a bit blue when he replied, 'Good idea. Yes, out with the long johns for my poor legs for these walks from now on, I think. Come on then, Rosie…let's go,' and he was off again.

Annie did her best to drag Gertie's nose away from what appeared to be a most interesting spot, but Gertie got the better of her and Annie knew before she was airborne what was going to happen; her feet slithered away from her, Gertie took the opportunity of less tension on her lead to move in the wrong direction, and Annie landed, face first, on the sharp, frozen grass, and felt the ice against her cheek.

She didn't cry out, she just lay there for a moment, her arm being pulled this way and that as Gertie followed the circuitous track of whatever it was that had left an irresistible scent trail on the village green. As she lifted her head, she caught the expression on Tudor's face when he turned to check that she was close behind him. She wondered if his eyes would drop out of his head, they were rolling so hard.

Rushing toward her, he said, 'Are you alright?'

'I think so.'

'Come on, let me help you up.'

Once Gertie and Rosie realized that Annie was down, they both decided they needed to help her get up, but that she required a thorough licking before they did that…so Tudor wrangled her arms, while she fended off tongues and tails and paws. Finally able to wipe away the chunks of ice that were stuck all over her coat, and jeans, and hat, Annie wriggled her wrists and ankles. 'No harm done,' she announced with as much relief as delight. 'Come on then, let's get back.'

She didn't dare stride off, so was able to catch Tudor swearing under his breath – in Welsh – as the foursome headed back toward the pub, where hot coffee and a change of clothes were in Annie's near future.

When Carol honked her horn outside the pub an hour later, Annie was disappointed to see that the day had hardly brightened at all; there wasn't even a hint of a break in the clouds, meaning that the ice was still covering every surface with a perilous, glossy gleam.

She got into the front passenger seat; the back seat was covered with a host of boxes and packages, which she and Carol had loaded in there the previous night at the office.

'Morning, Car. Dave's driving himself there, as we agreed?'

'Yes, so he can get back as soon as we've finished. We might need to hang around for a while.'

'Bertie with his grandparents for the morning?'

Carol sighed. Deeply. 'Yes. They mentioned taking him across to the duckpond later on, though the conversation about the extent to which he should be wrapped up to allow him to do that safely dragged on through breakfast until I wanted to… Yes. He'll be fine.'

Annie wondered what to say…for about three seconds. 'Your mum's getting on your nerves, in't she?'

Carol sighed. Again. 'A bit. Though I am grateful for everything she and Dad are doing. You know – looking after Albert, Mam doing a fair bit of the cooking, Dad getting little jobs done around the house while David's online, working with clients all around the world. But even he's…well, David's more than capable of doing most things, as you know, but he feels he has to let Dad do something, because he always seems to be at a bit of a loose end. I wish…I don't know, I wish they could be close by, just not…in the house. But it does mean we're able to call upon them whenever we need a hand, and I have to admit that's made a huge difference to our lives – me and David, I mean…not always having to negotiate who's on parenting duty while the other works. And David's got more work than he knows what to do with, at the moment. Like me. Did I tell you that I've just had another "urgent" request for two more deep-dive profiles for potential hires at the Zurich office of CZJ?'

Annie was impressed. 'They love you, don't they, Car? The work they're sending us – well, you – keeps growing and growing. I mean, let's be honest, what you do amounts to most of the income we have at the agency now. You could go out on your own and not have to share the money with us and be nicely set up.'

Carol laughed, which was music to Annie's ears. 'You know I'd never do that. I mean…why would I? It's working with you lot that keeps me sane. These deep dives are repetitive, and not particularly pleasant, especially when I find out things about people that their potential employer didn't suspect, and I'm the one who has to throw a giant spanner in the works. It weighs on me, you know, that I'm changing these people's lives forever.'

Annie dared to pat Carol on the arm, even though 'not touching the driver' was one of their unspoken rules. 'That's not your fault, doll. From what you've told me about it all, it's the people who write horrible comments on social media posts – and try to hide behind the anonymity of a weird online handle when they do it – that are to blame. In other words, themselves. Like that bloke you told me about who wrote all that racist stuff, then tried to get a job with an NGO that helps refugees. Did he think he'd get away with it? You finding out what he'd written wasn't the problem – him actually being the person he was, and writing it in the first place, while being devious enough to use a fake name, was the issue. And the potential employer deserved to know that. That's a good job, well done, that is, Car. You can't go blaming yourself for unmasking a two-faced liar.'

Carol smiled at Annie as they waited at a set of red lights. 'Thanks. I do understand that, but I still feel that sometimes…well, you know.'

'Yeah, I know you, Car – but you have to shove the weight of the world off your lovely shoulders now and again, right? Besides, like you say, it's days like today that keep us both sane. I mean, who wouldn't be uplifted by the prospect of secretly installing cameras in the house of a woman who thinks her own daughter is poisoning her? I'm not a mother, but that's got to sting, hasn't it? Even if, maybe, she's imagining it all. Can you imagine ever suspecting Bertie of doing that sort of thing to you? When he's a good bit older, of course.'

As she accelerated, Carol chuckled wryly. 'No…but there's been the odd occasion, recently, when I've looked at the medicine chest, then at my mother's tea, and…wondered.'

Annie guffawed. 'There you are – that's the Car I know and love. I get it that she's driving you a bit nuts at the moment, but I know you love her really. Like I do Eustelle. But let's talk about this job for a minute. Once we've got all the cameras sorted, we need to get digging into the daughter, and the entire family situation for Barb. Can you do the financials, and the online stuff and so on, and I'll concentrate on the people? I thought I'd start with the stepson, Tim – get what I can out of him about his stepsister. Then I'll tackle Nia herself, and try to get her to rat on him. She doesn't know we're investigators, and I'll aim to keep it that way. I'll get myself in to see her somehow.'

'You're good at that.'

'Ta.' Annie didn't see any point in disagreeing. She was good at getting to see people, and getting them to talk to her. Always had been, and – given her present job – always would be, she hoped.

Carol said, 'With that division of labor sorted, tell me more about this chip van thing. What's Tudor said about it all? And are we all going to buy our dinner from them tonight, as we planned? I need to let Mam know, if I am. It's supposed to be "her night to cook something nutritious", and she's mentioned it quite a few times already.'

'Yes, we're both still doing that. Tude definitely wants the "kebab-burger" and I'm going to try the curry sauce, and the gravy, because he wants to taste them himself. So if you could just choose any four other things to go with the chips – or even them too, if you fancy it – that would be great. And can you do photos, as well as explanations? You know, taste, texture, was it all nice and hot…anything that comes to mind, really.'

'Do you really think a lot of people will brave this weather to stand in a queue for chips, Annie?'

'I don't know. It's a novelty, that's one thing, and Tude reckons the weather doesn't ever make that much difference to how many people come to the pub for food at this time of year. It does when the weather's good, of course, because people like to sit outside, but when they're exchanging their living room for our bars? Not so much. Except for those who want to save a bit of money on their own heating. Though they don't tend to eat – that's the type who'll sit with a half of dark mild for an hour. Like Gwyn, who seems to think we'll keep him warm for the whole of the winter, and he'll have an electricity bill that's going to cost him less than the odd drink or two. He puts his money on the bar like he's feeding the meter.'

Carol laughed. 'You're showing your age now, Annie. I don't think anyone still puts money into a meter to get their electricity.'

'Not sure that's an age thing, Car – more to do with how brassic a person was. And I was, for a lot of my life. Nowadays it's all cards and prepayment, of course, but there's still a lot of people finding it hard to pay for their heating. Like Gwyn, I dare say.'

'Why's it "brassic", Annie? I know it means poor, but…why that word?'

'"Boracic lint" – rhymes with "skint". Come on, Car, you're better than that. Am I not keeping you up with Cockney rhyming slang enough these days? Comes of Eustelle and Rodney having been here for so long, I expect – even they stopped using it as much as they usually do…gave themselves over to your lot's sayings, like "over by here". I heard Eustelle say that to Rodney just before they left. Couldn't believe it. He thought it was hilarious. She pulled herself up about it, too. They are funny, Car. I hope me and Tude are like that when we've been together as long as they have been. Mind you, we'd both be over a hundred by then. It's their sixtieth wedding anniversary later this year. Sixty years. Imagine that. Of course, they married young. You and Dave could manage that. You were only in your twenties when you got married, weren't you?'

'I was, though my late twenties. Sixty years? That's their diamond anniversary, then. What are you going to give them, Annie?'

'I in't thought about it yet, Car. It's not for months. Look, we're nearly there. I can see Dave's car. He got here sharpish.'

'Set out before me, and I know you hate it when I drive too fast. Come on then, let's get this done.'

A couple of hours later, David Hill was waving to Annie as he drove off, and Carol was heading to Barbara's kitchen to put the kettle on. Again. Annie joined Barbara in her stuffy sitting room, wondering if she could face the second gallon of tea and third packet of Rich Tea biscuits of the day.

Looking relatively perky – having been surrounded by a buzz of activity for a while – Barbara asked, 'Why did I have to go into the kitchen when you put the cameras in here?'

Annie made sure Barbara's blanket was tucked around her ankles. 'Because we don't want you knowing where they are so that you don't keep looking at them. It's important that you act completely naturally when anyone else is in the house with you, and it's tricky to stop yourself from glancing toward their positions, especially if you're trying hard not to. You don't know where they are, so you can't give them away, see? It's for the best. Now, me and Car just need to check that everything's talking to your Wi-Fi properly, so that we can watch and record everything with our end of the system, then we can leave you in peace. I know you said you weren't expecting Nia today, but do you think Tim might drop in at any point?'

'We're really not that close, Annie.'

'But you were just rushed into hospital. I mean, I know you're back here now, but wouldn't he want to…check on you, at least?'

Barbara Newsom looked wistful. 'When Richard and I met, and married, Tim was already living his own life. He was happy that his dad was happy, but we two never really…gelled. No need to. Not a bad relationship, just not much of one, I suppose. I saw a bit more of him after his father died than I ever did before, as I think I mentioned, and the kerfuffle about his father's will? Well, Tim's understanding of his father's worth at the end of his life was quite out of line with reality, as I pointed out to him, and – what with me threatening to cut him out, or only give him less than half, a while back – I think I've seen the last of him for some time. Of course, he doesn't know I've given it all more thought, and plan to leave him half of it after all, so he's probably still cross with me. So…no Tim, I wouldn't have thought.'

Carol arrived with a tea tray that had been replenished for what Annie reckoned was the fourth, or maybe even the fifth time, and said, 'No more for me, thanks, Car, or I'll never make it back to the office without you having to stop for me. But you two go for it. I had no idea you liked your tea so much, Barb.'

Barbara smiled as Carol poured. 'I used to have coffee when I had my office, as I believe you'll remember, Annie. But coffee seemed to be a part of my working life, whereas tea has always been a big part of my home life, going back to my nan's time, I suppose. Though her idea of tea was to stew it for hours. I don't think I could face that, now. This suits me. It's a nice light, bright blend, don't you think? From that little place on the high street, in Brecon, called Fresh as a Daisy. Do you know it? The shop's got giant daisies painted all over it. This has a fair bit of orange pekoe in it. Nice and…fresh.' She laughed.

Annie observed, 'I didn't taste any orange in it.'

Barbara replied, 'I think the "orange" part of the name has something to do with the Dutch house of Orange. Pekoe's the name of the leaf. So no, there's no orange flavor. This mix is called "Tingle Tongue", which is nice. The girl at the shop's got a good nose and palate…mixes it there herself. But what am I doing talking about this? It's nice tea, though I do understand you might want no more of it…we've had quite a few pots this morning. Luckily, Nia's bringing some more when she picks me up tomorrow morning. She's taking me out for the day.'

Annie and Carol stared at each other, then Barbara. Annie said, 'What do you mean? Where's she taking you?'

'There's a group she's part of, something to do with female periodontists, and they've got their annual awards thing. This year it's being held at Plas Newydd, in Llangollen, and she's up for an award.'

Carol said, 'Heck, you'll be in the car for a long time. That's got to be…well, about a hundred miles from here. Are you staying over in Llangollen?'

Barbara shook her head. 'No, but it will be a full day, I knew that. And I've insisted upon going. I want to be there if she wins, and I need to be there if she doesn't.'

Annie couldn't fathom what Barbara was saying…and so calmly, too. She dared to say, 'You've said you suspect Nia of trying to kill you, Barb. Why on earth do you want to spend an entire day with her? Especially where we can't watch over you, even if only through cameras.'

Barbara's neck turned a deeper shade of pink. 'I've been feeling quite…bonny…since they let me come home, yesterday. No sickness at all, so I've kept all the goodness of my food inside me. Maybe it really is all in my head? Maybe I've been…oh, heck, I'm a psychologist, for heaven's sake, a professional counsellor for decades, yet I can't understand my own situation. Maybe I've just lost perspective. Maybe there's nothing physically wrong with me – these are all psychosomatic reactions to my grief for Richard. I find it impossible to diagnose my own mental health…so I've been thinking I might consult an old colleague of mine, as well as you, of course. Though I do think, upon reflection, that what you're more likely to be able to do is prove – to me – that no one is tampering with anything I consume, which might help to put my mind at rest.'

Despite being floored by her ex-counsellor's change of mind, Annie replied, 'It can't hurt to have a chat with a professional…as I know only too well. Nothing like belt and braces to make a person feel safe. But –' she made one last effort – 'do you really think you're up to it, Barb? I mean, look at you, all bundled up. This place is like an oven, and you're still shivering. Besides, when we asked if you could cope with not leaving this house for a week or so, you never mentioned this trip. Where's it popped up from, all of a sudden?'

Barabara wriggled in her seat. 'Yes, I'm so sorry, I forgot it was tomorrow. The back end of January seemed like such a long way off when Nia first told me about it, and now it's here.'

Annie glanced at Carol, who only partially met her gaze, then said, 'Well, you're the client, Barb, so if you want to go off with your daughter for the day, you have at it. Do you want us to shadow you? I dare say we could manage that.'

As she spoke, she could almost feel the metaphorical daggers being hurled in her direction by Carol, who, she knew, would have to drive.

Barbara's reply was very definite, and Annie saw Carol relax a bit as the woman spoke. 'I'll be fine, Annie. We'll each have our own meals, I might not even be sitting close to her – I'm not sure about the arrangements, except that I do know that this will be a very special gathering, because the place is closed to the public at this time of year. One of their docents will be there, though, to give us a private tour of the whole house, and the little museum. Such an interesting place – I've not been there for many years. It will be a pleasure to see it again. There's so much to take in there, that I dare say a person would never tire of it. Certainly the guests of the Ladies of Llangollen never did – just the carving of the entryway that greets you could keep you entertained all day, it's so intricate, and complex, with so many figures within it. They do say that Shelley and Wordsworth, and even Sir Walter Scott and the Duke of Wellington, stayed there…though maybe that wouldn't impress you two a great deal, given how close you are with the Twysts at Chellingworth Hall.'

Annie and Carol both chuckled. Annie said, 'Well, you're not wrong in one way, in that when you get to know someone with a title as a real person you think about all the others who have them a bit…differently. But, who were the Ladies of Llangollen? And I'm sorry I mangled that pronunciation. I keep trying, but it seems we English aren't too good with that double "L" sound.'

Carol grinned. 'The two "Ladies" were Irish, but moved to Wales back in the late 1700s to be able to live life on their own terms. They set up home at Plas Newydd, and became the darlings of the literary world, and high society in general. They rebuilt the house to meet their own, unique aesthetic – sort of Tudor-Gothic, I suppose you'd call it – and Wordsworth even dedicated a poem to them.'

Barbara clapped her hands. 'Oh yes, well done, Carol. I'm so pleased you're another one who finds their story interesting. But, to be accurate, Wordsworth actually addressed a sonnet "To The Lady E. B. And The Hon. Miss P." – Lady Eleanor Butler and the Honourable Miss Sarah Ponsonby, also known as "The Ladies of Llangollen". The poem ends with the lines: "Sisters in love, a love allowed to climb; Ev'n on this earth, above the reach of time." People disagree about whether they were a lesbian couple, as we would understand it these days, or two women who saw each other as spiritual sisters and…shared the same bed for the better part of fifty years. Whatever the case, they left a scandalized Ireland, referred to themselves as "fugitives", and found their niche in North Wales. Richard took me there one summer, and we had a wonderful time walking around the *parterre*, and the woodlands. Not that I'll be doing that tomorrow, of course. Not in this weather. But I do feel…well, I'm Nia's mother, and this – possible – award would be the crowning glory of her career, to date. I want to be there to support her – win, or lose. Though how on earth one judges one periodontist against another I have no idea.'

Annie was relieved when Carol was the one to say, 'Well, it's your decision, obviously, Barbara, though I believe that both Annie and I would advise against going. Not least because of the fact that we were the ones who witnessed how suddenly you became dangerously ill just a couple of days ago.'

Carol's tone suggested to Annie that she was feeling a bit miffed, something she became even more certain of when Carol added, 'As soon as we get back to the office, I'll email you a formal contract for our work – just so we have everything straight at our end. You don't need to sign it, just reply saying you accept the terms. That'll be fine, though if you could then sign your name on a piece of paper, with the date, and attach a photo of that to your email, that would be helpful.'

Barbara almost bristled. 'I have a printer in my office here, on the top floor. If there's a signature page I'll print that off, sign it, and scan it back to you. I didn't retire that long ago, and I executed all my own business undertakings right up to the end, so I know my way around contracts, thanks, Carol.'

Annie was starting to feel uncomfortable about how things were progressing between her ex-counsellor and her colleague and friend, so jumped in with: 'Always great when two pros are on the job, right? So, yes, let's get that all taken care of. We know our kit is all up and running, and you go and have a nice time with your daughter tomorrow. We'll keep an eye on you – when we can.'

'Thank you.'

Carol said, 'Come on then, Annie, let's get back to the office. I'll drive – it'll be faster.'

CHAPTER EIGHTEEN

Christine had enjoyed a delightful breakfast of Greek yoghurt, blueberries, granola, and wheat toast by the time Alexander arrived, and was feeling nice and fresh after a long, warm shower in her attached bathroom – seated and overseen, at all times, as required by her doctor. Her hair was still a little damp, but that didn't bother her too much, as her hospital room was quite warm.

His welcome of, 'And how's my darling fiancée this fine morning?' lifted Christine's spirits even more, as did the kiss he planted on her forehead. 'It's a cold one out there, so I'm glad you're tucked up in here. Your parents send their love. As we agreed – though it's against my better judgement – I haven't mentioned any of this to them, but I managed to get a number out of Sunny Dalton for the Fentons, and spoke to Lottie Fenton myself. She's…she's quite effusive, isn't she?'

Christine laughed. 'That's a good word for it. What did she say? Shall I phone her, or will she phone me?''

Alexander made the sort of grimacing face that Christine knew always preceded her fiancé telling her something she didn't want to hear. He forced a cheery smile, then said, 'Well…she sort of invited herself to pop in to see you this afternoon.'

Christine's heart fell. 'Oh no, I don't want anyone – let alone Lottie Flaming Fenton – seeing me like…this. Oh Alexander, why didn't you say I was too ill to have visitors?'

'Is that what you'd prefer people to think? That you're in here because you're at death's door…or that the baby's in trouble?'

'No. Okay. I'll see her. I suppose at least my hair's clean. But you did tell her that this isn't to get back to Mammy and Daddy, right? She won't say anything to them about me doing this teeny tiny bit of investigating while I lay here, will she?'

Alexander sat up. 'Now that is something she liked the idea of – that this would be a special secret between you and her. She promised she won't say anything to anyone at all.'

Christine flung her arms wide. 'You can't get too close because of you-know-what, but let me hug you, you wonderful man. Not only handsome and clever, but with a persuasive ability that would allow him to sell a shamrock to a leprechaun. I love you. So – what else do you have for me – news of any other great achievements?'

Alexander flopped into a chair and pulled the knitted hat off his shaved head. 'This thing doesn't like the cold weather, I can tell you that for nothing. Oh, and it appears that I've become superfluous to requirements at the antique shop in Anwen-by-Wye. Elizabeth Fernley is quite the woman, isn't she? Even when we move into Honeysuckle Cottage I don't think I'm going to have to spend too much time on that business – she's overseeing everything quite expertly. Of course, I briefed her well,' he chuckled, 'but she's a sharp one, and she emailed me to say she's enjoying not only the extra responsibilities, but also the extra hours. Of course, it's a quiet time of year, but, even so, she's handling it well. So that's good.'

Christine was pleased, but feared that might not bode well for the amount of time Alexander was prepared to spend in Wales once they'd set up home there; she was well aware that most of his business was in and around London, with only the shop and the school renovation – which was due to be completed quite soon – tying him to Anwen. She told herself she shouldn't worry about it. For now.

Smiling brightly, she asked, 'And what about your get-together with Bill Coggins yesterday afternoon? Was Nat there? How did that go?'

She felt her spirits fall with Alexander's face. 'Ah, yes, that. Nat was busy, and…there's nothing to worry about, really. It's a conversation I've had with Bill before, about him wanting to step away from the antiques trade in general, and from our company in particular. It's not the first time it's come up, and it probably won't be the last. But we're going to reduce things to just one auction a week, from now on. So he and Nat can have a bit more time together. I think it's the only compromise we could possibly both have agreed upon without him just chucking in the towel altogether.'

Christine wondered how far she should take the topic. 'How's the world of antiques looking these days? Not just in general, but for

Coggins and Sons, specifically. I know you own fifty-one percent of it now, with Bill and Nat owning the rest, and I also know he's said that he's keen for the business to survive for the next generation, now that there is one. So what does he propose? That you wind it down…or find someone to take his place? I rather imagined the fact that the company is called Coggins and Sons meant that he'd want only a Coggins to run it, even if not own it.'

'Generally I'd say the antiques business is becoming…more difficult. Online auctions aren't going to be the death of us – as we all feared, initially – but we have to use technology wisely. There's an awful lot of activity at what I'd call the bottom end of the market, but the part of it that we tend to operate within – the middle, quite honestly – is where things are a bit sticky at the moment. It might be a phase, because the business is certainly cyclical, and not just because of changing tastes, but because of generational shifts, too. Trouble is, we've found that more of what people would have brought to us to sell is being sold by them, direct to buyers, which means that reducing things to one public sale a week could work, though it doesn't bring our overhead down at all, because we need the storage, the auction site, and there's little we can do to cut staffing costs, which are more associated with the stuff coming in than going out.'

Christine said, 'So you're in a bit of a pickle. I can see why you're giving the one-sale-a-week model a go. Good idea.'

'Indeed.'

'Well, on a brighter note, I've learned a lot about wine as a possible investment, if that's of interest to you.'

Alexander grinned. 'Can I drink it, or is it going to be in a bonded warehouse somewhere, and the closest I'll get to it is to see a photograph of brown cardboard boxes?'

Christine swore. 'If you know that much, then why didn't you tell me yesterday?'

'You sent me packing, if you recall. And I know next to nothing, as I said – though Cliff Richards did drone on about it a lot, and I seem to have absorbed a bit more than I thought. Anyway – you've got me for the next hour, so impress me with your wealth of new-found knowledge. Did you manage to get hold of Sunny, or Cliff…or anyone else, by the way?'

'I had a minute with Sunny, who expected my call – thank you – but he did think it better if I spoke to his wife, Charlene, and she's due to phone me this morning. Out at something last evening and unavailable until some time after eleven today. James Onatade? I got voicemail – he's in New York this week. Cliff Richards? I have a telephone appointment with him at three. He sounds quite…precise. I didn't get the notes of "plonker" you mentioned, but there was a hint of "OCD" about the way he made me wait while he entered my details into his calendar, then repeated them back to me. Twice.'

Alexander laughed. 'As I said, Cliff's an interesting vintage. You must tell me about the aftertaste later today. So, I can see there are ducks in a row – anything else?'

Christine pressed buttons to get herself a little more upright. 'I wanted to know what to ask people about, so did some general research last evening after dinner. I feel a bit embarrassed to admit that I knew next to nothing at all about wine as an investment. I know Daddy has a cellar at our London house, but I've never paid it much attention. All I know is that he wanders upstairs into the kitchen from it, looking a little dusty, and whatever he has in his hand is what we drink…and it's usually enjoyable. You and I have our favorite wines, of course, and I've absorbed a bit over the years – as one does when one's being entertained or doing the entertaining – but it's never really interested me, so I suppose now's as good a time as any to fill a gap in my knowledge.'

Alexander leaned forward and took her hand in his; Christine felt immediately safe, and happier for feeling his touch. He whispered, 'Dazzle me with your insights.'

Laughing, Christine replied, 'Well, I've discovered that you can either treat wine like any other commodity investment – in other words, sink as much as you like into it, though you never get to drink the wine, and it sits, as you said, in a bonded warehouse somewhere where you never get to touch it, let alone open a bottle. You buy and sell it through a broker, and that's about that. Otherwise, you can have what's called a cellar plan, and I think – though I don't know until I've spoken to them – that's what Charlene and Sunny Dalton, as well as the Fentons, invested in, because it's a plan where you buy some wines to drink and some to act as a longer-term investment. You also have the opportunity to either rent cellar space for the "drinking" wine, or use your own. Now, if what you said was true – that there was a dispute about the Daltons' storage conditions – then it sounds to me as though they were storing their own wine to drink. If so, then they'd have been advised about an appropriate portfolio of wines to buy for each purpose – drinking, or laying down for future sale.'

'Got it so far. And that sounds about right, considering what I heard from Sunny. So that's what you'll talk to Charlene about? Who advised her to buy what, and about how to store it?'

'Exactly. I should be able to work out if the wine was poor wine – so she was ill-advised to buy it at all, or if it was supposed to be good wine that had spoiled – so was poorly stored. Of course, there's the good old stalwart of it should have been good wine, but it was counterfeit, to back things up. And that angle's fascinating. I learned that a chap named Rudy Kurniawan flooded the marketplace with millions of pounds' worth of faked fine wines back in the early 2000s. And, yes, the pun was intended. No one knows if everything he counterfeited was found, so there's still a great deal of speculation about the veracity of certain labels and vintages out there. Apparently even the product in the bottle of relatively mediocre wines is faked – fruit juice and sugar and all sorts of horrid chemicals being added just to make it go further. But that might not be what happened here. And, in the case of Mammy and Daddy's friends, it might just be that Lottie Fenton's lost the plot completely.'

'I bet you'll get to the bottom of it, Christine. You always do.'

Christine felt a little bereft. 'But that's when I'm part of our team. I'm missing the others. We've been texting, of course…well, until a few days ago, though even that's not the same. I knew I'd miss them, but I also know it's unreasonable to expect them to keep in touch with me about…well, whatever it is they might be working on at the moment. But I had hoped they'd just check in with me now and again.'

Christine noticed Alexander glance at his watch. He said, 'Do they even know you're in hospital?'

'I haven't told them that I'm stuck here. Why would I?'

'Don't you think they'd like to know? You all care about each other…wouldn't you want to know if one of them was hospitalized?'

Christine knew Alexander was right, but countered with: 'It's not as though I'm ill. I've just got a bit of high blood pressure, really.'

Alexander stood. 'Right, well, if that's the case, I'll let you wallow here, and get on my way. I won't give your pre-eclampsia another thought…just think of you lounging around being served first-class meals in a first-class hotel – with nurses and doctors wandering about with nothing useful to do, shall I?'

Christine attempted her most coquettish smile. 'You know what I mean. I am being good, and I know I have to be – what it means for me and our child. But, yes, you should go. If we both get done what we have to now, our time will be more our own when this one emerges into the daylight, right?'

'Correct. And I promised Geordie I'd give him the best of my day. Even though it's winter, we've got a lot on, and he's been juggling things while I've been putting out fires in Wales, at Honeysuckle Cottage. Not literally, just in terms of making sure that people are doing what they've promised, when they've promised to do it.'

'Give my best to Geordie, and thank him, from me?'

'Will do.'

Christine accepted the kiss she was given, and returned it.

CHAPTER NINETEEN

Mavis looked at the boat that Frank O'Malley was pointing toward and thought she must be seeing things. 'Your boat's called *The Wee Mavis*?'

Mavis noticed that Frank had at least the good grace to blush – or was that the effect on his cheeks of the biting wind coming off the sea?

He muttered, 'Aye, she is. The new chap said he'd keep the name too, so you'd best come up with some way for us to find out if there's anything underhand planned, because it'll be your name attached to it, as well as mine.'

Mavis tutted, then turned. 'Right then, where's all this paperwork you promised me a look at? I hope it's somewhere warmer than this bleak spot.'

'Ach, the sea's wild today, alright, but still beautiful.'

Mavis gazed back at the gray waves tipped with paler gray, mounding and roiling beneath gray skies. 'It looks like an old black and white film. All the color's gone. It's…sad, but, yes, beautiful. Though I'd no' wish to be out on it in that thing.'

'She's kept me safe all these years, Mavis. Thank you.'

Mavis chuckled. 'Ach, away with you. Come on – those papers?'

'Follow me.'

The pair trudged away from the jetty toward the arc of Port William's beach, then Frank led her to a row of structures that looked as though it would take only one particularly strong gust of wind to send them skittering into the sea, or away toward the village – where the folks living there would be grateful for the firewood, she reckoned. She also guessed that paint must be very expensive in this part of the world, otherwise more of it would have been used on the almost decaying structures.

Frank beamed proudly as he stood in front of a once yellow…shed. 'This one's mine.'

He grappled with a large padlock, then pulled open a small door, set into a larger one, through which he urged Mavis to step. The smell inside was overwhelming, and forced Mavis to breath only through her mouth.

Stepping in behind her, and closing the door, she felt Frank's arm on her shoulder as he reached forward for what turned out to be a light switch. A row of large, caged bulbs sputtered to life, and the scene in front of Mavis made her heart sink. Two long tables, a couple of battered old chest freezers, and a small part of a workbench where there were some box files, a kettle, and a couple of mugs – that was it. Frank O'Malley's empire was…unimpressive, though it was clear to her that he saw it all very differently.

Mavis took in the variety of rubberized garments hung on hooks along one wall, and the pairs of rubber boots, in various colors, ranged beneath them on the floor. Buckets, hosepipes, taps, and knives – lots of knives – added to the "ambience", along with the remnants of myriad fish – long since gone, but making their mark in her nostrils nonetheless.

Mavis observed, 'It could do with a bit of a spruce up, I'd say. Some gingham curtains at that window, and mebbe a little rug in the kitchen-slash-office area? All with yellow as the main color, to flow seamlessly from the exterior design choices, of course.'

When Frank O'Malley let out a loud, unfettered laugh, Mavis slid all the way back to the summer she'd turned sixteen, when the two of them had spent as little time apart as was humanly possible. Golden sand, golden days, and a golden boy. She careened back through her marriage, the births of her children, her career, and her present circumstances when something wet dropped onto her nose. She stepped aside before she dared to look up. 'I hope that's just water,' she said, wiping off the suspicious liquid with a tissue.

Frank beamed. 'Aye. Just water. Of course.'

Mavis swallowed hard, and continued to breathe through her mouth. 'Those papers?'

'In my office,' mugged Frank, his eyes sparkling, his chipped tooth on display at the center of his lopsided grin. 'Please follow me this way…but do be careful, the floor's slippery. Inevitable, I'm afraid. Here you go. Right where I left them.'

Mavis couldn't help but notice a small tremor in Frank's hand as he struggled with the button that released the cover of the file box. She also noticed that his hand was a dead white, almost blue, but said nothing.

'There you are. Daniel Carmady. From Lewisham, originally, now with an address in Hastings. Had a small boat there, but decided this was more his style, he said. I didn't get a sense of anything untoward when he approached me. And, no, I'm no' going to say "fishy", Mavis. Just a bloke wandering the beach until he pointed to my boat and asked about it. But now…well, I don't know."

'I can find out all about him, Frank. It's what I do. We do. That's where we should start. See if his story's true, find out what he does in life, then find out about his background. How about that?'

'You can do all that?'

Mavis nodded, knowing she'd be calling on Carol's expertise, soon. 'I do, with my colleagues. There's easy stuff, then more technical stuff. We do it all. And, in the spirit of you being an old friend, it's on the house.'

Frank beamed. 'Can't do better than free, can you? But…you should at least let me thank you with a meal. I know it was Althea who invited me for that fine lunch yesterday, but you'd be the one doing this – so lunch? Or…supper?'

Mavis smiled. 'There's a chip shop here that does a very good haggis supper, I believe. Though it's no' the weather for sitting on the sand to eat it, eh Frank?'

Mavis saw the warmth in his eyes when he smiled, and felt it in her tummy. So many years had passed, and yet there she was – in her mind's eye – sixteen again, and never been kissed, sharing chips and Irn-Bru with a boy she'd helped up after he'd fallen and chipped a tooth, though they did laugh later on about how he'd missed his footing on the path from the beach. The boy whose arms had kept her warm long after the midsummer sun had vanished from the sky, leaving behind a twilight that never, ever became true night throughout all of June. What a month that had been, and what a summer it had led to. Mavis sighed, then refocused on the papers in her hands.

She noted, 'You got a tidy sum, I see. Is that a fair price for that boat, your van, and – as the papers tell me – this "waterfront structure"?'

'Danny Boy thought so. The commercial fishing license is included in that – which accounts for about a quarter of the total – and you're forgetting my client list, Mavis. As you already know, I supply the best homes in the area.'

A stray thought flitted across Mavis's mind. 'Have you always supplied Twyst House, or only since Lady Clementine moved in there?'

Frank chuckled. 'Billy Stewart might tend the birds and beasts on the estate, with oversight of the river fishing there, but he likes sea fish more than most. And that he gets from me.'

'He seems a…gruff sort.'

'Hmm. I usually deal with the cook. Millie, she is. Been there a while now. Stuck it out longer than most of them, she has. He can't be easy to deal with, I reckon. If Millie's not about the place, Eileen comes in for her. Not often many other people there – which is to be expected, with there not having been a Twyst in residence for donkey's years.'

'But the Twysts are keen that the place is well maintained.'

Frank chuckled. 'If you say so. So, what's next for…us?'

Mavis answered starchily, 'I think I should get back to Twyst House and hit the internet, if I can. I might even have something for you by tomorrow – would that suit?'

'Pick you up at five, to go out for that meal? You can give me your report, or whatever, then.'

Mavis finally understood why Althea was so proud of her ability to summon a dimple at will, because – had it been within her power – she'd have dimpled at Frank at that moment. 'A little earlier mebbe? To allow for the drive. Half-four? Now, let me take some photos of all these sheets, and anything else you have in that box file that might be of use to me. If you could hold them, I'd be grateful. Thank you.'

She snapped away and, by the time they left half an hour later, she hardly noticed the smell, or the floor, or even the lack of a bit of gingham here and there.

CHAPTER TWENTY

Henry sat in his dressing room in his shirtsleeves and waistcoat, knowing he had to make the call, but couldn't for the life of him come up with the right phrases in his head. And he knew things always worked out better when he did that. Time was passing; Stephanie would expect him for luncheon at any moment, and still he hadn't the nerve to do it. It was all well and good asking his mother to ask her friends for a favor, but, this time, he was on his own. His mother was ensconced in Scotland with Clemmie and he really didn't want his sister to get involved, which she inevitably would once his mother knew about it all. Not even Christine Wilson-Smythe was available to him as she was, rather inconveniently, choosing to stay in London with her parents until her firstborn was delivered.

No, he had to summon the courage to phone Carol Hill; a woman with whom he'd shared a dinner table, and more, on many occasions, but not someone he felt he…knew. Of course she was one of his tenants – doubly so, as she and the rest of the WISE women used the converted barn on the Estate for their office, and the Hill family now resided in what he believed was the largest house in the village, at a rent that his mother had informed him was as low as it was because Carol deserved it. Rolling on his toes, Henry wondered if she was as good as everyone always said she was. She was a quiet one, that was true, and doted on her son, he knew; she and Albert had spent a fair amount of time with Stephanie and Hugo. But…yes…he would telephone her and explain.

He entered the number into his phone, half hoping there'd be no answer, but there was.

'Hello, this is Carol speaking.'

Henry managed to say, 'Good.'

'Hello? Is anyone there?'

'Yes, I'm here.'

'Hello, this is Carol.'

'You said that. This is…' Henry couldn't decide how to refer to himself. He knew that his mother's rule was that all the women at the agency should use no titles for anyone when they were at Chellingworth Hall – but telephone etiquette had never been discussed. Should he use Chellingworth? Twyst? Henry? He made up his mind. 'This is Hugo's father speaking.'

'Oh…um…hello,' said Carol.

Another voice cut in. 'Is everything alright? Mave and Althea haven't got into any trouble, have they?'

He asked – quite unnecessarily, 'Are you alone, Carol?'

'No, I'm driving and you're on speakerphone, Annie's in the car with me. We're about an hour from the office – or Chellingworth Hall. Would you like us to come to see you, for some reason?'

Henry snapped, 'Absolutely not. No. Please don't. In fact, before I say anything at all, I must ask you – both – to never speak of this conversation, or anything that might arise from it, to anyone, at all, ever. Do you understand that? I assume there's some sort of client confidentiality thing for private investigators?' He thought it best to get that matter clear, right away.

Carol replied, 'Well, we promise confidentiality, but – if there were a legal requirement for us to divulge something – it's not like the seal of the Catholic confessional, or the protected, legal privilege between a solicitor or barrister and their client, no. But we don't break confidences unless we're absolutely required to. Is that acceptable?'

Henry gave the matter some thought.

'Hello? Are you still there?' It was Annie.

Henry said, 'Yes, of course. And I accept. So I may speak openly?'

The two women chorused, 'Yes.'

'Very well. I have concerns about a certain man. A Mr Barry Walton. You might recall having met him here, at Chellingworth. He is a television producer.'

Annie's voice rang out clearly, 'He's the one who wanted to do that nasty little exposé of that ancestor of yours, wasn't he? He's dared to show his face again around these parts, has he? Well that takes some cheek that does.'

Henry admitted to himself that he always found Annie Parker to be a little intimidating, and she was none the less so on the telephone. 'Indeed, he was. Though he's not exactly…shown his face in these parts.'

Carol Hill was much more softly spoken when she urged, 'Go on…we'll listen, you just tell us.'

Henry decided he would. 'I shall. You both know Val Jenkins, and I hope you both understand how close my wife feels to her. Val is, after all, Hugo's godmother, and you know that means a great deal to us because Tudor is his godfather, Annie.' He paused, but hearing nothing other than something that sounded like hissing, he continued, 'It has come to my attention that Val Jenkins and this Barry Walton are…in a relationship. Which is, of course, nothing to do with me whatsoever. But they are not only personally…entangled…but are also undertaking certain joint business arrangements which I feel might not be in Val's best interests. And I want you to look into that, please. Professionally speaking, of course. I realize that, usually, my dear wife is your point of contact with our family – unless my mother's in play in some way, of course – but, in this instance, I do not want Stephanie to know anything about this. You see…she and I do not see eye to eye on this matter. She believes that everything is going swimmingly for Val, and is loathe to intervene. I believe that Val is blinded by…amorous intent. She's very much focused on bettering herself these days, which I think they refer to as a "red flag" in that – maybe – this Barry chap is making her feel less worthy than she should. In any case, that whole thing is leeching into my wife's life views, and I think it should all be looked into. There.'

Upon reflection, Henry thought he'd explained a rather complex set of circumstances really quite well.

There was a moment of silence, some sort of scuffling sounds, then Carol said, 'So, to be clear, Barry Walton and Val Jenkins are setting up together in business, and you think she might be missing something she should be noticing in these arrangements because she's romantically involved with Barry at the same time. You're concerned enough about this that you'd like us to undertake an examination of the business relationship involved, but not the personal aspects. To protect Val. Is that correct?'

Yes…Henry knew he'd done a good job of explaining. 'Exactly what I said. Could you do that? Maybe by…tomorrow?'

He heard some sort of explosive sound, then Carol's voice again; he assumed the women might be motoring over some rough terrain, because there seemed to be a definite tremor in her voice when she said, 'Well, we can try, but we can't promise anything. It's the middle of the day already, and we'd need to contact outside sources, who'd need to get back to us with information, you see. But, of course, we'll do our best. How should we communicate with you…without the chance of accidentally connecting with Stephanie?'

Henry panicked a little when he realized he hadn't thought of that. 'My mobile is private, of course, but my circumstances cannot always be said to be the same. I shall give the matter some thought, and telephone you again before dinner. Would that suit?'

Carol replied, 'Of course. But, before you go…do you have any more information about the business concerned? Its name? The nature of the business? When it was started? Anything would help.'

Henry wracked his brain. 'It's all about clothes and accessories for health nuts, I know that much. But as for when it began, or what it's called, I'm afraid I have no idea. No…wait…the name is something to do with their names – the two of them together, somehow. Drat, it's gone. Sorry. Wait…Jenwal? Something like that?'

'No worries, we'll do what we can, with what we have,' said Carol's calm voice. 'So I'll wait to hear from you later today, on this number – my mobile phone, correct?'

'Indeed. Thank you both.' Henry disconnected, and felt himself warmed by the glow of the satisfaction that came from a job well done…then realized he was late for lunch, and pulled on his jacket before he rushed downstairs to join his darling wife, and son.

CHAPTER TWENTY-ONE

Carol threw an arm across the front seat toward Annie, who still had her sleeve stuffed into her mouth. 'You can stop that now. He's gone. You're awful, Annie. You can't laugh at the poor man like that – he's a duke.'

Annie wiped the tears from her cheeks and panted, until she could speak. 'Oh Car, he's a one, in't he? Stephanie's quite normal compared to him – I don't know how she copes. Mind you, Althea's quite a turn, too – so the apple hasn't fallen far, has it?'

Carol had to smile. 'Everyone thinks their normal is the only normal, Annie. You probably frighten him to death, and he probably thinks of me as just a mumsy blob…but how would we know how he sees life? He's only ever lived at the Hall as an adult, hasn't he? Except when he was off in that artists' commune in the South of France, or whatever it was that he and his sister were doing when his big brother died. Anyway, let's not talk about him, as a person – what about him as a client?'

'I had no idea what he was on about, Car. Good for you for picking the sense out of all that, 'cos it was beyond me. So he reckons Val Jenkins is being…swindled, somehow? I never took to that Barry when we met him, so can't say I'm surprised. But didn't him and Clementine go swanning off to London together, after all that business about the other duke?'

Carol paused at a turning, checking both ways, twice. 'Well, Clementine's married now, so if there was anything going on there, it's way behind both of them. And I didn't get the impression that the man was any sort of…chancer, as such. He'd got hold of what he thought was a good story, and didn't seem to care that using it would impact a lot of people he'd been getting to know, which makes me think he's not the nicest, or least self-centered, of people, but who knows? Anyway, we haven't got a lot to go on, but I dare say that if I launch myself at Companies House as soon as we get back, I might at least be able to find out something, if the "business" is incorporated, that is. I'll start with Jenwal…though Henry did sound quite uncertain of that.'

'You could play around with all the bits of both of their names. And Henry said fitness gear was involved, which suggests to me that they'd need to be incorporated, but – as you like to say – who knows? We'll find out, shall we? So…how about I go back to the pub, and set myself up there to start overwatch on Barb, while you – well, you don't need to go out to the office, do you? Couldn't you do the Barb stuff, and the Henry stuff, from your home office? Then you'd be nice and close to be able to go to the chip van when it arrives.'

Carol sighed. 'You're right. The barn seems a bit…superfluous at the moment, doesn't it?'

'Yeah. I miss Chrissy. I hope she's doing alright. I'd give her a ring, but I don't want to butt in…you know? Maybe I could just text her? But, you're right, with just the two of us, we don't need the office really – except to meet clients, maybe. Oh heck, I said I wanted to have another good look around the place for Barb's notebook, didn't I? Mind you – we seemed to look everywhere yesterday…but it might be there, somewhere. She never did find those photos she said she took of it. I don't know, Car…maybe this is something and nothing after all – just her mind going a bit.'

Carol suggested, 'I know we both hope she's not really in danger, but if she's experiencing some sort of paranoia, that would need looking into, too. We know we're doing all we can – to prove, or disprove, what she suspects, or fears – and she's said she'll see a professional, who might be better equipped than we are to work out if it's all in her mind. But, for now, I'll drop you at the pub, so you can get the laptop set up, and I'll nip out to the office to check for the notebook, send a few emails, and I'll drive home while I wait, and hope, for replies. And everyone at my end is looking forward to a chip supper by the way, so – while I really hope they're horrible, and don't become a problem for Tudor and you – I sort of hope the Sglod Squad's chips are good.'

'Yeah, I know what you mean, Car. Got me mouth in shape for a good chip supper, I have. They're like that, chips, in't they? Which is…weird. They're just potatoes, after all.'

'Oh Annie, you're hopeless. Chips are the Great British Food – the way to not only let your tongue enjoy the tang of malt vinegar on the crunchy outer layer, but to also relish the fluffy interior…all while providing a method of delivering other tasty tidbits to your tongue. They're perfect – just enough flavor on their own, but not too much to overwhelm anything else. And they're cheap – as the saying confirms. Well, they always used to be. It'll be interesting to see what the Sglod Squad charge, and how big the portions are. I'll make sure to get both small and large portions, and weigh them, for comparison.'

Annie chuckled. 'I love the way you're taking this so seriously, Car. Ta, doll. Not everyone would understand how critical this could be for me and Tude. You're a good mate. Right, here we are then. Back to the office for me – well the kitchen table – and back to the office office, then your other office, for you. Talk later, Car. Love to the family. And give Bertie a squishy hug, from me.'

As Annie made her way toward the pub, Carol called, 'It's Albert, Annie,' but she knew she was wasting her breath.

CHAPTER TWENTY-TWO

Annie burst through the back door of the pub and headed for the bathroom in the flat upstairs before she dared to even think about finding Tudor to say hello. She knew that – if he were to be busy at all that day – this would be his rush time, so she gave herself a chance to pet the girls, change her clothes for something a bit comfier, and set up her laptop, where she opened up the connections to the cameras at Barbara Newsom's home.

With Barbara having such a large house, with so many rooms, it had been agreed that they'd concentrate only on those she'd be using, not those that were, essentially, set aside for – non-existent – guests. The entryway, sitting room, kitchen, stairs, her bedroom – not her bathroom, to allow for privacy – and the landing outside her bedroom, as well as the conservatory that led from the kitchen, were all covered.

Not having been into the kitchen the day before, Annie had taken the chance to have a bit of a nose about that morning, and had been impressed by its cleanliness, and the way Barbara had put things in cupboards arranged by height, and grouped together like they were in the shops. The one thing that had surprised her, though, was just how many bottles of ginger wine Barbara had about the place – some full, many empty. She was surprised the woman was ever sober, but – as Barbara had said when Annie had mentioned it – she'd tried all sorts of things to settle her tummy over the past months, and the ginger wine that Nia had suggested had turned out to be as good as anything, especially after dinner, with a drop of hot water in it. And it wasn't as though she ever wanted to drive anywhere after dinner, anyway.

Annie checked each camera, one at a time. They were all small, set up in places that would make them invisible – unless they came under close scrutiny – and gave wide-angled coverage of each space, while allowing for a little shift in direction, if needed. Each could be activated remotely, and had its own motion detector, so they would only record to the cloud if there was movement in the room, and they'd automatically shift to night-vision, if needed. She was glad they'd set up two cameras in the sitting room, because it meant she had a full view of the room Barbara was likely to use most. No motion was registering anywhere, which Annie could see was because Barbara was fast asleep, swaddled into her large armchair, much as they'd left her. Reviewing the recordings, she could see that the woman hadn't bothered to tackle the stairs after they'd left, but had used the cloakroom off the entryway, which made sense. She was pleased to see that Barbara had looked steady on her feet when she'd moved about. Other than that, it looked as though their client had tried a bit of daytime TV, but had given up on it. The set was still on though, because Annie could see it from the camera that also offered a rear view of Barbara's chair. She set her screen to show all camera feeds, then minimized it so she could attend to other matters.

Tudor called, 'Was that you coming in?' His voice attracted not only her attention, but that of Rosie and Gertie, who rushed to the top of the stairs in case something was about to happen that might involve them.

Annie checked her watch – good grief, she'd been in for half an hour already, and hadn't let Tude know. 'Yeah, sorry, had to do something up here. Do you need me down there?'

'No ta, it's quiet. Just checking if you'd had lunch, or if you wanted me to bring you something.'

Annie realized she'd forgotten all about lunch. 'I could do with a bite – anything that's going, ta. Surprise me – but no chips…we're having them tonight, remember?'

'How could I forget? It's the Sglod Squad night. Give me five minutes, and I'll bring something up. No chips.'

The door at the bottom of the stairs banged shut, and Annie returned her attention to her screen, while the dogs returned to their usual spots. 'Right, now let's track you down, Mr Tim Newsom…'

It seemed as though Tudor was at her elbow two seconds later, bearing a plate of cheese, a scotch egg, and a bowl of coleslaw. She looked up at him. 'Everyone wanted a hot lunch on this chilly day, and you've only got cold things left over?'

'Smart as a whip, like I always say. Lunch, m'lady.'

'Ta, Tude. Did you manage to have something?'

'The scotch eggs needed finishing up, so two of them. No coleslaw though – can't cope with it, as you know.'

'Without hot sauce, it's a mound of tasteless slimy stuff. With the addition of that one, magical ingredient, it's a luxurious accompaniment to…anything, really. You should try it sometime.'

Tudor laughed. 'Nope. Not for me. Right then – are you settled here for the rest of the day? Because, if so, there's something you can be doing for me…if you have the time.'

Annie mugged a salute. 'You command is my pleasure, sir. What's it to be?'

'Dig me up some dirt on those blokes you said run the Sglod Squad, will you? I know we're going to try their food, and that Carol's going to help on that front too, but you've no idea how many people have mentioned that blessed van coming here, so let's be forearmed, eh? I know you can do it…but can you do it now?'

Annie reached up, and grabbed Tudor's neck, pulling him down for a snuggle…which meant that both dogs wanted to join in, of course. 'It's already on my list of things to do, and only just below somehow finding a teacher named Newsom, somewhere in, or near, Brecon.'

Tudor petted the dogs, then stood upright. 'Well, why don't you make that an easier task for yourself by asking Iris Lewis about him? I know she's been retired for donkey's years, but she's still plugged in to what I can only describe as the equivalent of a super-network of teachers that covers not only the retirees, but all those who've followed after them. I bet she'd have some way of tracking him down.'

Annie blew him a kiss. 'See – I knew there was a reason for me loving you. Of course – I'll ask Iris. Then the quicker I've done that, the sooner I can get on with what you want me to do. You haven't got any advice for me on that one, have you?'

'You've already managed to get all their names, Annie, so no – I'll let you loose on that front. Text me if you need anything, okay? I've got to get back, now – Aled's got a few hours off. It might interest you to know that he's told me he's going to spend some time with Gwen Pike, so that Joan can have a bit of a break…she's popping into Brecon to do a bit of shopping, he said, while he sits with her mum. Nice bloke, eh?'

'You only pick the best, Tude. And he is named Evans, too, so…you know…you two might not be related, but the name must count for something. Okay, I'll do me, you do you, and we'll meet for chips around five – alright? Will he be back by then?'

'Oh yes – he'll be here by then. Good luck. Love you.'

'Good luck. Love you too.'

Alone again, except for the dogs – who she knew wouldn't leave her side until she'd cleared her plate – she picked at her scotch egg before she phoned Iris Lewis, because, now that she'd seen food, she was starving. She dared to leave her plate to collect her bottle of hot sauce from the cupboard, then slathered her plate with it, before tucking in.

CHAPTER TWENTY-THREE

Christine was surprised to note, upon her arrival, that Lottie Fenton had become a blonde. She told herself that lots of women of her mother's age – which Lottie was, roughly – lightened their hair, thinking it would disguise their grays. Personally, she thought her mother's solution – a balayage leaning darker, rather than lighter – was much more effective…less harsh-looking.

Swooping down to air-kiss her cheek, Lottie's perfume overpowered Christine, then she managed to drape her fresh-from-the-bottle ash-blonde hair into Christine's mouth, which was deeply unpleasant. With that *faux pas* dealt with, Lottie settled herself on a chair and placed her ruinously expensive handbag carefully on her lap, the sanitized floor being, apparently, unworthy of the little brass feet designed to protect the skin of whichever poor creature had been used to create the so-called 'work of art'.

With pleasantries exchanged, Christine realized she wasn't going to be able to cope with Lottie's nasal tones – which she'd managed to erase from her memory banks quite successfully – for very long, so decided to get to the point.

She adopted a chummy, conspiratorial persona, hoping it would get what she needed out of the woman, fast. 'So, come on then, Lottie, do tell me all about it. Why do you think this wine merchant of yours is up to something…questionable.'

Lottie's pained expression matched her whiny voice. 'It's nothing concrete, you understand, just a general…feeling. And it's the same chap that the Daltons used, and they were so terribly embarrassed when they served undrinkable wines to those wedding guests. We couldn't risk anything like that happening to us. I dare say they managed to get away with it because those who were served were their extended family, and their acquaintances. They're originally from somewhere north of London, and he's of Indian descent, so maybe they weren't all as used to fine wines as our circle would be.'

Christine noticed that, with a wave of her hand, Lottie had sought to include her within her 'circle', while simultaneously belittling the Daltons and giving herself the opportunity to reveal her thoughts about racial hierarchies.

She boiled internally as she did her best to come up with a telling retort, but Lottie didn't give her the chance, continuing immediately. 'We hadn't opened any of our wines until last evening, because we were planning to do so when George and I celebrate our thirtieth wedding anniversary next month – we married on Valentine's Day, you know.'

With Lottie's expression suggesting to Christine that she expected to be congratulated on such an achievement, Christine decided she couldn't be bothered to play nice with this woman. 'I dare say it was a white wedding, Lottie. Very white. In every sense. Like your "circle".'

Lottie tittered, suggesting to Christine that she'd taken her comment the wrong way. 'It most certainly was.' She continued, 'And the wine we tried last evening was not very…pleasant. We both felt it lacked body, and left a slightly metallic aftertaste, though the nose had been promising, and it had good legs.'

Christine could imagine the couple swirling, examining, sipping, and discussing the wine, and felt quite queasy. 'I'm so sorry to hear that. Was it an expensive bottle?'

Lottie bridled. 'That's not the point…the fact of the matter is that it was a disappointment, and we don't want our guests to be disappointed.'

The price is the point, and you don't want people to think you don't know your vintages, thought Christine. She said, 'Tell me more about the merchant in question.'

Lottie perked up. 'We met him at a function being hosted by one of our chums from our yacht club days. A small soirée held for those considering developing their appreciation of wine. It was great fun, and both George and I knew, that very evening, that we could both put our excellent palates to work, and gain a valuable alternative form of investment to diversify our portfolio. Hans's organization had provided the wines for the evening, and he was terribly impressed by our abilities when it came to spotting the better vintages among those being tasted. In fact, he took us under his wing after that, to help us develop our skills, and it was only a few months later that we both felt confident in placing our first order with him. He'd accompanied us on a specially arranged visit to one of the oldest vineyards in Bordeaux and managed to talk the owner into releasing a case of one of his exceptional vintages just for us. We were so lucky, and the owner was such a lovely man. He even spoke English when we were with him, because I'm not blessed with an ear for foreign languages.'

Christine could picture the set-up, and – having initially wondered if the Fentons were overreacting – she suspected the couple had fallen for a scam of some sort; they'd been flattered and groomed, then their funds plundered. 'How wonderful for you. And the merchant is…?'

'Hans. Hans van Ruud. Maybe you've heard of HVR Wines?'

Thanks to Alexander, Christine had, and her detailed examination of their website had already alarmed her, because its depths spoke far too often about 'spectacular' returns, she felt. Wanting to build, rather than duplicate, her knowledge, she asked, 'Have you met many of their other customers?' She was interested in trying to work out how the company accessed what she was already thinking of as its 'marks'.

Lottie fizzed, 'At first we did, at the exclusive evenings Hans organized. We were invited to lots of events because, he said, we're naturals when it comes to sharing our experience with others. There are so many people who know so little about fine wines, and George and I are only too happy to teach them a little of what we know.'

So you're being used as 'come hither' window dressing, and you don't even know it, thought Christine. 'What a treat for you all. Have many of the people with whom you've shared your passion and knowledge also become customers of HVR Wines?'

Lottie deflated a little. 'Well, people come and go at these sort of things, you know? And there's the element of confidentiality, of course, which is so critical when it comes to one's investments. But Hans liked to have us as the center of attention, of course, so we met lots of new people. And we're only too happy to show them the lovely photographs we took when we were in France, and not just on that first trip. We've been to a few other vineyards with Hans, since then.

But, now that you mention it, we did meet Sunny and his wife at one of those events. It was a little gathering where we led a tasting in a medieval cellar, somewhere in the City. Wonderful place – such atmosphere. Candlelit. Intimate. Delightful. And George was on top form that evening, I recall, him being on his home turf, so to speak. The City.'

Christine asked, 'Could you explain the plan you have with HVR Wines, please, Lottie?'

Lottie did, in excruciating detail. Christine felt her eyes glaze after about ten minutes, so jumped in with: 'So you personally store the wines that you plan to drink, and they store those you plan to keep as an investment. You give them a monthly budget of five thousand pounds which they spend on a balanced portfolio for both parts of your cellar. And they have the right to trade your investment wines for you – with your express permission – when they advise you that it's a good time to do so. Is that a fair summary, Lottie?'

Lottie blinked. 'Yes.'

'What's the most you've made on a trade, Lottie?'

Lottie looked taken aback. 'Oh, you mean actual numbers?'

'Yes, actual numbers.'

'Well, they advised us to trade a case for which we'd paid around six thousand, and it went for eight and a half. We thought that was rather good, because we'd only had it for about a month.'

Christine nodded. 'An excellent return, indeed. And do they pay you directly when they sell for you?'

Lottie giggled. 'Oh no, of course not. It goes into our account, where it either offsets our monthly spend and charges – because, of course, we pay fees for the storage they undertake on our behalf – or else, sometimes, we agree to additional expenditure, when the pot's looking full, and when Hans alerts us to a special something that's coming up at auction…though he's rather good at getting pre-auction access to a wide range of utterly exclusive offerings, all with the best possible provenance.'

Christine was beginning to see how the whole scheme could work. 'Do you ever see the wines that are being stored for you?'

Again, Lottie's face suggested that Christine was woefully lacking in knowledge. 'Of course not. Our cases are in a secure, bonded facility in Wiltshire, where the conditions are strictly controlled – temperature, humidity, that sort of thing. The gold standard in wine cellaring, in fact. We see photographs of our cases with our unique client number pinned to them, but the experts at the facility are the only ones who come into contact with the wine there.'

Christine nodded. Regurgitating what she'd read on the HVR Wines website, and several others of its ilk, she said, 'So the wine that has been purchased on your behalf, by your merchant, arrives at a closed facility, where it's examined for the veracity of the label and record of ownership by experts, also hired – on your behalf – by your merchant. When it's passed muster, it's then connected to your electronic account, adorned with your personal customer number, and placed with the rest of the cases being held for other customers of the same merchant, as well as those of all the other merchants who choose to use that particular facility. Is that a fair summary?'

'Well, yes…but we're clients, not customers. We're trading through the merchant, as one trades with any number of other investment experts. We're not just customers, of the sort a mere shop would have.'

Christine could tell that this distinction without a difference meant a great deal to Lottie; she was almost starting to feel sorry for the woman, however odious her views about some of her fellow humans being 'less than' herself might be. 'So you only get to see, and taste if you wish, the wines you've been advised by Hans would make good drinking wines? Not the investment wines?'

'Of course. The true investment wines should only be disturbed, or transported, when absolutely necessary. The wine we plan to drink is delivered to us – HVR has its own specially designed vehicle – and we keep it in our own cellar.'

Christine said, 'So you've added these new wines to an existing cellar that you've always had?'

Lottie sat a little more upright. 'No, it's a brand-new cellar. We had it installed last autumn. Hans put us in touch with the most wonderful people who designed it, and then installed it with absolutely no fuss or mess whatsoever. It's in a small room that used to be a pantry. They were impressed that we had a spot that could be converted with so little adaptation required, though, of course, we agreed that we needed the highest level of technological installation they could offer. It was a worthwhile investment.'

Christine asked, 'Do you happen to recall the name of that firm?'

Lottie nibbled her lower lip. 'Now it was something amusing, because they only do cellars. That's it – Plonk It In – because they install wine cellars, you see? Funny. Nice people. Very young. But they need to be to understand all the computer programs for the atmospheric control systems, I suppose. The actual building people were the usual type, but George kept an eye on them the entire time…just in case.'

You mean just in case they went after the family silver, Christine thought as she made a mental note to speak to Alexander about this construction element of the set-up…which she guessed also, somehow, managed to end up lining the pockets of Mr Hans van Ruud.

She asked, 'And did you have any concerns at all about the arrangement you have with HVR Wines prior to hearing about the incident with the Daltons, Lottie?'

Lottie shifted in her seat, and Christine noted that the enthusiasm of her tone diminished. 'Well, we haven't been to as many events with Hans, recently, and we'd heard that they were still happening, but without…us. Of course, we both have other commitments, so it was natural that we'd not been able to accept all of his kind invitations, but it came to our notice that the size and number of his events, overall, was increasing and I suppose we felt we were being…sidelined a little. Not that we're ever a couple to push ourselves forward, especially where we're clearly not wanted. But we noticed that the number of opportunities to sell that we were being offered was also decreasing, and George – who likes to check the value of our investment every day – began to notice a bit of a dip in the value of some of our holdings, but we weren't getting any advice to move on it, from the team, nor Hans himself – who, understandably, as the business grows, is often unavailable to take our calls. We're dealing more with a pleasant young woman named Isla these days, who certainly seems knowledgeable, but more about trading and values than actual wine, you know?'

Christine nodded. 'And how does George check the value of your holdings, exactly?'

Lottie perked up again. 'Now that's the wonder of the whole set-up, you see. We have our own exclusive client portal, where all our holdings are listed, and we can see what prices they're trading for on all the exchanges. There are several, internationally, and HVR's unique offering is that they allow us to keep an eye on all of them. There are very good quality photographs of bottles of our wines – each one has its own little profile, with its bottle and case identifier, and our client record attached. Sometimes the value changes while George is actually watching, so he knows exactly what's going on. Of course, one expects values to dip as well as improve, as Isla keeps reminding us, but you know the saying – once a vintage is bottled, there'll never be any more of it, so we're investing in a market where the demand will eventually outstrip supply, because no more supply is possible. And, of course, the more people who invest in wines, the more demand there is, and so their value goes up. Overall. Though we've always known we're looking at a mid- to longer-term investment for the bonded stock.'

Christine couldn't help but say, 'But Lottie, surely that means the value of the wine is dictated purely by the demand from people who will never, ever drink it. I mean what's the point of that? And, more importantly, how on earth is it sustainable? Won't it all just go "pop" one day? It's as though the wine isn't…real. You could be investing in anything – there could be lumps of rock in those boxes, for all you know. All it would take is for someone to open one of them, find out what's really in there, then you could wave goodbye to all of your so-called investment.'

Lottie preened. 'That's why the experts are called upon to examine every case, and every provenance, when it's taken on by a new client – so they've been checked many times in some instances, as the case is sold, and bought.'

Christine sighed; here was a True Believer. 'Lottie, I understand that – sometimes – things aren't real, in terms of what the rest of the world would imagine to be the true sense of the word, because they are constructs, or bets, about situations that may, or may not, arise at some point…like the future value of green coffee, for example. But, in this instance, you are truly relying upon what you believe to be in those bottles to be what's actually there. Or even that the bottles even exist.'

Lottie harrumphed. 'We've seen photos of the bottles. They're real. But…well, yes, what you're saying about what's inside them is what we've…developed concerns about.'

Christine was becoming increasingly aware of her bladder, so knew she had to hurry things along. 'One quick thing more, Lottie – the wine you and George drank last night was some sort of test, prior to you coming here today?' Lottie nodded. 'Okay, was that from your own stock, in your own cellar, at home?' More nodding. 'And had it been in your possession prior to the construction of the cellar that was installed by the Plonk It In people, who were referred to you by HVR Wines?'

'No. HVR held it for us until we were all happy that we had the correct facility at our own home, then they delivered it, placed it correctly within the cellar, and we prepared the bottle for consumption exactly as we should yesterday. We can't understand why it was so bad. We both recall sampling the exact same wine early in our tasting journey, which was when we decided it would be ideal for our celebration next month.'

'So there's no question that the bottle was ever improperly stored?'

'No. Certainly not since we've owned it. And the provenance proves that it was properly stored before that.'

'And do you plan to speak to Hans van Ruud about your…disappointment?'

Lottie fidgeted again. 'Well, George and I discussed that, of course, but we both thought we'd defer to you on that front. So…what would you advise?'

'Keeping your mouths shut, Lottie. Don't touch any of the bottles you have, and don't mention your experience to anyone else – got it?'

Despite looking somewhat taken aback, Lottie replied quietly, 'I understand.'

Christine dared, 'Good. Now – if you would excuse me, please – I am a very pregnant person who has certain needs, and they cannot be ignored. I'm about to ring for assistance, and you don't need to see me being hauled out of this bed. Bye, Lottie – and, yes, I think I can help, and will do all I can to get to the bottom of things. But for now – please…go! And don't forget – this is our secret – not a word to anyone. Promise?'

'Promise.'

Even as she pressed the buzzer on her bed with a sense of urgency that mounted by the second, Christine couldn't help but think that the entire industry that had sprung up around wine investment appeared as though it couldn't have been better designed to have the potential to bilk people out of their money…and that made her very angry indeed.

She'd grown up knowing and believing – because of her father's excellent example, and her own career in the City – that a person's word was their bond. But who really knew what was in the bottles, in the boxes, stored in all those climate-controlled warehouses around the world…other than those who were paid to give an opinion by the people doing the buying and selling, and taking a cut of every transaction? And, if the bottles were never actually opened, would they even know, for certain? Surely all they could do was give an opinion on the design of the bottle and label, and trust in whatever paperwork existed to 'prove' ownership of the bottle since it had been filled. She needed to speak to Alexander, and Carol, and was already formulating the questions she'd ask Cliff Richards that afternoon, and Charlene Dalton – who'd phoned earlier to say she was unexpectedly detained away from home, and would it be alright if she phoned Christine back around teatime. But, first, she needed someone to respond to the buzzer.

CHAPTER TWENTY-FOUR

Mavis stood in her drafty bedroom, looked at her phone, and swore, silently. She didn't believe that using bad language was something that should be done often – indeed, she thought it suggested that a person possessed a poor range of vocabulary. However, having spent so many years tending to the needs of members of the armed forces when they were in medical distress, she was more than familiar with most epithets that existed – and their many, and varied, applications. On this instance she allowed herself a relatively mild expletive, directed at the lump of useless plastic she held in her hand.

With the question, *Why now?* rolling around her head, she moved about, her phone held high, seeking an adequate signal. But there was none. Not even one bar. She tried to access the internet. Nothing. Her phone, unhelpfully, told her it was connected to Twyst House's Wi-Fi, but that there was no signal. She dreaded another visit to the gruff Billy Stewart, but realized she had little option; she had no idea how the house was set up for internet access, so had to resort to…asking for help. Again.

She resigned herself to the situation, and headed toward the rear of the ground floor of the house, where the kitchen and estate office were located, hoping to find someone – anyone other than grumpy old Billy Stewart himself – who could help. The entire house appeared to be deserted. She was aware that Julian would be at his smithy, that Clementine had announced at breakfast that she would, once again, be spending the day in her studio, and Althea had muttered something about getting Ian Cottesloe to drive her somewhere where she intended to enquire about a dozen haggis. Mavis had only half heard what Althea had said at the time, but now, as she tried to work out where everyone had gone, she wondered why on earth the dowager would need so many haggis.

Mavis was relieved when she found a cook in the kitchen, though not the same one she'd met upon her arrival, which puzzled her.

'Hello there, I'm Mavis MacDonald, and I wondered if you could help me, please.'

The woman stared at her, put her hands on her substantial hips, and said, 'I know who you are. The dowager's companion. Billy told me. I'm Eileen. I do the odd day, when I'm needed. There's a lot of you here at the moment, and Millie's not feeling too bonny, which is a shame for her, and me. What do you want?'

Mavis wondered if everyone who worked at the house was rude, or if she were just catching them all at an exceptionally busy time. 'I hoped you might know how the internet is set up here. I can't get onto the Wi-Fi system at all, and it's urgent that I do.

Eileen shrugged. 'No idea. Ask Billy.'

Mavis had been afraid of that. 'Any idea where I might find him?'

'Out. Or in his office. One or the other. I'm no' his keeper.'

Mavis bit her tongue. 'I'll try his office first. It's through there, right?'

'Yes.'

Mavis dared, 'Will we be seeing Millie again?'

'Mebbe. I'm the backup. Have been for more years than I can recall. But the main ones? They come and go. Can't cope with Billy. No idea why. He's no' a bad man, just direct. Knows what he wants. Millie though…she seems to be able to handle him.'

'I understand Billy's a great fan of fish. Sea fish. Frank O'Malley was telling me he delivers here often.'

Eileen looked Mavis up and down. 'Not a lot, I'd say. He likes a bit of fish now and again. Doesn't everyone? Know Frank, do you?'

'We were at school together.'

Eileen dropped her hands. 'You're from around here?'

Mavis gave the woman a potted version of her life's journey. She finished with: 'Are you local, too?'

'Glasgow. Came out here for a bit of peace. Enjoy cooking. This suits me. It's a quiet place. Usually.'

Mavis was trying to work out why a cook would be needed when there wasn't normally a Twyst in residence. 'So who would you – or any other cook – cook for? You know, before Lady Clementine and her husband moved in.'

'Billy. Whoever's here doing a bit of cleaning, or fixing things up. The blokes who take care of the gardens. And the woodlands. The Twysts like everyone to be fed, if they work here. Which is very nice of them, I'm sure. And it's good for me, too. It's not usually a lot, and I'm happy to be here for a few days at a time. The only time it's busy is when the fishing lot's around.'

'The fishing lot?'

'The people who come to do all the fishing. You know.'

Mavis didn't know, but she realized she'd never talked to Althea about how, exactly, the estate was run. She decided to allow her general curiosity to take a back seat to her main concern. 'Well, nice chatting, Eileen. I'll let you get on with preparing dinner, and I'll try to hunt down Billy. Thanks.'

'Wherever he's been, he'll be back soon. End of the day, for him.'

'Thanks again.' Mavis headed toward the office, steeled herself, and knocked at the door upon which resided a brass plate engraved with the words 'Steward Stewart'. Mavis rolled her eyes and knocked again. There still being no answer, she tried the handle, hoping to be able to open the door and find a modem of some sort that she could at least reboot. The door opened, but the room she found behind it looked as though it would chew up and spit out something as hideously modern as an internet modem; it appeared as though the room had been left to itself at some point during the 1950s. Or maybe even the 1930s. One corner housed a radiogram with matched flame walnut veneers and a fabric-lined section in the pattern of a sunburst. The massive desk at the center of the room had an in tray, an out tray, and a blotter between them, in front of which stood a dual-potted ink well, which appeared to still be in use, if the blottings on the paper were anything to go by. There was no overhead light, and the room was deep in shadow, but there were standard lamps in each of two corners, adorned with ruched and tasseled bottle green shades, and there was a curved, stainless-steel lamp which arced from a side table toward the one easy chair in the room, which was upholstered in a tartan that was so worn its pattern was almost unidentifiable. Mavis suspected it was the Galloway tartan, in green, which would be appropriate, not because she was currently standing in Dumfries and Galloway, but because the Galloway tartans had been invented in the twentieth century for Scots without a clan tartan of their own, so using it to upholster a chair seemed reasonable.

Suspecting this office was not where she was about to find the solution to her technological problem, Mavis turned to leave, and inadvertently knocked into a large roll of…something…that had been propped against the frame of the door. As she picked it up, she grew curious about what it was. Around four feet tall, she laid it on the floor and kicked it. The roll was hessian sacking, single thickness, and was printed with a recurring design. Mavis – now completely curious – flipped over a part of the fabric to get a better look at it. A red circular outline was filled with the same tartan as the chair – yes, definitely Galloway – and also featured a smiling fish of indeterminate species that appeared to have steam coming off it. Above the circle was the word 'TRADITION', below it the word 'DELIVERED'. Mavis was completely mystified, but took a photo of it in any case. She'd ask…someone…what it meant when she had the chance, though knew it wasn't a priority.

She rolled the hessian back around the cardboard core, and stood it up again in the spot it had occupied before she'd knocked it over. She'd taken just two steps away from the office when Steward Stewart rounded the corner, and almost bumped into her.

Mavis was pleased to see that the man appeared to be genuinely embarrassed by the fact that he'd almost knocked her over, and took advantage of his softened mood to enquire about the fact that she was unable to communicate with the outside world.

His response of: 'The satellite's down. Again. Fell off the roof in the winds last night,' flummoxed Mavis. When he added, 'They'll be out next week to put it back up again,' her spirits plummeted. How on earth was she going to be able to make the enquiries she'd promised Frank she'd undertake?

She spluttered, 'So there's no internet? But my phone won't work either. That can't be anything to do with the satellite, surely.'

'Your mobile phone?'

Mavis nodded.

'Signals come and go as they please, out here. You could try walking out to the summer house, that might get you a few bars.'

'It's getting dark out there already,' she said, knowing from her experience the previous evening that she didn't want to walk the path to the summer house alone, at night; it would be treacherous underfoot.

Billy Stewart spoke accusingly. 'Is the landline nae working?'

She realized it hadn't even occurred to her that there might be a functioning landline at the place, so asked, 'Where might I find a handset?'

'Library. And I have one, in my office. But I'd prefer you to use the one in the library. I'll no' be needing the line myself this late in the day, so feel free.' With that, he opened his office door, stepped inside, and shut it firmly behind him.

Mavis stood still for a moment, and seethed silently at the man's rudeness, then made a decision: she'd try to get in touch with Carol, and fill her in with all the salient details about Frank's Danny Carmady, so that she could use all her online powers to find out more about him. She was cross that she wouldn't be able to send the photographs she'd taken of the paperwork, but would refer to them, so that Carol could take notes.

Having decided this was the best way to proceed, Mavis beetled to the corridor that doubled as a library and hunted for something that looked like a telephone. Nothing leaped out at her. It wasn't until she looked on the shelves just higher than her eyeline that she spotted an instrument of such age that she wondered if it could possibly work; she hadn't seen a 'trimphone' for decades. The line was certainly open, she discovered, which lifted her spirits, but then she realized she didn't know Carol's number, so had to check it on her mobile and dial, carefully.

The angular plastic handset felt strange to her as she stood in the middle of the corridor, which was where she had to hover, there being a wire of about three feet in length plugged into the wall at a very strange height. She got Carol's voicemail and left a garbled message. After she'd hung up, she composed herself and made a second call, getting the voicemail again, but doing a much better job of her message this time. She admitted to herself that she wasn't used to not being able to text and email to back up what she was saying, so made a third call to ensure that Carol had the names, dates, and locations of the contract signed by Frank and Danny, so she could at least get started with her digging. It would have to do until the morning, when she'd head off to the summer house to try to get a signal. Having done all she could, she retired to her room, where she sat down to compose a series of lengthy texts to Carol which she sent, knowing that — if a signal deigned to waft its way to her phone — they'd be on their way in milliseconds.

CHAPTER TWENTY-FIVE

Other than the too-short visit by Alexander, and the time when she'd been graced by the company of the rather-too-fragrant Lottie Fenton, Christine had endured being monitored in her bed all day, then found she had to engage with various professionals for what felt like hours; she was feeling thoroughly fed up with her situation. Alexander wasn't answering her calls – which didn't surprise her – and she'd had no time to herself to do even a little bit of online research on her phone that might help with what she told herself she was allowed to think of as a real case, despite the fact she was just doing a favor for her parents, though they didn't know it.

Eventually, she and Cliff Richards spoke for about half an hour – no, it had been exactly half an hour, and Christine suspected that was the time slot he'd allowed for her in his schedule, because he'd proved to be nothing if not precise. The upshot of their conversation was that she hadn't learned a great deal more about HVR Wines specifically, other than to confirm that they were one of the faster growing companies in their field. But she felt she'd gained a better overall perspective on the marketplace.

Generous with his insights, Cliff had confirmed for Christine that she was, in fact, correct in her characterization that an organization could – if they chose to – exploit the system, but they both agreed that could be said of any type of marketplace, given a determined enough, and crooked enough, operator. He was unable to allay her fears that HVR Wines was such an operator, though, which left her feeling disconsolate when they disconnected. She really wanted to talk the whole thing though with Alexander, but he still couldn't be reached at all – which meant she found her frustration increasing. She capitulated and put a call through to Carol – but only got her voicemail, so she left a general message, not mentioning her hospitalization. Then she did the same with Annie – whose phone also went straight to voicemail. She couldn't help but wonder if they were engaged in some sort of activity together, and felt a pang of jealousy; it might be a long time before she'd be running around the place, nose down, and tail up…following a hot lead.

She turned on the television, where she found her spirits being dragged down by consecutive news stories about skyrocketing levels of illicit drugs finding their way into rural areas, then something to do with the way that climate change was impacting the seas and fish stocks, followed by something to do with infant mortality rates being on the rise again. She turned the screen off at that point, and lay down instead, trying to ignore the constant, background beeping of the machine which was monitoring her blood pressure…then realized she needed to go to the loo…yet again.

She reached for her buzzer, her spirits low, and her sense of independence having completely evaporated.

CHAPTER TWENTY-SIX

Carol sat at the table in the kitchen which still felt fresh and new – and enormous – to her, with her mother, father, husband, and son, and handed around the copies she'd made of the list of things she wanted their opinions about when it came to the plate of food in front of each of them.

'I got talking to a couple of people on my way back from the Sglod Squad van, so things might have gone a bit cold, but I want your honest opinions, please. Taste and texture, marks out of ten for each…then the other questions are open-ended, as you can see. Let's begin.'

'There's nowhere here to comment on the packaging, which I think is very important,' said Carol's mother.

'You can put that under "Other Comments", Non,' replied her father. 'See? There at the end.'

'Thanks, Emyr, I'd seen that, but I think it's more important than that. How they give you your food is critical – it's got to keep everything hot, and be easy to carry about, hasn't it? Those box things they use are very good at both. And the design is excellent – look, the name and the pop art styling is vivid, and fun. It makes you think that what's inside will be…exciting.'

Carol intervened, 'You're right, Mam – I hadn't thought of that, but it's just us, and Annie'll understand, so do your best.'

Her mother shrugged, then stuck her fork into a chip. Silent eating followed for a while – except in the case of Albert, who seemed to think that the quietness was unnatural and he had to fill it with chatter, most of it nonsense, possibly to everyone but himself, thought Carol. He had his own little plate of chips, which Carol had cut up and allowed to cool before she gave them to him. And he didn't have salt and vinegar on his, of course.

She'd chosen the curry sauce to accompany her chips, and she had to admit that it was delicious: good flavor and consistency, and there were no lumps, which got bonus marks. As for the chips themselves?

Carol was impressed; they'd looked good when she'd opened the boxes, and the portions were massive…something she wasn't sorry about as she ate them rather more quickly than she should have done.

'My gravy's fantastic,' said David. 'It's velvety, smooth, and tastes like a proper beef gravy should, with a hint of onion in the background. Do you want to try some, Carol? Anyone?'

'Go on then,' replied Emyr. 'And do you want a bit of my sausage? It's…well, it's one of the best sausages I've had in a long time. Lovely texture and flavor. Go on, it's massive, I could cut off a bit for everyone, if you like. I wouldn't mind dunking a bit in your gravy, David, or your curry sauce, Carol. And how's your rissole, Non? Fishy enough for you?'

Carol's mother pushed her plate away and said, 'That rissole there has got more fish in it than there was crab in those crab cakes we had at that so-called gastro pub in Solva, Emyr. It's lovely, it is. But it's not very big, so I'll let Carol have a bite, if she wants – for research purposes – but you two men will just have to take my word for it.'

Moments later, with arms reaching, and oh's and ah's being exchanged, Carol realized that what should have been a test period was turning into a delightful family event – even Albert was enjoying his chips, the majority of which were actually finding their way into his mouth, rather than onto the floor…which wasn't pleasing Bunty too much, who seemed to be giving Carol's mother most attention, maybe because of the fishcake.

By the time they'd finished their food, and discussing what scores should be given to which products that had been tasted by multiple people, it was way past Albert's normal bedtime, though Carol reckoned it would be good to let him have a bit of a sit up after his four big, fat chips, which he'd managed to polish off completely.

With the dishes in the dishwasher, her mother and father happy to get Albert ready for bed, and David having to settle down at his desk to make some calls to a client in Florida, Carol phoned Annie; she suspected her chum would want feedback as soon as possible.

When Annie answered her phone, Carol could picture her sitting at her kitchen table above the Coach and Horses. She could hear the dogs in the background, and took comfort in the warmth of Bunty, who was curled up, purring, on her lap. She opened with a challenging question. 'So, what did you and Tudor think?'

Annie didn't need any more encouragement. 'Flamin' heck, Car, it was all lovely, weren't it? Well, ours was. And that kebab-burger thing? Looked like a burger, but tasted like a kebab, as we suspected. So clever. As Tude pointed out, by serving it in a bun like a burger, they got rid of the need to have pita breads on hand, and he pointed out to me – at some length, I have to say – how awkward those things are to slice open properly…they slow down service something terrible, he said. So, yes, a clever move on their part – use buns for beef burgers and kebab-burgers and there's not only faster service, but less chance of wasting pita bread, or buns. And they did a very good job of the mushy peas, and the fish. The only thing that neither of us liked were the chicken nugget things. They were definitely commercial, cooked from frozen, and they were not nice at all. But, otherwise – yeah, even the chips were lovely, weren't they?'

Carol had to agree. They went on to discuss the scores her family had given each item they'd tried, and she made a point of mentioning the packaging, which her mother had insisted she should. She ended with: 'I know when we met up in the car park of the old school that you thought the two blokes serving were a bit rude, but I've got to be honest and tell you that, fair dos, they were very polite and efficient when they served me.'

Annie made a grumbling noise at her end of the line, and Carol could visualize her chum rolling her shoulders the way she did whenever she felt put out about something. Eventually Annie said, 'You know I try not to jump to conclusions that I'm being treated…differently, because I'm Black?'

Carol nodded, realized Annie couldn't see her, so said, 'I know you do. Though, I have to say, I don't quite know how you manage it. Everyone around here who knows you, also likes you, but with strangers? Well, you're made of stronger stuff than me, Annie. But…do you mean you think the blokes were rude to you when they served you, because you're Black?'

Carol could hear Annie sigh. 'I don't know, Car…maybe it was just me. You know very well I went there all worked up because what they're doing could really knock our food business for six, so I was probably a bit prickly meself. But they were short with me. Almost stuffed the boxes into my hands, they did. And said they'd have preferred it if I'd had the right money – though I bet I wasn't the only one who didn't have it. Until I got there, I didn't know how much anything was going to cost, did I? It was…well, Tude reckons it was all dirt cheap. A lot less than he'd have to charge for the same.'

Carol could hear the hopelessness in Annie's voice, so made sure she sounded doubly bright when she said, 'Look – Tudor's got the overhead of the pub itself, and I think people will realize that. It's a lovely place, and it's always so warm and welcoming, as are you two, and Aled. This van? People were standing out in the freezing weather, then having to try to get everything home without it getting cold, and not slip on the ice while they did it. Of course it's going to be cheaper – they've only got the van to pay for, and they're not providing the heat, or light, or comfort, and traditional meeting place that the pub does. And, you know what, Annie – I really think there were quite a few people there tonight who only made the trek out of curiosity. They aren't going to have a queue like that every week – especially not through the rest of the winter.'

Annie managed a wry chuckle. 'Ta, Car…that's almost exactly what I said to Tude when it was my turn to console him, so it's nice to know your thinking is the same. But, yeah, it was cheap, and it was good, and…well, almost no one bought food tonight in the pub. Which Tude was expecting, so he'd allowed for it, which was good. But the Sglod Squad will be back again next week, and I haven't found out anything about them that could be…helpful.'

Carol was genuinely surprised. 'So you're really trying to dig up some dirt about them? To get them run out of town?' She laughed.

Annie replied seriously. 'Exactly. And Tude's following up with the village social committee, and the Chellingworth Estate, to see if they need some sort of permission to come here, especially since they just assumed that the car park by the old school was theirs to commandeer.'

Carol realized that the potential to put a dent in Tudor's business was something that he, and Annie, were taking seriously. 'Can I help? I mean, if Barbara's off for the day tomorrow, there's not much we can be doing on her case, so how about I have a bit of a dig into the Sglod Squad blokes, while I'm chasing up the stuff that Henry asked us to look into, and doing the CZJ deep-dives? I could manage it, given the free childcare I've got on tap here at the moment.'

Annie replied, 'Why don't you do the Henry, Val, and Barry thing, and I'll focus on the Sglod Squad? That seems more fair for the two of us…oh, speaking of which, I got a voicemail from Chrissy. It sounds like she's bored to tears down in London. I dare say her parents are treating her like Lady Muck, and she hasn't got to raise a finger. Or else she's out and about having endless cups of tea – in bone china cups, of course – with all the other Hon. Misses she knows.'

Carol couldn't help but laugh. 'Oh Annie, it's obvious you've never been pregnant. It wouldn't matter if she was drinking tea from cups and saucers made of pure gold, she'd still end up having to go to the loo umpteen times, feeling as though someone had squeezed her body into a sausage skin that was five sizes too small, and be constantly battling an aching back, swollen ankles, and a fuse on her temper that had shrunk to a tiny percentage of a millimeter. It's no holiday, the last month or so of carrying a child, I can tell you that.'

'Yeah…I know I don't know, really, Car – never will, neither – but the idea of having someone to bring me everything I need while I just sit around sounds very attractive, sometimes. Anyway, her message was quite…jolly. Sounds like she's doing alright.'

Carol replied, 'I got one too – and ditto. Sounded strong, and happy. I wonder if she's even missing us, to be honest. I know I miss her, though I think it's a bit late to phone her now. Or even send a text. I bet her mother's got her going to bed early – mine would…tried to do it when I was having Albert, even though she was in Carmarthen and I was here.'

'Still…um…getting on your nerves a bit, is she?'

Carol was honest in her response. 'We actually had a lovely evening. We all tried each other's food, as I told you, and…well, it was a bit like a party. So that was nice. No sniping. Well, a bit between her and Dad, as usual. But not generally. And Albert was so well behaved. I just hope he goes down nicely after those chips. Which reminds me – I need to get off and see that everything's alright in that department. Shall we both work from our homes tomorrow, Annie? I'll drop Barbara's notepad over to you in the morning, by the way – imagine it managing to get all the way to the floor at the back of the sofa like that…when it's not even going to roll there, because it's not round. Amazing where things can end up.'

'I'm glad you found it, Car. I'll let Barbara know when she gets back from her jaunt being a supportive mother tomorrow. Now, off you go and be the same thing, and we'll talk in the morning. I could do with an early night myself…though being full of chips doesn't help. Mind you, I think I could squeeze in just one G and T…if I tried hard enough.'

'You never finished them all, did you? Those portions were massive.' Carol couldn't believe it.

'I did. Eustelle brought me up with haunting tales of children starving around the world who'd starve even worse if I didn't clear my plate. I'm never going to shake the dreadful sense of guilt I feel if I haven't mopped up every last morsel I've been served…so, next time – if there is a next time – one small portion between me and Tude and that'll be it.'

Carol laughed, and disconnected, then whispered at her handset, 'Of course, Annie…of course.'

21ˢᵗ JANUARY

CHAPTER TWENTY-SEVEN

Henry made sure the coast was clear – it was – then crept toward the kitchen, hoping he wouldn't bump into anyone at all; he didn't believe he'd be able to hide his emotions adequately if he did. Having endured a dreadful breakfast, he was in a less-than-charitable mood, and needed to seek out Cook Davies as a matter of great urgency. However, he didn't want his wife to know what he was doing, and certainly didn't want word that he'd done it reaching her from any other quarter; that could make for a terrifically awkward situation. He stayed as close to the walls as he could, then took each turn with his hearing on full alert, and – finally – made it to the kitchen without having encountered another living soul, which he knew took some doing in Chellingworth Hall where there always seemed to be someone, hurrying somewhere, at all times.

Cook Davies was, as he'd expected, fully involved in her duties, though he couldn't be sure what she was doing exactly. It looked as though she were working her way through a list of…something…rather than actually cooking, or preparing food. He stuck his thumbs into the pockets of his waistcoat, adopted a nonchalant appearance, and strolled into the kitchen with what he hoped was a confident, if vague, smile on his face, and a bouncing step. As Cook Davies's head rose, along with those of her assistant and Edward, his butler – who was washing his hands at the sink – three sets of sharp eyes judged him; he wished he'd brought Hugo with him, which would have at least given him a reason to be there.

Cook Davies straightened her back, and said, 'And what can I be doing for Your Grace this fine, if perishing cold morning?'

Henry didn't want to talk about the topic that was playing on his nerves in front of anyone else, but also didn't want anybody – Edward included – to know that he needed to talk to Cook on a matter that required secrecy…which he realized put him in a bit of a tight spot. As he did his best to come up with some bright idea that would fit the bill, Cook moved toward him and said quietly, 'Of course – you said you wanted to look at those old jars I found at the back of the pantry, Your Grace. Silly old me almost forgot. Come with me – there's no one in the pantry at the moment.'

Henry had no idea what Cook Davies was talking about. 'Jars? I don't recall you mentioning any…oh, yes, I see. Absolutely, Cook – that would be splendid. I'd be most interested to see them. And you say the pantry isn't being used by anyone else at the moment? Even better. Let's make haste.'

He couldn't work out why Cook Davies was staring at him the way she was, but he followed her and the two of them went into the pantry. Cook closed the door firmly behind them, saying loudly, 'We don't want any of that warm air from the kitchen getting in here, do we?'

Henry all but shouted, 'Indeed not, Cook.'

He was most taken aback when she hissed, 'There's no need to shout – no one can hear you. The door's got a good seal on it. Now then – I suppose you want to grumble about that excuse for a breakfast I served up to you this morning, would that be right?'

Henry nodded, and thought it best to say nothing; the woman had hit the nail on the head.

'My apologies, Your Grace. I knew the changes would not go unnoticed, but I was…following orders. From Her Grace. And I know that's no excuse, but I'm stuck in a terrible position, and I had to make a decision. And the decision was to follow Her Grace's clear instructions. Though I had no doubt they'd cause an upset for you. I am truly sorry.'

Henry hadn't expected this, so resorted to what he hoped was a noncommittal response. 'Well, yes. Thank you.' As an afterthought he added, 'What was it I ate? Those sausage-like things weren't…real, were they? And the bacon was…well, quite peculiarly flavored. I couldn't put my finger on it, but it wasn't…right. And my eggs weren't…right…either. I wondered, at first, if there was something wrong with me. If I were maybe coming down with my wife's head cold, but I haven't an elevated temperature, and feel quite well in myself – hence my trip to your…domain.'

'Vegetarian sausages, turkey bacon, and a mixture of half eggs with half egg whites only, scrambled together, Your Grace. Grilled tomatoes, not fried as usual, and the mushrooms were boiled, not fried. That's what I was told to serve, and that's what I served.'

Henry took it all on board. 'Well, no wonder it was an excruciating experience, Cook. Thank you for telling me. I feel…well, at least I'm pleased to know that I'm still able to tell the difference between real food and a range of entirely unsatisfactory alternatives. And these instructions came directly from my wife?'

'Yes.'

Henry felt…well, he wondered if 'betrayed' were too strong a word, but he certainly felt quite put out about the entire matter. 'I had to drink an unusually large amount of tea just to try to get rid of the unpleasant tastes,' he noted.

'I spotted that, Your Grace.'

'You would, Cook Davies – your attention to detail is something I admire tremendously. So, what's to be done? Has Her Grace requested that you make other changes…about which she expects you to keep me in the dark?'

Cook Davies's eyes glittered in the dim interior of the pantry, and Henry wondered what the woman was working up to, because she was certainly working up to something. He noticed her shoulders droop, and then she shook her head, but she didn't speak. After a moment of him wondering what would happen next – and her seeming to contemplate her feet – her head snapped up and she glared at him with what he took to be anger.

She said, 'I know Her Grace runs the household, you've both made that clear to me, and it's an arrangement with which I am, of course, quite happy. But it's your family I've served these many years, Your Grace, so I hope you'll understand me breaking a promise I've made, and I hope Her Grace forgives me. I've been given a list – a very comprehensive list, I might say – of substitutions I'm to make across the entire range of what we create in my kitchen. Now, please don't think I'm grumbling about all the extra work that will be involved in sourcing new ingredients, and then having to amend – and test, of course – recipes we've been using here for years, because that's not at all where my concerns lie. Indeed, if you're in agreement with what's been asked of me, my team will, of course, undertake all the work necessary to make the changes required. So with the understanding that it's not that I don't want to do the work, I have to say that I feel the very essence of what I cook will be changed, you see? And I don't think that's right. Not without telling you, Your Grace.'

Henry was at a loss – this sounded like a much bigger issue than having a strangely textured sausage, or a slice of bacon that didn't taste remotely bacon-y. 'Could you – briefly – explain the extent of said changes, Cook?'

A few moments later, Henry realized that Cook Davies wasn't overly familiar with the meaning of the word 'briefly' as she was still listing the ways in which 'simply' replacing butter with a substitute would mean she'd have to work through dozens of recipes that she could usually 'knock up in her sleep', and how replacing sugar with its best alternative would have to be dealt with as a separate, yet nonetheless equally disruptive, matter. It seemed that the idea of having to amend the recipe of every one of the items she baked in her kitchen – twice – had led to her experiencing a very poor night's sleep indeed…which he could tell had shortened her temper as she testily paced around the pantry that had felt large, until she'd begun to wander about in it.

Eventually, she appeared to be winding down. 'You can see what I mean, can't you, Your Grace? Ordering in a few fake sausages is the least of it – though I should warn you that it's not just you who didn't take to the vegetarian ones. Her Grace has made it quite clear that the new rules apply to everyone, and I think you'd better be aware that Bob Fernley had quite a lot to say about that this morning, him being a man who's always liked a big breakfast on account of the fact he spends most of his day gadding about the Estate to see what's what. And being out in this weather's got to be a bit easier when you've lined your stomach with something with a bit of substance that'll get you through to lunchtime. Even so, that's not the worst of it. No, baking is chemistry – you can't change one element without impacting its interactions with all the others. Yes, I can manage to make some mashed potatoes with a butter substitute, or pull together a lovely warming *cawl* with leaner meat and more veggies…but a Victoria sponge only works when it's got exactly the right recipe. And it's all well and good to say that low-sodium salt tastes the same as the stuff they say these days is bad for your blood pressure, but I need to try things, at least once, to make sure they're to my satisfaction, before I foist them upon your lot…sorry, before I serve them to Your Graces, I mean. And…well, I'm at the end of my tether. So – what do you say, Your Grace? Should I do as Her Grace says, or will you…speak to her about this?'

Henry felt his breath catch, and his tummy tighten. This was all Val Jenkins's fault, he knew that much, and suspected that Stephanie wouldn't listen to him bleating about what she, apparently, imagined were a few manageable changes to her, and – by extension – his diet. Though he was surprised to discover that Stephanie had seen fit to impose such draconian measures upon everyone who lived, or worked, at the Hall. Cook Davies was, as he knew Stephanie agreed, a most valued member of the Twysts' staff…and she deserved – and obviously currently required – his support. He'd already begun to fight on one front, by asking Carol Hill to try to find out about Barry Walton…maybe he could use Cook Davies herself to open up a second line of attack? He'd think about how he could best achieve that…

Henry said, 'Could you leave this with me for a few hours, Cook? If you could maybe come to the library just before tea, I'll make sure I'm there alone, and we can plan a course of action. Would that suit?'

Cook Davies nodded. 'You'll be having a fruit flan for tea, which I shall do my very best to make look appealing, even if it's just fruit laid out on a plain – fat-free – sponge. But there won't be any cream today. Sorry. Forewarned is forearmed, they say. So I'll come to see how you want me to proceed then, Your Grace. Oh, and – in case you were wondering – it's grilled fish with broccoli, cauliflower, and green beans for lunch. Which I can manage without having to rework everything Mrs. Beeton ever wrote, thank heavens. And, when you go back out into the kitchen, don't forget that we hid in here to look at some old jars I'd found at the back of the shelves…though you don't really need to make a big fuss about it. It's your home – you don't need a reason to be in the pantry with me…though, yes, it is a bit unusual, now that I come to think of it, isn't it?'

'Indeed,' replied Henry, then he ventured through the door, doing his best to look completely natural, while chattering loudly about non-existent jam jars, and how lovely it was to revisit memories of his youth, reliving the excitement he'd felt all those long years ago when he'd collected stickers to send away for little badges…then he couldn't help but wonder what had become of them all.

CHAPTER TWENTY-EIGHT

Annie was ninety-nine percent sure that she'd cheated death by a hair, having endured a terrible night as a result of food poisoning. What she'd called the Sglod Squad through the small hours wouldn't bear repeating, ever, and now she felt as though someone had wrung her out and left her to flop about with no hope of real recovery, ever. She'd managed to drag herself out of bed, but had only been able to face a mug of boiled, though cooled, water. The idea of anything else made her groan…and she'd only drunk the water to have something to wash down the painkillers she needed; her temperature was all over the place, she reckoned she had to be completely empty, and now her head was thumping. Tudor – who'd suffered no ill effects at all – had suggested that she was completely dehydrated…another reason for the water.

Rosie and Gertie were giving her sympathetic looks, but, generally, a wide berth; Annie had fallen over each of them at one point or another during the night, when she'd been dashing to the bathroom. Now? Now she had to steel herself: she'd texted Carol, to check if all her lot were unaffected by whatever had ripped through Annie's system, and it seemed that she was the only one who'd been taken ill; next, she was due to talk to Tim Newsom.

She pushed off her slippers under the kitchen table, and settled herself as best she could. She'd managed to track down Barbara Newsom's stepson thanks to the encyclopedic knowledge of the local teaching fraternity possessed by Iris Lewis – her one-time next door neighbor – who hadn't known Tim himself, nor had she even known of him, but she'd put Annie in touch with a science teacher in Builth Wells who had known him, had kindly got in touch with him, and they'd made an arrangement for him to call her first thing, because he had a free period at the beginning of the day. Something for which she was – sort of – grateful…but she wondered why such a thing would happen.

Prior to actually talking to her stepson, Annie had sipped water and watched Barbara Newsom – in double-quick time – getting ready for her outing with her daughter, then taking her leave of her camera-festooned home before half past eight that morning. Annie had applauded the way Barbara had wrapped herself up in what looked to be a knitted suit, in a heathery hue, with a cape on top of it. She'd learned, since she'd arrived in Wales, that such capes were made of Welsh tapestry, with the signature complex geometrical pattern composed, in Barbara's case, of a striking variety of blues and greens. A matching cap had finished off the outfit, which Annie had thought looked rather dashing, especially given the way that her own woolen hat had gone to look a bit tatty.

Knowing she could relax as far as keeping an eye on Barbara was concerned, and having almost died at their hands, Annie turned her attention to trying to unearth something damning about the Sglod Squad. She let her fingers tap away, sipped more water, and gradually felt her nausea and headache subside, much to her relief. All of which meant that – by half past nine – she was starting to feel a little better about her prospects of surviving, after all…and about her morning.

When her phone rang, she warned the dogs to be quiet – which they, thankfully were, curled up in front of the TV which was on, but muted. 'Hello, this is Annie Parker.'

'Hiya – Tim Newsom here. As I said in my email, I haven't got long, so how can I help you? You said this was connected to me being related to Barbara Newsom? I'm only related to her by marriage…so I'm not sure I'm going to be of any help.'

Annie had framed her message to Tim that way, because she hoped it would get him to contact her, but was a bit taken aback by his opening…though, if he and Barbara had had a falling out over his inheritance, maybe it made sense.

She aimed for jolly, and fussy with her tone. 'Yes, that's right. Thanks for doing this. See, I used to be one of Barbara's clients, and we met for coffee a few days back. I'm sorry to say she was taken rather ill. My friend and I managed to get her into an ambulance, and she's out of hospital, now, but…well, I did have some concerns.'

'Ah. I see. Right. Yes, Nia phoned me about that. Out of politeness, I suppose, though that's not like her. Anyway, if it's you who got Barbara sorted, and to safety, thanks for that, of course. But Nia said there were no bones broken, or anything. That can be dangerous at Barbara's age, I know.'

Annie wondered why Tim was talking about Barbara as though she were a woman he knew in passing, and in her eighties, not in her sixties, but decided to let that slide. 'To be honest with you, I was shocked to see how much she'd changed in the last five or six months. She's lost such a lot of weight, and looks so frail. Have you got any idea what's going on?'

Tim's, 'Errr…' was a study in uncertainty. 'Well, I haven't actually seen my late father's wife for a few months myself. You know how it is…busy life…work, kids, so much to do in the evenings and at weekends. Maybe she just wanted to lose a few pounds? Being a counsellor's a bit…well, they sit down a lot, I'd imagine.'

Annie said, 'I don't think anyone would want to lose as much weight as she's done, in so short a time.'

'Not on those injections, is she? You know, the ones that make you lose weight really fast? A friend of mine's been doing that, and he's half the man he was. Not a bad thing, in his case. Maybe she is and it's too much for her? They do say that happens a lot. People get addicted to the weight loss, even when they've really gone too far.'

Annie was starting to wonder how insightful this man could manage to be when it came to explaining anything of a scientific nature to schoolchildren, and wanted to follow his line of thought, but knew she really wanted to shift the conversation to focus on Nia.

To that end she asked, 'Has Nia talked to you about this? She indicated to me it was something she was very concerned about.' Nia had done no such thing, but Annie thought she should have done, so made no excuses – even to herself – for putting words in the woman's mouth.

Wondering if she could actually hear him scratching his head, Annie listened intently as Tim spoke more quietly. 'It's not very private here, in the staff room, and…well Barbara and I aren't really related, you know? Especially now that Dad's gone. I mean, there's no question they were a close couple. In fact, he always seemed much…happier, jollier with Barbara than I ever remember him being with my mother. Of course, I told myself that might have been because he no longer bore the responsibility of having to support and raise a sometimes annoyingly nerdy boy, but…with all due respect, Miss Parker, why talk to me about Barbara's health? Shouldn't you be having this chat with Nia? She is her daughter, after all. And I don't feel that…well, Barbara's health problems aren't really something I'm involved with at all. Not that we're estranged, exactly, but…well, yes, none of my business. And, well…maybe not even yours?'

Annie pounced. 'Well, I'm not saying you're wrong, but I thought I'd start with you because I only know Barbara, see, and I wondered if you could fill me in a bit on Nia. I want to understand how best to approach her. She's a bit…' Annie let the sentence hang, hoping that Tim would finish it for her.

He did.

'Unapproachable is what you're aiming for, I think. I have to say I was surprised that she bothered to let me know about her mother's recent collapse. Nia and I didn't not get on at whatever family events we attended, but we didn't…build what you might call a relationship. To be honest, she's rarely had much good to say about her mother, which is understandable. Barbara's not the most thoughtful of people, and Nia's very suited to her profession as a dentist. Sorry, periodontist. She mentions that a lot. It's not a profession that suggests a warm personality, is it? I know I'd like to never have to see my dentist ever again…and I dare say I'd feel the same way about a periodontist, if I had one. But, as for how to get her to talk to you – someone she doesn't know – about her mother? I couldn't say, I'm sure.'

Annie gave one last shove. 'So I don't need to invite her out for a drink or anything?'

'A drink? Nia? Oh no. She doesn't drink alcohol at all – tea and coffee, yes, but only ever water with a meal. Probably something to do with it inflaming your gums, though she's never averse to anyone else taking a tipple of something.'

Annie sighed with frustration. 'So is she close enough to her mum to talk to Barbara like a person, and would Barbara listen – or are they…not that close?'

Tim said, 'Nia and Barbara? Well suited to each other. Not…close, close, but not a bad relationship.'

Annie didn't feel as though she was getting very far. She tried a different approach. 'I have to say that I got the impression that Nia's being a bit impatient with Barbara…according to Barbara. Might there have been a souring of their relationship, do you think?'

'I have to say that Nia was a bit dismissive of this latest turn that Barbara had taken. She took the time to let me know about it, which was unusual, but I felt she was…well, I don't know if I could say she sounded like she was accusing Barbara of bringing it all on herself, but she didn't give me the impression that she was knocking down doctors' doors to try to find out why her mother has been collapsing right, left, and center.'

Annie tensed. 'She's lost consciousness before? Neither Barbara, nor Nia, mentioned that to me.'

Tim replied, 'To be fair, that might not be something Barbara, or Nia, thought it was appropriate to discuss with one of Barbara's ex-clients. And maybe I should respect Barbara's privacy, too. I think it's best if you talk to Barbara herself about this, Miss Parker. It's good of you to be concerned, of course, but when it's a person's health, it's hard to know where they'd like to draw the line, isn't it? You know…outside the family.'

Annie feared the man had decided he'd already said too much. 'Oh, I know what you mean,' she gushed, 'my mother's a good bit older than Barbara and I sometimes find myself telling her off like she's a child, especially when she won't do things she knows are good for her. Getting her to drink water's a challenge, and she will insist upon eating all sorts of things we both know she shouldn't. But, when you love someone, it's hard to make them unhappy, when all you really want is the best for them, don't you think?'

'I know what you mean – it's the same with actual children, not just your elders. But, like I said, best to talk to Barbara about it, or, if you think it's the right way to go, approach Nia. I dare say that any daughter would want to help, wouldn't they? Especially one who's in the process of buttering up the mother in question.'

Annie pounced. 'Why would Nia be buttering up her mother?' She wasn't supposed to know about the issue over Tim's inheritance.

'Errr…oh, nothing really. Not that's got anything to do with you…or anyone outside the family. Anyway, it's back to the chalk face for me, as we used to say…though now it's more about laptops and projectors, of course. Sorry I couldn't help. Best of luck with it. Goodbye.'

After they'd disconnected, Annie felt a bit disappointed; she'd not gained any real insights into Nia…except that Tim thought she was 'buttering up' her mother. Which, now that Annie thought about it, could explain all the extra time Nia was spending with Barbara, and why Nia had urged her to wait before she wrote a new will; Nia would get everything if Barbara died intestate. But Nia had a good career…didn't she? Annie immediately decided to dig into the background of Nia's practice as a periodontist; she'd ask Carol for some pointers on that one, or maybe Barbara herself would have some idea of how successful her daughter really was. But, no, Nia wasn't the type to give that away, not even to someone like her mum.

It made sense to Annie that Tim wasn't overly worried about his late father's widow having dropped a fair bit of weight since she'd lost her mate, given that they were, in fact, estranged – despite what he'd said. Though she was concerned to learn that what she and Carol had witnessed hadn't been Barbara's first collapse; she'd need to winkle the truth out of Barbara on that front. But as for Nia being a more, or less, likely suspect for attempted murder? Well…that might depend upon how much she needed what Barbara had suggested was a fair lump of money, and then there was that house, too…it was very big, and Annie knew that the market was getting more and more expensive for housing, as Carol's parents' research into finding a new home was proving.

She opened up a screen and began to delve into the world of periodontists, found Nia's practice quickly, and established that what she did was, in fact, quite unusual. She worked with National Health Service and private patients, and didn't just have her own surgery, but was the periodontist used by several dental general practices in the area, too. But…well, Annie reckoned the photos of Nia's workspace suggested it needed a few upgrades, when compared with another company that was new to the area. They had state-of-the-art equipment, much fancier rooms and chairs, and so on, and there were testimonials by smiling patients talking about how they'd had a 'lovely warm-wax hand treatment' while they'd been in the multi-function chairs, and how they'd never felt as pampered. Nia's offering didn't look as though pampering was on the schedule; in fact, although she looked professional, Annie thought she looked a bit forbidding in her photographs.

Sitting back, sipping more water, Annie wondered how much it might cost to significantly upgrade Nia's business premises…or even find new ones. Might she see this new competitor as a real threat to her standing in the periodontal community – which Annie knew must exist, or else they wouldn't have an awards ceremony. The new company appeared to be backed by a lot of money, and had clearly established itself in what had, until recently, been Nia's 'own' business area. So…yes, maybe a nice inheritance from Mummy would be a good thing at this time, but…would Nia really go as far as to poison her mother for just…money? Or, was Nia the sort of woman for whom her career was her everything? Annie knew, from experience, that people killed for what seemed, to others, ridiculously petty reasons. Could the threat of losing one's professional standing – and, maybe, therefore, one's personal place in society, or even entire identity – lead someone to murder?

She opened some documents she'd been studying as part of an online psychology course she was following, and decided a bit more reading was needed, then she'd discuss it with Carol; everything made more sense when she talked things through with her.

CHAPTER TWENTY-NINE

Mavis gazed across the well-used dining table at Althea, who was working her way through her second pot of breakfast tea, and – quite obviously – sulking. Mavis knew why; it was Clementine's fault, of course, who, it appeared, was either completely oblivious to the fact that her mother, and Mavis, had trekked to the wilds of Dumfries and Galloway simply so that Althea could spend time with her daughter, or else was willfully choosing to ignore it. Either way, another fraught breakfast had been endured, where Althea had grumbled, Clementine had snapped, Julian had tried to be the peacemaker, and Mavis had done her very best to hold her tongue.

The lumpy porridge they'd been served hadn't helped matters, and Mavis had wondered how an experienced cook, and one from Glasgow at that, was unable to produce porridge that was smooth and flavorful; the woman had to have been making the stuff for most of her adult life. That disaster aside, some toast made from bread that seemed to comprise only seeds had transported great globs of blackcurrant jam into Althea's mouth, and that, at least, had served to make the dowager smile, though Mavis suspected she might be the one to experience the bad end of the inevitable sugar crash that Althea would experience in a couple of hours, if not sooner.

She dared, 'Althea, you need to try to put Clementine's attitude to one side, and come up with a plan for your day, dear. Plans that don't include her, I'd have said.'

'Oh, I have plans, Mavis. I have a meeting with Billy at ten, then with Eileen at eleven. We need to get everything arranged.'

Mavis decided to bite. 'Arranged for what, dear?' She dreaded the answer.

'Burns Night, of course. There hasn't been a proper celebration here since Chelly and I last hosted one and that's many moons ago. I want Clementine and Julian to see how it's done, properly, so they can carry the tradition forward.'

Mavis's heart sank: of course, Burns Night…she should have guessed. This was Althea, after all. 'And what do you have in mind?' She needed to know, in case she had to try to temper Althea's expectations.

'We used to do everything, me and Chelly. Piping in the haggis, all the toasts and addresses, you know…then dancing until very, very late…though maybe I won't be up to that. I'm a good deal older, now – and those traditional reels are for the fleet of foot, and the young ones with all the energy.'

Mavis smiled to herself – yes, she could imagine how this dining hall could have hosted some wonderful dances: swirling tartan, pipes resounding, the shouts and cheers of the assembled diners, their mood improved by any number of drams of amber nectar throughout the evening. As she looked at her friend, she imagined how Althea must have once glowed, and felt the woman's loss, almost as keenly as though it were her own. In her youth the idea of such a fancy party, with pipes and everything else, had been an alien concept; her family had been too poor for all that sort of thing. Maybe it was one of those occasions where you needed to belong to some sort of community association, or club – or else a wealthy family – to be able to go the whole hog. The Scots she'd encountered in the armed forces had certainly thrown themselves into it when they could, and she'd been invited to attend enough of those events to know how they could start well, but descend into chaos soon enough. As she recalled a certain Burns Night when she'd been in her thirties, she smiled at the remembrance of the men dancing reels together, the thudding noise as they leaped had almost drowned out the two pipers who'd been roped into playing for them.

Feeling a bit misty-eyed about the whole thing, she was torn: should she encourage Althea, or throw cold water on the whole idea? She asked, 'Is that why you were out trying to track down an unusually large quantity of haggis with Ian yesterday?'

Althea nodded. 'That's no problem – the butcher in Garven will do it for me. As many as I want – as long as I give him enough notice. I knew his father well. Dead now, of course.'

Mavis didn't want to go down that road; talking about all the people she knew who'd died never did Althea any good, which Mavis realized was quite natural. She beamed when she asked, 'So who would be invited?'

Althea perked up. 'Obviously anyone and everyone who's still living who's ever worked here – that's what Chelly and I made our Burns Night about – a sort of thank-you evening, for everyone who'd supported the Estate through the year. There are suppliers as well, of course – which means that your Frank will be invited…so you'll have a partner for the dancing, Mavis.' She dimpled and flared her nostrils, which Mavis knew was a sign that she was thinking especially wicked thoughts. 'And, of course,' she continued, 'it would be lovely if your two boys and their families would join us…and that might be it. Which should amount to about forty people. But that's why I want to consult Billy – he'd know much more about what's been going on here while I've been *in absentia*, so to speak.'

Mavis said, 'If Eileen – your backup cook – is right, the "fishing people" she has to prepare food for could be quite a group. Have you included them?'

Althea looked puzzled. 'The "fishing people"? Who on earth are they? Did Eileen mean people who pay to fish our loch and rivers? Why would I invite them? They come, they go, and they're asked to take every item they brought onto the Estate with them when they leave – the wrappings and leftovers from their own meals included. You must have misheard, or misunderstood, dear.'

Mavis was quite sure she hadn't, but knew Althea well enough to not bother pursuing the topic. But now she was finding the situation at Twyst House even more…confusing. Realizing she sometimes had to admonish herself for suspecting the worst of any situation, she ventured, 'You know that you, and Henry, often refer to the cost of keeping this place in good order?' Althea nodded. 'And I cannae help but recall how you talked about the…changes that Clementine made when she moved here from the London house – and, I must say, some of her choices of décor have made an unmissable impact on the place.' Her mind's eye flew to the portrait of a naked woman at the top of the staircase that everyone would see the minute they walked through the imposing front door, the impact of which seemed to be heightened, rather than diminished, by the fact that the woman had two heads, and was purple.

'Clemmie's her own woman, Mavis, as I know we're both only too well aware. She deserves to be allowed to have her way here – she's making this place her home, after all.'

Mavis demurred, and continued, 'Aye…as you say. And she's made some…bold choices, to be sure. But they seem to be decorative alterations, rather than structural ones. So my question is this – if your family's been sinking money into this place, where's it all gone? You and I, and Clementine and Julian themselves, cannot fail to see that the windows let in the wind, the furnishings have seen better days and – while it's all generally clean, and tidy – the place is…tired out. There are cracks in the plaster, whole areas of the house that could do with a lick of paint, and the plumbing leaves a great deal to be desired. I got the impression, from what Henry's always said, that there's been an ongoing investment in this place. But…it seems not.'

Althea waved a small hand dismissively. 'Everything costs such a lot, these days, dear. To be honest, I have no idea what we spend on Twyst House. Billy keeps the books here, then Bob Fernley at Chellingworth gets them, gives them the once-over and that's all I know. Of course, Bob reports to Henry, not me, and Henry's the one who bemoans how much the place costs – but that's Henry for you. We all know how he likes to have something – anything – to worry, or moan, about. And he never, ever comes here, at all – so it's all expenditure from which he'll never, personally, benefit, which I dare say makes him see it as a complete waste of money…however little, or much, it might be.'

Mavis saw the sense in what Althea was saying, and was pleased to at least understand how the financial management system – such as it was – worked. She wondered if it might be worth having a word with Bob Fernley about it, because she seriously doubted that Henry would have a clue about what was an appropriate amount of money to spend on the upkeep of a seventeenth-century hunting lodge-cum-mansion in Scotland…even if he was the one doing the actual spending.

Telling herself that this was yet another thing that might have to wait until she could be bothered to stand in a chilly hallway to use an ancient landline, she turned her thoughts to Billy Stewart himself; maybe she was worrying about nothing? She had to admit to the possibility that she was only feeling a sense of creeping suspicion because she'd not warmed to the man himself.

She said, 'You told me that Billy's been the steward here for a good time.'

Althea's smile came out like the sun on a winter's morning…exactly what was happening outside – brightening the room, and the mood of the two women in it. 'Chelly and I appointed him, together. We'd both benefitted from the oversight of a wonderful steward before him, but he suffered a heart attack – nonfatal, but serious enough that he had to retire immediately – so we had to replace him with some haste. We used an agency, of course, and we wanted someone who was looking for a small estate where they'd have full control, which they'd want to oversee for their whole career – not view Twyst House as a steppingstone to something larger. The moment we met Billy Stewart, we knew he was the right man for the job…and not just because of his name, though we did laugh about that, I recall. Billy was dour even as a young man, which he was, back then – though, to be honest, I never thought of him as a young man at all. One of those people who seem to be somewhere in their middle age even when they're a child, I dare say. I'm sure you know what I mean. Anyway, he was available to move in right away, though he had a smaller cottage when he began, because the previous steward had the cottage Billy's in now until his death. As will Billy, of course.'

'So it really is a job for life for him then?'

'Indeed.'

'No need of a pension? You'll have him here, for nothing, until he no longer needs a place to live…at all.'

Althea nodded. 'Of course. A steward is a part of the Estate – they deserve to live within it for life. That's what Chelly and I believed, and it's what I still believe. Of course, Billy's free to leave whenever he wants, but I would never push him – he'd have to want to walk away.'

Mavis asked, 'What happens when he goes on holiday? Who looks after everything then? He's no…deputy, or backup, has he? You know, like Eileen is the backup cook.'

Althea looked puzzled, and thoughtful. 'What an interesting question, Mavis. I can't ever recall Billy having taken a holiday away from the Estate. Maybe he has done, and it's been during the period when I haven't been here, and no one's mentioned it to me. But…well, where would he go? This is such a lovely place.'

Despite the weak sunlight streaming through the slightly grubby windows, Mavis could still hear the whistle of the wind, and noted that the motes of dust illuminated by the sun were dancing quite wildly. She said, 'At this time of year, when it's this bleak? I'd have thought somewhere warm.'

Althea's laugh tinkled in the echoing room. 'I don't think Billy's a sand and sangria type, Mavis – do you? He has the typical Scottish skin color – white, with a tinge of blue – so I imagine he'd burn to a crisp and need to be hospitalized after a few hours beneath anything other than a Scottish sun.'

'He must like woodlands, and the gardens here, Althea. There are lots of places around the world where gardening aficionados make pilgrimages during the winter months.'

Althea dimpled. 'I say, has Dennis Moore – he of the lupins, and The Lavender Mob fame – asked you to accompany him on some sort of exotic garden exploration, in foreign climes? You should go, Mavis…you're only young once. Or…or has seeing Frank O'Malley again thrown a spanner in the works – reawakening long-forgotten passion in your heart?'

Mavis had to laugh. 'Ach, you're a wee scamp, Althea. One, I'm no' young…though I'll grant you I'm no' as old as you.' She winked. 'Two, the topic of garden tours during the British winter came up during a conversation between me and Dennis – no more than that. And neither of us could run to a holiday overseas, exotic or not. And three, Frank O'Malley has awakened nothing in me, other than a desire to help him address the fear he has that the young man who's buying his boat, van, and business is some sort of ne'er do well. But the fact that the satellite dish was blown off the roof has cramped my ability to get anything done on that front, I'm afraid.'

'How so?'

'No internet access, Althea. And my mobile can't find a signal – which doesnae help matters. Maybe, at some point, I'll take Billy's advice and head out to the summer house to see if I can get a signal for long enough that I can make a few calls and, more importantly, send some emails and photos. My battery's fully charged, and I intend to make use of it.'

'I had no idea the internet was down, dear. But, instead of wandering the Estate like a lost soul, you could borrow Ian and get him to drive you to the nearest library. That would be a good deal warmer, and you could get everything done that you want.'

Mavis stood and clapped. 'You're a marvel, Althea. I should have thought of that.'

Althea shrugged. 'Indeed. You're usually the first to come up with bright ideas. Like your observations about the upkeep of this place – that's something that wouldn't have occurred to me. Yes, I must say, this has been a very interesting conversation. Lots of food for thought.'

'Umm…you're welcome.'

CHAPTER THIRTY

Christine hadn't slept well; it hadn't surprised her, because, other than making a new human being, she was doing nothing, so how could she expect to need sleep? But the night had seemed endless, and her thoughts had become very bleak at times…which had led to a bit of a tearful start to the day, which – in turn – hadn't helped her blood pressure. She was acutely aware that every move she made, and every action her body performed, was being scrutinized, and the more she told herself it was all for the best – that all she had to do was stay healthy so that her baby could grow as much as possible inside her before the doctors encouraged it to make an early appearance in the outside world – the more she was annoyed with herself. She was bored of hearing her own rationalities and platitudes, let alone those that might be offered by anyone else, however well-meaning their intent.

Thus, she'd been glad to see the back of Priti's temporary replacement that morning, who seemed to think that Christine needed to hear about how careful she'd had to be through her own fourth pregnancy. All Christine could think was that the woman must be mad to want to go through what she was currently enduring more than once. Then she tried to work out how young the woman must have been when she'd first become a mother, because Christine reckoned she couldn't be that much older than herself, and she already had four children. *Four.*

Finally alone, and fed, and as comfortable as she was likely to be able to get, Christine found her thoughts taking refuge in the wine problem being faced by the whiney Lottie Fenton, rather than dealing with her…reality.

She was – at last! – due to speak to the perpetually postponing Charlene Dalton in a few hours, and hoped she'd get more out of the presumably disgruntled woman than she had out of the anodyne, if precise, Cliff Richards. But she admitted to herself that she found it hard to muster any real concern for people who'd – by the sound of it

– invested in a scheme where they thought they could turn a large profit, even if not a quick one, and out-game the markets, all while getting the chance to swan about and lord it over the poor plebs who drank the sort of swill one could buy at the supermarket.

She said aloud, 'If it sounds too good to be true, it usually is,' then she sighed, and reconciled herself, yet again, to helping some rather unpleasant people – well, certainly one unpleasant woman, in the shape of Lottie Fenton – because it mattered to her mother and father, whom she loved a great deal.

A knock at the door startled her, then made her heart sink. A doctor, or nurse to tell her it was time for another test of some sort? 'Come in – it's open.'

Seeing Alexander's head pop around the door was the best tonic she could have wished for. 'I hope there's an entire person to go with that head,' she said, then scooted up the bed a little, and couldn't help but flick her hair about until – she hoped – it looked as though it had a bit of life in it.

Alexander's kiss revived her spirits, and when he said, 'Good morning, gorgeous,' she knew she didn't deserve it, but accepted the compliment with a gracious smile.

He looked concerned when he asked, 'Did you sleep well?'

Christine decided to lie. 'Just tickety-boo, thanks. You?'

Alexander sighed. 'Sort of, but not for long enough. There's a site we've got a few issues with, and Geordie and I had to go to meet a few blokes for a quick drink when they knocked off, to thank them for putting in a lot of extra hours at short notice…and a quick one led to a much slower several more. You know how it goes.'

Christine did, though it hadn't gone that way for her for a while, nor would it for some time to come, and she wondered how that would all work out when she and the baby were finally installed in the cottage in Wales and Alexander's business requirements led him into situations like the one he'd faced the previous night. Not well, was what she immediately feared.

Alexander snapped, 'Why's that machine doing that? It's beeping differently.'

Christine glared at the monitor beside her. 'Oh…something must have pushed my blood pressure a bit higher. Watch, all I have to do is some deep breathing and it'll come back down again. See?'

She closed her eyes, concentrated on her diaphragm, and did what the nurse practitioner had suggested until the beeping lost some of its urgent undertone, then both she, and Alexander, settled back into their conversation, which hardly flowed at all, beyond discussing the quality of the food at the hospital. Alexander was seemingly unprepared to elaborate upon who he'd met the previous evening or why he'd felt compelled to do so, and Christine didn't feel inclined to pursue the matter. With the number of options available for three meals a day within the menu app exhausted, the pair fell silent.

After a few moments, Alexander appeared to rally, and sounded almost enthusiastic when he asked, 'How's the wine thing coming along?'

Christine took her chance. 'There's a company called Plonk It In – they install wine cellars in people's homes. Do you know them?'

Alexander shook his head. 'Doesn't ring a bell. Have they got a website?'

Christine watched as he pulled his phone out of his pocket and started tapping away. She said, 'Just Google the name – they're easy to find.'

'Got them. Let's have a look…see who's involved.'

Christine continued to watch the man she loved as he read, and clicked, and scrolled, then she grinned when he looked up, surprised, and said, 'I feel ancient. The lot who run this outfit all look as though they're about fifteen. I'm going to have to watch myself if this is the future of construction.'

'You're not old, Alexander…if fifty-something is the new forty-something, then surely being forty-something is the same as being thirty-something? You're safe from a walker and commode for a while yet, I think. But you're right, they are all young, aren't they? Is that because they do installations within existing structures – as the website makes it appear – rather than constructing new buildings, or carrying out major renovations, like you do most of the time? You know –

hence the name – Plonk It In, rather than Build From Scratch, or something.'

'First, thank you. Second, maybe. It looks like their main focus is the technology needed for modern, high-end cellars. I reckon the adaptations they need to make to someone's home is something they'll organize job by job, depending upon needs. This business model suggests to me that they'll be calling on sub-trades as they need them, not keeping people on staff, like I'm able to, moving them from site to site, as needed…because I always need them, somewhere, and they know that. This lot? Might need a brickie one week, then a metal worker the next – they'd hire people in, subcontract them, as required.'

'That's what I thought. See – all this knowledge about construction practices must be rubbing off on me.'

Alexander smiled wryly. 'As long as it's just the good bits, that's great.' Christine was just about to dare to ask him what he meant when he added, 'I tell you what, there's a bloke I've used a few times who's a dab hand at making new bricks look like old ones. See this photo here – this massive cellar with all the wine racks, that looks like it's ancient? That's the sort of thing he does. I've used him to get new bricks to match up with old ones when we've had to do some filling in, or patching around something. Uses paints and glazes like magic, he does – he's an artist as much as anything. Tony…let me think. I can see him now…short bloke, long hair, leather jacket. Tony…Mulligan, that's it. Let's see if I've got his number…yes. Shall I try to reach him now – see if he knows them?'

Christine waited as Alexander made the call, got an answer then said, 'Hang on a sec, Tony.' He looked at her, rose, and said, 'I'll do this outside. Back when I've got something.'

Christine's monitor told her she needed to focus on her diaphragm again, as she couldn't help but wonder if this pattern of Alexander trying his best to shield her from his business contacts would go on…forever. Even the blessed monitor knew she didn't like it.

Long minutes passed, during which a nurse stuck her head around the door and said, 'I just need to check something.' She entered, looked at the machine, checked the attachments to Christine's body, then leaned in and whispered, 'Is that the dad outside, in the hall?' Christine nodded. 'You're lucky – my blood pressure'd go up if he was visiting me, too…but you need to do some of your exercises, okay? You know?'

Christine nodded, and focused with more effort as the nurse stood beside her bed. The beeping returned to normal just before Alexander popped back in.

The nurse looked at Christine, smiled at Alexander, and said, 'Please be careful with our patient. She's carrying precious cargo,' and left.

Alexander asked, 'More tests?'

'No more than usual. Did you get anything?'

Retaking his seat, Alexander nodded. 'Tony's done a few jobs for them. Fair people to deal with, he says – from his side of things. Good briefing, payments on time, no funny business. But he happened to overhear one client talking about what they were paying for their installation, and he reckons that Plonk It In charges way over the odds for what they're providing. He said it sounded like the client in question was boasting to someone on the phone – quite happily – about how much the whole job was costing, particularly the brick finishing Tony was providing, which had been a late addition. He said they'd quoted the client four times what he was charging them. He put up his prices after that, but they've paid them without any haggling. He reckons they've found their niche and they're going to ride the market as best they can. Said that the kids who run it, and sell it, present the technology as hard as possible, and they've all got posh accents, so know how to butter up the sort of person they're dealing with in all the right ways.'

'Ah well, a fool and their money are easily parted,' said Christine, suddenly feeling very tired.

Alexander stood. 'You need a nap, but, before I go, there's one more thing. Tony said it's not common knowledge, but the bloke who owns Plonk It In has a brother-in-law in the wine business who gives him hot leads. The brother-in-law in question is Hans van Ruud. His sister's married to this Jocelyn bloke, of Plonk It In. Keeping it in the family, by the looks of it. Could be a good business move – meaning Hans has a supplier he can trust – or it might just be to keep the money all flowing into a small number of closely related pockets. I'll leave that up to the detective in the family.' He kissed her on the forehead. 'Now I'm off, and you're going to sleep. Promise?'

Christine couldn't fathom what was wrong with her – she could feel herself dropping off as she smiled up at Alexander's receding figure. She tried to say goodbye, but couldn't be sure she'd managed to form any words.

CHAPTER THIRTY-ONE

Carol Hill hadn't slept well, and she knew why – those chips! She'd eaten too much, had shoved all sorts of things into herself that she shouldn't have done, and she'd paid the price, having to get up twice to take antacids. Though it sounded as though Annie had suffered a worse fate; she'd got a text from her before she was really awake, asking if anyone in Carol's house had been ill. Thinking about the chips Albert had eaten, Carol wondered if her family had had a lucky escape.

She'd also got off to a bit of a strange start that morning – other than because of poor Annie's texts – finding three messages from Mavis on her phone, and not having been able to reach Mavis at all; the warning her colleague had given her about the unreliability of her mobile phone in Scotland seemed to be true, and the landline number she'd given Carol just rang and rang, with no answer, and not even offering the opportunity to leave a message.

She'd spent a little time noting all the information Mavis had shouted at her when she'd left the messages, did her best to make sense of it all, and she'd done a few, quick searches to make a start on that front. However, then she'd had to stop Mavis's work to give her attention to Henry's problems which she was contemplating naming 'The Case of the Naïve Nutritionist'. She'd run that one past Annie.

Finally, she was ready to organize her thoughts, then her desk. Regarding Henry's case – whatever it ended up being named – she'd had a really cracking morning, and was feeling rather pleased with herself, because her investigations into Barry Walton had been…well, successful in a way. At least she felt confident that the duke would be pleased to discover what she'd found out about the man, even if the news was bleak. She checked her notes, and dialed the duke's mobile number at half past eleven on the dot, the time when he'd promised her he'd be 'somewhere he could talk'.

When Henry answered his phone, Carol could hear Hugo crying in the background, and Stephanie doing her best to pacify him. She also heard Stephanie ask, 'Who on earth is phoning you, Henry?' so suspected this clandestine phone call wasn't going to turn out to be quite as secret as she, and certainly the duke, had hoped.

She heard Henry say, 'It's something to do with some art supplies I've ordered, dear. I'd better take it now. I'll just step outside.'

Stephanie called, 'You can't be painting out in your studio at this time of year, Henry, the folly is hardly suitable for winter temperatures.'

Carol could hear the panic in Henry's voice when he replied to his wife, 'It's for a special project, dear. I shan't be long.' There was a pause, the sound of a door closing, then Henry whispered, 'I'm here. Just wait a tick – I need to get a little farther away.'

Carol held on, and was rewarded with an eventual: 'There, I'm in another room entirely. She'll never hear me now.'

Carol envisaged Chellingworth Hall, and wasn't surprised that Henry had managed to find one out of its two hundred and sixty-eight rooms where he could take refuge. 'Good,' she replied, 'because I have news, and you might want to ask me questions. Shall I begin?'

'Please do. Should I…um, should I be taking notes, do you think?'

Carol sighed, as quietly as possible. 'I'll send you a report, because you'll want to have access to the details, I'm sure, but – for now – how about you just listen, and I give you the…broad brushstrokes?' She hoped she'd engage the duke by using terminology related to art, since that was what she'd observed was pretty much all he truly cared about…and his wife and son, of course.

'Always a good place to begin,' said Henry, and Carol reckoned she'd adopted the correct approach, because he sounded quite enthusiastic.

She said, 'I'm about to paint a picture of a man with a long and varied history, some of which is good, but, unfortunately, some of which is a little less…shiny and bright. Where would you like me to start?'

Henry didn't hesitate, she noted. 'Oh, with the bad stuff, of course. Thank you.'

Carol stifled a laugh. 'Very well. He's had a company under his control go into liquidation. This was only about nine months ago, so after the time when he was filming at Chellingworth Hall. I don't know when he and Val…connected, personally, but – from what you've told me – that would be within the same general window. From what I've unearthed, he owed a lot of people a great deal of money when he went bust, which might be why he's moved away from television production and is now working on much smaller projects where he does everything himself. I'd say it's likely that word would have spread around what I understand to be a relatively small world, to the point where people would be unprepared to work for him any longer…without being paid up front, in any case.'

Henry said, 'Oh, I say…that's good, isn't it? I mean, do you think he's latched onto Val just to get at her money?'

Carol wondered if she was being unfair to Henry when she was surprised by his ability to hit the heart of the matter straight away. 'Well, I'm not sure we should jump to conclusions quite so quickly,' was what came out her mouth, when she knew full well that was exactly what she'd done herself when she'd found out.

Henry immediately backpedaled with a gruff: 'Of course, you're quite right. Their personal entanglement might be perfectly aboveboard, though it does make one wonder.'

Carol knew that Henry was keen for ammunition he could use against Barry, and thus Val's influence over his wife, but she still felt a little bad about doing all of this behind Stephanie's back. She told herself she'd done the work already, so she should get on with sharing her findings, so added, 'There's more. I was finally able to find the company Barry and Val have set up. It's called Barval.'

Henry spluttered, 'Yes, I know, I told you that.'

Oh no you didn't, thought Carol. She said, 'I believe you mentioned Jenwal.'

'That's quite close.'

Carol didn't pursue the matter. 'Well, I found them, and Val Jenkins isn't listed as a director, but someone called Judy Walton is. She's Barry's sister. She's twenty-five. She's been in and out of rehab facilities for the past six years. Seems to be clean now, but doesn't sound suitable to be the director of a company that's going to be making clothing and accessories for the health and wellness marketplace.'

'Might she turn out to be one of those influencer people – you know…turned her life around, and all because of…whatever it might be that they're selling?'

Carol was astonished; such a scenario hadn't even occurred to her. 'Well…you might have a point. That would be an excellent sales pitch, after all.'

'So this company might make a go of it?'

Carol wasn't sure how to respond: she'd picked up the phone ready to tell Henry that Val's boyfriend was a gold digger, but now she wasn't feeling quite as sure of herself. 'I tell you what, with your brilliant idea as inspiration, could you let me have a few more hours on this?'

'Oh, I wouldn't call it brilliant, but, certainly…take a little more time. Though I'm seeing Cook Davies just before four, so knowing whatever you have to tell me by then would be most helpful.'

Carol couldn't connect Henry's cook with what she was doing for him, but needed to get on; she agreed she'd text Henry when she had news, so he could get himself to a private spot where they could talk.

When she disconnected, she prepared herself for a deep online dive into Judy Walton, about whom she'd thought she'd known everything relevant, but now she had a different angle to research. As her fingers flew, she hummed to herself…though she wasn't sure about the tune. She was just getting into the swing of things when she got a text from Annie asking her to phone her when she could. She sighed – she'd already been interrupted, so she thought she might as well make the call right away.

'Hiya, Annie – how are you feeling now? Any better?'

'Oh, I don't know, Car…I feel wrung out. Completely exhausted, to be honest with you. Can't face much, but I'll try to keep plodding on.'

'Well, maybe take it a bit easy today? And, obviously, only eat and drink what you can. Food poisoning can be nasty. Anyway…what's up?' She listened as Annie recounted her conversation with Tim Newsom, her summary of what she'd found out about Nia Williams's periodontal practice, then her thoughts about why the woman might, after all, have a significant motive for wanting her mother out of the way…and sooner, rather than later.

When Annie stopped talking, Carol felt compelled to add, 'I get what you're saying – and well done for following through like that – but do you really think someone would plan to murder their mother just so they could get some new kit for their business? It sounds a bit…extreme, to me.'

Annie countered with: 'Her stepbrother reckons Nia's been sucking up to Barb, Car. And what Barb said makes it sound that way, too. I know we've hardly met her, really, but what if Nia really is a cold, calculating person, who only sees her self-worth in terms of her profession? That it means more to her than her mother does. It's possible.'

A penny dropped. 'Have you been working on that online psychology course you said you were going to do?'

'Might have been.'

Carol dared, 'A little bit of knowledge can be a dangerous thing, Annie.'

She could hear the defensive note in Annie's voice when she replied, 'Oi…we all agreed that the course was worth the money, didn't we? And I am taking it seriously. You've no idea how much I've had to read for it. No one mentioned that bit when I signed up for it, did they? Oh no…it was all, "Yes, Annie, if that's what you want to do, Annie," but no one said, "That might mean a lot of reading, Annie," did they? No. But I'm doing that, and my driving lessons, because I want to be the best investigator I can be, and you've got the online research thing all sewn up, so I'm going down the "understand people better" route…as we all agreed, if you recall. And yeah, that's where this is coming from. Self-worth, self-value, how people define themselves – if you threaten that, they can do some terrible things, apparently, Car.'

Carol nodded. 'I see. Well, you're the one reading the books, Annie, so I'll defer to your knew-found understanding of the human condition and tell you that you might have a point. To be honest, I think I'm seeing first-hand what can happen when you take away someone's role in the community – as represented by their job, or, in the case of my parents, their entire way of life. Mam and Dad are at a complete loss since they sold the farm. They don't really seem to know who they even are, these days, which is what I keep telling myself when Mam is driving me mad. They've…well, their entire lives revolved around the needs of their sheep, and the business of caring for them. Now? They seem to be struggling to find any sense of purpose…so, maybe, if Nia Williams sees herself as a periodontist first, and a daughter second, maybe she would think of her mother as simply a source of funds to be able to improve her business potential, or standing…or save herself from being second best in her field in the area…'

Annie jumped in. 'Exactly, and if they've never been that close until recently – which is the impression I got from Barb and Tim – maybe Nia's not being a good daughter and supporting her mother in her time of grief, but being on the spot to make sure her mother doesn't write a new will before she manages to bump her off…which she's also trying to do.'

'That's a very cavalier thing to say, Annie, let alone do. Nia would have to be a monster to even think about her mother that way.'

'Or a sociopath, Car. Or even a psychopath. They're different, you know? One knows that what they're doing is wrong, but does it anyway, while the other one doesn't believe that what they're doing is even a little bit weird. But…I don't think I know Nia well enough to be able to diagnose her.'

Carol chuckled, 'Well, at least you're aware of that, Annie, which I'd say is good. But, listen, being realistic for a moment…I can see that someone might do what you're suggesting Nia is doing, if they wanted to get their hands on what we're assuming is a fair amount of money, in order to either save, or improve, their business, and thereby their standing in the community. But we're still no closer to working out how she might be doing it, are we? Besides – and with all due respect to the course you're doing, Annie – Barbara is a trained counsellor, and psychologist, herself, so don't you think she'd be able to spot such…tendencies…in her own daughter?'

'You know she told us she's been going back and forth on that, Car. It's like she's spending all this time with Nia to try to convince herself that her daughter's not out to get her after all, but there's something niggling at the back of her mind that's telling her to be careful, nonetheless. That could be her subconscious picking up on cues that Nia's giving her. We do that all the time, we humans.'

Carol feared a psychology primer on the horizon. 'Look, Annie, I do get what you're saying…but, how about I do a little bit of digging to see if I can get my hands on any of Nia's business financials? She might be hugely successful, and more than able to fund her own business upgrades without having to resort to murder. Would that help?'

Carol heard Annie laugh. 'Oh Car, you're brilliant. I was going to ask, because I've hit a bit of a brick wall…but you'll know what to do. To save you the three seconds it would take you, I'll send you the addresses of the websites for Nia and the big, new, shiny competitor in town…which makes it sound a bit like *High Noon*, with periodontists wearing white coats, leather chaps, and big hats in the middle of Brecon, waggling pointy periodontal instruments at each other, with lethal intent. There – I texted them to you. Thanks, Car. All we need to know is if she's rolling in it, or on her uppers – and I know you can find that out in your sleep. Ta, Car…I know you can do it.'

After she'd checked the websites, and did some basic financial reporting searches, Carol was in little doubt that a well-funded organization had, clearly, decided that periodontics was worth investing in across the UK, and they were gobbling up the independent practitioners as they went. It looked as though Nia Williams might be the next to fall, and Carol had a sneaking suspicion that Nia might not fancy that idea. If her website made anything clear at all, it was that she was incredibly proud of being an independent, female periodontist in a profession where that was something that couldn't be said very often. She wondered if Annie had a point about the woman being desperate to invest in herself, and emailed her findings to her colleague.

CHAPTER THIRTY-TWO

Pleased that she'd sorted things in her mind about Barbara and Nia, after her chat with Carol, Annie kept glancing at the camera feed from Barbara Newsom's house, but – of course – nothing was happening. The only time any of the boxes on the screen came to life was when a local cat jumped up onto the windowsill of the sitting room, and one of the cameras there recorded the fact that Barbara wasn't in her chair, nor watching TV.

Annie was definitely starting to feel a little stronger, and was quite enjoying going down online rabbit-holes in her search for mud that would stick to the Sglod Squad people, and it was starting to look as though Dylan Tanner – especially – had a rather colorful background.

When her phone rang on the kitchen table, she picked it up and said, 'Hello, Annie here,' without thinking. No one spoke at the other end, but she could hear a lot of muffled, scuffling noises. Checking the number, she could see it was Barbara Newsom – though the screen said 'SHRINKY BARB'. She tried again. 'Hello, Barb…is that you?' More indeterminate noises. She wondered if she should hang up – maybe Barbara had somehow rung her without meaning to? But she allowed her curiosity to get the better of her, so tucked the phone under her chin as she continued to tap at her keyboard to open photographs from Dylan Tanner's social media feeds showing him at various parties where he appeared to specialize in setting fire to something in a shot glass then drinking it while it was still alight…which she found quite terrifying.

Her attention was diverted when she heard a gruff male voice saying, 'Get her onto her back…' followed by a louder, female voice shouting, 'No…don't move her…'

Annie stopped tapping, and shouted into the handset, 'Barb? Barb…are you alright?'

Now there were loud grating sounds coming from Annie's phone, which she immediately set to record and switched to speakerphone.

Every fiber of her body was on full alert; she knew something was wrong, but felt helpless. She checked her watch: if what Barbara had told them was right, she and Nia would still be at Plas Newydd, at the periodontists' awards lunch…maybe actually at the table. Had Barbara fainted again? Then she told herself that – if that was what had happened – at least Barbara was surrounded by people who, presumably, knew the ins and out of the human body to some extent, and Nia would be at her side too. However, even as she thought this, she realized that knowledge didn't bring her any comfort.

Looking around the large room that comprised their living, cooking, and eating area above the pub, Annie desperately searched for something she could use to more effectively attract the attention of those at the other end of the line than her voice. At the end of a lariat tangled onto on a hook at the top of the stairs she spotted the large, stainless-steel whistle that Tudor had given her when she'd first got Gertie – a gift to help with training, he'd said – it always worked on rugby players he'd said – though it had proved useless in terms of getting Gertie to do anything but run away. Annie grabbed her phone, kept on shouting into it, then grabbed the whistle and blew it into the phone. Until then, Gertie and Rosie had only reacted to Annie's shouting by getting up from their curled positions and showing mild interest – now, they went berserk. Gertie started barking, growling, and showing her teeth, the usually glossy fur on her back standing to attention, while poor Rosie leaped onto the sofa and began to howl – not something Annie was aware she'd ever done before. Annie kept blowing the whistle and shouting, 'Gert – it's alright, Gert…calm down,' until the door at the bottom of the stairs was wrenched open and Tudor ran up toward her, shouting, 'What's the matter? What's going on up here? Are you alright?'

Annie managed, 'I'm fine – but please come up and sort the dogs,' then blew the whistle again.

Tudor's expression as he finished clambering up the stairs suggested she'd lost her mind, but she was pleased to see that he did his best to calm Gertie, and was even more relieved when a clear voice came through on the line. 'Hello? Is someone there?'

Annie shouted, 'Yes, my name's Annie – has something happened to Barb? Barbara Newsom. My phone rang…is she alright?'

The voice didn't respond to Annie, but she could hear it relaying what Annie had said to another party. Next, she heard Nia Williams's voice. 'Who is this?'

'It's Annie Parker. Your mother phoned me, but no one there could hear me. Is Barb alright?'

Nia's response was curt. 'No. She's dead. Now go away. I've got better things to do than talk to you.' Then she was gone.

Annie was stunned…then felt Gertie's head battering her legs…then the phone falling from her hand…then the room shifted, and the top of the flight of stairs beside her seemed to be getting closer, and closer…and, somewhere in the distance, Tudor was shouting, 'Nooooooo…'

CHAPTER THIRTY-THREE

Mavis had decided that she couldn't babysit Althea for another moment; the woman had a bee in her bonnet about something that she was muttering about, and Mavis thought she'd let her get on with it, so she'd told her that she'd be off to try to get a signal on her mobile, rather than dragging Ian into the local library. Being honest with herself, Mavis couldn't envisage using a small, local library to carry out research anyway; much too public a place. Besides, she knew she could rely on Carol's diligence and expertise, but just wanted to make sure that her messages of the previous evening had got through, had been understood, and were being actioned in a timely manner.

Having taken instruction about how to reach the so-called summer house prior to her meeting there with Frank O'Malley, Mavis felt confident she'd be able to make her way back to the place without any problems. However, as she walked, she realized there was a great deal about her surroundings that she'd not taken in properly when she'd made the trip the first time. She admitted to herself – though she'd never, ever admit it to Althea, nor even Frank – that, as she'd walked to meet him that evening, her head had been filled with thoughts of a long, relatively hot summer, when she'd fallen in love for the first time…and had her heart broken for the first time, too.

Not that she'd had her heart broken since, she told herself, which wasn't a bad thing at all. Once was enough. And it hadn't even been Frank's fault. No, it had all been because of her parents, and that was that. In those days she'd lived under the normal sway of 'my roof, my rules' and her parents had been dead set against Frank O'Malley from the moment they'd heard his name. A name with Irish roots. A name for a Roman Catholic family. A name that meant – as far as they were concerned – Trouble, very definitely with a capital 'T'. Mavis sighed and shook her head as she wondered, again, how different her life might have been if Frank's name had been McTavish, or even Smith. Then she managed a chuckle as she recalled the hours of pleading, and tears, as she'd explained that Frank's family never went to church, let alone confession, and there was no way that them being allowed to see each other would lead to her becoming a rabid papist…though she couldn't see why that would matter, anyway. It was her last point that had led her father to put his foot down, and insist that she get back to regular church attendance right away. It was no wonder to Mavis that her relationship with organized religion had been soured, though she had to admit she very much enjoyed going to St David's in Anwen with Althea every week, nowadays, because it seemed to be as much of a social as a religious gathering.

Pausing to put such thoughts from her mind, and determined not to miss the part of the Estate through which she was making her way for a second time – it had been dark when she and Frank had made their slightly stumbling way back to Twyst House that evening – she looked around her, and noted the pleasant, gently mounded shape of the broader landscape, the familiar mixture of deciduous and evergreen trees, and the surprising vibrancy of the color of the grass, despite the fact that it was the depth of winter. Those slightly warmer winds that allowed this part of the world to enjoy a less rugged climate were doing their job, she noted.

Tucked into a deciduous copse, she noticed a small stone cottage, painted white. It looked inviting and picturesque, so she made her way toward it. As she approached, she became aware of the lingering scent of woodsmoke, though she could see none coming from the cottage's chimney. A wooden crosspiece stuck a few feet away from the little path that led to the front door told her this was 'THE COTTAGE', which Mavis thought might be one of the least informative signs she'd ever seen in her life.

She wanted to take some photographs – the scene was so idyllic – but wondered about the privacy element; should she get permission from the residents? Reasoning that this might be the cottage where Billy Stewart lived, she approached the front door and used the black-painted metal knocker in the shape of a leaping salmon. It made a satisfyingly resounding noise, but brought no response. Mavis tried again, then shouted, 'Hello-ooo.' Nothing.

She said out loud to herself, 'Ach well, if there's no one here, it cannae do any harm to take a few snaps,' then wandered away from the cottage again, to try to get the best angle to show off its structure and its setting. Clicking away with her phone, Mavis realized she'd get a nice shot if she got down lower, and, as she was getting back up off her knees – something she found strangely difficult – she spotted a structure tucked almost out of sight in the woodlands behind the cottage. Curious, she wandered over to it, and found the smell of woodsmoke and…fish?…getting stronger as she did so. The surprisingly large wooden structure had a sloping, newer metal roof and a small door. No windows. Mavis suspected she'd found a traditional Scottish smokehouse. Maybe Billy smoked fish from the loch and the river as part of his duties? She'd heard about no such thing, but told herself she'd only been at Twyst House for two minutes, in the scheme of things, so she might not have done.

Outside the building, she noted a row of what appeared to be old, metal dustbins, that were charred and blackened, as well as discarded wooden boxes – and some of the hessian fabric she'd seen in Billy's office; the logo was unmistakable. So smoked fish from the Twyst Estate was 'TRADITION DELIVERED'? Mavis didn't see why not. Even more curious, she flipped the simple wooden latch that was holding the door closed, and stuck her head inside…then she heard a rustling noise and felt – as much as saw – a shadow pass above her line of sight as she turned to see who was behind her. Then…nothing.

CHAPTER THIRTY-FOUR

Christine wondered why her monitor was screaming at her, then peeled her eyes open to realize that it wasn't her monitor making the noise, but her phone…which she managed to grab and answer.

She even sounded groggy to herself when she said, 'Hello? Alexander?'

'This is Charlene Dalton. Is that Christine Wilson-Smythe?'

Christine did her best to pull herself together. 'Yes…just a second, though…sorry, I was…napping.' She chastised herself for having told the woman that; she needed to be professional. 'There you are. My apologies, I don't know if Alexander told you, but we're expecting a baby and I'm confined to a hospital bed at the moment, and I find that I drop off now and again. I'm quite wide awake now though – thanks for phoning, Charlene.'

'You're alright. Our second was a nightmare – twenty-seven hours of labor, and I needed two lots of surgery to get my undercarriage back into working order after him. Needless to say, we never had a third. Alexander told me this is your first. Good luck with it. What hospital are you in?'

Christine told her.

Charlene laughed. 'Oh my gawd…they'll be all ready to shove a silver spoon in its mouth the minute it pops out, won't they? You make the most of being pampered, Christine, and sleep while you can. But, there, I used to hate it when other mums went on and on about what they'd gone through when I was first pregnant, so I'll shut up now and ask: what can I tell you about these rip-off merchants?'

Christine felt a bit blindsided by Charlene Dalton's more than breezy personality, and took a second to compose herself. 'Thanks, Charlene. Though I think the way you've just referred to them gives me the headline, could you tell me about your dealings with HVR Wines, please? I don't know exactly what Alexander told you, but some chums of my parents are having…misgivings about them, and I understand you had a bit of a bad experience. So anything you could tell me would be helpful. Thanks. But, obviously, only what you're comfortable with. Thanks.' Christine wondered why she was being so…pathetic was the word that came to mind, so she put aside all thoughts of the nagging pain in her back, and her side, and listened intently.

Charlene Dalton had a hearty laugh, that much was obvious, and Christine was grateful that the woman seemed to pull the phone away from her mouth as she let it rip, because it might have been quite deafening otherwise.

'I'm not known for holding back, Christine, so be careful what you wish for. And I'd be quite happy to tell you what color knickers I'm wearing if it means these wide boys don't get away with ripping anyone else off. Blue, by the way – to which my Sunny's quite partial…but that's another story.'

Christine was starting to feel a bit dizzy trying to keep up with Charlene's enthusiastic flow.

Charlene laughed again. 'TMI from me – again! Right. This shower? HVR Wines? Well, we first met the ever-so-chummy Hans van Ruud at some candlelight evening that Sunny got invited to by one of his old roofing clients. I didn't fancy it, but he did, so we went. See, Christine, as far as I'm concerned, wine is for drinking, and as long as I like it, I don't care much about any of the rest of it…all the vintages, and terroirs, and all that stuff. But I'm like that anyway, about everything. Sunny, on the other hand, has spent his whole life having to deal with people in business – and he's met all sorts, I can tell you – so he's probably got a different view of life than me. Now that he's retired and the boys have taken over the company, he's a bit lost, so I thought the wine thing might be a good idea. We've always liked France, and Spain, and Italy, so going to vineyards has given it all a different dimension, see? And there's always something on offer that I enjoy, though – oddly – not usually the really expensive ones. Must be something wrong with me, I suppose. But Sunny? Yeah…he's loved it. And I will say that for Hans, he knew his vineyard owners – always showing us around, they were…nice as anything. And the entire thing went really well for about a year.'

Christine asked, 'Did you invest through Hans early on, or did you wait a while?'

Charlene replied, 'Ah yes, Alexander said you were sharp. Well, that's the thing, see – Sunny was enjoying it all, but he said it could be up to me how much we invested in the wines, as opposed to going to vineyards and getting the odd case or ten delivered directly. And I'm no slouch when it comes to the markets – that's my little hobby, see? Well, we all need one, don't we? Anyway, I wasn't so sure about the investment angle. Thought it was a bit risky to be honest with you, because wines come into and go out of fashion, and what I've noticed is that our boys and their age group – ha…our boys…our sons I should say, they're young men, really – well, none of them seem interested in wine at all. In fact, quite a lot of them hardly drink. I can't say I understand it myself, because Sunny and I have always enjoyed a tipple, but the younger generation? I've never seen as many "mocktail" things listed when you go to a nice bar somewhere as you do these days, have you?'

She didn't pause for Christine to be able to answer. 'We're in Epping, so we have some decent places around here, which is good. So, yes, I wasn't sure about the long-term future of wine as a viable investment, but Sunny reckons that the young ones will come around to wanting to drink wines the older they get, and that'll safeguard future demand – which will dictate the value. Flavored fizzy waters…that's where we should be putting our money, I think. They can't get enough of them, can they? But I let him sway me…so we jumped in with both feet.'

As Charlene paused to take a breath, Christine ventured, 'So how much have you got tied up with them?' She thought it best to be direct.

'A couple of hundred thousand. After that fiasco at Sunny's cousin's wedding where we proudly gave the bride and groom a dozen cases of what turned out to be drinkable, but in no way exceptional wine, and the one case of what should have been an excellent wine, which was completely disgusting, I've sent any number of emails to the nowadays much less contactable Mr Hans van Ruud telling him that I want to liquidate the lot. And, no, I didn't intend that pun…but I'll enjoy it anyway.' She laughed – loudly.

Christine felt a pang in her left side that was…unpleasantly different. She did her best to ignore it. 'And have you made any progress toward retrieving your money?'

Charlene swore. 'Not so you'd notice. I've been playing text, email, and telephone tag with him for weeks now. Our arrangement is supposed to be that I can organize all my trading transactions through someone called Isla, but she's informed me – ever so politely – that closing my account, and getting us our money, is not something she can do. That can only be done by Hans van Ruud himself, and he's somewhere in Africa with clients, at the moment, and they're on safari so that's that until he emerges from there, she said.'

Christine managed to not make a little noise of discomfort when she replied, 'I'm sorry to hear that, Charlene. And I wish you luck with tracking him down and getting your money back. Could you just confirm for me – the case of undrinkable wine…was that always meant to be for drinking, or was it for investment purposes?'

'Ha – that's the thing. Sunny thought he was being so generous when he pulled that one, special, case from our collection in bond. The wine cost enough in the first place, and then, of course, he had to pay all the taxes on it when he took it out. They charged us through the nose to deliver it to the venue where the wedding was taking place, too, and we even hired a qualified sommelier to look after it and serve it correctly. Sunny doesn't do anything by halves when it comes to family, which is why it was so devastating when the main wedding party all drank a toast, and lots of us had to spit the stuff out – and not in the way you do when you're at these tasting things…we didn't have a load of little buckets around the place, so there was quite a scene. I felt ever so sorry for Sunny, and the bride and groom, of course. She even got some on her dress. Oh Christine, it was awful. And then for that lot to tell us we'd stored the stuff incorrectly when they'd done all of that for us? The cheek of it. Tried to tell us it must have got overheated the night before the wedding, which was rubbish. That case of wine was treated like it had the crown jewels in it.'

Christine could hear her monitor starting to make the most peculiar noises, and a nurse banged through her door – without even knocking.

Not needing to be told, she knew something wasn't right. 'Thanks, Charlene. Sorry. Got to go.' She dropped the phone and looked up at the nurse who rushed to the wall behind Christine's bed and slammed her hand against a big red button, then Christine gave into the need to close her eyes…just for a minute or two…

CHAPTER THIRTY-FIVE

Annie sat at her kitchen table and glared at Gertie, who was half on the sofa, her head buried beneath a cushion. Rosie was beside her littermate, poking at her back with her paw and giving Annie the most baleful side-eye look she'd seen in a long time. Both dogs were fully aware that they'd almost caused a catastrophe, and were acting either guiltily, in the case of Gertie, or with bravado and empathy, as was being currently displayed by Rosie. Tudor had gone back down to attend to the bar, having ensured that the tumble Annie had taken perilously close to the top of the stairs hadn't resulted in any injury to her. To be fair, he had admonished both dogs, though he'd told Annie they'd only gone bonkers because she'd been blowing that stupid whistle, which he'd taken away with him, promising to throw it out.

Annie's ego was bruised, but the rest of her felt – relatively – alright. She knew Tudor was right about the whistle, but she'd defended herself as heartily as possible, and he'd conceded that – given the circumstances – she'd, probably, done the right thing.

Now she didn't know what to do; phoning Carol was top of her list, because she'd sent Annie a long email about Nia's business situation, and she deserved to know about Barbara…but…Annie's heart sank. Poor Barbara. Not knowing what had happened, she had to guess, and that meant she envisaged all sorts of dreadful scenarios…so she picked up her phone to speak to Carol.

'Hello, Annie – make it quick, I'm busy.'

'Barb's dead.'

'What?'

'Barb. Barbara Newsom. My ex-counsellor. Our client. She's dead.'

'I know who she is. What do you mean…dead? When did she die? How? How do you know? What happened?'

'All good questions Car, but – other than that her daughter told me on the phone about ten minutes ago that Barb was dead – I don't know anything else. Though I can make a few guesses.'

Silence.

'Car?'

'Yes. Sorry. I'm taking it in. Right. Well, that's…awful. The poor woman. How…how are you doing with it? You okay? I know she meant a lot to you.'

Annie realized she hadn't really considered how Barbara's death had impacted her on a personal level. She sat back, allowed Gertie and Rosie to be in their own little world without her staring at them for a moment, and said, 'Honestly, I don't know how I feel about it. I mean, obviously shocked. Sorry for Barb, of course. And I hope she didn't…suffer. But…she was the one who helped me get over those terrible feelings of guilt I had when I thought I could have saved that poor man in Swansea. She's the one who helped me sleep at night without dreaming about his eyes staring at me…accusing me of having done nothing, when I could have done…something. She's the one…oh Car…Barb's dead! Barb!'

Annie felt the unusual sensation of filling up with tears and being horribly aware that a human being with whom she'd shared a unique connection didn't…exist any longer. For some reason she thought about Barb's empty chair, facing her blank TV screen, and the cat that had jumped onto the windowsill. As she felt herself succumbing to an unbidden flurry of heaving sobs, she heard Carol shout, 'Put the phone down, put me on speakerphone, and find yourself some hankies, Annie. We can blub together.'

Annie did as Carol suggested, and grabbed the roll of paper towels off the kitchen counter. When she retook her seat, Rosie sniffed her way toward Annie, looking a little timid, and even Gertie took her head from beneath the cushion and gave Annie a pitiful look, leading Annie to pat her thigh, encouraging the dogs to approach her. She felt enormous gratitude when Rosie licked her hand, and Gertie finally came close enough to offer a paw, then a nuzzle. With one hand attending to two dogs, and the other wiping away tears with rough paper that might be all well and good when it came to mopping up spilled orange juice, but left a lot to be desired when it came to blowing your nose, Annie spent the next few minutes sobbing her heart out, and forming incoherent words, hoping Carol would make sense of them. Meanwhile, Carol offered comforting phrases like 'Cry it out, Annie,' and 'It's alright,' which, along with the dogs' attention, helped.

Bleary-eyed, and still suffering the occasional sob, Annie said thickly, 'Ta, Car…I'll be alright now. Well…you know. I wish I knew what happened. Not that it makes much difference. She'd still be dead.'

Carol said, 'What did you mean when you said you could guess what had happened?'

Annie rallied a little, and explained, 'First off, all I could hear was scuffling sounds. I reckon Barb's phone must have been in her pocket, and she somehow dialed my number. But I heard someone say they should put her on her back – which I think might mean she was on the floor. So I reckon Barb had collapsed, like she did at our office.'

Carol sighed. 'Maybe it was on the cards, Annie. I think she was luckier to get through that episode she had at our place than any of us knew.'

Annie bleated, 'But they let her out of hospital quicker than you could shake a stick. There couldn't have been anything much wrong with her if they did that, could there? And goodness knows she'd been tested for everything under the sun over the past few months. So why was she so thin? Why couldn't she keep food inside her? What made her so weak? That's the question, Car. I mean, you might well be right – she might have had a repeat of the last time, but they didn't have someone doing what we did to her, and maybe she was just that bit weaker this time. Though, to be honest, she looked to be in good shape yesterday, didn't she? And so excited about today. I…I don't know what happened, in truth, but that comment did make me think she'd gone down again. But, this time – given how soon afterwards Nia told me she was dead – it looks like maybe her heart just couldn't take it all again.'

Carol replied, 'Other than phoning the daughter, there's no way to find out, I suppose – no, wait, we could phone the venue. Plas Newydd, right? Let me find their number…right, here it is…got it. I'll phone them – see what I can find out. Tell you what, you hang up, I'll call you back in a min.'

'Alright, doll. Thanks. Maybe they'll speak Welsh, too…that might help.'

Carol said, 'I'll give it a go…'

Annie gave her attention to the dogs while she waited to hear back from Carol. 'It's alright, Gert, I forgive you. I'm sorry I frightened you both with that nasty old whistle. I won't do that again. Yes, there you are, let's give you a good old scratch there, shall we? Oh you like that, don't you? Yes, you too, Rosie my love. Oh, look, I've found your spot…oh that's funny.'

By the time Carol called her back, Annie discovered she was feeling less down, and incredibly grateful for the unconditional love of two wonderful pups. 'You were quick. So, what did you find out, Car…anything?'

Carol chuckled. 'Lucky for us my call was answered by a lovely woman by the name of Gwyneth who was just glad of the chance to tell someone everything that had happened. And you were right, being another Welsh-speaking Welshwoman helped a lot.'

'And?'

'Long story short – because she did like to throw in more than the odd aside…not something you'd ever do, of course, Annie.'

'I'm LOL-ing over here, Car. Get on with it.'

'You were right – Barabara collapsed during the lunch, just after it had been announced that Nia didn't win the award…some woman from Rhyl took top honors, it seems. This Gwyneth was serving the drinks at the lunch, and said she'd taken a shine to Barbara as they were joking about her being one of the few people there who wasn't driving, so she could have a couple of extra glasses of wine. Said Barbara wasn't drunk, by any means, but she had been to the loo a few times, and had got up looking as though she was about to make the same trip again when she keeled over and was – as Gwyneth put it – as dead as a dodo before she even hit the floor. It seems Gwyneth could tell by Barbara's face, which was as gray as old newspaper. Gwyneth might fancy herself as a bit of a poet, I suspect. Anyway, people fussed around, as you'd imagine. Fortunately, there were three medical doctors in attendance – which Gwyneth remarked upon. The one who took control said

Barbara was dead, but they went through the motions of trying to revive her anyway. Sounds like they had the same sort of defibrillator kit there that we have at the office. No luck. But it sounds like everyone there did all they could for her, Annie. Not that it's any comfort, but – if she did die before she collapsed, like Gwyneth maintained – it would have been quick for her. She'd probably have been unaware of any pain.'

Annie felt no comfort whatsoever. 'She's still dead. And we don't know why. Did anyone venture an opinion at the scene? As far as this Gwyneth knew?'

'The belief, among the attendees, was a heart attack. Though I've no idea if that came from one of the doctors, or just spontaneously arose from within the assorted periodontists and accompanying others. Sorry. Gwyneth was called away then – people were wanting their coats, and she was also in charge of the cloakroom. Oh, she did mention that the daughter – Nia – seemed resigned to her mother's death. Didn't have any of the screaming ab-dabs that Gwyneth would have expected, it appears.'

'Not the screaming type, is she, though, our Nia?'

'Not exactly. No.'

Annie sighed. 'Any suggestions about next steps? I can't imagine that we'd be a welcomed interruption to Nia's…grief. Besides, I've only got Barb's number, not Nia's.'

'There's bound to be a post-mortem, I'd have thought. Try to find out how that goes? But, as for all our cameras at Barbara's house – well, that's going to be tricky, isn't it? How on earth will we get them out of there now that she's…gone?'

Annie hadn't thought of that. 'No idea. But maybe now's not the time to worry about that. I'll…oh, I don't know, I'll try to get on with something else at this end, while you do whatever it is you're doing, but I'll give it all some more thought. Won't be able to help myself, I dare say. But…thanks, Car. You're brilliant, you are. Thanks for everything.'

'Phone me if you need to talk…or whatever. Bye for now. I'll get on, alright?'

'Yeah. Bye.'

Annie stroked Gertie and shoved her feet into her slippers; she suddenly felt cold. 'Oh Gert…what should I do next, eh? I can't do anything to help poor old Barb, so who can I help? I know. Let's help ourselves, shall we? Let's find out about these horrible Sglod Squad people, and get them out of our hair. That's right, yes. No, give me my hand back, and let me find out whatever there is to find out about them.'

Annie pushed several pieces of damp kitchen paper into the bin under the sink, rolled up her sleeves, literally, and got back to her laptop. She pounded away until she found a glimmer of hope: Liam Tanner's full name turned out to be Liam Noel Tanner – Annie reckoned his mother must have been a really big fan of Oasis – and it appeared in several newspaper reports of the young man having been found guilty of minor drug possession charges over the past few years, when he'd had an address in Ystradgynlais.

Annie wasn't sure if Ystradgynlais was within the area over which her chum DI Carys James had responsibility, though a quick check of a Google map suggested it might be. She'd noted that the cases had been heard at Swansea Crown Court, the city where Carys was based, so she dared a text, containing all the relevant information. And then wondered if she should follow up with a phone call, but decided to make herself a pot of tea instead.

She sauntered back to her phone when it pinged as the kettle was boiling. 'Gordon Bennett! Oi, Gert – what do you think of that? Carys has answered me already.' She read the reply, and laughed to herself, then told Gertie, 'Carys says she'll never forget the Tanners because the whole family's a court case waiting to happen, and Liam's the least of their problems. It sounds as though his father's been in and out of prison for years, and the two boys are just starting their criminal careers. Which is good, for us, in't it, Gert? Because I bet if they're setting up a business that allows them to work with cash, and be at the heart of a variety of villages, at predetermined times – out in the open, so to speak – they could be getting up to all sorts, couldn't they? Tude's going to love this.'

CHAPTER THIRTY-SIX

When Althea invited Frank O'Malley to take a seat beside her in the sitting room at Twyst House that offered a view of the last of the sunset beyond the gardens, she thought he looked as though he'd been completely renovated, from head to foot. He'd shaved and had a haircut, that much was obvious, but his skin seemed to glow with health, his trousers were freshly pressed, and his jacket hadn't seen much wear. He seemed to be having a bit of a problem with his shirt collar and tie, but Althea suspected the man was unused to how they felt around his neck, which would explain why he kept pulling at them with those shaky hands of his. Was he feeling nervous? About taking Mavis out for a meal?

'If you made an arrangement, I'm sure she'll join us, soon, Frank,' said Althea, graciously hosting her chum's beau – as she most definitely viewed him – while Mavis no doubt, was putting the finishing touches to her own titivations.

'I'd offer you tea, but have no way to summon anyone from the kitchen to deliver us any. With Clementine and Julian being the only residents, and both quite young and fit enough to buzz off to the kitchen to make their own beverages, should they so choose, I dare say that the lack of a functioning bell-pull in this room isn't something they've seen fit to bother themselves about, given all the settling in here they've had to do.

Frank stood upright before he'd even settled in his seat. 'If you'd like a cuppa, I'm sure I could organize one for you,' he offered.

Althea dimpled. 'Thank you for offering, but no, thank you. Absolutely not. You're my guest, Frank, even if only temporarily, while we wait for Mavis to join us. Please, sit awhile and tell me all about yourself. More than you told me the other morning, in any case. How are you and Mavis hitting it off? Lots of lovely reminiscences? Wandering down memory lane hand in hand, are you?'

Althea did her best not to giggle when Frank's ears went red.

He stammered, 'No' exactly hand in hand, no. I wouldnae say that. But there's no question that Mavis was a beautiful girl, and she's grown into a handsome woman.'

Althea observed, 'Handsome? Mavis? I'd have said pleasant-looking, myself, but I'm not a man, and maybe that term has connotations you'd prefer not to imply. In any case, she – like you – brushes up well, when required, so I'm sure she'll present herself very nicely for your date.'

Frank snapped, 'It's no' a date. Though…well, yes, we agreed a time and place for me to collect her. But it's no' a "date", date. Not like we used to have.'

Althea was delighted. 'Do tell, Frank, I'm all ears. What was she like as a girl? Did she have any of the sauce she has now, or was she meek, and mild?' She thought Frank O'Malley was quite handsome when he laughed.

He said, 'She always was one for saying what she thought, was my wee Mavis, and had strong opinions on many matters that most of her age didn't give a thought to. Never one to let a bully get away with anything, when that sort of thing went on in school all the time. Not one for violent outbursts, she wasn't, but I've seen her drag more than one lump of a boy off to the headmaster's office by the ear seeking justice for someone who'd been picked on, or made to feel small. Always wanted to help people, she did. Like…like it was in her DNA.'

Althea nodded. 'A life of service to others, that's what she's lived, and the world's a better place for her being in it, Frank. She has a lot of people who love her, and look out for her, too. So bear that in mind, if you've any thought of leading her on, then breaking her heart. Again.'

Althea was both amused by Frank's increasingly mottled neck, and felt some sympathy for him as he struggled to come up with a response.

Eventually he managed: 'Hers was no' the only heart broken back then. And none of it was any of my fault. Her parents were the ones who got in our way, and mine helped out.' He sighed. 'But that's a long time back, and we're older now than our parents were then…by a good amount. So, now, it's just us. Though I'd no' want you thinking I've any ideas in my head. Mavis and I were good friends before we were anything else, and I'd hope we could renew at least that friendship. And, as mebbe you know, she's helping me with…a little matter.'

Althea noticed Frank sneak a glimpse at his watch as she said, 'I do, indeed, Frank. And from what she's told me, I'd say you're quite correct to have…reservations. Look, rather than fidgeting there, would you like to knock on her door? I can't see why such a thing would be a problem – she can always tell you to go away, after all. Go up the stairs, turn right, and hers is the…third door along. Or maybe the second. Try both. Go on – she's late, and that's not like her. Give her a quick kick up the you-know-what.'

She noticed that Frank didn't need to be told twice, and he was out of the sitting room in an instant.

Althea watched the muddy horizon, and wondered how McFli was getting along without her. She hoped he was missing her as much as she was missing him; she kept feeling as though she'd forgotten something all the time…that she'd placed something, somewhere, and had walked away without it and needed it, now, urgently. It reminded her of how she'd felt for years after Chelly had gone.

Frank's dramatic reentrance was accompanied by a loud: 'She's no' there. Not in any of the rooms up there. She's…gone. Did she go out earlier? Did she say where she was going? She might have taken a tumble out there…' He ran to the window and stared out of it. 'It's getting dark. She could be in trouble.'

Althea was alarmed by his wild-eyed reaction to Mavis not being in her room, but remained sufficiently composed to suggest, 'Why don't I phone her?' She pulled her phone from the handbag at her feet, and punched the button that connected to Mavis's number. Nothing happened. She looked at her phone. 'Oh dear, I must have forgotten to charge it up. There's a telephone in the library you could use…if only I can recall her number. It's number one on my list on this thing, you see, so I never have to remember it. Oh dear, silly old me.'

Frank was hopping about the place as though the floor were made of red-hot lava. 'I need to get out there. Look for her. That's what I'll do. Why on earth did I wear these stupid things on my feet? They're no good for wandering about here, in the dark.'

Althea thought his shoes were perfectly pleasant – brown leather with a stout heel and a highly-polished finish. She accepted they might not look as good after a bit of a scout around the Estate, but they'd probably be adequate.

She suggested, 'Why don't you try to find out if Mavis told anyone where she was planning on going earlier on? She didn't mention a particular destination to me, I don't think…or did she? I know she was keen to get a signal for her mobile. That's right…she said she might head to the summer house. According to Billy, apparently that's where one can often pick up a more reliable signal than here, inside the house itself. You know where that is, of course.'

'I do. Thank you. I'll head there myself, now. Maybe you could…oh, hello.'

Julian Treforest's enormous body entered the sitting room and immediately seemed to fill half of it. 'Hello there. I heard voices and thought I'd just pop in to find out if any of you have seen Billy Stewart before I get ready for dinner. Eileen seems to have…misplaced him, she says. He was supposed to bring her some vegetables for our dinner, but he hasn't done, so I think we might be resorting to something from tins. I hear from Althea that you're taking Mavis out for a bite to eat this evening, Frank. That'll be nice for you both. Especially if we're relying upon tins.'

Althea explained, 'Mavis is nowhere to be found, either, Julian. Might she and Billy be doing something together? It sounds unlikely, I know but…you haven't seen her by any chance, have you? My last sighting of her was late this morning, when she was bleating on about needing to use her mobile, so I've suggested to Frank that he gives the summer house a try. But, if that is where she went, I cannot imagine why she wouldn't have returned here long ago. So – any sightings of her, by you?'

Julian shook his head. 'No. And she wouldn't be with Clemmie – she's still in the barn…her studio. I can see the lights in there – and she locks the door, though now that the sun's set, she won't be long. Says she can't work when there's only "false illumination". Tell you what – why don't I come with you, Frank? Two sets of lungs shouting

Mavis's name, and two sets of eyes to keep peeled for her, are better than one, right?'

Frank appeared to relax a little. 'That would be very kind.' He turned to Althea, 'And, if you could plug in your phone and find her number – try to phone her mobile – that might help, too. She might be somewhere where she can pick up a signal and…well, I don't know, but it's a chance, agreed? Unless you don't have a signal yourself of course…oh, dear.'

Althea stood up to her full four feet and eleven inches – or whatever it was that she measured these days – and mugged a salute. 'All over it, like…a ghillie at a shoot. Leave it to me. But get hold of Ian Cottesloe before you go – he's younger than either of you and has a voice that carries tremendously well because he's always shouting at boys who play football, or at the Scouts, or something. He'll probably be in his room…mooning over the fact that he can't get hold of Wendy Jenkins, I dare say.'

Just as the pair was about to leave to hunt down Ian, Clementine Treforest-Twyst entered the sitting room. She had smudges of paint on her face and hands, and looked…as radiant as Althea had ever seen her daughter look.

Althea gasped. 'You look extraordinarily well, dear. Your eyes are alight with…well, something. You're…glowing.'

Clementine laughed, a sound with which her mother wasn't overly familiar, but which made her heart swell.

Tossing her long, scarlet hair, Clementine said, 'I think I've cracked it. It's not finished yet, but now I know I shall be able to get it done…properly. It's the most…the most electrifying feeling. I feel fully alive for the first time in so long.'

Althea said, 'Well, I'm delighted to hear that, dear. Now, will you sit with me, or will you join these two in trying to track down Ian, and then Mavis, who seems to have gone AWOL? As has Billy.'

Clementine looked from her mother, to her husband, to Frank. She held out her hand. 'I'm sorry, we haven't been introduced.'

Althea tutted. 'That's Frank, Mavis's first love who's here to take her out on a date, and this is my daughter, Frank. Stop dawdling – if you're going, go. Now. And if you're joining them, wear a coat, Clementine. It's going to get very cold indeed out there tonight – they said so on the radio. Clear skies. Plummeting to well below freezing they said. And I hope you brought more than that jacket, Frank. It would have looked lovely beside a plate of something in a local hostelry, but it won't do you much good out there. Julian – do you have something he might wear?'

Frank, Julian, and Clementine all stared at Althea. She snapped, 'I haven't grown a second head, have I? Mavis is out there, in this weather…somewhere…and you all need to find her. Go!'

And they went.

CHAPTER THIRTY-SEVEN

Christine wanted to kill someone, and knew that anyone would do. This wasn't the way things were supposed to be, and she was going to do her best to make sure that someone would pay, at some point in the future, for what was happening to her. Alexander was completely to blame, she knew that much, and if he thought he was getting near her ever again, he had another think coming. She screamed, again, and once again the brainless twerp beside her who, apparently, had conned people into believing she was a nurse, told her to 'breathe through the pain' as though that were a possibility.

Christine wanted to yell so many things, but hadn't the strength – not in the face of possibly being burst into a million pieces by the oil tanker that was, obviously, grinding around inside her body. As she squeezed her eyes shut, she saw flashes of light, heard noises that couldn't possibly be coming from her, and then…in a moment of blessed relief, she fell back – wet with sweat – on the moist, yet welcoming pillows behind her.

She growled, 'Where's Alexander?'

'Mr Bright is on his way, and your parents, too. But it's rush hour, so they might be a little while,' said the annoyingly calm nurse. 'But don't worry, they'll be here in time – you've only just started.'

'How long?'

'How long will it take them to get here?'

'No. How long will this baby be?'

The nurse laughed. Actually laughed. 'Well, they take their own time. We're keeping a close eye on you, and you're doing very well. But it could be quite a while yet. You went straight into established labor, and that TENS machine should help your back a bit, but you'll recall, from all your classes, that this stage could go on for a while. Maybe as long as eighteen hours. Who knows? We'll let nature take its course, though not if you or Baby are in any danger. Then the team will take action. And either I, or someone else, will be with you every minute.'

Christine sighed. Her intellect told her that she'd studied everything she should expect and was, in fact, expecting it. What she hadn't accounted for was the crashing realization that she was no longer in control of her own body, that – to all intents and purposes – the baby had already taken over her very existence. And she was also horribly aware that the contractions she'd felt so far were just the start of it all; the books all said that the pain during the delivery process was in an entirely different league when compared with these early stages. She had no idea how she'd cope.

She said, 'Can we revisit which drugs you're going to use, and when? I might not have made the best decisions.'

The nurse laughed. Again. 'Of course we can. That's a normal thing to do at this stage. I'll fetch the doctor, shall I?'

'Please. And would you be so kind as to pass me my phone before you go?'

The so-called nurse paused and turned. 'You want to phone someone? Now? But…everyone you wanted to be here is on their way. Is there someone else you'd like us to notify?'

'No, I'd like my phone so I can make a phone call, please.'

Handing over Christine's phone, the young woman said, 'Well, if you think you're up to it. I'll be back as soon as I can be.'

Christine did the breathing thing again, and hoped it would help, then scrolled madly through her contacts, seeing the names of people she'd encountered through her previous life in the City, as well as those she'd met during her pre-City years. There he was…she punched numbers, then waited.

'Archie Pitcher speaking. Is that you Christine?'

'Hello, Tubby. Yes, it's me.'

The man with the light tenor on the other end of the call cleared his throat. 'It's Archie nowadays, Christine…which you'd know if you hadn't abandoned me in Cornwall all those years ago when we were on that wretched camping holiday. Anyway – to what do I owe the pleasure? Didn't I read that you'd become engaged to be married to some chap in antiques? Or was it something else that he did? I can't recall. Sorry.'

'Hang on a tick, Archie…' Christine shoved a pillow into her face and screamed, then said, 'I'd love to catch up, at some point, but I'm a bit busy at the moment. Tell me, is your father still something to do with the Fraud Squad?'

Archie laughed. 'He retired. Lives on the Isle of Man, now. Mummy died, and he remarried, you know.'

Christine did her best to sound concerned. 'I'm sorry, Archie. My condolences. That's very sad for you, though I'm pleased for him. However, as I said, I'm pressed for time…so, I don't suppose it would be possible for you to give me his number, would it? If you recall I did meet him on several occasions, and it's important that I talk to him. Urgently.'

Archie hemmed and hawed for a moment, during which Christine did the shouting into the pillow thing again. Eventually he said, 'Don't see why not. Will you write it down, or shall I text it to you?'

'Text. Now. Please. And please immediately text your father – he was Harry, wasn't he? – to tell him I shall be calling him. I don't want him to not answer an unknown number. It's important, Archie, and…sorry about Cornwall.' More silent shouting. 'Would chat but must go. Thanks. Talk soon.'

The nurse arrived and stared at Christine with a mixture of horror and disbelief. 'You still need your phone?'

'Just one more quick call. But…it's private.'

She thought she heard something about 'toffs' as the nurse left, then she clearly said, 'I'm outside the door. Waiting.'

Christine punched in the numbers that Archie had sent, and waited, hoping she'd get an answer.

'Pitcher here.'

'Christine Wilson-Smythe here. May I call you Harry?'

'Of course. Any friend of my—'

'Sorry, Harry. I can't natter. Thanks for taking my call. I need help with a matter concerning a serious fraud, and I think you can help me.'

The baritone replied, 'I recall you clearly, Christine, of course…but I have to decline. I'm no longer in a position to help anyone, I'm afraid. Did Archie not tell you that I've retired?'

'Hang on a second…right…Mr Pitcher, I am about to have a baby, and I mean that literally. So please listen, and, if you can, record this call. I'm asking you to do whatever you can to help – through whatever contacts you might have. I'm now a private investigator, and I've discovered a scheme to defraud people. The company doing it is called HVR Wines. It's a wine investment scam. They recruit unsuspecting potential investors, talk them up, then use them to lure in more marks. I believe they're offering investments in wines that either do not exist at all, or are a sham – with possibly fake bottles, or else fake wine inside them. A Sunny and Charlene Dalton from Epping are already chasing them to retrieve their investment, with no luck. The owner, one Hans van Ruud has gone to ground. A George and Lottie Fenton, of Chiswick, are also highly suspicious that they've been duped. HVR Wines is growing rapidly, so they must have many more marks, possibly all believing they own good wine, or, possibly, even the same wine as others do. Hang on…' Christine was on the verge of tears, the pain was now so bad. 'Sorry. Like I said…literally having a baby. Please…can you help? I believe time is of the essence. The van Ruud chap knows that the Daltons want their money back, and I think that an employee – or more than that – named Isla will have tipped him off that the Daltons might make a big stink if it isn't forthcoming, pronto. There's also a company named Plonk It In which installs wine cellars. Hans van Ruud's brother-in-law runs it, and they're overcharging wildly for their services. Probably nothing to be done about them, but I fear van Ruud will be making investors' money disappear very soon, if he's not already done so. Please act…now. Thank you.'

Christine lay back, panting. She vaguely heard the words, 'Got it. Leave it with me, I know just who to get in touch with…'

She didn't bother ending the call, but shouted, 'Nurse, I need you…and I need drugs…now…'

CHAPTER THIRTY-EIGHT

Mavis couldn't feel her hands. She knew they must be there, because she still couldn't release her arms from behind her back, which meant her wrists had to still be fastened together, which meant her hands were…still there. So…why couldn't she feel them?

She'd been awake for some time. She'd been conked on the head by something and had passed out – though maybe not for long. Long enough to be carried into the fish-smoking shed and tied up, but that wouldn't have taken more than five or ten minutes at most – she'd already been almost inside the place. It had been late morning when it had happened and, when she'd initially regained consciousness, the interior of the shed had been very dim, but she'd at least known that it was still daylight outside. Now the shed was completely dark, and a chilly day had become a frigid night.

After she'd first come to, she'd put a great deal of effort into trying to get herself loose, but her hands were tied to one of the uprights of the shed, so she couldn't move at all. Couldn't even move her hands up and down the upright to create some useful friction. Couldn't scoot about. Couldn't get to any of those appealing bits of broken metal she'd spotted just feet away from her – though they might as well have been on the moon. She'd shouted through the tape on her mouth with no effect – other than to give herself a nasty headache…unless that was the result of the bang on the head. Probably a combination of the two, she reckoned. And she was quite certain that the skin on her wrists was broken, bleeding, and likely to become infected, if the ropes that had been used to constrain her were anything like the manky old things coiled on the floor beside her that looked as though they'd been used – and reused, probably, over the years – to tie fish to the beams that stretched the length of the shed, ready for smoking.

But she had made some progress with her feet. Luckily, she'd decided to pull on her walking boots to go out to the summer house, which meant that her ankles were protected, so she'd been able to strain against the rope around them without hurting herself, and she'd managed to create some slack there. Not that it was going to do her any good, but she clung to that small achievement in the face of diminishing hope that she'd be found…in time. She wasn't concerned about the lack of water, or food – it was the cold that would get her, she knew that. Hypothermia was a sneaky condition, and she knew she had to keep trying to free herself, but also that she had to conserve energy so that she would stay as warm as possible. But now her entire body was shivering uncontrollably, and she wondered how long she'd be able to remain alert, and conscious.

She kept trying to wiggle her fingers; being gloveless, and the closest part of her body to the uninsulated wooden wall, she reasoned they must be getting the worst of the cold temperatures, so wasn't entirely surprised that she couldn't tell if they were moving, or not…if they were banging against the wall, or not…if they'd dropped off, or not. But she could at least feel her toes wriggling in her boots, and she could still feel her arms and legs, and her nose, which felt…hot.

Once again, Mavis told herself she was lucky – she'd dressed in layers, was wearing a decent coat, and trousers, and socks…though no hat, which was a great shame, but that might have been taken from her even if she'd been wearing one to start with. The great thing to her advantage was that she was dry, and the weather forecast had been for a cold night, not a wet one, though she suspected that the smokehouse roof was watertight – it would have to be, to be able to fulfil its function.

She'd wondered, at first, if her captor would come back to scoop her up and take her…elsewhere, but so many hours had passed that she thought that was a non-starter now. Then she thought of Frank coming to Twyst House to collect her for dinner, and how he'd not find her there. And what would happen then? Would he think she'd stood him up? Would Althea poo-poo Mavis as a flighty one and off he'd go – and here she'd stay, until someone found her desiccated remains at some point in the distant future?

She was past the angry tears stage, and the sad ones, too. She'd imagined how her grandchildren would grow up not knowing her, and how her sons would have to bear the weight of the knowledge of the circumstances of her death – that she'd died because of her job, her need to know everything…her nosiness, as James had once put it, when she'd told him she was going to become a private investigator. Should she have retired to a little place in Dumfries that would have allowed her to babysit for both families, be a part of their high days and holidays, and become Grannie MacDonald on a full-time basis? Maybe. She wouldn't have found herself in this situation if she had. But then she thought of all the other things she wouldn't have done too, of all the people she wouldn't have met, the places she wouldn't have gone, the clients she wouldn't have helped.

At which point her thoughts turned to Althea, of course, who she knew would miss her bitterly. The poor woman had taken a few knocks recently – to her confidence, not her person – and Mavis's death, at the Twysts' Scottish retreat, would hit her hard. Mavis hoped she'd recover from it. Rally. Fight on…and maybe even find a good replacement for Mavis at the head of the MacDonald Trust, which she sincerely hoped – no, knew – would continue without her. It had to. People needed it.

In fact, as she sat there, in the dark, her breath billowing from her nostrils as though she were a raging bull, Mavis MacDonald suddenly realized that it was actually through that charity – the one set up by Althea, for her to run – that she could achieve most, and possibly had done already. Of course, she'd patched up thousands of serving and retired members of the armed services throughout her nursing career, but setting up pods of people who could reach into the community to help prevent and treat addiction to prescription medications was, in all likelihood, the achievement of which she was most proud. If only she'd been given longer, to be able to do more.

She felt her entire body jump when her mobile phone started to ring in her pocket…the pocket she couldn't reach. But, if she wriggled, could she get the pocket to at least dump the phone onto the floor? If it was ringing, there must be a signal. If she could get it onto the floor she could maybe, somehow, work out how to press some buttons on it. It stopped ringing before she managed to writhe enough for it to fall, but she was sure she could feel it shifting in there…though her coat was riding up, and she really needed it under her bottom for just a little bit of warmth between her and the floor. Now the phone was ringing again, and, yes, it was on the floor, and the ringing was really, really loud – that was because she'd turned up the volume so she'd hear it when it was in her pocket. Yes, she was glad she'd done that – but now it had stopped again. She was feeling dizzier and dizzier. The phone was on the floor; she'd achieved that, but the floor was moving, heaving like the sea. How could she get at the phone if it was floating on the sea? How would she manage to press some buttons if it sank? It rang again, though, this time, the ring sounded like…music…lovely music. And it seemed to be getting farther and farther away. And…why did it sound like McFli barking? No, that wasn't barking it was…shouting? She made as much noise behind the tape across her mouth as possible…

The door flew open and there were very bright lights.

A voice. Was it a man? 'She's here. She's alive – oh my wee Mavis…you're alive. But look at you…oh my Lord, just look at her. Come on, we've got to get her loose, get her warm.'

It was Frank O'Malley…Mavis knew it. She felt herself being shoved this way and that, then was aware that her arms weighed a great deal, and that someone, not Frank, was staring at her. Red…lots of red. She blinked, then closed her eyes.

Another voice. A woman? 'This will hurt, I'm sorry.'

Mavis felt slight pressure on her lips, then she was being given water to drink, though she couldn't. The idea that she was going to get wet terrified her – more than anything had ever terrified her in her life before, and she did what she could to shove the deadly liquid away from her…to protect herself.

The voice again. 'It's tea. Drink it. It's warm.'

Mavis wanted to shout that it was burning her lips, but just shoved her arm about again and moved her head.

Frank said, 'It'll be too hot for her. Look at her – she's blue.'

Mavis felt a weight on her entire body, and looked up at Frank as he covered her with something large and dark.

He came close to her and she screamed, 'Smokehouse!'

He bent closer to her lips. 'What was that, Mavis? You'll have to try a bit harder to speak.'

Again, Mavis shouted, 'Smokehouse!'

Frank's face moved away. She heard him say, 'She croaked "smokehouse", I think, which I know is what we're in. Does she think we don't know what it is? And…why does that matter?'

Another voice, another man: 'I didn't even know it was here.'

The woman: 'Me neither.'

Mavis screamed, 'Smoke! Fire!'

Four confused faces. Frank said, 'Did she whisper "fire"?'

A man: 'You need fire for smoke. There's wood here, must be…somewhere. We can make a fire, in here…use those old metal bins outside…warm her where she is. I have matches…always carry them. Be prepared, you know?'

The woman: 'And I've phoned for an ambulance.'

Mavis closed her eyes for a nap. She could tell them all about who had knocked her out and tied her up – and why they'd done it – when she'd had a nap.

22nd JANUARY

CHAPTER THIRTY-NINE

Christine knew that death was near. All she had to do was give in to it, and it would all be over. She could almost feel the light, though she couldn't see it…then her body was filled with the pain again, and she did as she was told, and pushed.

The people surrounding her kept congratulating her, but she didn't feel as though she were achieving anything. The pain was indescribable, and whatever drugs they'd given her had obviously been defective. And Alexander? Nowhere to be seen. Her parents were, she knew, outside the delivery room…somewhere…but he'd never arrived. No one had heard from him at all, and he wasn't answering his phone. She was angry with the world, but mainly with him…unless he showed up dead, she'd kill him…at least, that was what she knew she'd been shouting for the past hour.

'You're doing really well. This is all so fast that anyone would think this was your third or fourth,' said a voice somewhere behind her, or down below her waist.

'If anyone else tells me again that I'm doing well, I swear to God I'll kick them in the face,' she shouted, knowing she couldn't, because there was nothing at all she could do with her feet.

The door flew open, and there – at last – was Alexander swaddled in a blue gown, his face covered with a surgical mask, and with…only one arm?

Christine spat at him, 'Where the Hell have you been? And where's your arm?'

Alexander stood beside her, and grabbed her hand with…his only hand. 'It's in a sling, under this thing. Broken. Nice clean break. Nothing to worry about. Sorry I'm so late. How's my darling doing? Are we having a baby?'

Christine pulled his hand toward her, bringing him closer. 'No – *we're* not having a baby, *I* am having a baby. And I think it's going to be the biggest one ever born. But you listen to me, Alexander Bloody Bright – if that arm of yours got that way because of any of your shady stuff, we're finished.' She could tell that he was about to say something, but she stopped him.

'Hold on…' The pain came again, and she followed her instructions. She didn't care that she was mashing the hand of the man she theoretically loved as she did it. When the tide subsided, she wailed, 'I needed you…you should have been here. Where were you?'

Alexander bent close to her. 'None of this, here, now, should be about me…it's all about you. Suffice to say my Aston's a write off. I had not been drinking. Black ice. A van hit me. He's…in another hospital. Geordie's there…keeping an eye on him, and reporting back. I will be fine. Now…let's focus on this wonderful thing you're doing, my darling.'

Christine hissed, 'Oh…my poor Alexander. Sorry about your arm. And your car. But this is not…wonderful. And I need you to make a phone call, then talk to my parents. Just one call. I have to know if it's all been done properly.'

Alexander seemed confused. 'What are you talking about?'

'You need to get onto Harry Pitcher. Check my phone for the number. He knows all about the wine thing…said he'd help. Used to be Fraud Squad. You have to do this for me because they won't let me have a phone. Find out what he's done. Did they manage to get the van Ruud bloke? I can't ask my parents to phone him, obviously, and this lot are holding me here…incommunicado.'

Alexander said, 'You're having a baby, and it's four in the morning, Christine. What do you expect me to do about…that? It's all completely unimportant – this is what matters…you, and the baby.'

Through gritted teeth, and between pants, Christine growled, 'I won't let my child be born to a…a complete failure of a woman, Alexander. Promise me you'll phone Harry Pitcher. My parents are as good as my clients. You have to help me finish this. For them. For me. For us…aaahh…'

A disembodied voice said, 'This is it, Christine – we really need you to help Baby now…come along, you're doing really well…one more big effort…'

'I warned you about congratulating me,' shouted Christine – then the air turned blue.

CHAPTER FORTY

Having managed to eat some soup the previous evening, and having kept it down, Annie had enjoyed a good night's sleep, though she'd got up at six, knowing she wouldn't even nap after that. By half past, she was slouched over her plain, buttered toast, and doing her best to ignore the girls, who'd just had the quickest of dashes outside before she'd put the kettle on. 'Gert, you can't have any…and you know it. Be nice, like Rosie…yes, go on back to your spot. Good girl.'

Tudor ambled in from the bathroom, looking a bit sleepy, and petted both dogs. 'You still look worn out this morning. How are you feeling? A bit better again? You wouldn't let me cuddle you through the night…how about now? Need a hug?'

Annie said, 'Don't need consolation, Tude, ta. I do feel a lot better, yes thanks, but what I really need is…answers. I can't stop it all whirling around in my head. Why did Barb die? Should we have talked her into going to the police with her concerns? That's what I can't help but wonder. If we had, she might be alive today…and don't tell me I'm talking rubbish, because we both know it's a consideration. Car and me have been texting already this morning. She didn't sleep much. And Bertie was grizzling, she said.'

Tudor sat beside her, and buttered his own toast. 'If you don't want consolation, how about this – a dose of reality. Annie…a woman to whom – yes – you owe a great deal, turned up out of the blue asking for help, and was already a very sick person. She had suspicions, that you weren't able to substantiate – and which even she wavered on – that her daughter was carrying out some stealthy program of poisoning her. Now, four days later, she's dead. Four days, Annie. Do you think that if you'd driven her yourself to the police station directly from the hospital when they released her, that you could have saved her? I'm sorry – if the woman had suspected she was being poisoned over a period of months, she should have done something about it before her body was so weakened that her heart couldn't take it any more…if that's what killed her. It's not your fault, Annie. It's either her fault, for not acting sooner or – if she was being poisoned – then it's the poisoner's fault…obviously.'

Annie patted his hand. 'Thanks, but you can lower the high-dudgeon setting, Tude…I know all that. Car and I both do. But that's it, see – if her daughter really was poisoning her, she's going to get away with it, in't she? And…well, Car and I have agreed, we can't let that happen. So we're still on the case, until Mave comes back from swanning about on her holiday in Scotland and tells us off for wasting time on it. But, even then, I think Car and I would still do whatever we could, to make it…right.'

'By which you mean…have the daughter arrested?'

'If Nia Williams poisoned Barb, she deserves to be done for it. You can't take a life – or bring a person's body to the point that it goes and gives up all on its own – without consequences, Tude.'

'I agree.'

'Of course you do. I couldn't love a man who didn't.'

Tudor chuckled. 'Well, that's a relief. I wasn't expecting a test, before I've even finished my Marmite.'

'I'm like the Spanish Inquisition, me, Tude. Oh heck, I think Althea's love of Monty Python's starting to rub off on me, and I haven't even seen her in a week.'

'When are they back, by the way?'

'Middle of next week, I think. Or maybe next Friday.'

'I'll be good to have at least Mavis back. With Christine out of play, you'll need another body back in full working order to lighten your workload. Any news from London, yet?'

'Nah, Chrissy's not due to pop for weeks yet. I dare say we'll chat soon…she left me a message a day or so ago. Sounded great. Bored, more than anything, I suppose. It's got to be boring, hasn't it? Just sitting around in the lap of luxury, with servants to do everything for you – or else out shopping for the nursery and having tea at Fortnum's with Mummy.'

Tudor laughed, making both dogs meander toward the table again. 'I know that's not what you think of her, Annie, and you know that's not what she's like. And I don't know about tea – but I've seen her drink a few blokes under the table in this pub, and the last one I ran. She can't half tuck it away.'

'Well, we're not going to make our fortune if everyone follows Gwyn's example. We need heavy drinkers, Tude, not people who nurse a half of dark mild for an hour – regular as clockwork – then go home to their place to eat their own food.'

'Ha – and not even Gwyn's going to be drinking for a while. He was on the fizzy water last night – dental problems. On some sort of antibiotics that you can't drink with. Very special, he said. Because he's allergic to penicillin, he said. Well, Gwyn would be, wouldn't he? Even had the box with him. Something with one of those long names – umm, metro…nida…zoll. Poor dab, he's on them for a week.'

Annie stood. 'You know what, Tude – the fizzy water costs almost as much as the beer for our customers, but there's less of a profit margin on it for us, so that's a shame. But maybe he'll sneak in the odd half of dark mild before the week's out.'

'Oh no, he was telling me all about it last night. In great detail. He's taking it very seriously – has to, he says. It's not that alcohol would stop the antibiotics working – 'cos that's what happens, I believe, which is why you shouldn't drink when you're taking them – no, this one would make him very poorly if he drank with it. Nasty, it is. Acts a bit like the stuff they give to alcoholics to make them really ill if they drink. Nothing to muck about with, he said. His dentist, and the chemist, were both very firm with him, he said. The chemist gave him a leaflet – an extra one, I mean, not just the one that comes in the box. And I know he might like to benefit from our heating bill rather than his own in the winter, but he's not a natural rule-breaker, is he, Gwyn? More your silent protest type, if anything, really.'

'Well, that means we'll have to take a light bulb out of the fixture in the bathroom, then, if Gwyn's got a week of fizzy waters, Tude. That'll save us the profit we're not making out of him until his…whatever it is that's wrong with him is sorted.'

'Abscess on his gum, he said. Very painful, he said. As best he could, anyway. Came out of nowhere, he reckons. No warning.'

Annie pushed her plate into soapy water. 'How would an abscess warn you?'

'I said that, too.'

'And what did Gwyn say?'

'He said, "Well, you'd think it would start small so you could do something before it got big, but it was massive, overnight." Oh – and he told me to: "Hold the slice of lemon, ta". Too much acid, apparently. Not that I was thinking of giving him one anyway. I don't know what he's been watching on the telly. Lemon in fizzy water? In a G and T, yes. But in water? It's…water.'

Annie blew him a kiss when her phone rang. 'It's Car – got to take this. If you've gone down to see to the cellar before I've finished, I'll pop down to let you know what my plans are. Hello, Car, how are you doing, now?'

'Albert's still not right, and I think I can feel a lump on his gum. Screamed his face off when I had a look inside there, and it does seem a bit red, I must say.'

'Get him to wash his mouth out with warm salty water, that's the best thing,' offered Annie. 'Or else he'll end up like Gwyn, with an abscess.'

'Says the woman with no kids. He's a bit young to be swilling his mouth out, without drinking it down…though if I don't try, I won't know, I suppose. But swallowing salt water isn't good for you – it's an emetic.'

Annie sighed. 'Now that's an idea. You don't think someone – in other words, Nia Williams – was somehow getting Barb to drink gallons of salt water every day, do you? You know – so that's why she was throwing up all the time, and kept losing weight.'

Carol's laugh was…dark. 'Unlikely, I'd say. And we might never know what killed her, anyway, as we've both discussed…at length. It might have been her heart that went, but we won't know why she was so weak.'

'Do you think they'll test for all those poisons again, when they do the post-mortem, Car? You know she said they'd done lead, and zinc, and all sorts of things.'

'I don't know – though I don't see why they would.'

'If only we could get hold of whoever's going to do it, without having to go through the prime suspect. I tell you what, Mave would know how things work – you know, medical stuff like who does what, and where you might be able to track them down in a hospital, or laboratory – I could ask her. If I can get hold of her. Didn't you say she'd left you messages?'

'Said the internet was down at Twyst House, and her mobile couldn't always get a signal. She used a landline to phone me, and I've been ringing it, but no one answers. I've got no idea of the set-up there, so can't say why that might be. In any case, she briefed me well, and I think I've got what she wants – now all I have to do is wait for her to get back to me, I suppose.'

Annie chuckled. 'Typical Mave – can't help but get involved, can she? What's she got you doing for her? Much?'

Carol sighed. 'I know it's nice to be thought of as good at your job, but, honestly, Annie, sometimes I don't see why I always… No, never mind. Mavis? It's all to do with a fishing boat and some bloke in Hastings who's buying it from some old mate of hers in Scotland, and was the Hastings bloke to be trusted? And, basically, he's not. You know you told me that Carys James said that the Sglod Squad's Tanner family was just a series of court cases waiting to happen?'

'Yeah.'

'They sound just like the Carmadys, of Lewisham, and areas surrounding. This Danny that Mavis put me onto has had a bit of bother himself, but nothing close to how much his brother, father, and most of his cousins, have had. Though…maybe that's why he moved from Lewisham to Hastings, to get away from them. And maybe that's why the move to Scotland, too.'

'What sort of trouble?' Annie poured herself another mug of tea – the last from the pot.

Carol laughed, 'Well, the nice thing is, the Carmadys all seem to specialize in their own thing, without treading on any toes within the family. Petty theft, car theft, pickpocketing, breaking and entering, one armed robber – of a jeweler in Lewisham – and drugs, drugs, and more drugs. But they seem to divvie up the types of drugs. This Daniel Carmady – Danny, to his mates – he's been done for possession in both the Lewisham area, and again close to Hastings. So…yeah, maybe moving wasn't about escaping the clutches of the family, but about expanding their criminal footprint. His favorite seems to be magic mushrooms, which are a Class A drug. Not big quantities, but enough that he's done some community service. He's got a cousin who's been done for Class C steroids, twice. See – demarcation of crime, within the family. Nice.'

Annie sipped her tea. 'So…this Danny's buying a boat in Scotland from this mate of Mave's to – what? – deliver magic mushrooms?'

'No idea, but I did a bit of digging, and it looks like the area around Twyst House would be an ideal place to grow magic mushrooms – moist, and with the right range of temperatures. Nothing at this time of year, of course, it would be too cold, but during the growing season. They've even got the right type of grass there.'

Annie had to laugh. 'How do you find out all this stuff, Car?'

Carol surprised Annie when she said, 'Not so hard, in this instance – you can download an app for it. Shows you all the best places to find magic mushrooms, or grow them. And there are loads of places where you can buy the spores to be able to start up your own…colony.'

'But…they're illegal. You said. Class A, right?'

'Yes. But looking at them isn't. Not even photographing them is illegal. Having the spores to do scientific research isn't, either. Not that I think a Carmady would be stopped by the idea of doing something illegal. So…there's that.'

'Well, I hope Mave's grateful. You've got a full plate, what with that, and the Barb thing, and the stuff Henry wanted you to look into. And here's me just having to wait on Carys to come back to me with all the stuff about the Tanners so that I can show it all to Tude. Oh, by the way, when you talk to Henry, could you ask him to phone Tude, please? Bob Fernley's established that the rules of the Chellingworth Estate do apply to the entire village of Anwen-by-Wye in that the Sglod Squad need the written permission of the Twysts to be able to "set up shop" down here. Reckons that if Tudor appeals to Henry directly, he's much more likely to say yes to the action that Bob would need to take to get them to just drive away the next time they arrive – which would be, to start with, a letter from a solicitor telling them about the rules. Bob says Henry will do everything he can to avoid a course of action that costs money – which a solicitor's letter would – and Bob doesn't like the idea of having to come down to explain to a couple of well-built young lads, with a criminal background, that they need to move on. So, short of asking everyone in the village to dust off their pitchforks and show the Tanners the road out, he suggests the softly-softly approach. So that would help. You will be talking to Henry today, right?'

'Yes. Just before eleven o'clock. I think he's quite enjoying all this cloak and dagger stuff…though I know he doesn't like the idea of upsetting Stephanie. Do you think Carys will have what you need on the Tanners by then?'

Annie shrugged, realized Carol couldn't see her, and said, 'I can't imagine it's high on her list of priorities, and I hate chasing up on a favor, so…we'll see. I'll let you know right after I find out – okay?'

'Okay. So…what have you got planned for today?'

Annie was at a loss. 'Well, I'm waiting for Carys on the Sglod Squad stuff. I'll try to reach Mave about the Barb post-mortem thing, or else I might just work out which health authority would deal with it and try to wangle myself a chat with the doctor or pathologist in charge on that one. I dare say I'll try and have a chat with Chrissy, at some point – we've missed each other's messages, so I'll try again. And…well, is there anything I can do to help you with the Barry Walton, Val Jenkins, Henry, and Stephanie thing?'

'Yes.'

'Oh, okay then – what's that?'

'I've got a lot on Barry Walton, but you could do some online shopping for me, if you like…without spending any money, of course.'

Annie liked the sound of that, not that she was a big shopper. 'Go on then…brief me!'

Carol chuckled. 'It'll be a bit boring, but what I could do with is a list of comparables, so we can get some idea of the market that Barval is trying to, theoretically, enter. If I send you a list of items, could you make up a spreadsheet of comparables, and then get that to me? Include small, niche brands, and global titans, too. Length of time in the market, and anything you can get me about market share, and investment in market, would help too. Thanks.'

'You don't want much, do you, Car? And getting me going with the idea of "shopping" was a bit mean. Go on then, send me the list. But you know I'm not as fast as you, especially with spreadsheets. I suppose you want this…yesterday?'

'By eleven?'

'I'll need more caffeine…oh hang on a tick, there's Carys. Send the list. Bye.' She ended the call and accepted the next one quickly. 'Hello, Carys, sorry, I was talking to Carol.'

Gertie'd had enough of sitting alone, and decided that Annie's feet needed warming, which Annie didn't mind at all…though she'd been planning to get up and put the kettle on: she'd almost finished her tea, but didn't want to disturb Gertie, so she took smaller sips as she listened to Carys James talking to someone in – presumably – her office in Swansea.

Eventually, Carys said, 'Sorry, Annie – I thought I'd picked a good moment to phone you. I sent you an email, which I need to update. Already. As you asked, I sent a list of the Tanner boys' records, but the news is that a Shaznay Tanner, wife of Liam Tanner – which I thought was weird, because of, you know, Nicole – anyway, she's just been arrested on suspicion of handling stolen goods, namely a couple of cardboard boxes full of mobile phones. Found in the boot of her car when she was pulled over for having a brake light out, and an almost flat tire, last evening. I only found out just now, and I sent the email…oh, an hour ago? You did get it, didn't you?'

Annie had been frantically opening her laptop as Carys had been speaking. Sounding as casual as possible, she said, 'Yeah, and it's just what I needed. Thanks, Carys. And for taking the time to phone me about this Shaznay, too. Ta. You alright? You sound a bit…stressed.'

Carys laughed. A bit manically, thought Annie. 'Normal state of affairs here. Loads of people off sick with colds and flu. Best they don't spread it around, I know, but…well, the work doesn't go away at this time of year. You doing alright? You don't sound…quite yourself.'

Annie explained about the food poisoning that had been inflicted upon her by the Tanner brothers, then about Barbara Newsom's death. Carys sympathized about the loss of her counsellor, then Annie said, 'We reckon her daughter killed her, but don't think we can prove it.'

Carys was quiet for a moment, then said, 'You kept the juiciest bit until the end, I see. Okay, I can take five minutes to listen. Tell me everything.'

Annie did.

When she'd finished, Carys was quiet again. 'That's a tough one, Annie. To be honest, if you'd taken her to your local station with her suspicions, they'd not have been able to act. Nothing to act upon, see? In fact, even now she's dead, there's nothing in what you've told me that I could…do anything about. Well, I could talk to the medics and get them to check the body for signs of poisoning that might not have been obvious in blood or organ functionality tests, which is, I daresay, what they'd have been doing when she was alive. But I'm no doctor…though you do pick up a lot of stuff through experience. I had a case a little bit like this when I was starting out. Woman died. Had been wasting away. People who lived around her suspected undiagnosed cancer – she was one of those who never went to the doctor. When they cut her open…oh heck…sorry, Annie, that was thoughtless of me, this Barbara was important to you, I know. When they did the post-mortem, they found she'd been poisoned, over a long period of time, with…oh, what was it? Some sort of essential oil. Pennyroyal. That was it. The husband had talked her into taking it every day – too much of it – and it just destroyed her liver and kidneys. She'd been throwing up for months – literally wasted away.'

Annie tensed up. 'How'd they find out, Carys?'

Carys half chuckled. 'The smell. She smelled minty, inside. The effect of the pennyroyal, too, it seems.'

'Gordon Bennett, Carys – Barb's house reeked of mint. She had those essential oil bottle things, with little sticks coming out of them, all over the place. Could that have killed her?'

'Calm down, Annie. I don't think so…not unless she'd been taking the stuff orally, no. It's not fatal if it's just…in the air. But I suppose you could ask the pathologist to investigate it, during the post-mortem.'

Annie chuckled. 'Yeah, right-o, Carys…I'll just phone them on their private number – that I just happen to have on speed dial – and ask them to do that, after we hang up.'

Annie heard Carys sigh. 'Ah…alright. Where did you say she died, and when – exactly? One phone call, Annie. Because I owe you.'

Annie punched the air. 'You're a wonderful person, Carys. I must mention that to your brother, when I see him. Plas Newydd, Llangollen, one-ish, yesterday afternoon. Thanks, Carys. And sorry about mangling your language. It's always those two Ls that get me.'

'I forgive you. I'll text you. Bye.'

Annie couldn't wait any longer – she headed to the loo, then, since she'd already had to disturb Gertie, she made a pot of tea, and settled herself back at her kitchen table.

She'd just entered a few search parameters onto the world's biggest online shopping platform, to help Carol, when her phone told her she'd received a text: **Check emails Docs name & number for Newsom PM there. Told him your suspicions. He got excited. Pathologists are WEIRD. Shes now top of his list. CJ**

Annie was excited too, but put her head down and started to build the spreadsheet Carol had asked for. It took longer, and was much more tedious, than she'd feared, but she sent it to Carol with five minutes to spare – meaning her chum would be better armed when she spoke to Henry Twyst…at any moment.

Needing another pot of tea – both the previous ones had gone cold, she'd been so immersed in her tasks for a couple of hours – Annie promised herself she'd give her eyes a rest by phoning Chrissy, once she had a hot mug in her hand…but another text came in that shifted her mood: **Newsom PM done. Heart failure COD due to failure of internal organs – liver & kidneys. Doc said no poisons not even pulegone (poison in pennyroyal). Got test results EXTRA FAST just for ME but some still pending waiting for** reactions he said. Any more ideas? He asked me I'm asking you. He's kept extra samples for extra tests. Can hold body for a little but daughter is already nagging. Text me ASAP. CJ

Annie didn't feel very bouncy-trouncy, so decided to wait until she did to call Christine; it didn't seem fair to phone someone who was probably bored when you felt a bit down.

'I need a biscuit, Gert. What about you?'

Both dogs beat her to the cupboard where the treats were kept – of both human and doggie varieties.

CHAPTER FORTY-ONE

Mavis was cold…cold to her bones, and everything around her was dark. She knew she'd been asleep, but now she knew the end was near. She'd hallucinated being rescued, being cared for, carried about, and made safe. But now…this was it. It had to be. She couldn't fight it any longer…

'I think she's waking up. Put some lights on, or open those curtains. I want to see her.'

Mavis knew it was Althea speaking, but wondered why the woman wouldn't let her just die in peace. She tried to wave the blurry vision of the woman away…but connected with…something.

'How wonderful – she hit me. James, come on, get the nurse.'

Mavis tried to make sense of what she was hearing, what she was seeing…then things came into focus. Her son, James, was beside her, as was Althea. As soon as she'd uttered them, Mavis hated the fact that her first words were: 'Where am I?'

Althea twittered, 'There – her eyes are open. Oh, James, she's going to be alright. Mavis, you're going to be alright. Where's that nurse?'

Mavis managed to croak, 'I'm in hospital. Was in a smokehouse. Hypothermia. Billy Stewart knocked me out. Get him, Althea. He's been swindling you. No money spent on Twyst House. All in his pocket. Taking your fish. Smoking them. Business called "Tradition Delivered". Get his books. Get hold of his bank accounts. Tell the police. Get him.'

James said, 'Ach, will you stop, Ma? You've been rambling in your sleep about the same thing for hours. We know. They got him. Your health is all that matters. Stop mithering. Rest.'

Mavis wasn't going to be told off by her son like that. Not even by James, the older of the two. She wriggled a bit so she was able to see him better.

She cleared her throat. 'I'm no' in Intensive Care, which is good. I dare say this thing in my arm's been warming me up, slowly –' she nodded toward the drip – 'and I expect they're monitoring my heart and such. Good. So there's basically nothing wrong with me.'

James snapped, 'There's a lump on your head the size of an egg, you might have a concussion, your wrists look like they've been flayed, and you were lucky you didnae lose one of your little fingers to frostbite. That huge bandage wrapped around your hand, the bindings on your wrists, and that massive one on your head aren't there for fun. You could have died, Ma – so don't you go talking to me as though I was the one acting recklessly.'

Mavis snapped back, 'Ach, I was no' acting recklessly. And don't you go speaking to your mother like that in public, nor in private, young man. How would you feel if one of your bairns gave you such cheek?'

James shrugged. 'If I deserved it, I'd take it. Ma – you're no spring chicken. You can't go chasing crooks all the time. You're our ma. We need you.'

Mavis bit her tongue, then said quietly, 'I wasnae chasing him. I was just having a wander about trying to find a mobile signal, and one of the people I was going to phone was you, to invite you to the Burns Night shindig this one's throwing at Twyst House. It's really no' my fault the man had a go at me. To be honest, I hadnae put two and two together about him when he attacked me. I only worked it all out when I was sitting there alone. I had the time to think about what I'd been talking to you about, Althea…all the money Henry and you said you were spending on Twyst House – and the state of the place when we got there. And there's the company logo for the smoked fish…and the likelihood that the fishing people that the kitchen's been feeding are there to catch a heck of a lot more fish than you thought Billy was taking out of the loch. I do hope he's been putting stock in too, dear, because he might have completely messed up the ecosystem in that lovely loch of yours.'

Althea cooed, 'Like your son says, Mavis, don't worry yourself about it. Especially not the fish. It turns out Billy's been using the loch for years – that company he's got has been going for over a decade. Imagine that! He's been stocking the loch, then harvesting the fish – did a good job of it, by the sounds of it…though not at all what I imagined was happening with the loch, you know? Trout, of course.' Althea sighed. 'Much though I hate to admit it, we've had that brand of smoked trout at Chellingworth Hall for some time, and I've always thought it rather good. Had no idea the fish came from our loch. The things you find out, eh? And as for the money – yes, you're right. It's no wonder the place is almost falling down – not a penny's been spent on it for years…and years. I…well, I might have mentioned a thing or two about that when I had my meeting with him, after we parted company yesterday morning, Mavis. Though that couldn't have been what set him off, could it? No…I didn't raise his suspicions that he was about to be found out any further than they'd already been raised by…well, by our arrival, I suppose. Yes, not my doing at all.'

'Aye…well,' said Mavis, glaring at James, then Althea. 'They got him, you say? Where? When?'

James said, 'He'd arrived at Glasgow airport to catch a flight to Alicante. Him, three dogs, and a woman.'

Mavis said, 'A redhead named Millie, no doubt. She was the cook on duty when Althea and I arrived, but she'd gone by the next day, and she'd called in her backup, Eileen. I expect Millie saw the writing on the wall, and she and Billy agreed to start packing things up. Oh dear – Millie and Billy. A couple, of course. Ah well, got them both. Sorry to hear there are three dogs who'll have lost their humans for a while.'

Althea jumped in. 'Don't worry, dear, the dogs lived with Billy at the cottage on the Estate, and they will remain as Estate dogs – though with an upgrade to their accommodations, because Julian and Clementine have agreed to take them on. Though, honestly, I'm not at all sure that the main house is an upgrade – I think some of the money that's missing has been spent on making the cottage as warm and cozy as possible. And you should see the electronics Billy had in there…such a massive television. In fact, that might be why you got a signal at the smokehouse – he had his own satellite on the cottage, you know.'

Mavis managed a chuckle. 'No. I had no idea. It must have been around the back of the place, where I didnae see it. Though I can understand why a person would want one.'

'It's what saved you,' said a voice from the corner.

Mavis tried to move, but failed. 'Is that you, Frank?'

'Aye, it's me.'

Frank O'Malley stepped out of the gloom, and Mavis was shocked by how dreadful he looked. His hair was all over the place, his face covered with stubble, his clothes all smudged with – was that charcoal? – and the bags beneath his eyes suggested he'd not slept for a week. Mavis could tell he was feeling emotional; he was trembling when he reached toward her, and touched her gently on her shoulder.

Mavis said quietly, 'Did you find me, Frank? I seem to remember…something, though I might have been hallucinating. Sorry – it's all a bit muddled.'

She could tell that Frank was fighting back tears when he said, 'Me, Julian, Ian, and Clementine spent hours looking for you. We were out there until about nine at night, then we went back to the house and Althea'd phoned the police, of course, and they advised waiting until the morning before searching again. But we disagreed with that idea, and decided we couldn't risk you maybe being outside all night, not with the way the weather was. So we all put on some more clothes and…started again. None of us even knew that smokehouse was there, and we'd been past the cottage before – but we didn't even see it in the dark. I'm so sorry, Mavis – we could have got to you earlier if only we'd gone a bit farther out into the woodland behind the cottage. But we might never have found you if it hadn't been for us hearing your phone ringing. We followed the sound, and…there you were.'

Althea butted in. 'I phoned you, Mavis. They left me at the house you see, the first time, and the second time. But my phone's battery had died, so I couldn't find your number, then I charged it a bit and found it, but I still had no signal, and I rang and rang you on the landline but got no answer. So I just kept trying. I'll never forget your phone number ever again, I rang it so often. But I have to say that I'm not at all sure that old handset in the library actually makes calls properly all the time, so eventually I had another bright idea, and went to Billy's office to use his handset. And it was not long after that, that Clementine answered your phone and told me they'd found you. I'm just glad that your phone rang when it did. When it really mattered – when they were close enough to hear it.'

Mavis smiled her thanks at her friend. 'I was lucky to have all of you trying to find me. But, look – word of all this does no' need to be passed around all and sundry. I'll tell the folks back in Anwen-by-Wye, or even London, when I'm good and ready. They don't all need to be worrying about me when they've babies to birth, and an agency to keep running…though I dare say they'll all be interested to hear about The Case of the Swindling Steward – and I'll fight Annie if she wants to change that one.'

'Oh, Ma, stop thinking about other people and think of yourself, and your family, will you?' James sounded angry. 'Look at all the people it took to save you, Ma. You've given us all a terrible fright.'

'That's as mebbe,' said Mavis, knowing she was one of the people who'd been frightened. 'But all's well that ends well, eh? I'll be out of here in no time, I'm sure. Though I dare say your plans for a big party for Burns Night are cancelled, Althea?'

Althea looked uncertain. 'Hmm…well, it certainly won't be what I'd originally hoped for, but I have promised the butcher that I'll take a dozen haggis, and it's the day after tomorrow, and I can't let him down. So…maybe a family gathering? You and your brother plus all of your families, of course, James. And you should be there, Frank. A smaller gathering. More intimate. And I could tell the butcher to donate some of the haggis to people who might like them.'

'And mebbe not as many speeches, or dancing,' said Mavis, her eyelids feeling suddenly leaden.

'Oh, there has to be dancing,' said Althea. 'Clementine was most insistent about that – she and Julian have been practicing, it seems…and she's got the proper regalia for them to do it in, too.'

Mavis tried to imagine the sight as she drifted off, but found herself unable to form a thought, and realized she didn't care that she couldn't.

CHAPTER FORTY-TWO

When she put down the phone, Carol felt she couldn't have made a worse job of her conversation with Henry. She'd made the call when she'd been in a foul mood, almost immediately after she and her mother had a bit of a run in about – of all things – which way the toilet paper should be put on the holder in the bathroom. She had no idea why they'd both dug their heels in so forcefully on such a stupid matter, but it seemed that it was the final straw that had managed to break a pair of camels' backs.

Henry had been as annoyingly dithery as usual during their call, and she'd ended up sounding like her old history teacher, who'd been a snappish dragon with a penchant for making pupils feel small. Carol had hated her, and was beginning to hate the version of herself she'd become over the past hour or so.

She'd been polite when she'd told Henry everything that she'd found out about Barry Walton and his sister – who, it turned out, wasn't a reformed addict with a great recovery story that might help sell the idea of a company hawking wellness products, but rather a young woman with a mass of tattoos and piercings who liked to post reels of herself in the most extraordinary situations, often doing something that bordered on the illegal. Not the best person to be introduced as the Managing Director of…anything. As she'd pointed out.

But then Henry had become annoyingly pathetic, droning on about how best she thought he might relay her findings to his wife, which Carol had felt compelled to tell him she believed was something he needed to decide for himself. As he bleated that, maybe, there was some way for her and her colleagues to become involved – to back up the opinion of one poor man with the voices of four strong, independent women – she'd found herself reacting, seemingly uncontrollably, by becoming more and more assertive. No…bossy. Yes, she'd been bossy. Maybe more like her mother than her old history teacher, now that she thought about it.

At one point, she'd actually gone as far as telling off a duke of the realm – and her landlord, no less – for being dim. As she recalled her exact words: 'I don't know how anyone can be so obtuse,' – at least she'd used a big word, correctly – she felt everything within her gathering into an acidic little ball in her tummy. How could she have done it?

She supposed that at least, now, she had a little insight into why Althea moaned on about her son, and the nannies she'd retained to raise him. But it didn't help. Carol didn't like bullies, and she'd come close to being one, despite all the real power being held by the man she'd been berating. How could she make amends?

She shook her hands as if to rid herself of the guilt she felt, then placed them both on her beloved calico's gloriously silky fur, and accepted Bunty's purring by way of comfort. How on earth did cats manage to do it? While she'd been on the phone, Bunty had leaped onto her lap, had worked at Carol's body with her paws as though she were a mere cushion, then had closed her eyes with pure contentment. She knew she'd enjoyed the calming effects of Bunty's purrs even as her blood pressure was being elevated by Henry, so now thanked her companion, because without that bit of support, who knew what she might have ended up saying.

Carol told herself it was too late to do anything about it all, sent the email to Henry that she'd promised, then dialed Annie's number. At least she, and Tudor, should be pleased by how the part of the conversation had gone regarding the scaring off of the Sglod Squad; Henry was going to phone Tudor to discuss his son's godfather's concerns after lunch…so, some time soon.

As she cradled her phone, Carol told herself that at least the conversation had ended without Henry threatening to throw her and her family out into what was, truly, the bleak midwinter landscape, and he'd even make a jocular remark about not having realized that the people he'd asked to look after his son's spiritual welfare *in loco parentis*, would, themselves, require him to intervene to improve their lot. Which she hoped bode well for her continued living situation, and both Val Jenkins and Tudor Evans.

Annie's bright voice answered, 'Hiya, Car – how's it going?'

Carol's spirits lifted. 'Henry's going to phone Tudor after lunch. Let him know, so he's ready? I didn't tell Henry anything about the Tanner brothers – I'd just given him a lot of information about Barry Walton, and didn't want to overwhelm him. So Tudor can fill him in – the police records you got hold of, how they aren't the sort to be encouraged into the village, that sort of thing. Or…however you two are planning to play it to get what you want, you know?'

Annie didn't reply immediately, then said, 'Thanks, Car. I'll put you on speakerphone for a second while I send him a text – he's downstairs, already tending to a huge pot of *cawl*, ready for dinner tonight. Though you know what we want – we want anyone trying to elbow in on our evening food monopoly in Anwen-by-Wye to be ground to dust beneath the unforgiving and ever-present heel of the patrimony.'

Carol paused, dealt with her surprise…then laughed. 'Very good, Annie. You got me there for a minute.'

She heard her friend chuckle. 'Yeah – I don't mean it of course. Except – now I've said it out loud – that is what we're trying to do, in't it? Which makes me feel a bit bad. I mean, the Tanners could have decided to make a go of something to keep them on the straight and narrow, couldn't they? Something that would help them, and their wives, build a good life without having to resort to the established family tactics of robbing people blind. And we'd be throwing a massive spanner in the works. Those phones they found in Shaznay's boot? Could be part of a big clear-out before they all become law-abiding citizens.'

Carol knew that her friend would be hoping for support. 'There are lots of other places that don't have a great pub with an excellent cook like Tudor, who'd be glad of the Sglod Squad being there every other night, Annie. It's taken them a while to even add Anwen to their schedule, so I dare say they'll survive without it.'

'Yeah…you're right. Ta, doll. And the other thing went well? I know you'll have done a good job of gathering all the ammunition Henry would need, but do you think he'll be able to sell it to Stephanie? 'Cos

I dare say she's the one who'll have to break it to Val. He wouldn't do that, would he? Best done between women, I'd say.'

Carol decided to be truthful. 'No idea. I gave him the information, and told him it was up to him to deal with it.'

Annie chuckled. 'That doesn't sound like you, Car. You're the quiet, polite one among us. Are you…over-simplifying?'

Carol confessed what she'd done, what she'd felt at the time, and then explained about the argument with her mother.

Annie's reply buoyed her up a little. 'Right-o, let me give Tude a bit of a warning on that front too, then, and let's see if he can sound Henry out about how he feels it went, eh? I'll let you go, and grab a couple of minutes with him down in the kitchen, alright? But, listen, Car – I think maybe it's time for you and your mum to have a bit of a heart-to-heart. But…that's just my opinion. Take it, or leave it. But have a think about it, eh? Anyway, bye for now.'

'Bye.'

Carol hoped that Henry hadn't taken umbrage…and tried to calm herself by stroking Bunty. But it seemed that her beloved cat had been petted enough, because she leaped down, gave Carol a baleful glance, then writhed out of the half-open door, her tail high, with her final little wiggle looking quite disdainful.

She whispered, 'Traitor,' then gave Annie's words some thought. Yes, she needed to talk to her mother, but had no idea how she was going to be able to even start that conversation.

She needed a plan…

CHAPTER FORTY-THREE

When he put down the phone, Annie felt Tudor couldn't have made a better job of his conversation with Henry. The duke's call had come through just as she'd finished briefing Tudor about how Carol had felt her chat with him had gone, so she hung around to listen in, with Tudor's half-blessing. Well…he hadn't shooed her out of the kitchen, and he could have done, if he'd really wanted to.

Henry had listened patiently to Tudor's – very natural, and apparently understandable – concerns about an unknown van offering foodstuffs being operated in Anwen by two sons of a family with a long, and alarming, police record, as well as the fact that Annie was convinced she'd been served something by them that had given her a terrible dose of food poisoning. Henry had agreed that a solicitor's letter would be forthcoming, though explained that he would double-check with Bob Fernley on the exact required content. Henry had also said that he'd make sure it would be available for presentation to the owners of said business when they arrived in Anwen next Wednesday, and had even said that Tudor could present it to them himself, if he so chose. At that point, Annie had run around the kitchen silently cheering, but Tudor had said he'd think about it.

Tudor had then – quite nonchalantly, for him – managed to raise the topic of Hugo's co-godparent, Val, and it transpired that Henry thought Carol had done a wonderful job, and was planning to broach the topic with his wife that evening.

With all that put to bed, Annie texted Carol, assuring her chum she wasn't going to be chucked out into the snow any time soon – because there was definitely a threat of snow on the way – and that she could rest easy on the Barry Walton front. Then she happily climbed the stairs to the flat, nuzzled both her pups, whose fur was warm and extremely nuzzle-able, and told herself that a fourth pot of tea was probably one too many, but that she was in a good enough mood to be able to phone Christine, to try to cheer her up a bit.

Her phone buzzed in her pocket. A text from Carys read: **Check your email CJ** so she did, where she found more information from the pathologist regarding tests that had been carried out on poor Barbara's remains. They'd detected no poisons, and the toxicology panel they'd run had been extensive; once again, the pathologist was seeking helpful input from Carys. Annie liked the way the bloke seemed to have really sunk his teeth into Barbara's case, and suspected it was a situation of someone liking a challenge. She wished she could help him fight on, but didn't know where to start. As she was scratching her fingers across her scalp, hoping that would help her come up with some sort of bright idea, Tudor raced up the stairs.

Puffing a bit, he asked, 'You haven't seen that bottle of ginger wine we had left over from Christmas, have you? Marjorie Pritchard fancies one – to help her warm up, she says – and I haven't got a bottle in the bar. Remiss of me, really, because it's a good winter drink, that is…though it's a bit strong for Marjorie, I'd have thought.'

Annie looked up. 'Nah, haven't seen it. But it might be in the top cupboard, over the sink. I should have brought one back from Barb's. She had loads of the stuff. For her stomach, she said.'

Tudor clattered about in the cupboard, placing all sorts of tins and jars on the counter. 'You told me earlier that her liver was in a mess. No wonder, if she'd been knocking back that stuff. It's stronger than most wines…though it's not as strong as spirits, I suppose. There it is…I'll put all this away later on. Got to go. See you.'

Tudor disappeared with his precious bottle, and Annie wondered about the wine. She'd tried it at Christmas, and had liked it – it was spicy, which suited her palate. The flavor of ginger was quite strong…could that have been used to disguise some sort of foul-tasting, harmful substance? Barbara had said that Nia had suggested she should try it. Annie wondered how much Barbara had drunk of it, then remembered she still had Barbara's little notepad, and grabbed it out of her handbag.

She'd been through it all before, of course, as soon as Carol had given it to her. In fact, she'd pored over it, trying to spot any discernable patterns. Now it made her sad to see how Barbara had taken the time to note everything she'd eaten and drunk, and what her daily routines had been, all in the hope of spotting some sort of pattern herself that might have allowed her to understand why she was always so nauseous, unable to keep food down, and suffering palpitations, sweating, and headaches. She'd listed every pill she'd taken, every meal she'd eaten, everything she'd drunk, and every dreadful symptom as it had arisen. The only patterns Annie had spotted before – or could spot now – were that the woman had drunk almost as much tea as Annie did herself, and had a particular fondness for Rich Tea biscuits; she'd enjoyed a wide variety of foods, some plain, some spicy; she'd enjoyed a small glass of wine with her dinner, and that she 'took' – as Barbara put it – 'a small ginger wine with hot water' as an after-dinner staple.

Thinking about the huge number of prescription drugs she'd seen in Barbara's home, Annie wondered again about the idea of drugs and alcohol interacting badly. Surely such a potential problem would be explained to a person when they collected their medications at a chemist shop? Tudor had told her that Gwyn had received a special leaflet with his antibiotics, which he'd said were called…no, she couldn't remember. She texted Tudor to ask him if he recalled the name of Gwyn's tablets, and he replied with three words: **Metro Nida Zoll** which she Googled, to discover it was one word: metronidazole.

Annie sat at the kitchen table again, and let her mind, and her fingers, wander. She could see why Gwyn had been warned off drinking while he was taking the stuff: alcohol made it act like something called disulfiram, which was – as Tudor had said Gwyn had mentioned – a medication used to help people to stop drinking alcohol, which it did by, basically, making a body do a whole host of nasty things to get rid of the stuff. Which more than deserved its own little leaflet, she thought. In fact, as she read more, she discovered that most of the symptoms that Barbara had been complaining of – and had listed, in her notebook – were consistent with the negative interactions a person could expect to experience if they drank alcohol while taking either metronidazole or disulfiram.

She sat back in her chair. Clearly Barbara had been drinking alcohol. Had someone – Nia? – been somehow spiking her booze with a prescription drug that would create all those symptoms? Might Barbara's daughter have injected something into the box of red wine that had been sitting on Barbara's kitchen counter? Or what about somehow being able to get it through the metal screw top of a bottle of ginger wine? But…even then, how would a person be able to get antibiotics or a drug given to alcoholics without a prescription? Surely you'd need an actual prescription to get hold of prescription drugs? Annie swore silently in frustration at her own stupidity when it dawned on her: what if you were a periodontist who could write prescriptions for an antibiotic that had a specific use for oral abscesses, like the one Gwyn had?

She immediately opened the screen that showed the camera feeds from Barbara's home, to which she'd given no attention since she'd heard about the poor woman's death. Yes, they'd been activated an hour earlier. She watched as Nia Williams entered the hallway, carrying a paper sack with a large logo of a daisy on it, walked directly into her late mother's kitchen, opened the cabinet above the kettle – which Annie happened to know contained Barbara's stock of loose-leaf, orange pekoe tea, and all the accompaniments – removed three bags from the cupboard, and replaced them with three she took from the daisy-bedecked sack. She popped the bags from the cupboard into the sack, turned around, and left the house. She'd been there all of two minutes, and went nowhere near the ginger wine, nor the box of wine…nor anything else at all. Just the bags in the cupboard…

Annie grabbed her phone and texted Carys, realized that what she wanted to say was too complicated and texted instead: **We need to talk NOW** then sent a follow-up text saying: **PLEASE!** A moment later, her phone rang, and she babbled into it, hardly drawing breath.

'Ta. Listen, Carys…Nia Williams has been poisoning her mother, and I know how she did it. With an antibiotic that dentists use for gum abscesses. At least, I think she has. If she has, I think she wrote dodgy prescriptions – somehow – for it, ground up pills and mixed them into her mother's loose-leaf tea. Been doing it for months. The stuff's not dangerous unless you also drink alcohol, then it does all the things to a person that were happening to Barbara. But it wouldn't show on any tests, see…because it's just an antibiotic. But, I did find out that some tests would show if a person's on antibiotics – and Barbara had some tests done when she was, once…but she said she'd been feeling better that week. Now I reckon that was because she hadn't been drinking – because she *knew* she was on antibiotics that time. Not that I'm saying she was a lush, but she certainly drank every day…except that week. I've got her notepad that lists everything she ate and drank, and her symptoms. And…Gordon Bennett! I think I was poisoned too! I drank a lot of tea at Barb's place, and that night I had a load of chips and stuff, and fancied a gin and tonic after I'd eaten…and I was as sick as a dog. So…maybe it wasn't the Sglod Squad who poisoned me, after all, but Nia…with the tea, and because I had a drink. See? Anyway – the main thing to do is to grab Nia Williams while she's got the tea with the stuff in it actually with her.'

Carys said, 'Slow down, Annie…'

'No…no…let me finish. I've got Nia Williams on camera taking three bags out of a cupboard at her mother's house and replacing them with similar ones that she had in a sack with the logo of the place where her mother got her tea. I bet those were three bags of contaminated tea. She'd have driven there. I don't know what she drives, or the license plate number, but you can find out, and someone should search her car before she dumps the stuff. And get them to check Barbara's body for signs she'd been taking metronidazole, though, of course, I have no idea if you can even do that. Right – that's…it.'

Carys didn't say anything.

Annie snapped, 'Are you still there? Did you hear what I said?'

'I'm typing, not talking, and texting too. Hold on, Annie. Right…I need to do things. And, more importantly, I need to get other people – over whom I have no direct line of control – to do things. I've got everything you said. I'll need the recordings of Nia at her mother's house. And…leave it with me. And don't go phoning me every five minutes. Trust me, Annie. But…thanks for handing it over to me. You did the right thing. I'll text you when I have news. Bye now.'

Annie looked at the phone in her hand, and nodded at it. 'Yeah, I did the right thing…now I'd better phone Car to tell her what's what.'

23rd JANUARY

CHAPTER FORTY-FOUR

Henry Devereaux Twyst, eighteenth duke of Chellingworth, was…terrified. The recognition of the depth of his emotion only added to the turmoil in his, rather empty, tummy. So he decided that he'd have to face it, not crumple in its presence. At least…that was what he'd told himself at the table that morning – where he'd once again endured what he was now referring to mentally as his 'faux' breakfast – over which his wife had glowered at him. He'd repeated his intention to his reflection as he'd prepared himself for elevenses.

However, now that he was actually walking down the staircase in the Great Hall to join his wife, his beloved son, and his son's godmother, Val Jenkins…the terror was winning in the face of his diminishing resolve.

When he'd broken the news to Stephanie over dinner the previous evening about Barry Walton's questionable sister's ownership of the company into which he was seeking an investment by Val, and the fact that he didn't own it himself because he had a track record of crashing business failure, Stephanie had, initially, become very still, and very quiet. Then she'd grown…icy. Hard. Then she'd…well, the word 'exploded' came closest to what he'd witnessed, he supposed – though it had been an alarmingly controlled explosion.

As the words had poured out of her – so quietly that it chilled him – about trust within loving couples, how friendship was something to be admired not undermined, that relationships could bend until they broke, and that she would have to rethink a great number of the life decisions she'd made, Henry had told himself that she was pregnant, that her hormones were probably raging, and that she'd forgive him once she'd had a chance to think about things.

He'd slept on the sofa in his dressing room last night.

He knew he could have used one of the huge number of other rooms available to him, but then the staff would have twigged that something was amiss, and he didn't want that. No, this had to remain private. Which, he believed, it was…so far. But he, too, felt slighted. Wounded. His wife had expressly told people to lie to him – Cook Davies being at the top of the list. And he didn't care very much for how that made him feel. He hadn't mentioned that at any point during Stephanie's tirade, of course, because he hadn't wanted an argument. All he wanted was for Stephanie to realize that he'd asked Carol to do what she'd done for the sake of all concerned.

Of course, he also hoped that Stephanie wouldn't put two and two together and see that his ultimate desire was that she would realize that Val could make poor decisions about men and business investments, and that she might, therefore – by extension – see that Val could be wrong about other matters too…especially the list of things Henry should no longer be allowed to eat or drink.

But he wondered again about his plan: would it be a step too far, or would it be a masterstroke? Only time would tell.

The grandfather clock chimed eleven as Henry entered the sitting room. Hugo was safely corralled within his portable playpen, while Stephanie and Val were seated close together. He suspected that the redness of Val's eyes, and the damp handkerchief in her hand, meant that Stephanie had already tackled what was, after all, a delicate subject.

He hesitated, then knew that he had to follow the plan. Carol had agreed to it when he'd spoken to her around ten o'clock the night before. He'd explained how he'd told his wife everything, had described how she'd reacted, and begged for Carol's help, which she'd agreed to give in return for a favor…to which he'd readily agreed. Then she'd promised to make all the necessary arrangements. He knew she had, because his phone had been pinging with incoming texts. The tray was already on the table beside Stephanie. There was no cake. Just tea. Which gave him pause…then he walked to the fireplace, warmed his hands for a moment, then turned to face his…accusers.

Carol had told him to pull the bell rope at five past eleven. He checked his watch. He had three minutes to go.

He opened with a booming, 'Good morning, Val. You were able to reach us safely, despite the snow, I see. There's not a great deal of it. They say it should clear by this afternoon. One can only hope there are no remnants that could freeze overnight, and prove treacherous.' He felt he'd acquitted himself well, under trying circumstances.

Val and Stephanie glared at him. Hugo stopped his chattering, burped, then chuckled and squealed. The logs shifted in the fireplace. Henry felt suddenly hot, so stepped away, in the general direction of the bell. A minute early wouldn't matter, surely? He rang it.

Stephanie observed cooly, 'We have everything we require already, Henry. Elevenses will be a simple cup of tea, from now on.'

Henry almost held his breath…then there was a knock at the door and Bob Fernley entered, followed by two of his staff, one carrying a small table, the other a laptop and an extension cable.

Henry said, 'Where Her Grace and our guest can see it, please. Thank you all.'

Stephanie and Val sat in surprised, and stony, silence as arrangements were made, the two younger men disappeared, and Bob Fernley woke up the laptop and said to Henry, 'You just need to click here, Your Grace,' then left.

When Henry heard Stephanie sigh, he knew that something was coming, so he jumped in with: 'I am just…a man. I have taken certain steps that have caused you to be hurt, Stephanie, and have also, undoubtedly, caused sorrow for you too, Val. I took these steps with the best of intentions.' He ran a finger around his collar. 'I suspected that my actions would, indeed, cause such wounds, but believed it was my duty as a loving husband, and friend, to take them, nonetheless. But I do not think I am the best person to explain those reasons to you. That is why I have done…this.'

He clicked where Bob had indicated, and the screen came to life, showing four quadrants.

The half-interested glances Stephanie and Val gave the laptop were immediately replaced by looks of concern on both their faces. Henry peered at the laptop himself to find out why…and saw that two of the boxes were showing what were quite obviously hospital beds.

In one there was a very poorly-looking Mavis: her hands were crossed on her chest, both heavily bandaged, and her head was sporting an enormous cap made of something white, set at a jaunty angle – at least that was the impression it gave Henry.

In the other was Christine Wilson-Smythe who looked a bit worn out, but generally not too bad.

Annie Parker was sitting in what appeared to be a kitchen, and Carol Hill was in front of a wall that was covered with some rather busy wallpaper. They were all speaking to each other, he assumed, though there was no sound. Knowing that he'd pressed the button Bob had told him to, Henry was at a loss, though he did his best to work things out by peering at the keyboard, hoping something would say 'SOUND'. Nothing did.

Stephanie reached forward. 'Get out of the way, Henry. Stand behind me. Let me do it. There.'

As Stephanie unmuted the system, the chattering diminished, then she said, 'Ladies, we're here, and we can hear you. Can you see and hear all of us?'

Heads nodded in four boxes.

Stephanie continued, 'Henry has foisted this upon Val and myself. You would all only be where you are now if you know what's going on. So, I shall start by thanking you, on behalf of my family, and my friend, for taking the time to be…here.'

Henry was taken aback when his mother's head popped into the shot showing Mavis. She shouted, 'I'm here too but there's no way for me to be on the camera, unless Mavis agrees to half-turn her phone toward me, and she won't do it. But I'm here. And don't be too long because she needs her rest. She almost died, you know, and all to help save our Scottish seat from the clutches of a swindling steward.'

Henry couldn't help but ask. 'What on earth do you mean by saying that, Mother? What swindling steward? We only have one – Billy Stewart – and he's no swindler. You simply cannot say things like that about people.'

His mother's head popped in again. 'Well, you can tell that to the police who have him in custody. He's been robbing us for years,

Henry. We've even been eating our own blessed fish, had we but known it. I'll tell you all about it when we get home. Soon. But Mavis sorted it out, and risked her life to do it. So, as I said, be quick about this…whatever it is. What is this all about, Mavis? You never told me…what's going on back at the Hall?'

Mavis turned her camera so only she was visible and said, 'Ignore her. But, yes, please, let's get on. I see you're in hospital too, Christine. No problems with your pregnancy, I hope. Anything you can tell us…that you're prepared to mention…here?'

Henry focused on Christine's square. She smiled – well, she beamed, in fact – and replied, 'Yes, I'm in hospital. No, no one needs to worry. And yes, please get on with it – there's someone I need to spend time with. Thank you.'

Annie said, 'If Alexander's there, give him our best, and it's good to see you looking so chipper, Chrissy, though you should have told us they'd taken you in. Have they got you there for the duration now?'

Christine shook her head. 'Just a couple of days.'

Carol added, 'Mavis, it's good to see you, and thanks for holding the phone for me and Annie to be able to talk to her last night, Althea. Christine, you should have said in one of our texts that you were in hospital – we really could have done this without you.'

Henry heard the warmth in Christine's voice when she replied, 'We're a team and we all care about Stephanie, and we all care about Val – so let's do this, ladies. I'll start, because I really do know what I'm talking about. Val – there's no easy way to say this, so I'll just say it – you've picked a wrong 'un. Sorry. We've probably all done it, and this time you've done it. I read everything that Carol dug up, and it looks to me as though Barry Walton latched on to you because he knew you had a pot of money he could dip into to get his "wellness" company set up. We've all met him, and we all agreed he wasn't unpleasant, but his record suggests he hasn't got the best of heads for business, and – to be honest – I can't see this business doing well in any case. The market's flooded, and there's no angle…no unique selling proposition. I've just managed to uncover a scam wine investment company down here in London – and I'll tell you all about it, soon, I promise – but it just proved to me something we all know, and do. Val, when we want something to be true, we ignore the warning signs that it's not. In my case, the people who wanted the story they were being sold to be true felt that way because they were greedy. I know that's not the same for you – but there isn't a person in the world who doesn't want to believe they can be loved. And that's what you believed…that Barry loved you. Wanted you…not your money.'

Mavis said, 'Ach, Val, my dear…trust me when I tell you I've had quite a bit of time to think through a lot of things this past couple of days, and you've no idea how being chilled to the bone can focus your mind on what's really important. As Christine said, the desire to be loved, to be wanted, to share your life with someone who understands you, is one of life's most basic driving forces. On a purely biological level, it's about reproduction – the continuation of the species. But on a psychological level, it's about the need to belong not to a tribe, or a group, but with one special person, with whom you can be…all of yourself. Not everyone is fortunate enough to find that one person…some, on the other hand do seem to go through them like a dose of salts. But just because we want a person to be the right one, it doesnae make them so…no matter how much we might want it to be them. And I fear that's where you are with this man who was your friend, and who became more.'

Henry watched Stephanie as she watched Val…and had no idea what either woman might be thinking.

Annie said, 'I've got to be honest, Val, and say I don't know you very well, but – having met Tude so late in my life – all I can tell you is that you never actually know when your partner will show up, if they ever do…but it's worth waiting for. Well, you know, not waiting, waiting, but…you know what I mean. Anyway, I was the one who did the market research. About the company stuff. There are some huge players out there, Val, and Barry's business plan – that you gave Stephanie, that Henry managed to nab for us – isn't much of one, and it won't work. Even I can see that. It's just too…thin. Sorry.'

Henry noted that Carol spoke more quietly than the others, and what she said seemed to carry more weight for that reason. 'I'm sorry that what I did hurt you, Stephanie, and Val. But, let's all be honest here, we did the same sort of thing for Annie once, when we believed there was someone who was using her natural desire to find a significant other to their advantage…and – although there were a few rocky days within our relationships because of it – I know that Mavis, Christine, and I would do the same for Annie again. Not that we'll ever need to, I don't think. I could have declined Henry's request, but I knew that if there was nothing bad to unearth, then it wouldn't matter that I'd dug around. But if I did find something questionable – like I did – that that was something you would deserve to know. But let's be clear, Val – none of us can possibly know for sure that Barry doesn't feel about you the way you believe he does. It is possible for two things to be true at the same time – he can love you, and he can also be trying to feather his nest at your expense. So what you do with what we've told you is up to you. But, please, don't blame Henry for this. He knows how much Stephanie cares about you, and I think we can all appreciate that he must think highly of you, himself, for you to have been invited to become Hugo's godmother.'

Henry could feel his heart in his chest…which he hoped wasn't a bad sign. He could see looks passing between his wife and Val, and felt the frustration build inside him as he realized he had absolutely no idea what they meant. He hardly dared breathe…

Eventually, Val spoke; Henry noted the shakiness of her voice, but hoped the fact she didn't need the damp handkerchief was a good sign.

She said, 'I don't blame Henry. I don't blame any of you. And thank you all so very much for taking the time to be here, as best you can, to support me at this difficult time. And it is a difficult time, because, sadly, what you've brought to my attention about Barry is…only too believable. I appreciate what you said, Carol – that he could feel something for me, and still try to rip me off – but…well, I think I've…I've been fooling myself. I wanted him to love me as much as…he said he did. I wanted to start up a company that would set the world alight. To build something that's more important than a bookshop in, albeit a wonderful place like Hay-on-Wye, but…it's just a bookshop. I wanted to…be significant.'

Henry jumped when Annie shouted, 'Oi – Val – hang on there…you are significant. You saved that bookshop, and loads of people love it. I know I do, and Eustelle loved it too when I took her there, didn't she? And you're a real, honest-to-goodness telly star, Val. No one else has been, or will be, the *Curious Cook* – that was you. And you're so clever when it comes to food, and cooking, and old ingredients, and nutrition and all that, that you will do more significant things. Just…not this business, right? It'll flop. Honest it will. But do something that comes from your heart, Val. I'm not wrong, am I, girls?'

Henry was exceedingly gratified by the chorus of female voices which echoed Annie's sentiments, and felt quite warm inside when he saw Stephanie hugging Val, and the two of them smiling, and crying and…oh dear, they'd set Hugo off.

Wanting them to have their moment, he strode to pacify his son in his pram, but Hugo was fast asleep. So where was that baby crying?

Annie made him jump, again, when she shouted, 'Gordon Bennett! Is that yours, Chrissy? You've had the baby already? Is it alright? Are you alright? Good grief…you managed to keep that quiet.'

Everyone in the sitting room, and on the screen, was beaming as Christine Wilson-Smythe showed off her child's face – well, a few square inches of wrinkled skin was all Henry could see – to the camera.

She said, 'Everyone – this is Robbie…the most beautiful child ever born – sorry to all those of you who've had children before me. Mother and baby are both doing just fine. Father? Well, that remains to be seen. But, I hope you don't mind – we don't get much time together because Robbie popped out a bit early, so needs a little bit of special attention, and this is our bonding time. We'll see you all soon, but I'm saying goodbye now. No – *we're* saying goodbye…for now.'

There was a rush of chatter, within which Henry heard Annie say, 'So is it a boy or a girl, then? Robbie's one of them names that can be either…' Stephanie and Val were consoling each other, or else celebrating the new arrival – Henry wasn't sure – and the women on the screen were disappearing, one at a time. He knew that the event, such as it had been, was over, but wasn't certain if he'd come out of it smelling of roses. But he'd done his best, and he hoped it was enough.

25th JANUARY

CHAPTER FORTY-FIVE

Sitting in what had now become a true family bedroom at the Wilson-Smythes' house in London, Christine looked around and sighed with pure contentment. There were the flowers she'd received from Mavis and Althea, and Stephanie and Henry, plus the jolly balloons from Annie and Carol, as well as the antique – and newly hand-painted – cot that had been erected there, courtesy of Bill Coggins and his designer wife Nat Smith. And there was…Robbie.

As she gazed at her perfect child's perfect nose, she said, 'Mammy's livid with me, of course. Called me devious, so she did…but she'll get over it, I know.'

Alexander chuckled. 'What, livid with you because you did all that work on – what was it…The Case of the Whining Wine Snobs? – when you should have been resting? Or because we've decided to name this gorgeous one Robbie, and she and your father think that's not an Irish enough name?'

'Both. The fact we've brought Robbie home from the hospital on the afternoon of Burns Night doesn't help, does it? Robbie Burns? Yes, I suppose it is a bit of a Scottish name. But Robbie Bright sounds…wonderful. And she will be Bright, once we're married. I've decided.'

Alexander felt something shift in his psyche. 'You're going to take my name? When we marry? I thought you'd decided that you'd stick with Wilson-Smythe. That's what you've always said…until now.'

Christine dared to touch the downy hair just above her infant's ear. 'I know that's what I said…then. But now? She deserves to be one of…us, not one of the Wilson-Smythes. Mammy kept the Wilson, because that was important to her. Do you think I should become Bright-Smythe? Smythe-Bright? I think both sound a bit…clumsy. Unnatural. I don't really feel the need to trumpet the fact that I'm

Daddy's daughter. Not any longer. But I'd like people to know I'm your wife. Mrs. Christine Bright sounds…wonderful.'

Beaming, Alexander asked, 'Did they dose you up with something before they wheeled you to the door of that hospital? You're sounding a bit…dreamy – for you. Not that I'm complaining, by the way.'

'Oh Alexander, let's get married – as soon as that cast is off your arm. I'm sorry I shouted at you – and I'm so sorry about your poor Aston Martin. I know it was insured and all that…and, at least it kept you safe. So that's good. Trust you to find a patch of black ice as you were rushing to the hospital, and then to get side-swiped by that van. By the way – is poor old Geordie still camped out beside that bloke's hospital bed? Couldn't he just get the hospital to phone him when the bloke can talk? Why does he have to be there, sitting beside him?'

Alexander shrugged. 'Bit of a…coincidence, really. Turns out the van driver works for a supplier of ours. Sliding doors. You know…for balconies? Geordie got to the scene before the firemen got me out of my car, and he spotted the other bloke. Recognized him. I knew as soon as the paramedics had a look at me that I'd be fine, so we agreed that Geordie would go in the ambulance with him. He was unconscious, you see. Geordie just wants to make sure there's someone there for him when he wakes up. But, don't panic, he's not doing it all on his own – we've worked out a rota, so there'll definitely be a smiling face to welcome him, when he opens his eyes.'

Christine gazed up lovingly at the man she knew she was going to spend the rest of her life with; her daughter's father. 'You're so good to people, Alexander. And, of course, I'm so grateful to everyone who got you and your arm sorted out. And I'm so, so pleased you were able to be there when Robbie joined us. Thank you…for everything.'

Alexander kissed the top of Christine's head. 'Oh my darling, you're the one who deserves the thanks. Mine, of course, for creating this little wonder, and I know your mum will come around – and be grateful, too – when she realizes that what you did for the Fentons and the Daltons was as much for her and your father, as for them. I'm amazed you had the mental capacity to get hold of someone who was able to do something about it all – and so fast, too. Whoever that bloke on the Isle of Man was, he must still have some clout at the Met. They grabbed that Hans van Ruud bloke before he could scarper with any of the funds, and they'll get back whatever he managed to syphon off they said, didn't they? As far as possible, anyway.'

'I should imagine a lot of the money's just…gone. Spent, already. From what Harry Pitcher told me on the phone this morning, Hans van Ruud's lifestyle was quite something. No expense spared on jets, yachts, cars, and dining out. Which is why they won't let him out on bail, he said. But I think the high life will be over for van Ruud for a while. Though, who knows…he might just end up with a slap on the wrist, metaphorically speaking. I hope not. I know he was ripping off people who have more than most, and that they were all sinking their money into a scheme that seemed just a little too good to be true. But they're people, nonetheless, and I bet some of them worked hard to amass whatever wealth they have.'

'I know Sonny Dalton, did,' mused Alexander. 'Like I said – a fair bloke, and reliable. But…enough about all that. What about us? I'm not only amazed by you, but so proud of you, too. And now there are the three of us. I know your parents have said we can all stay here for as long as we like, but – after you've rested up for a week or so – let's start to make plans to move to our own place? Honeysuckle Cottage is ready for us…I made sure of that. And I bet I can do anything your mother could…though having one arm out of commission for a while won't help. I want to be completely involved as a father, Christine, really I do. So – whenever you say you're ready – we'll take Robbie to Wales, with her too-Scottish, insufficiently Irish name, where an Englishman will give her a new surname and we can all just…be. And don't listen to your mother when she says you were being devious by working when you were in that hospital bed, because you were just being…you. And, except for this one here, you're the most perfect person in the world.'

'Thank you. I love you. And I love you too, Robbie.'

Christine kissed her newborn's forehead, and breathed in…and felt her heart swell.

Carol and David were sitting with Annie beside the bar at the Coach and Horses, where Tudor was serving. Carol noted, 'That's a lovely sign you made, Tudor. It really highlights the fact that your chips are handmade, here, by you. That should shift a few more portions.'

Tudor beamed. 'That's the hope. And I think I can outdo what any old chip van can offer by way of curry sauce – seeing as how our curry nights have been going down so well, and my gravy's second to none, I'd say. So, chips and dips it is…something between a snack and a proper meal, see? And Annie's come up with just the right amount of hot sauce to go into mayonnaise for that to be a good offering too…and we're going to keep coming up with new ideas on that front – so if you've got any suggestions, just tell me.'

David suggested, 'Barbecue sauce? How about that? That might go down a treat. And you could try something cheesy, too. They have chips with cheese curds on them, with gravy, in Canada, so maybe a thick cheese sauce?'

Annie made a noise that sounded like someone in the throes of ecstasy. 'Oh yes, Tude – cheese sauce and chips. Oh, and a blue cheese one, too. I'd eat that. Let's try a recipe for that, shall we? It would be fun trying to get it right, if nothing else.'

Carol laughed. 'Oh heck – this could go on for a long time, I bet. But you're right, Tudor, it's a good idea. And now that you've got the Sglod Squad out of your hair, you can rule supreme as the king of chips in Anwen-by-Wye.'

Tudor raised his glass to the three of them. 'And long may I reign. Yes, I'm glad that all went…well.'

Annie added, 'All the better for you telling Henry that you didn't want to be the one to rock up to the chip van waving a letter from his solicitor. Getting it delivered to them by hand at their so-called office yesterday was a much better idea. And knowing that they're not planning to ever come here again is the best possible news we could have had – not that I think they'll be doing much business in many other places either. Carys told me that a lot of the mobile phones they found in Shaznay Tanner's car were stolen from people in the very villages they've been servicing. Imagine that – pickpocketing people as they queued for chips. Terrible. I bet they'd have tried that on here, too. I can't imagine how I'd cope without my phone. Oh, and I've named it The Case of the Sticky-fingered Sglod Squad. Because they were. Especially about them phones.'

Tudor said, 'Well, they've gone, and we don't ever have to think about them again. Thanks to you two. We've got a couple of wonders here, haven't we, David? Sorted out the Sglod Squad lot, and all that business up at Chellingworth Hall, too. Poor Val Jenkins, though, eh? He was a devious one, that Barry Walton. I hope she hasn't lost the money she put into that company of his – or his sister's – for good. It's bad enough that he led her on.'

David shifted on his barstool. 'Your Annie seems to have told you a lot more about all of that than my Carol has.' He turned to face his wife. 'What, I'm not in the circle of trust on this one?'

Carol smiled as she play-thumped him. 'You've had enough on your plate without me going through the ins and outs of all our cases, David. And, you know, things haven't been all they could be at home, so we've had other stuff to talk about…when we've had the time.'

Annie asked, 'So, when do your mum and dad move out, Car? Tude was telling me earlier on about what you did…talking Henry into letting them become the new tenants at my old cottage as a favor to you – now that it's had the bathroom redone, and all that. Will they fit? I had a few problems, but they are a good bit shorter than me, I suppose.'

Carol almost spat out her drink. 'What, will Mam and Dad fit into your old cottage? Of course they will. You brought mountains of stuff with you from London when you moved here, Annie. They've come from a farmhouse in Carmarthenshire with no furniture – thank goodness, because it had all seen a lot of wear – and they've never been people to have a lot of things about the place. Not only will they fit in nicely – and, yes, they're a lot less likely to bump their heads when they walk through the front door than you were, Annie – but their possessions will, too. And it is, I believe, the perfect solution. They'll rent – at a lovely low rent, as agreed by Henry – while they keep searching for somewhere to buy, and they'll be just across the village green from us to be able to help with Albert. But they can do their own thing, and not always be trying to "help us out" all the time.'

'It was a brilliant idea, Car,' said Annie.

David smiled. 'It was a bit…what was it that you called Barry Walton, Tudor? Yes, it was a bit devious of her, really.'

Annie snapped, 'Oi, you, don't go using Tude's words against Car. That horrible Nia Williams gets the word devious all to herself. She was most certainly a devious daughter…or maybe Car was, and Nia was a deadly daughter, I don't know…because there's a lot of different levels of deviousness, in't there? But I've written the name of The Case of the Devious Daughter on poor old Barb's file folder now, in indelible felt-tipped pen, so she can keep it.'

David said, 'Carol did tell me all about that case, but do you think there'll be enough evidence to take it to court? Let alone find that Nia Williams guilty of – well, what would it be? Was it murder? Or manslaughter? Or…what?'

Carol shook her head. 'That's for the police and the courts to decide, but Annie and I provided the authorities with the best evidence we could. Poor Barbara's notebook, reports of our interviews with Barbara herself, her stepson, and what little interaction we had with Nia, plus the camera recordings. And they did nab Nia with the tea that they proved she'd tainted with that nasty antibiotic. Ground up tablets through the lot of it, there was. And that was down to Annie.'

Annie mugged a bow and graciously accepted a silent round of applause. As if waving off the plaudits, she said, 'Nah – team effort that was, as always.'

'As was The Case of the Naïve Nutritionist,' replied Carol. 'You dug up the information that we showed to Val to back up the fact that Barry's business could never make it.'

Tudor poured a fresh pint for David as he asked, 'Do you reckon Stephanie will stop getting Cook Davies to rework all the recipes she holds near and dear to her heart…and to Henry's heart, of course?'

'I reckon that's something that only time will tell,' replied Carol. 'Though Annie and I aren't usually privy to Henry's gripes about the food he eats at the Hall, so we might never know. The thing is, I see that Stephanie's got a point about that, but I also feel for Henry. It's not nice when you think you're not in charge of your own little world. We've been on the receiving end of that for a while, haven't we, David? Though that'll change…soon. But – for now – it's nice of Mam and Dad to shoo us out to come and have a drink tonight. And now that Barbara's tainted tea is out of our system, we can both enjoy a G and T or two without any fear of being ill afterwards, can't we, Annie?'

'Or three, more like, doll. When you've finished topping off that pint for David, Tude, mine's a large one, ta. Once Mave and Althea get back from their jaunt up north there'll be no more late nights for me – back to all my coursework, and my driving lessons…though I haven't got one for a couple of days, given this weather. Too slippery, said Josie, and I don't mind. You talked to Mave today, didn't you, Car? Did she say when they were coming back?'

Carol shook her head. 'She's out of hospital, as you know, and she was excited that she was going to be able to spend time with both her sons, their wives, and all her grandchildren tonight, at Althea's Burns Night Bash, as she's apparently calling it. Goodness knows how that'll go, but I dare say we'll hear all about it. When they get back.'

David said, 'I know Mavis won't be able to contribute fully immediately, poor thing, but I'll be glad when she can take some of the load off my poor wife…and you, of course, Annie. And, yes, Carol did brief me on both The Case of the Swindling Steward, and The Case of the Fearful Fisherman. Nice title, Annie, for that thing Carol was looking into for Mavis's friend Frank, about the bloke down in Hastings. Another good "catch" by you two – well done.'

David chuckled at the groans from the other three at his 'fishy' pun, then continued, 'I understand that Mavis's old flame gets to keep the money he was paid, but the bloke in question doesn't actually get the boat or the van because he's about to be serving time – not fish – due to being nabbed in Hastings with a load of magic mushrooms, and this not being the first, or even the second time, he's done it. And all thanks to my Carol – who dug up the dirt on him, at Mavis's request – then managed to get the local bobbies to go sniffing around him, which I happen to know took a lot of doing.'

'Mave'll get back up to full speed as soon as she can, I bet,' noted Annie. 'And I'll raise a glass with you to having her back…and to Chrissy and little Robbie, too. Cheers, folks!'

Carol replied, 'Cheers…and here's to the four of us – two loving couples – on St Dwynwen's Day. She's the Welsh patron saint for lovers, Annie, in case you'd forgotten – our St Valentine. So, with Tudor and me being Welsh, and you and David being English, Annie, we're two couples who prove it's possible for love to conquer all…until there's rugby on the telly, of course, then – well…it's every man and woman for themselves, isn't it?'

Mavis MacDonald felt as though she were in her eighties, and wondered if she'd swapped bodies with Althea, who was still tripping around the dining hall, swooshing her surprising tartan kaftan, with sash, and humming the tunes that had surrounded them all evening; there being no piper, Clementine had, resourcefully, downloaded a great number of pieces of traditional Scottish music, utilizing the newly-replaced satellite dish at Twyst House. Mavis had to admit she was feeling more than a bit done in…but it had been such an evening, she wasn't really surprised.

'Look at it – wasn't I magnificent, Mavis?' Althea was, once again, drawing Mavis's attention to the life-size portrait of herself and her late husband that Clementine had spent weeks painting out in her – apparently – incredibly chilly barn-cum-studio. 'If I'd known what Clementine was up to, I'd not have been so hurt by her abandoning me every day.'

'But then it would no' have been a surprise, Althea. And, let me tell you, seeing your face when she pulled off that sheet made putting up with all your pouting when you thought she was ignoring you absolutely worth it. It's a splendid portrait of you, and I dare say it is of your late husband, too. I know you've shown me photographs of him, but to see him looking so…vibrant, is quite something.'

Althea sighed. 'We never really know how our children see us, think of us, or feel about us, do we, Mavis? This…this masterpiece tells me that Clementine must have seen the lifeforce in Chelly that I did, or she'd never have been able to paint him like this. As for her portrayal of me? Well, of course I'm younger in it than I am now – because she's shown us as we were back about thirty years ago – but I think she's portrayed me as a gentle, happy woman, and she captured my dimples perfectly, didn't she? How very clever of her. And to show us here, in front of this house, where we were always very happy…that means a great deal.' She leaned toward Mavis and stage-whispered, 'The poor girl has no idea she was conceived here…but I didn't think I'd mention that, given her recent flirtation with the idea of having a child.'

Mavis blanched. 'I dare say we should be thankful for wee mercies.'

Althea dimpled. 'You're even more Scottish when you're with your boys, you know? And that's charming. Though…thinking about that portrait, which, of course, I cannot help but do…I have to wonder how we'll get it back to Chellingworth Hall. I dare say that Ian will come up with a good idea – he usually does.'

Mavis replied, 'Well, I don't know about that, but he certainly managed to be a wonderful part of the team who saved me, and he pulled a rabbit out of a hat for tonight. The way he managed to help make up rooms, and get the place all set for the meal…and didn't Eileen do us proud with the food? I have to say, Althea, that being able to have my boys, and all their lot, here tonight, meant a great deal, dear. I still cannae quite believe that they're all upstairs, now, above me…sleeping. All of them – under one roof, for one night, with me here with them. That might never ever happen again. So…you'll have that portrait, and I'll have the memory of this night.'

'And Frank O'Malley got to meet them all, too, didn't he? I thought your two boys were very polite to him, Mavis. You did a good job with those two.'

'Why would they no' be polite?'

'They might think Frank's trying to take their father's place.'

'For heaven's sake, Althea, I've told you and told you – and so has Frank – that there's nae chance of anything like that between us.'

'I noticed that the two of you had your heads very close together when Clementine and Julian were showing us their dancing skills…which means you missed part of a grand exhibition, by the way. The way their kilts flew about was spectacular. Clementine did a very good job of getting their costumes sorted out. And Julian really looked the part, didn't he? So big, and…beardy.'

Mavis shrugged. 'Aye, well, the music was deafening, Clementine's kilt was a wee bit shorter than it needed to be, I think…and Frank was telling me about his plans for his Canada trip. I had to get close to hear what he was saying. And…well, I had a few private things I needed to say to him that I wanted no one else to hear, too…but no' of a personal nature. At least, not in the way you might think.'

Althea sniffed. 'Did you talk to him about the tremor he has?'

Mavis looked amazed, then said, 'You noticed it, too? Aye, I did. Turns out it's one of the reasons he sold up when he did, and sharpish, too. He's afraid he might have the early stages of Parkinson's Disease, but willnae see a doctor about it, because he's concerned that a diagnosis will mean he'd no' be able to travel – or else no' be able to afford the insurance to travel.'

'I dare say that means you gave him a piece of your mind.'

'Well…I did point out that, given the life he's led – at sea, dealing with cold fish, and so on, for so many years – there could be lots of other reasons why he has such poor circulation in his hands, and a tremor. But I don't think he'll take my advice to get it looked into, not until he's met his granddaughter, anyway. That was one thing about Frank – even when he was young, he never really understood when persistence crossed the line and became stubbornness. And that can be…problematic.'

Althea twittered, 'Especially given how stubborn you are, dear. No…maybe you're right, maybe you weren't meant to be a couple. You were just the right two people, in the right place, when you needed each other…back then. So, with him being able to keep all that money – because the chap in Hastings actually sold a boat to buy Frank's business, so they can't prove it's drug money which they'd confiscate…for which we're all grateful – he'll be off, then. And will you stay on here at Twyst House for a while, dear? You'd be more than welcome, as would all your family.'

Mavis shook her head sadly. 'I think both James and Duncan felt they could use the "Grannie's in hospital" card to get the children out of school for a couple of days, but they'll all need to be in their own beds tomorrow night, and back at their desks the next morning – either in school or at their offices. And that's as it should be. But I won't impose on any of them by going to stay at their houses when I'm not quite myself, so I'll come back and stay with them some other time. And I'll make sure I see that new manager for our charity in Dumfries at that time, too. He deserves to get me when I'm feeling one hundred percent, which I'll admit I'm not. So, I'll join you in the car when Ian drives you back to Chellingworth after all, if that's alright with you, my dear.'

Althea beamed. 'You don't need to ask, Mavis. I shall leave the day after tomorrow, so you can have the day with your lot, and I'll enjoy some time with Clementine…now that we're on much better terms. She and I need to have a good look around this place and come up with some plans that we can pass on to Henry. Though goodness knows how he'll react to that. Do you think there's any chance that the money Billy swindled out of my family will ever be…found?'

Mavis sighed. 'Ach, Althea – that's going to be hard to say for some time. I think it's clear Billy spent a fair bit making that cottage of his as fancy as it is, and – as the police mentioned when I spoke to them – he bought that wee house of his in Alicante, so he probably sunk a lump of it into that. So…who knows.'

Althea managed a wry chuckle. 'I can't imagine Billy Stewart swanning about in Spain, can you? And to think I hadn't even been aware he'd ever taken any holidays…though a three-hour flight from Glasgow airport for a long weekend, or a mid-week jaunt, isn't going to be something I'd ever hear about, I suppose. Didn't they say he'd been such a regular at the airport that he knew most of the security guards by name? It was so fortunate that he'd missed the last flight of the day when he scarpered, and was trying to get the first one the next morning…and that those very security guards he'd palled up with were able to spot him so easily. And he was definitely going for good, or why would he have taken the dogs?'

'Aye, there was no hanging about, on his part. But, if they'd no' found me when they did, he might have got away with it…and it might no' have ended well for me. Mebbe my boys have a point – I'm getting a bit long in the tooth for this investigating business, Althea.'

'Nonsense. You're feeling sorry for yourself, that's all. Can you imagine being content to play at grandmothering full time? There'd be a grandchild or two who'd get the sharp end of your tongue within a week, and who knows what would happen after that. No, come home, with me. Carol and Annie will be glad to have you back. We could even pop to London to see Christine and her baby.'

Mavis said quickly, 'I think mebbe we'd best wait until she and Alexander are ready to bring wee Robbie to Wales, don't you? Let them set the pace.'

Althea sighed. 'I dare say. But, before all that, there's all…this, to sort out. Would you like to help me and Clementine as we reconnoiter the entire house, to work out what fixes need to be made?'

Mavis smiled. 'I think I might enjoy that – though, of course, what needs fixing, and the way that it gets fixed, are two very different things, and opinions might…not align. How will you cope with Clementine putting her stamp on the place?'

Althea smiled. 'She's already begun to do it, my dear. She's quite devious in her own, quiet way…and she knows I won't object. At least, not loudly enough that anyone would notice.'

'Of course not – you're such a mouse about the place, Althea.'

Althea tittered. 'Hoots mon…there's a moose, loose aboot this hoose…'

Henry lay his head on his pillow and hoped that sleep would find him swiftly…because he suspected that if he didn't manage to drop off within the next half an hour, he'd be compelled to sneak down to the kitchen to find something to eat. His tummy had been rumbling for ages, and he was convinced it wasn't good for him. But he didn't dare mention it to Stephanie…she might not understand. He was sure a nanny had mentioned something called 'night starvation' to him once upon a time – maybe that was what he was experiencing now?

When Stephanie turned off the bathroom light and got into bed – Hugo had been asleep for at least an hour – he whispered, 'How are you feeling tonight, my dear? A little better?'

Sephanie replied, 'My head is quite clear now, and – in other regards – I'm not ill, Henry. My dyspepsia is quite normal. Please don't concern yourself about my well-being.'

Henry dared, 'But I worry about you, because I care about you.'

Stephanie sat up, and stared down at him. She said, 'And I feel the same about you. Which is exactly why I've been trying to take steps to get you to eat and live more healthily, Henry. It's because I care about you – not because I want to punish you. But…but it seems that I've upset you, deeply. Thank you for telling me how you felt about my going behind your back to Cook Davies. It's much better that we discuss our feelings, dear. And I realize now that trying to…hoodwink you was quite wrong. Though your use of the term "devious" was uncalled for, I feel. Going forward, I shall be open about the changes I want to be made.'

Henry couldn't believe his ears. He spluttered, 'But…but earlier today, when we had our heart-to-heart, you said you apologized completely, and would tell Cook Davies to not amend any of her recipes at all. So…so what do you mean by "changes"?'

'I hadn't understood how difficult I was making life for Cook Davies, and that, too, was wrong of me. There is no way she should be expected to make alterations to recipes she's been making for decades.'

Henry relaxed a little. 'Good.'

'But she's agreed to try some brand-new recipes – things with which she's not familiar. She says it will spice up her life a little, and even mentioned that an old dog is never too old to learn new tricks. So, I'll be sharing some recipes with Cook Davies that Val has developed. Recipes that will not, now, be used as part of any wellness business. We're going to start testing and tasting them next week. I look forward to your feedback.'

Henry's spirits plummeted. 'I'm sure I shall find the whole experience…interesting.'

'Indeed, Henry.'

Acknowledgements

Writing any book that's set in Anwen-by-Wye, or on the Chellingworth Estate, is a joy for me, because it means I get to 'spend time' in Wales with people who've become my friends. I've also given Christine's family a home near where I used to have a flat in London, and now I've allowed the Twysts to have one close to where I spent a lot of time at a cottage in Scotland. Yes, I know, it's all a bit selfish of me, choosing locations that I love, but, there it is. I hope you can feel the joy I have when I 'visit' these places; even if the specifics are fictional, there's great warmth for the real locations in my heart.

I'd also like to thank Rebecca (Bex): your gift of a flat cap has made it to Althea's head. You're a brilliant woman, and a constant source of inspiration – thank you for your wonderful support, and friendship.

Once again, the story I've told has been improved by my editor, Anna Harrisson – thanks Anna. My proofer, Sue Vincent, has also been as assiduous as ever, thanks Sue. We've all done our very best to not let any errors get through, but we're only human (no AI used here, folks) so please forgive us if something slipped past us that pulled you out of the story. If you want to let me know about that, so we can fix it – if possible – just email me (the address is at my website, noted below).

My thanks to all the reviewers, bloggers, folks who leave stars or reviews at online platforms (that's always useful, you know!), booksellers, or librarians, who've helped you, and others, find this book, and this series. Without all of them I'd be telling stories to myself…which I'd probably do, but it wouldn't be as much fun. And last, but absolutely not least: I know there are a LOT of books out there, so thank *you* for choosing to spend time with the WISE women.

Cathy Ace
December 2025
www.cathyace.com

About The Author

CATHY ACE was born and raised in Swansea, Wales, and migrated to British Columbia, Canada aged forty. She is the author of *The Cait Morgan Mysteries*, *The WISE Enquiries Agency Mysteries*, the standalone novel of psychological suspense, *The Wrong Boy*, and short stories and novellas. As well as being passionate about writing crime fiction, she's also a keen gardener.

You can find out more about Cathy and all her works at her website: **www.cathyace.com**